UNSPOKEN LOVE

By
Christmas Carol Kauffman

D1378054

Conestoga Valley Bookbindery
505 Musser School Road
Leola, PA 17540

CHRISTIAN LIGHT PUBLICATIONS INC.
P.O. BOX 1212
Harrisonburg, Virginia 22803-1212
(540) 434-0768

FOREWORD

You have in your grasp a life changing story. It's been over twenty years since my mother laid down her pen and said her last words. Yet, I continue to receive letters like these:

From Mission, Kansas: "I grew up with two alcoholic parents. I have been in six mental hospitals. In desperation I went to a bookstore. I don't know why, but I bought one of your mother's books. Until that day I had never heard of Christmas Carol Kauffman. During the next two weeks I devoured all of her books that I could buy or borrow. Her books helped me see what real life is all about. I now have an understanding of true Christianity. I can face hurt and trial with new assurance that God will see me through."

From Paden, Oklahoma: "I would like at least fifty copies of each of your mother's books. I want to give them to Christian schools and young friends. Christmas Carol Kauffman's writings are so helpful to Christian living. Please tell me where I can buy her books."

Mother became ill with hepatitis as she was writing her tenth book. She was unable to complete it before she passed away. It was the story of a black woman who lived in a small second story flat on the south side of Chicago.

This woman had enough love to mother over thirty children, none of them her own.

In such true stories real life and true Christianity have spoken to many persons around the world. Mother's books have been printed in several languages.

Some of her books are out of print. Fortunately one of her stories has come alive again in the edition you now hold. I pray you will be blessed as you read <u>Unspoken Love</u>.

Stanlee D. Kauffman
Pastor of Waynesboro Mennonite Church, Waynesboro, VA

INTRODUCTION

Unspoken Love was originally published as a serial in <u>Youth's Christian Companion</u> in 1949. This story is now presented in book form. Those who have enjoyed reading <u>Lucy Winchester, Light From Heaven, Hidden Rainbow</u>, and numerous other titles by Mrs. Kauffman can now enjoy another one of her stories.

This is a true story about real people. Find out how Millard's "Unspoken Love" affects his family and his decisions and see the faithfulness of God in bringing victory. We hope the experiences this family faced will challenge each reader to a deeper faith in Christ.

—The Publishers

Chapter 1

A strange sensation went through Mrs. Grinstead like a sudden shock! She caught her breath and held it. The hand that had reached up to pull down the blind grabbed the lace curtain instead. She stood at the window as if paralyzed, watching—listening. All she heard was her own heart pounding. Then the clock in the dining room struck ten. She pulled the blind and swallowed hard. Perhaps she had been mistaken.

But for some reason Mrs. Grinstead was not satisfied. She walked to the kitchen, crossed the room without snapping on the light, and looked out both windows. It was not altogether dark outside, for the small sickle of a November moon fastened in the havens above Harper's Valley, gave a soft tarnished-silver cast to the frosty ground and roofs. She walked stocking-footed through the dining room and hesitated at each window. She saw nothing.

Strange. Myra Grinstead was not a woman to be easily frightened. Seldom had she had apparitions. Long ago she had received complete victory over being afraid when Jeth did not get home early. Of course when Orpha was only two, and Don Millard a wee thing yet, she sometimes felt plenty anxious if Jeth wasn't home by ten; but not more. My, no. What was there to be afraid of? No one had ever tried to rob or molest them. Myra got used to being alone with the children nights, for Jeth had business in town at least three nights out of every week. How could a common laboring man rent ten acres and a comfortable modern house three miles out of the city of Doddridge on the slab, and support a wife and seven children without doing something else besides ordinary carpenter work? It couldn't be done. At least Jethro Grinstead couldn't make ends meet and have enough left to twist even a small French knot. So he stood on the street corners of Doddridge three nights a week selling popcorn he

5

raised on the ten acres. Orpha, Don Millard, Liticia, Homer Jo, and Derwood shelled and sacked the popcorn and Pop sold it. Glen didn't help because he was the baby.

For almost five years before Glen came Myra had had a rest from washing small baby clothes. The three boys before Glen were just far enough apart that the shirts and overalls could be handed down without any alterations. Socks never lasted long enough to be worn by the second child—that was after they (the boys) once learned to crawl. Orpha was fifteen and Liticia eleven. They had a room of their own upstairs. Don Millard and Homer Jo slept together in the big room over the kitchen, and Richard and Derwood occupied the other bed in the same room.

Baby Glen had been tucked in at seven and fifteen minutes later his mother heard his bottle fall on the rag rug beside the crib with that familiar thud, and she knew he had rolled over on his stomach and was ready to drop off. After little Glen went to sleep was the time when Myra Grinstead really got things done that stayed done until morning. At least such things as winding up threads, closing the sewing machine drawers for the last time, straightening the pans and lids in the bottom of the kitchen cabinet that Glen was forever changing around and cluttering up, picking up the blocks and placing the throw rugs where they belonged. After that she could sometimes sit down and sew on buttons, darn socks, or patch overalls and underwear. There were four boys and a husband to patch and darn and mend for, besides two girls and a baby. Myra was never idle.

Before Glen was asleep Jeth had started for town with his basket of sacked popcorn. All he needed to do was start out and someone would pick him up. He had no car of his own, not as yet.

It was Thursday.

"I hope you sell it all tonight, Pop," Myra said as Jeth put on his overcoat and picked up the basket. She walked toward him all the while smoothing out her blue percale apron.

"I mor'an likely will," he answered, putting on his black cap. His thick grayish hair curled below it, almost resting on his coat collar. Pop needed a haircut. He almost always did. Very rarely had he come home with any popcorn left. The basket held twenty one-pound sacks. At fifteen cents a pound that would buy groceries, at least some of the most necessary items and things to put in the school lunches—five of them!

After Jeth left Liticia finished wiping the supper dishes, then worked on her sentences. There were fifteen she had to diagram before she went to bed. They were hard.

"Help me a little, Millard," she exclaimed tiredly, with a big sigh. "There you sit behind the stove again with that book."

Millard kept on reading. He heard Liticia, but he had to finish that paragraph about the crippled beggar outside the Beautiful Gate, who at last got more than a coin tossed at him. The story touched him, for somehow he pitied anyone who was ignored or ill treated in any way. Millard was very tender hearted.

"Don Millard," repeated Liticia, "Don Millard Grinstead—if—" She always called him Don Millard whenever anything was especially urgent. "If you know how important this English lesson of mine is you'd come and help me just a little. Please, Millard, then you can return to your blessed book."

"Don't make fun of Millard, Liticia," reprimanded Mrs. Grinstead gently. "I'm glad he loves to read."

"I'm not making fun of him, Mother," spoke Liticia repentingly. "He can read till midnight if he wants to, if he'll only help me just a minute. Come here and see if I'm doing this sentence right. Homer Jo, you and the boys go to the dining room to play your spinning game. I can hardly hear myself think straight. Is this right, Millard?"

Don Millard's brown eyes scanned Liticia's paper and he ran one hand right through the pretty wave of his thick black hair, as though he didn't care one bit how badly he mussed it up. Millard was a serious-minded boy for thirteen, always wanting to lie on the floor behind the kitchen stove and read, rather than play with other boys. He was handsome too—and didn't know it.

Liticia was next to Millard, next to him in the family, in school, and in everything. She had a peculiar fondness for her big brother. It seemed Pop always sort of picked on Millard and scolded him for things that weren't worth being scolded for.

Homer Jo was Pop's pet. That was easy to see. Homer Jo almost always got what he wanted, and did as he pleased. It was Homer Jo who always got to go along places with Pop if anyone did.

"It's this sentence right here." She pointed to it with her pencil.

"Well, Liticia," said Millard warmly, "what is the subject of this sentence?" He placed one hand on the kitchen table, the other on her shoulder.

"I guess it's 'mountain'," she answered without looking up.

"That's right. And what is the predicate?"

Liticia scratched her head like many or most girls do when they're thinking hard. It was always Millard she went to for help. Orpha didn't like to rethink those lessons she so much detested. She'd rather do anything else.

"I suppose it's 'rise'."

"They rise above the deep blue river, running swiftly toward the gulf some thousand and sixty miles to the south of —" Millard hesitated. "This is a little hard, I'll admit. Let me read it again."

Liticia was soon satisfied. Millard always knew. He made excellent grades in school. He resumed his favorite reading place behind the kitchen stove, and continued where he left off.

Grandmother Winegar had given a good many story books to her grandchildren. Being very fond of reading herself, she took genuine pleasure in selecting the best books for Myra's children. Don Millard was reading the one grandmother had given him for his birthday, "Special Friends of the Lord." He had read it through once and was half through its three hundred and forty-seven pages for the second time.

Orpha, who was large and strong for her age, would rather work bread, or iron, or hoe the popcorn any day than go to school. Jeth insisted going to school was a waste of time, and when Orpha wanted to quit as soon as she had completed the eighth grade, her father was heartily pleased. She quit, of course!

"It's nine o'clock, Millard." Mrs. Grinstead folded the sixth pair of blue jean overalls and glanced at the clock before she spoke.

"Is it? Well, Mother," spoke Millard, "let me read while I have a chance, for Pop told me this morning I'm to start working away as soon as school is out."

"Away where?" Mrs. Grinstead's needle stopped in mid-air.

"Over at Beabout's dairy farm."

"Beabout's. Are you sure?" Myra dropped her arm.

"That's what Pop told me this morning. He's already asked Mr. Beabout if he'd hire me and he said he would."

"And you mean-a-a," Mrs. Grinstead's pleasant round face suddenly took on a sober expression. She knew what it would mean, and so did Millard. It meant he would work like a man, and get a boy's wages, only to hand it all over to his father, so he could have more popcorn money to gamble with at the Daisy Del Lunchroom. And Liticia knew what it would mean, too, for hadn't she been sent away the past three summers to live with Mr. and Mrs. Elisha Grape, an elderly couple on Fourth Street in Doddridge, and didn't her father ask for her wages every month? Liticia would gladly have worked to get her mother new linoleum for the kitchen, or some dishes, or a spread for her bed. She got none of those—nothing she had dreamed of getting. She didn't even get a new print dress for herself out of her summer's wages. Mrs. Grape liked to sew while Liticia scrubbed and dusted, so she made her several school dresses out of her own cast-off ones.

Liticia closed her English book and looked at her brother lovingly. How strong and handsome he seemed tonight. How manly for only thirteen. Her admiration was drenched with pity, and, although she said nothing, Millard read in her face a volume of words.

"Good night, Millard," she said gently as she walked toward the stair door; "and thanks a lot for helping me tonight. I'll do something nice for you someday if I can."

He looked straight into her face. "You most likely can," came his ready answer.

"And what do you mean?" She searched his face carefully. There was both reverence and seriousness in her voice.

"Nothing in particular—tonight, Ticia." (Only on very rare occasions did Millard call his sister Ticia.) Always and every time he called her that, it made her feel extra close to him. He never said it absently or with frivolity, but with warmth of meaning and confidence. No one else ever called her that. Only Don Millard. Liticia Ann had been named after a favorite aunt on her mother's side.

"Homer Jo," called Liticia, "you boys put your game away now, and go on up to bed. It's nine o'clock and Mother is tired and wants to go to bed too. You're almost done mending, aren't you, Mother?"

"Just about."

"You'll not be up till Pop comes home will you?"

"I hope not. He never comes home before ten thirty—hardly ever," she added with a stifled sigh.

Orpha was already asleep. Quietly Liticia undressed, said her prayers, and slipped into bed. One by one the boys went up, and Myra Grinstead was alone downstairs—alone with baby Glen fast asleep in his crib.

9

There is something so restful about the quietness of one's own home—that sort of peaceful quietness that accompanies a house full of healthy sleeping children at the close of a full day of hard work. She stuck her needle in the spool of black darning cotton and just rocked for a while. How thankful she was for all the children. They all were normal and bright. She walked through the house once more and put the last thing in place. It was such a satisfaction to get up with the house in order.

And then, just as she went to pull the blind at the bedroom window she thought she saw a large man duck out of sight. No, Mrs. Grinstead was not in the habit of seeing things. To be afraid never entered her mind any more. But—how strange! If that wasn't a man she saw in the dusty silver light of the sickle moon, what was it?

Chapter 2

SHOULD she go on to bed or wait for Jeth? Myra was tired. She could go up and tell Millard what she saw—what she thought she saw, or she could waken Orpha and have her come down and sleep with her until Pop came home. Myra thought. She stood at the foot of her bed and rubbed her right hand up her plump left arm. Unconsciously she did the same with her other hand on her other arm.

Why be afraid? If she did see a man—and if he did break in—(but there was nothing to break, for Myra never locked the house) if he did enter somewhere, through a cellar window, or by one of the doors, what would he get? What could he get? Mrs. Grinstead's handbag hanging on the bedroom doorknob had only a nickel in it besides her comb and a handkerchief, a letter from her sister, Idella, and a few throat lozengers. Myra seldom had much cash in her possession. She'd look to make sure. No. What was the use? She knew without looking. They had no expensive silverware, no jewels, no valuables a robber could want—not even a gold watch. None of the children had savings banks.

Oh! A new thought struck Myra Grinstead with sudden alarm. Panic caused goose pimples to come out on both arms, and she stepped quickly to Glen's crib and clutched at her throat. What if he wanted her baby? It could be that and not money or jewels. Hadn't she read just in Tuesday night's paper about a kidnapping in the suburbs of Chicago, and the week before about a similar kidnapping nearer home than that, yes much nearer—and in the country—and—and both had been baby boys, one younger than little Glen and one a little older? Pretty baby boys no doubt. Myra Grinstead bent over Glen's little crib and felt his soft dark hair. It was beginning to get curly. He was still on his stomach, face half hidden, nose smashed

11

into the outing drawsheet. She turned him gently face up and straightened out his gown. She refastened the corners. Glen never could rest well with his arms inside.

"He's not going to get you," said Myra to herself well imagining how glad someone would be for a beautiful child like hers. "I'll sit here beside you till Jeth comes. Why doesn't he come? He should be coming soon. Few people would be buying popcorn after ten o'clock. Most folks were on their way home by ten—the kind who were likely to buy popcorn anyway. Not many couples would want to carry a sack of unpopped corn along to the last show. The Daisy Del. Was it really true Jeth went in there to gamble? Myra wondered. She couldn't prove it with her own eyes. Why would Myra Grinstead ever have an occasion or an excuse to walk past the Daisy Del lunch room on any of the three nights Pop went to town to sell corn?

If she had heard this from any one else but her own brother-in-law, Myra Grinstead would have put a big question mark to that statement. But Arne Randolph wasn't the type to imagine things or tell tales about anyone. Quite the opposite. Arne always trusted folks until he found out he couldn't. He always gave the other person the benefit of the doubt, and put the best possible construction on everyone's motives.

Myra pulled a chair close to Glen's crib and sat. She did not rock. It was a straight chair. She wouldn't have rocked had it been a rocker. Just an hour ago she rocked, so easily, so freely, so contentedly. The squeak of the rocker did not bother her. In fact she rather enjoyed it after the clatter and racket of the three boys. Just the peaceful quietness of home after a day's work, no sounds but the ticking of the clock on the mantel shelf and the cozy companionable squeak of her favorite rocker. To be afraid never entered Myra's mind. It would have been contrary to her make-up and her religion as well.

Was Jeth at the Daisy Del? She could call and find out. That's what she could do and tell Pop to hurry home. Hurry fast. But Pop never hurried. He never got excited. Not even when Millard ate too many green grapes once when he was four and swelled up like a balloon. Not even when he fell into Yock O'Leary's well and nearly drowned. Pop wouldn't get excited now either. She wouldn't call after all. Myra didn't like to use the telephone anyway, and if she'd act scared over nothing at all, she'd feel silly the rest of her life.

Myra Grinstead was secretly surprised at herself and somewhat

12

ashamed. Maybe after all she just imagined she saw a man. To be real honest it was almost too dark to be sure of anything. She sat. She lifted the loose strands of black hair up from her ears and fastened them behind the bows of her glasses. Maybe she could hear better. Glen puckered up his little face and whimpered in his sleep. Myra patted his arm gently. He smiled faintly.

She heard a car door slam—soon a step on the porch—the knob turned and Myra was on her feet.

"Is that you, Jeth?"

"Aren't you in bed yet?" Jeth put the basket on the kitchen table. He looked at the clock.

"I couldn't."

"Couldn't?" asked Jeth, knitting his brows. "Did you have company?"

"Why do you ask that, Pop?"

"I saw a car—"

"A car?" cut in Myra. "Where?"

"Myra, what's wrong? Yes, I said a car, an automobile was just leaving our lane when we were ready to turn in."

"Who's we?"

"Ginger Hanckins toted me home from town."

"What sort of a car was it, Jeth, and who was in it?"

"Why are you whispering, Myra?"

"I'm not, Pop. I mean—I'm not now—anyway, but when I was ready to go to bed, I went to pull down the blind at the bedroom window, and I—saw a man duck below the window."

"Oh, Myra," chided Jeth.

"I surely did, Jeth. I thought I did, and now I'm more sure of it than ever—since you say you saw a car leaving our lane. What kind of car was it?"

"I don't know. I didn't pay much attention. Me and Ginger were 'a-talkin'."

"Was it a big car?"

"Sorta."

"A sedan?"

"I 'spect so."

"Don't you know, Jeth?"

"I didn't pay no mind, only it was black I think, an' right shinin' an' new lookin'."

"Was a man driving it, Pop?"

"I couldn't say if my life depended on it, Myra. I jes' figured you had company an' would be tellin' me who it was."

"Well, it wasn't company, Jeth. No one knocked, and I didn't hear a car drive in or anything. Of course the boys were playing and making lots of noise like they always do, and at nine o'clock Millard and all of them went up to bed, and at ten I saw a man."

"Tush, tush, Myra," Jeth said, taking off his shoes. "Let's go to bed. What would a man be wantin' around here?"

"That's what I wonder. It couldn't be money."

"It couldn't be gas, for we haven't that."

"I hadn't thought of that," Myra said somewhat relieved. "I thought of everything else but gas."

"I really don't think you saw any one," continued Jeth, pulling off his socks and squinting his lazy brown eyes. He yawned. "You weren't scared, were you?"

"Well—sorta," Myra bit her lip. She took the groceries out of the basket.

"You sold all the popcorn?" she asked.

"Yep." Jeth took a drink.

"Did you stop at the Daisy Del tonight?" Myra put the crackers in the top of the cabinet and opened the sack of sugar.

"Long enough to get me a sandwich an' a cup of coffee." Silence. Myra put the peanut butter and mustard in the cupboard. "Why?" Jeth coughed.

"Oh, I had a notion to call and see if you were there and ask if—"

"Ask what?" Jeth's eyebrows twitched. He held his breath awkwardly.

"Oh," came Myra's slow answer, "ask if you wouldn't hurry on home."

"You mean you were really that scared, Myra?" His heart pounded quietly.

"Oh, I don't know, Pop. I couldn't think of anything but Glen."

"Glen? What about Glen?" He drew a breath of partial relief.

"I mean," Myra walked toward the bedroom, "maybe it does sound silly now, Pop," she said over her shoulder, "but you know how a person feels after reading those kidnapping stories in the newspapers."

"Maybe we'd better quit takin' the paper then, Myra. Anyhow, who'd take one of ours? We ain't got no ransom money."

"But those babies weren't stolen for ransom money," reminded Myra. "They were just stolen because babies are in demand and folks who haven't any want them."

"Don't you never again get such an idea inter your head, Myra Grinstead. An' don't you tell the children you saw a man at that winder. I'm surprised. I thought you were brave." He crossed the kitchen and stood close to Myra.

"I thought so, too, Jeth, until—tonight."

"You mustn't be afraid again," Jeth said quite tenderly. "You must go on ter bed an' get your rest. You know I never come in," Jeth hesitated awkwardly, "so late, Myra. Remember, it's three miles ter town an' three miles back, an' when I don't get a ride, I have ter hoof it." He touched her shoulder, then patted it gently.

"You almost always get a ride, don't you, Pop?"

"Usually. Say, Ginger Hanckins is goin' ter butcher tomorrow— two hogs an' he's goin' ter send some over fer us." He wanted to change the subject.

"Are you good friends with Ginger Hanckins, Jeth?"

"That depends on what you call good. We're friends when it comes ter ridin' in the same car from town out. Tuesday night Anthony Beabout brought me home."

"Oh, yes, Pop. Millard told me tonight you have him hired out to Mr. Beabout as soon as school closes in the spring. Are you sure— I—a—aren't you afraid he will work him too hard?"

"Too hard? Why Myra, Millard will soon be fourteen. He ought to be workin' out now."

"But you didn't talk it over with Millard first, did you, Pop?"

"Did I have to? Let's get ter bed, Myra."

"He takes such an interest in books and he's such a serious minded boy that sometimes I feel we must let him go on to school if he wants to. Who knows, Jeth, maybe Millard will become a —" For some reason Mrs. Grinstead did not say what she was thinking.

Chapter 3

JETHRO Grinstead was twenty-one when he married Myra Winegar. She was eighteen but mature in more ways than one. Myra was a girl who at the age of fourteen could prepare a complete meal by herself and make her own clothes. More than that, at an early age she wore a womanly dignity that was not ordinary. Myra Winegar was very attractive. She was blessed with a crowning glory of black silken wavy hair, a peach-bloom complexion, high intelligent forehead, and a full honest face, just round enough to be pleasant. Jeth (for everyone called Jethro Jeth from little up) also had black hair, but it was not wavy; his eyes like hers were brown. Jeth had a physique any girl would admire, or boy, too, for that matter. His straight broad shoulders were square and usually erect. Once in a while he did forget himself and let them slump. At the age of twenty-one Jeth inherited sixty acres of good farming land, and he purchased from his younger brother, Oaty, his sixty. He built a brand new house four miles from Doddridge, a prosperous young city of twenty-five thousand or more. Jeth and Myra were married by a middle-aged bishop of the faith in which both had been brought up.

They were as happy as they knew how to be. To work and work hard, do her work well, and help Jeth pay for their new home was Myra's daily ambition. She planned and tried and strove to that end to her utmost, but in spite of all her trying the day came when they both knew the wisest and only sensible thing to do was to put the nice new house and 120 acres up for sale and start all over again on a smaller scale.

There is nothing so depressing and demoralizing to one's spiritual and mental state as debts—big debts. There was little difficulty in obtaining a buyer for the farm, but it was rather heartbreaking to

16

leave it and purchase a much smaller one. At least they could always have the memory of Orpha and Don Millard being born in the new house.

Myra always reminded herself of that. She could never forget when she heard Millard laugh for the first time as he lay kicking in the blue-lined clothesbasket by the bay window in the spring of the year. A happy robin had lighted for a minute on the white window sill to snatch some bread crumbs Myra had put there. Baby Millard caught sight of the trembling bird and waved both his hands and feet and laughed.

"Baby laugh," little Orpha had said, stretching up on her tiptoes and pointing to her little brother in the basket.

It was strange how certain pictures stayed in Myra's memory for years and years. Beautiful memories gave her inspiration, helped her build personality, deepened her love and sympathy, and even made for peace and confidence in sweetening her soul. Myra Grinstead was a quiet, deep thinker. She was not a woman of many words, but conversed in her thoughts.

That incident in particular made a lasting colorful impression on Myra. Soon after that they moved to a house that had no bay window, no white window sills, only lead colored ones that needed paint badly.

Somehow the necessity of selling, less than four years after they were married, and moving to a smaller farm had a peculiar inexacting, and inexorable effect on Jeth. Hadn't he tried? Were the fates against him? Other young couples were getting ahead. Leroy Slapp, Levi Chapman, and Ernest Hackleman had all been married by the same bishop that same spring, and not one of them had had to sell. If they weren't getting ahead financially, no one found it out. And it couldn't be that he had picked a shiftless, spendthrift wife. No, Jeth could never accuse Myra either, nor did he offer to. Jeth knew Myra was a worker and a saver—not only in the kitchen, but with the scissors and even with soap.

But around the coming of Don Millard came that down feeling. It came upon Jeth like an avalanche. Now most avalanches slide down the side of a mountain with swift, irresistible force, and suddenly bury or smash objects below. It was not exactly like that with Jeth. For months he was under the shadow of that slowly moving avalanche, but could not get out of its way. When he finally decided

17

he must sell the new house, he was almost overwhelmed with despair. He felt buried.

Don Millard was Myra's choice of the name. Jeth didn't exactly object to it, nor was he enthusiastic. He was nonchalant. But after the baby came, the name Don gave him such a depressed feeling he didn't know what to do.

"Don Grinstead," he muttered feebly. "Down Grinstead it ought ter be maybe."

"Jeth," said Myra, a little disappointed, "we'll call him Millard. Leave the Don off. We will only use it when we sign his full name, or when he grows up, he can sign his name D. Millard or D. M. Grinstead. See, Jeth? You like that, don't you?"

"That's better."

Jeth's steps lagged somewhat. His square shoulders slumped oftener. Maybe it would have been better had he not purchased Oaty's sixty.

"I will not let this make me feel too bad. Jeth," Myra said when they were beginning to load their furniture. "We have many pleasant memories of this our first home, and we have our two children now, and neither of them is puny—nor are we. Jeth, brace up and let's both smile through this. Please don't act so blue, Jeth. You haven't heard me complain, have you? We have our friends and our church."

"That's it," Jeth said somewhat fretfully, "all the rest of our friends are makin' a better go of it fer some reason. It's either our pigs die, or the chickens don't lay, or not enough rain, or too much wind, or I don't know what. And—as fer the church—oh, well."

Myra turned and facing Jeth, looked him straight in the eyes. Her own brown sparkling ones met his less sparkling ones.

"Oh, well—what—Jeth?"

"Well," he shrugged his shoulders, "what do we get out of it?"

"Out of it, Jeth? Do we go to get something out of it?"

"Why, certainly. Isn't that why we go?"

"You don't mean—things—do you, Jeth? Things like money and —"

"Of course not, Myra. I mean help. Help in here," he smote his breast. "You know what I mean."

Myra was surprised. She had seldom seen Jeth that dramatic.

"Oh." Myra put both hands in her apron pockets. She looked at Jeth a while, then bit her lip. "I guess that depends on us, doesn't it?

I always want to go. Don't you, Jeth?"

She waited. He did not answer.

"I always get something out of it—the services. Don't you?"

Jeth shook his head. "Not always," he said heavily, drawing a deep breath with his words, "and too often nothin'."

"I know I always get more whenever Reverend Jacobs preaches than when Reverend Euellsizer does."

"You mean when Reverend Euellsizer tries to."

"Well," added Myra thinkingly, "everyone I'm sure agrees that Reverend Jacobs is the best speaker, and the best all-around Bible thinker, and perhaps between just you and me, the best everyday Christian, but we must respect Reverend Euellsizer, too. Remember, Jeth, he is getting up in years."

"Well, it's the same old thing every time he gets up. Never anything new. Our church is too much form and rules and—"

"Not all, Jeth," Myra spoke the words gently.

"Let's go to Rugsbush Sunday."

"You mean it, Jeth?" questioned Myra. Her brows as well as her voice denoted the interrogative.

"Sure I do. Maybe I mean join, too."

"No! Why, Jeth! So soon you'd make such a decision? Think what all that would mean. We've been brought up—"

"I've been a thinkin', Myra. A plenty. It would mean better people to chum with, better preachin', better ways of livin'—"

"How's that, Jeth?"

"Well you know. Not so much custom an' ritual an' rules an' more freedom an' maybe a better job, too."

"A better job? What do you mean, Jeth? Don't we farm like anyone else does?"

"But I could maybe get on a real carpenter gang. Maybe Joe Pundle would hire me. He pays big. I—"

"But the farm."

"I'd do that on the side."

"Oh." Myra's chin dropped.

"We might get ahead that way," Jeth said. He seemed to be scrambling for words. Myra looked so surprised. Maybe he was saying plenty all at once.

"We're losin' time here," he said presently, rubbing his hands. "I'll finish packin' these pans, and you begin on those dishes. The

19

truck will be here any minute."

"The dishes are all packed. And—and, Jeth, did you really and truly mean it—you want to break away and join the Rugsbush Church, Jeth?" Myra's eyes opened wide, real wide, but there were not any tears in her eyes. Myra wasn't a woman to cry easily.

"Yes," answered Jeth.

"Well, I tell you," Myra said slowly but with meaning, "if you join first and can prove to me you're a better Christian in that church than in ours—Oh, Jeth—Jeth, I'm not hurting your feelings am I—I——don't mean to be hurting you, but anyway if you can—why, then I'll join, too."

Jeth's mouth fell open but no words came out. He looked at Myra in utter astonishment. How intelligent and pretty she was. Jeth knew his wife wasn't a stupid woman. He loved Myra.

Then the truck came and the Grinstead's four moved out of the nice new house where Myra was Jethro's pretty bride.

No one would have wanted to tell Jeth Grinstead he was a poor manager. No one would have dared to—not even his own wife, Myra. It seemed to her that was why they never got ahead, because it was the only reason left. It wasn't because Jeth didn't have a good job that brought him good wages. Every reason but the one she couldn't mention she crossed out. In her mind she had gone over the situation for years.

The smaller farm was soon sold for a still smaller one. This happened again and still again, until when Glen was a baby the Grinsteads had moved twelve times, always to where Jeth thought it was a wise move and for the welfare of the family.

Now in spite of everything Jeth was a good provider. He saw to it that his family had plenty of wholesome food. And whenever the children got sick he took them to a doctor or called one out. One of the greatest drawbacks about moving around so much was that the children had to change schools every year. The problem for Orpha was over with now, for she had finished the eighth grade and that without any honors. Was it any wonder? Poor Orpha. But Liticia and Millard. Even though they were both brilliant, having to enter a different school each year made the adjustment problem a real one—not only for them but for the three younger boys as well.

"Mother," called Liticia the next evening after the scare her mother had said nothing of. No answer.

"Where's mother?" Mother was always in the kitchen when she came home from school. Always. Liticia hurried to the bedroom. She stopped short. Her mother was kneeling beside her bed as though in prayer. Liticia backed away on tiptoe. What had taken mother to her knees at this time of day?

Chapter 4

IT was not an uncommon thing for Myra Grinstead to pray. Liticia was as certain her mother prayed every day as she was that she washed her face and combed her hair. But she had never before found her on her knees at this hour. Had something sad happened—like Grandmother dying—Grandmother Winegar? That would be about one of the saddest things Liticia could think of happening. Orpha was outside feeding the chickens, and she knew the four boys were all right, for they had all come home together in the same school bus. They were loitering outside playing with a slingshot Millard had helped them make. Maybe Glen was sick. Quietly Liticia pulled the bedroom door half shut. Just then the boys came in on the bound, and the next minute Mother stepped out of her bedroom smiling.

"Is Glen sick?"

"No," answered her mother. "Why?"

"Oh, I just wondered," Liticia hung up her coat. "Is he sleeping?"

"Yes. He's sleeping unusually long today for some reason." Mother turned her head. "But he's awake now." She chuckled good-naturedly. "Who could sleep with all this noise in here? Where does your cap belong, Derwood?"

"Let me get Glen, Mother," Liticia said.

Derwood picked up his cap and put it where it belonged. Richard and Homer Jo were pretty well trained by this time. Myra Grinstead was an excellent housekeeper.

And she was an excellent cook, too. Three times a week she baked seven loaves of snowy white light bread—Monday, Thursday, and Saturday. Jeth would have loved her for that alone, if for no other reason. "It even beats the bread my own mother used to bake," he had told her long ago.

And very recently he said, "It gets better every time."

22

"But Orpha made it this time, Pop," Myra said beaming on Orpha across the table.

* * * * *

"I'm hungry," shouted Richard.

"Hungry?" echoed Mother, "well, this is Friday night, you know, so you boys start shelling the corn right away, and I'll fix each of you a slice of catchup bread."

"Make mine good and thick," instructed Richard.

"Mine too," added Homer Jo. "Did you make the bread last time, Mother, or did Orpha?"

"I forget. Oh, yes, Orpha did. It doesn't matter who, does it?"

Mother spread the butter on generously, then homemade catchup over that. One slice called for another, but she said more than one would spoil their supper.

And what a supper they had that night, for sure enough Ginger Hanckins did as Pop had said he said he would; he sent his oldest boy over with a yard and a half of fresh sausage and some backbone Mother said she'd cook with kraut for Saturday dinner, since the children would all be at home.

"Better save jes a little of that back fer me fer supper," suggested Pop, and Mother said she would.

Just because Jeth Grinstead lacked the ability to get ahead financially wasn't saying Myra didn't love him. Nor did it indicate he lacked in every other respect. Secretly and quite naturally, of course, Myra did wish that they owned their own home like most of their friends and relatives did. However, she seldom complained. This now was the nicest house they had lived in since they had sold their first new one. There were hardwood floors in the living and dining rooms, a completely furnished bathroom, and a furnace. How fortunate they were to find such a place with ten acres of rich fertile ground and rent not exorbitant!

Myra wished Jeth would get a little excited just once in a while; for instance when something extraordinary happened or extra-unfortunate like Richard stepping on a rusty nail, or a motorcycle accident right in front of their house and two men getting hurt, or their nearest neighbor's house being struck by lightning. But truly the nearest Jeth had ever reached the excitable stage was when big overgrown Bud Tidlett claimed a pocketknife he found on the playground and Jeth knew it belonged to Homer Jo. He got pretty much excited and roused up that time when Homer Jo came home and said Bud wouldn't hand over that knife. Jeth looked mighty aggravated and excited like.

"Are you sure it was your knife, Homer Jo?" And Pop's lazy brown eyes snapped when he asked it.

"Yes, Pop. That blue speckled one you bought me the last time we went to town."

"An' no one else in school had one like it, did they?"

"No," Homer Jo affirmed strongly.

"Then he'll hand it over or—" Pop swallowed hard and added, half winking his left eye with a certain meaning, "You tell him I'll be over ter see the teacher."

He most likely would have gone, too, because Jeth Grinstead took a special interest in everything that concerned his second son, Homer Jo. Somehow he just liked that boy more than ordinary. Homer Jo got his knife back. Pop's fondness for the other boys in comparison was quite ordinary, because Pop never showed that much emotion or offered to spend that much energy trying to redeem anything they ever lost or broke. They had learned to help each other or suffer the consequences. Homer Jo had a way with Pop that seemed to work something like the law of magnetism. That was another thing Myra wished was different. There was still another thing Myra wished and wished Pop wouldn't do and that was stopping at the Daisy Del after he finished selling popcorn. Of course, Pop said Daisy made the best and biggest sandwiches in all Doddridge, and maybe she did; true enough the Daisy Del was on Franklin Street and that led into the road home. Myra really didn't object to Jeth getting a warm sandwich after he'd stood on the street corners for two hours, and after he'd worked hard all day. It was only natural that he'd be hungry. Jeth always was a hearty eater, as most strong men are. Nor did she object to his getting a cup of coffee or even a dish of ice cream to go with it. Myra loved Jeth. But if only Daisy wouldn't allow gambling in the Daisy Del. Pop never would admit he gambled; neither did he exactly deny it outright. Whenever his wife asked him about it he acted kind of shocked (not excited) and looked so hurt, and every time he answered with a strange mingling of both chagrin and mortification, and in a low tone that was next to a whisper, "Why, Myra Grinstead! Whatever makes you ask me such a question? Do I look like a gambler?" And Myra could honestly say he didn't, because he didn't. Jeth looked like an honest, upright, respectable laboring man.

Pop started being Pop when Homer Jo was four years old. This is how it happened. Homer Jo begged to go along to work with his father one morning, and since it was a barn Joe Pundle's gang was putting up, and since the barn was on Harvey Flitche's farm and Harvey had two small boys, Jeth saw no reason why Homer Jo couldn't go along and play with Harvey's boys and at the same time get an idea how men built barns. Homer Jo always did like to play with a hammer and nails from tiny up. So when Homer Jo begged, Jeth told Myra to put an extra sandwich and an extra banana in his lunch bucket. Prior to this Millard had begged to go along several times, but to no avail. Fathers never took their boys along with them to work. Jeth couldn't be responsible for watching a boy, and Joe Pundle never would allow such.

Well, that day during the noon hour and after Jeth was through eating his lunch, Russie Richmond (Jeth had been working next to him all forenoon) handed Homer Jo his box of smoking tobacco and said, "Here, kid, take this over ter your Pop; he wants to borrow some."

Homer Jo took the can over to his father and said, "Here Pop, he said take some."

"Pop?" Jeth asked with an inquiring inflection as he reached for the can. Then he laughed. It was the strangest sort of laugh, however, and even little Homer Jo thought so.

"Why do you call me Pop?" Jeth didn't take any tobacco out right away. He just stared at his boy.

"He did." Homer Jo pointed to Russie Richmond standing about twelve feet away. "Papa, Pop." Then Homer Jo laughed, too. That was how Jeth started being Pop. If any of the other children would have started it, it wouldn't have started. But because it started with Homer Jo, it was all right. Jeth even thought it was sorta cute. He'd been Pop now for three years. It seemed longer than that. Jeth was quite gray already and not yet forty.

That noon at Harvey Flitche's barn building, Jeth didn't laugh the way he did because Homer Jo called him Pop for the first time. Not altogether. When Homer Jo looked up at him, it put him on a little tension. Rather unexpectedly, too. Maybe he should have left Homer Jo at home.

Jeth had been smoking a pipe since the day his voice changed from a boy's to a man's. And that was before he married Myra, quite some while before. Jeth's father didn't seem to object, at least he never said anything against smoking. How could he, for he himself smoked. But Jeth. Somehow he couldn't bring himself to being reconciled to the thought of his own boys smoking. It was a habit that didn't do any man any good. To himself he admitted this over and over. It was an expensive habit, too—of course, not as expensive as drinking would be, but to himself Jeth admitted this every day. It was like burning money.

On several occasions he had told Myra he wished he'd never started. But all his chums smoked and he certainly did not want to be called a sissy or a cream puff. The other boys said it made a fellow strong to smoke, especially a pipe. Maybe it did and maybe it didn't. Secretly Jeth wondered. He'd quit some time and find out. In the forenoon he decided to quit at noon. At noon he decided to smoke once more and quit after work. At five o'clock he thought, "Oh, what's the use? My father smoked from the day I can first remember anything. Grandfather smoked to his dying day, and so does Reverend Euellsizer. There can be habits that aren't sinful." In these secret one-man debates "Resolved that I should quit smoking," Jeth Grinstead always allowed the negative to win, but in his heart he knew the affirmative deserved it by weight of the arguments. His five boys made a large percent of that weight, Homer Jo in particular. When he was four, Derwood was the baby, and Glen wasn't yet. The debate started before he had five boys. Of course Myra wished Jeth didn't smoke, and her main reason too was the boys. She didn't let the habit bother her. She knew Jeth smoked before she married him. It was after Don Millard was walking and talking that she developed a conscience against it.

That was one reason why Myra wouldn't care if Jeth would change his membership to the Rugsbush Church. She knew that Preacher did not smoke, and she also knew that Jeth had a deep admiration for him. Jeth had talked off and on about making the change for more than twelve years. At first the proposition he conceived was this: it would mean getting away from so many rituals and forms and belonging to a church where he'd have more religious freedom. But after twelve years of deliberating and considering the question, and also attending the Rugsbush Church frequently, he came to realize that there were as many rules in the Rugsbush Church as in his own but that every single one was an aid to finding joy and freedom in the Lord, and that the something he called freedom he thought he wanted was careful discipline by men of God, in love, and according to the Word.

Jeth was pretty certain he would feel out of place smoking a pipe if he were received into the Rugsbush congregation. For twelve years the one-man debate had continued and the decision of the one judge was always the same.

Constant defeat puts chivalry on the wane. That was true of the most gallant heroes of the knighted era. And Jeth Grinstead never had made a record of being strikingly brave about overcoming any obstacle. He had some brilliant plans broken time after time and felt many a high ambition crumble. He had not yet learned where to go for help or was not quite willing or ready. Which was it.

"You're sleepy already, aren't you, Pop?" Myra saw the newspaper drop and Jeth's chin touched his chest.

"Guess I am."

"Then why don't you go on to bed and sleep in comfort?"

Jeth glanced at the clock and scratched his head.

"Only eight?"

"It wouldn't hurt you to get a few extra hours, would it? You look tired, Jeth," Myra said with concern. He was three years older.

"Guess I will then." And Jeth went to bed.

"Millard," said his mother after she heard Pop's regular hard breathing, "I would like to talk to you a little while."

Millard stood beside his mother, and his eyes met hers—not on the level for Millard was all of two inches taller. They were standing at the stair door.

"What about?" he asked.

"A number of things. Let's sit down."

Chapter 5

MILLARD followed her across the dining room. He sat beside her.

"You're thirteen, Millard," she began, "the oldest of the boys, and I'm depending on you. I hope—you've never taken a smoke yet."

"Did you think I had, Mother?" Millard's face showed surprise.

"Not that I know of, Millard. I just hope you won't start. It's so hard to quit once you get started. I read something like this that a habit is like cable. We weave a thread of it every day but at last it cannot be broken. It's hard, you know."

"Yes, I know."

"You know? How do you know, Millard?" His mother bent forward and looked into his face searchingly.

"I can guess that much about Pop and—besides, he told Homer Jo so." "When?"

"Oh, I don't know when. More than once."

"Did you hear him say it?" "No, but Homer Jo said he did. He told me so just yesterday or the day before. He said Pop told him he wished he'd never started and he hoped his boys won't."

"Did he ever talk to you like that?"

"Who, Pop?"

"Yes."

"No, of course not. Pop never talks to me much about anything." Millard's glance dropped to the floor and lingered there. "Wished sometimes he would," he added, reducing the tone of his voice.

"That's why I want to talk to you, Millard," answered his mother quickly. "Did you mean then you've never taken a smoke?"

"I never have," Millard's voice was clear and positive. He raised his glance. He could see his mother's fingers trembling slightly as she picked at the bias tape on the edge of her blue percale apron.

"You've never been tempted to?"

"I—well I can't say that, Mother. I suppose I've been tempted a few times."

"No doubt you have," his mother's voice sounded a little tired, and he heard a note of anxiety in it, too. "Why do you suppose Pop doesn't want his boys to smoke?"

"I don't know unless it would cost too much. At least I don't suppose he'd want us to be spending money for smoke until we go on our own."

"Can you think of any other reason why you think he doesn't want you boys to start smoking?"

"Yes, I can think of one more reason."

"What is that?"

"Because he knows you don't want us to."

Myra Grinstead sat up very straight. She folded her plump arms across her breast and sat for a moment in deep thought.

"You mean," she spoke softly, choosing her words carefully— "You mean—you think—Pop wants you boys to do the things that would make me happy?"

"I think Pop wants us to do what he knows is right, and don't do himself, and if we listen to you—oh, well, I don't know how to say it, Mother, but," Millard reached down and straightened the cuff on his trousers, "he surely knows you've got something he hasn't. I don't know what it is myself exactly, but Pop—he—knows you're right."

"Right about what?"

"About everything, I guess."

"You mean—that, Millard. Oh, Millard."

"Sure I mean it. Pop could show it more than he does sometimes maybe—but I think he—" Millard stopped abruptly. He chewed at his smallest fingernail. Millard was not in the habit of chewing his nails.

"Loves me?" whispered his mother. She surprised herself. Oh! that was the first thought that had come to her mind—but—she didn't mean to say it.

"Don't you think he does?" Millard dropped his hand.

"Yes. Of course, he does," came Mother's ready answer. In spite of a few things about Jeth she wished were different, and in spite of his shortcomings, she was positive he had loved her when they were married, and over the years he had proved it in more ways than one. But if there was any one thing that ever made her doubt the sincerity of Jeth's love, it was his treatment of Millard. Myra didn't approve of showing partiality. Just why Jeth took more interest in Homer Jo, and showed so much more affection toward him than toward any of the other children, Myra could never quite figure out—unless it was because he looked more like his father than any of the others. And why Jeth ignored Millard except when he thought he had to be scolded had been puzzling her for years. Millard had been an obedient, well-behaved boy from the time he understood yes from no. Millard had been normal in every respect, intelligent, and even clever. The past nine months or so, his mother had taken particular notice to a growing seriousness about him. She noticed that when he wasn't reading he seemed to be in deep thought about something.

"Have you ever thought," she continued in a soft undertone, because the three boys were playing with their toy horses on the opposite side of the room, "that perhaps Pop might be struggling with—with conviction?"

"Conviction?" Millard turned abruptly. The color left his face.

"You know what I mean, don't you?" she asked.

"I'm not sure."

"Well, it seems to me, Millard, that for a long time Pop has been dissatisfied with himself. He wants to join the Rugsbush Church, because he seems to think our church is all form and ritual, and yet he can't quite give up some things he knows he should and make a new start. You remember that evening when that minister from Rugsbush, Brother Dungan, came here to visit us and, Pop asked him to conduct our family worship?" "You mean Pop acted like we always had it?"

"Yes."

Millard ran both hands into his pockets and stiffened his back. "That night, Mother, I said to myself that if I'm ever a Christian I want to be a real one—and all the time."

Myra's breath came fast. Almost too fast. "Oh, Millard—do you mean then—that you have been thinking of it? That's really what I wanted to talk to you about tonight. Have you, Millard?"

"Some," he whispered.

"I'm glad then. You see I felt perhaps you were old enough to be hearing the voice of God."

Millard stopped breathing. No one had ever talked to him like this before or on this subject—not even his own mother. They had been confidential with each other, but Myra had not until today felt led to speak to him alone on this point. She did not believe in hindering or urging young children into the kingdom. But Millard had been attending the Rugsbush Church with the family often enough now, that if he listened at all, he surely knew everyone had sinned and everyone must repent. Then, too, if Millard read with understanding (and he surely did) the books her mother had given him, he could not help but be face to face with what it meant to be a friend of God or an enemy. Why was Millard so serious of late and unusually quiet?

"Of course it's some months yet until school will be out," his mother continued, "and if Pop wants you to work for Mr. Beabout, it will most likely mean you will have to live there." She hesitated so long it seemed like a full minute. Orpha and Liticia wondered what Mother was talking to Millard about, but neither tried to listen.

"It must be three miles over there." "It's four."

"Four? And you have no bicycle, no horse, no way of getting back and forth unless Mr. Beabout would see that you have a way."

"Maybe Pop will have a car by that time."

"Do you think? Well, maybe he will. He's been talking about getting one for several years."

"Not a new one."

"My, no. Millard, you know we couldn't afford a new one."

"Well, if he doesn't get some kind of a car pretty soon, we're going to be left way behind in everything. The neighbors are going to get tired hauling us around, and there's so many of us, there's never room for all of us. I think sometimes," Millard's face beclouded and a desolate expression crossed it, "maybe that's the reason why Pop hired me out—because there's too many of us here."

"Oh, Millard," cried his mother and her big brown eyes got suddenly misty, "I don't know why he'd feel that way. Surely— surely," and she reached over and touched his arm gently, "surely, Millard, you don't think I feel that way, do you?"

Slowly Millard shook his head. He bit his lip hard.

"I don't want to be in anybody's way." His lower lip trembled slightly. He drew his one foot up to his knee. He fumbled with his shoestring, twisting it nervously. It wasn't at all like Millard to be nervous.

"You're not, Millard," his mother's hand on his arm felt warm. "If we had two dozen children, I would never say there were too many, or that any of them were in my way. I do think it would have been best if Pop would have talked this over with you first before he actually hired you to Mr. Beabout."

"But he didn't."

"Well, maybe he means only for the summer."

"He told me he promised me for a year."

"A year?" gasped Mrs. Grinstead, "but Millard, you're not through school yet."

"That's it. If I have to work as hard as I've heard Anthony Beabout's hired men always do, I can't make very good grades, and I was hoping to be able to finish school—well at least with above average marks."

"The eighth grade won't be too hard for you," his mother said comfortingly. "It will be easier than the seventh. But what I wanted to say is this, Millard: if when school closes, Pop still expects you to go over there, I hope that by that time you'll be strong enough in your own convictions that you can stand up for what you believe and know is right. Mr. Beabout—well, I doubt if he's a Christian, Millard. That's all for tonight. I just wanted to encourage you not to begin smoking. So many boys your age do these days. Then if they do want to give it up, it makes it that much harder."

"Well, if I ever join a church, Mother, it will be the Rugsbush Church; I'm sure of that."

"Why?"

"I just like it best. The preachers act like they care about us boys."

"I'm glad you feel that way. I think Pop will change over before so long now. I am praying every day especially for you, Millard. Good night now. I believe I'll go to bed early, too."

"Good night," Millard said. "Come on, boys, let's go upstairs, so Mother can go to bed."

* * * * *

Saturday forenoon, and the Grinstead house smelled of baking sugar cookies, pumpkin pies, and warm rolls. A light skiff of snow had fallen during the night. Having the oven on made the house cozy and warm. Both girls liked to help in the kitchen and learn Mother's methods of making ordinary foods tasty.

Myra herself answered the knock. It was the landlady.

"Good morning, Mrs. Grinstead." The woman on the porch had a voice that chimed like a bell.

"Good morning," answered Mrs. Grinstead. "Come in. It's chilly outside this morning, isn't it?"

"Oh, yes, a little," smiled Mrs. Morris, "but we have a heater in our car."

Myra hadn't noticed the car drive in. The woman motioned to someone. "Come on in, Christopher," she called. A large man got out of the car and followed Mrs. Morris into the house.

"This is my brother, Mrs. Grinstead. He brought me over in his car. Mr. Morris is down again with rheumatism. And, oh, how that man suffers! So we must hurry back, Mrs. Grinstead. I'd like to go up in the attic and get the rest of our things. There's a rocking chair up there yet, and my large mirror. I brought Christopher along to help me." The woman unbuttoned her fur coat.

"All right," Myra said, "go on up."

"And does it ever smell good in here." Mrs. Morris sniffed. "That's the way it used to smell in my grandmother's house half the time. Baking everything that's good, I'll bet. Mrs. Grinstead, you'd better start a bakeshop. You could work up a big business in Demerious, I'll bet. Couldn't she, Chris?"

"Wouldn't wonder that a bit."

The two went to the attic.

"The beds are all made, aren't they, girls?" asked Mother. The girls said they were.

Before long Mrs. Morris came down carrying the gold-framed mirror, her brother Christopher following with the rocking chair.

"You are a very nice housekeeper, Mrs. Grinstead," Mrs. Morris lingered at the door. "We appreciate that. We're thinking of doing a little remodeling here before long. We want to make an open stairway right here and put in a pretty new kitchen sink."

Of course Myra wondered if that would mean paying more rent, but she didn't ask.

"The furnace is working all right, I guess, isn't it, Mrs. Grinstead?"

"Yes, just fine."

"Keeping warm, I suppose?"

"Yes. Here are a few cookies for you."

"Oh, thank you."

Beaming from eardrop to eardrop, Mrs. Morris took the sack of cookies and hurried off, leaving a trail of some rare spicy perfume from the door to the attic.

Chapter 6

SATURDAY night as usual found Jeth Grinstead on the streets of Doddridge selling popcorn. The temperature was dropping fast until it was too cold for anyone to be standing long in any one spot. At nine o'clock he pulled up his overcoat collar and started cracking his feet together.

He had seven more sacks in his basket, and he didn't want to take any of them along home. He seldom did, for anyone who liked popcorn and anyone who had tried Jeth Grinstead's thereupon became a regular customer.

* * * * *

The girls helped their mother make preparations for the Sabbath day dinner such as peeling the potatoes, fixing the dressing for the chicken, making the jello, bringing up sweet pickles from the cellar, and spreading the cloth on the diningroom table. Myra Grinstead never liked to work more than was necessary on the Lord's day. Having company naturally meant extra dish-washing, but the company usually helped, so it wasn't much more work than ordinary. The extra potatoes could easily be peeled on Saturday night after supper, the butter pats could be made, the celery cleaned, and what not, to make less work for Sunday morning. That was as much a part of Myra's religion as her daily prayers. Then, too, the girls agreed with her that having company was that much more pleasure, and they could sit in church and relax and enjoy the services more, when everything possible was prepared before Sunday morning.

Tomorrow Uncle Levi (Myra's oldest brother) from Granger was coming with his new second wife, and Grandmother and Grandfather Winegar were invited, too. Uncle Levi and his bride (Myra was anxious to meet her) were over at Grandfather's now, and in the morning they would stop by and take Jeth's along to church in their

35

new Plymouth sedan. They would all visit the Rugsbush Church. They were agreed on that, for Uncle Levi knew Rev. Dungan well. In fact, as boys they used to go to school together back in Granger. Myra would have liked to invite all the Dungans, too, but there were eight of them, and she had only twelve nice dinner plates. "Of course, she could borrow anything she wanted from her mother, but then they would have to set two tables, and the children always get so hungry and restless if the have to do the waiting," Myra reasoned. "Anyway, it would be nice to sit around as a family, just twelve, and to eat slowly and to visit as long as they liked. Having to get up and hurry around and set for the second table just naturally spoiled the visit. With Uncle Levi's and the grandparents there would be exactly twelve. Glen would be in his high chair to the side. They would invite the Dungans some other time," Myra decided.

Myra walked through the house once more. Not a thing was out of place, or her observing eye would have seen it. She pulled off both shoes and sat stocking-footed in her favorite rocking chair. The clean warm floor felt restful. It was nearly ten. Jeth would soon be coming. Myra folded her plump arms and rocked back and forth in satisfaction with the day's work. Everything had gone so smoothly all day. Glen had been extra good, or the little boys had done an extra good job of keeping him entertained. Orpha's cake turned out perfectly, and the bread was never nicer.

Myra was happy. The children had gone to bed happily. Nothing hurt. There was only that good tired feeling one expects to have on Saturday night. Myra felt like curling up like a big Persian cat and sleeping. That's what she'd do. She'd go to bed. Tomorrow would be a big day. A happy day.

How nice and warm it was inside. She could hear the cold wind blowing outside. It could not penetrate. How thankful she was for their home. It was the nicest place they'd had to live in for years and years—twelve years. They'd lived in some mighty poor, rickety cold houses. This was the first time they ever enjoyed a furnace. These hardwood floors were tight, keeping out the cold November wind. Mrs. Morris had said they were going to do some remodeling soon. Myra wondered how soon. A nice new kitchen sink! Maybe like some of those in the catalogue? The open stairway would be pretty enough, but maybe it would take more coal to keep the house warm, too. Jeth might not like buying more coal. Maybe if the rent went up

Jeth would want to move again. Myra hoped not. She was tired moving so often.

Myra jumped. What was that strange noise? She waited. She thought she heard a car start and then slowly and quietly leave the driveway. Yet she wasn't sure. She wiped her forehead with the corner of her apron. Why was she so warm? Millard must have forgotten to check the furnace. She'd do it.

Mrs. Grinstead crossed the dining room. The floor felt terribly hot to her stocking feet. It felt scorching hot! What was wrong? She stepped to the cellar door. Her hand trembled as it gripped the knob. Her whole body trembled. She did not want to open the door—but—she must. Her happy face grew rigid with fear. She opened the door and looked down. Horror-stricken she clutched at her throat. Then as fast as her feet would take her, she crossed the hot floor and dashed up the stairsteps, two at a time.

"Millard!" she called. "Millard! get up this minute! Orpha! Liticia! Get the boys up! Hurry! Our house is on fire!"

Half blinded, not by smoke, but by excitement, Myra ran down the stairs into the bedroom and snatched Glen from his crib. Millard and the three sleepy-eyed boys came down in their pajamas.

"Go back and grab your clothes," cried Mrs. Grinstead. "grab what you can and come! No! No, I mean you, Millard. Just you. You other boys get on out of the house. Hurry, something might explode!" Mrs. Grinstead stood in the open door, unmindful of the cold wind blowing across her warm body.

"Go on out, girls," she demanded.

"But—but—Mother," gasped Liticia half crying. "Where's the fire? How did it start?"

"In the cellar. Don't ask me how, for—I don't know. See, it's coming through the floor now! It's coming up the cellar way! Oh. Oh! look! Go on out and stay out. Millard, do come! Oh, please don't go back in there for anything."

"I'll jump out—the bedroom window."

He was gone. Into his mother's bedroom he dashed. In no time he came around the house, blankets and comforters trailing on the snowy ground behind him.

"Here," he said, "you and the boys wrap up in these. You'll get pneumonia, Mother." He wound a blanket around her shoulders. "Here," he pushed her back, "you get clear away. You've got Glen

37

in your arms, you know. Where's Pop?"

"He didn't come yet," Mother was crying now. "Oh, Jeth. Oh, Pop. Why don't you come?"

"Please don't cry, Mother. I'm here." Millard put both arms around her. "I could maybe go back in—and grab something, yet."

"Don't you do it! Millard! Look! Oh, my, oh! It's coming up everywhere now. Where's Liticia? Liticia!" she screamed, "everybody's here except Liticia! Liticia!"

"What? Then I am going back in."

Over the blazing floor Millard sprang and disappeared in the stairway calling at the top of his voice.

"Licia, Licia!"

"She's not up here, Mother." Millard was hanging out an upstairs window. "Liticia's not up here. Where is she?"

"My God! Millard! Where could she be? Millard, don't you dare come down the stairway now. Oh, Millard! The flames are working up that way. Jump!"

Millard jumped.

Then Pop came.

"What in the world?" But before he was out of Ginger Hanckin's car he could see. So could Ginger.

"Don't cry, Myra," Jeth said, putting an arm around her shoulders. "How did it start?" Myra just cried and shook her head. She wanted to scream and couldn't. She was going to fall.

Three—four—five cars stopped. Men offered to help, but there was nothing to do now but sympathize and watch.

"Jes' be glad it's not our house," Jeth said hoarsely. Through the windows they could see the flames leaping to the ceiling now.

"But—where's—Liticia!" sobbed Myra brokenly. Oh, she did get the words out. "Jeth! Jeth! Liticia's missing!"

"Here she comes," shouted Richard jumping up and down and clapping his hands.

"Child!" cried her mother, "where were you?"

"Why," gasped Liticia, "don't—you—see? I got—Grand—fath—er." She would have fallen but Millard caught her. Her bare cold feet were bruised and bleeding.

"You ran—way down there!" choked Mother. "Barefooted?"

"Why, sure."

"Must have run like—a young deer," Grandfather said. He was

out of breath, too, and could scarcely talk. "We came back—on the—horse. Levi was asleep. Grandma said she'd tell him."

"Everybody's out? Thank God." Grandfather blew his nose. "Too bad, too bad. Nothin' to do but take it now, I guess," he said, wiping away the unbidden tears that blinded him. He shivered and looked away when the mad raging flames fed by the wind roared up through the attic. Then the roof crashed in! Richard and Derwood clung to their father on one side and Homer Jo on the other.

Uncle Levi came. He stood speechless. Someone called the Doddridge fire department, but it was too late.

"Sure is too bad, Myra," Grandfather said. "You must all come on over with us. Come at once. Jeth, get the children together. It's too cold to stand here any longer. Get into Levi's car, children."

At least ten men offered to help take the Grinsteads over to Grandfather Winegar's place about a mile south. But why be divided now? They all crowded into Uncle Levi's car. Several men volunteered to stay until the fire was completely out. One went to a neighbor to call the landlord by phone.

Grandfather and Grandmother Winegar lived in a handsome, spacious, white frame house trimmed with green shutters. Whether or not they would have room for all of Jeth's family was not a question. Every room upstairs was furnished with two full-sized beds, and there were six rooms. Even though Uncle Levi was there with his new wife there was plenty of room.

Poor Jeth. Could he ever get ahead? Just when he thought he was about able to buy a car, now this! Everything gone up in smoke in so short a time. They hadn't even saved enough clothes to go to church the next day.

"Myra," Jeth began after the children were all placed for the night, "do you have any idea how that fire started?"

"Not the least idea, Jeth. Orpha went to the cellar for pickles, and everything was all right then. I was ready to go to bed when I heard a strange noise—"

"What kind of a noise?"

"Kind-a like something falling—like coal rolling down, maybe. I don't know exactly, but it made me jump because it was quiet in the house. Soon after that I am almost certain I heard a car leaving our driveway."

"You think then—that maybe—someone—started the fire?"

asked Jeth, panting.

"I don't know, Jeth. All I know is that it started in the basement somewhere, and the fire seemed to be right up under the floor when I first discovered it. At least, Jeth, it must have started after all the children had gone to bed."

"Wasn't that Thursday night—you—thought—you—seen a man by the bedroom winder, Myra?" Jeth bent forward and looked into Myra's face.

"Yes," she whispered. She clutched at her throat nervously.

"We must tell Mr. and Mrs. Morris this. If they come out ter night yet, I told Mr. Forbes where they could find us." Jeth slapped his knee.

"They'll hardly come tonight, Jeth, because Mrs. Morris and her brother were just out this forenoon, and Mr. Morris is down sick in bed."

"What were they out fer this mornin'?"

"They got the last of her things that she had up in the attic."

"I see." Jeth paced back and forth looking at the floor.

"She'll be terribly upset over this, Jeth. Mrs. Morris will. Oh! I dread to hear what all she'll say, for she just told me this very morning how she is going to put in a new sink and make an open stairway soon. Oh, I do hope she won't blame any of us." Myra covered her face with both hands.

"Now don't worry about that, Myra," said her father. "They know you folks better than to think anything of that kind. And don't worry about a place to live, either, for you can stay here until you find somethin'. And if you can't find a place—well—I'll talk it over with Grandma first."

Chapter 7

IT was high noon when Mrs. Morris and her brother Christopher knocked at Grandfather Winegar's side door. They were talking in low tones as they approached the house slowly. Both Jeth and Myra saw them coming, for they had been expecting them all forenoon.

"Do you want ter go to the door, Myra?" Jeth cleared his throat. Jeth was not nervous. He was not going to let himself look nervous, let alone act it. He walked toward the door..

"I will if you don't want to, Jeth—but go ahead. You're closest to the door."

Jeth opened the door. "Good mornin'," he said.

"Good morning, Mr. Grinstead," Mrs. Morris began. "This—ah—fire was quite a shock. We just couldn't get here sooner, Mr. Grinstead. You see—ah—Mr. Morris is sick, and I had to get someone to stay with him till we get back. I do hope you all got out in—good time."

"Come on in, Mrs. Morris," called Myra over Jeth's shoulder. "You'll get cold standing out there."

"Let's step inside, Christopher," and Christopher did as his sister told him.

"We did, Mrs. Morris," Myra said, "we all got out."

"Well, good," Mrs. Morris drew a long deep breath. "That's all I care about, I mean—what I care about mostly. Of course—I hated to come out here-and—see the house in ashes, but what's that compared to a life. That's the first thing we thought of, wasn't it Christopher?" She drew another long deep breath, longer than the first.

"Yes, yes, of course," answered Christopher, shifting from one big foot to the other. He gripped his hat tightly.

41

"Were you at home when it happened, Mr. Grinstead—I mean when it started?" Mrs. Morris half closed her eyes.

"No, I'm sorry, Mrs. Morris, but I wasn't. If I only had been, I might have discovered it in time."

"Yes, that's what I thought. I mean that's just what I told Christopher. It would have to happen on a night when you go to town to sell popcorn. I—I—don't suppose you tried to call the Doddridge fire department, did you? Of course not. They couldn't have done much anyway with their little old extinguishers. When a fire starts out in the country, it's just about hopeless to try to do much with a wind like we had last night." Mrs. Morris was twisting the leather strap on her pocketbook as fast as she was talking. Christopher stood with his mouth open and stared in the direction of Jeth's knees. He gripped his hat tighter.

"You've been such nice renters all the way through. It's grand you have a place like this to come to. Are the children all here with you?" Mrs. Morris seemed confused for a moment. She swayed a little, then gathered herself together.

"Yes, we're all here together. We told them to stay in bed till dinnertime." Myra said this. "I am very anxious about Liticia in particular, because she ran clear over here barefooted and woke up Grandfather."

"Oh, you don't say!" gasped Mrs. Morris. "Why, the brave little rascal. I hope she won't get sick. When a person is excited they don't catch a cold so easily. And tell me, Mr. Grinstead, do you folks have any insurance—on—your household goods?"

"No, we haven't," answered Jeth. "Do you?"

"We have our furniture insured against fire. Oh, yes. Mr. Morris was always very particular about that. He always did have a horror for fires for some reason."

"I mean on the house." Jeth frowned slightly.

"Oh, we have some, Mr. Grinstead; I don't know if it will cover or not—but—I'm not going to let this spoil the rest of my life, I know that. There are things that could be lots worse than a house—" Mrs. Morris twisted and twisted the strap on her pocketbook—"burning down." She seemed out of breath.

"I'm glad you can take it this way," smiled Myra. She drew a long breath of relief. Wasn't Mrs. Morris going to blame them? Wasn't she going even to insinuate or act vexed?.

"Well, I can't understand what caused this fire to get started, can you Mrs. Grinstead?"

"I haven't the least idea, Mrs. Morris. I had everything fixed for company for today and was about ready to go to bed when I heard a strange noise—"

"A noise?" Mrs. Morris looked at her brother. She caught her breath awkwardly and held it. "Where?"

"In the cellar, Mrs. Morris. Then I thought I heard a car driving away. Soon afterwards I noticed that the floor in the dining room felt hot, and when I opened the cellar door the fire seemed to be under the floor or on the cellar ceiling."

Mrs. Morris made a stifled moan and shook her head. She drew her fur coat up around her neck and snapped and unsnapped her pocketbook several times. Christopher took her by the arm. Was she going to faint?

"Just so you folks are all right," she said. "That's my first concern." Her eyes filled with sudden tears. "I hope the Red Cross will come out to investigate and give you help. If they don't, just let me know and I'll see what I can get them to do for you. This will no doubt be in tomorrow night's paper. We just must go now. Guess I'm upset about this more than I thought I was. Come, Christopher. I feel sort of sick." She inched her way toward the door.

"You should stay for dinner," Myra said. "My parents went to church, but they will soon be home."

"No, indeed, Mrs. Grinstead, we wouldn't think of staying. Thanks anyway, but we must go back. Come, Christopher."

Jeth and Myra stood at the door and watched the shiny black car turn around and start down the lane. Then suddenly Myra turned and looked at Jeth straight in the face. His lazy brown eyes met hers with an unusual understanding twinkle. Millard stepped into the room.

"Maybe you're thinkin' the same thing I am," he heard Pop say to his mother in a low tone.

"Maybe so," Mother answered. Then they both saw Millard and said no more.

Difficulties and a taste of anxiety often bring about a keener relish to life and in the end prove to be a blessing. To Jeth's surprise it was no more than ten days from the night of the fire until they were settled once more in not as nice a house as the Morris place, but in a place they could call home. They could have stayed with Myra's parents all winter had it been necessary, but Grandmother Winegar was getting old, and Myra knew six children in the house might be a little too much on her mother's nerves, even if the house was large. A small five-room house (one-half mile from the school), though in a badly run-down condition, could answer the purpose until something better could be located.

Uncle Levi took Jeth and Myra and the four oldest children to Doddridge on Monday and bought them each clothing, nor did he stop until he had also purchased some for the three younger boys, and bedding, one bed, and a large box of groceries. Few were the neighbors who didn't give something to help furnish the Grinstead house, and besides that, Jeth's congregation made itself responsible for seeing they lacked nothing from a can opener to a heating stove.

But the greatest impression on Jeth and Myra both was a personal visit paid by Rev. Dungan and his wife. Before they left Rev. Dungan handed Jeth a fifty-dollar check from his congregation and the promise of a hog that would be butchered for them the following week. Jeth didn't know exactly where to look nor what to say when he unfolded the piece of yellow paper the minister handed him.

"What's this fer?" asked Jeth, clearing his throat.

"Just a little gift from our congregation, Mr. Grinstead. It isn't a whole lot, but maybe it will buy some coal to keep the family warm over these winter months. I don't know how much time you lost on your job through this misfortune, but I'm sure you can use it. We suggest you use it for some coal so the whole family can benefit from it, but if you need something else worse, it's for you and your wife to decide that."

Jeth looked at the floor, then at Myra, then at the minister. He picked at the corner of the check and said in a subdued tone, "I can't quite understand this, Rev. Dungan, but it will certainly help us out a lot, an' we thank you."

"We surely do," Myra said sweetly, trying at the same time to keep back the tears, "but we're not members of your church, Rev. Dungan. What would Reverend Jacob say to this?"

"But you've been attending our church for some time, so we feel quite confident you must like our group a little, and we hope we've made you feel at home. Then, too, your oldest daughter has expressed her desire to me of wanting to become a Christian, and I think—"

Jeth looked up in surprise.

"I think," continued Rev. Dungan, somewhat cautiously, "she is waiting to see what her parents are going to do." The minister smiled.

Jeth coughed.

"You understand, Mr. Grinstead, and your wife too, that we do not believe in proselyting. If you are satisfied in your own church, I'd advise you to stay there. If you are not and our church appeals to you, I'd advise you to investigate our doctrines thoroughly before you fully make up your minds."

Jeth nodded and kept looking at the check in his hand.

"Jeth's been talking of changing to your church for twelve years," Myra said softly.

"That long?"

Jeth smiled.

"Well, I tell you, Mr. Grinstead," Rev. Dungan said, "if we teach anything that is not Scriptural, I'd be glad if you would draw my attention to it, or if there is anything you do not quite understand, I'd be glad to explain it to you."

"It's not that," Jeth said. "It's not that."

"What is it then?"

"Well, it's jes' the breakin' away, I reckon." Jeth stroked his face.

"Yes," Rev. Dungan said genially, "I think I understand how you feel, but you see this way, you're really not faithful to either denomination, are you?"

"Guess not."

"For the sake of your children think it through prayerfully, Mr. Grinstead."

"Well, my wife here knows how I lean." Jeth looked at Myra and smiled faintly.

"Just so you both lean the same way," ventured sweet-faced Sister Dungan. "Do your parents object to the change?"

"No," answered Myra. "They want us to be satisfied. It's all right with them."

That night Myra and Jeth talked until near midnight.

Jeth Grinstead might have been classed as a nominal Christian. His spiritual experience probably was average. Over the years since his baptism he had not lost out, because one can't lose what one never had. For Myra, being baptized and becoming a member of the body of believers meant something definite and real. Jeth and Myra had joined the same church, the same bishop baptized both of them, and their vows and denunciations had been identical. But for some reason Myra really felt her religion. It was more to her than a mechanical, conventional, formal thing that the young people of her church were expected to do before they got married. At an early age she had developed an appetite for things spiritual. Her purity of motive for seeking the truth was revealed on her face. She beamed with an unclouded peace that was not found on Jeth's face. However, Jeth did not have the appearance of a wicked man. Indeed not. He did believe, but just didn't beam.

Before spring Jeth got a secondhand car. The family started attending the Rugsbush church for evening services. Myra sat rapt as she drank in salvation truths in such simple but attractive programs. She sat rapt because she could see that her own children, Orpha, Millard,and maybe Liticia, too were listening with understanding ears. There was only one thing that Jeth complained about, and that was that it took quite a bit of gas to drive to church twice a Sunday.

*   *   *   *   *

"Millard," said his teacher one evening after school had been dismissed, "I am well pleased with the work you have been doing this year. I heard the other day that the Smith's are moving to Oklahoma and the McMasters to California. That will take three from our eighth grade next year. But I'm glad you will be one of my pupils."

Millard smiled and his big brown eyes sparkled in appreciation. He liked Miss Butterfield and she liked Millard. But Miss Butterfield was not the first teacher who had shown a fondness for Millard Grinstead. He was a boy who did not try only by spurts, as some others did; he tried every day. He handed in his work neatly done, he was punctual, and he was careful to follow directions. Such characteristics endear a pupil to a teacher more than look, or rank in society, or family name. In spite of Millard's faded shirts and patched overalls Miss Butterfield esteemed him for his aptitude. School work for Millard had never been a drudgery.

*   *   *   *   *

Millard looked up from his history book with a quick glance. What was Grandmother Winegar telling his father and mother in the kitchen?

46

Chapter 8

I T'S just like this, Myra and Jeth," Grandfather was saying. "Grandma an' I have talked this over among ourselves before we decided to come over here and make the proposition. If it doesn't appeal to you, you don't need to make the move, but we feel with your boys growin' up you need a bigger place." Jeth was leaning hard against the casing of the cellar door, his hands clasping his suspenders, ready to snap them any minute. The whole family but Liticia and Millard was in the kitchen. As usual they had lessons to study. Millard's head remained up. What was that Grandfather was saying?

"We knew you didn't go to town on Friday night, so we came over. If you want to accept our help we're ready to buy. Your boys, especially Millard, are gettin' to the place where they could be a lot of help on a farm."

Jeth snapped his suspenders. He was thinking fast.

"I wisht it wouldn't be so fer away," Jeth said musingly. "I have my popcorn trade here an' my job. It's not too bad pay."

"They don't need to decide tonight," Grandmother put in.

"No, of course not," answered Grandfather. "We wouldn't expect you to make up your minds right away. I wisht, too, the farm was closer but that's how it is. It wouldn't be like goin' where you didn't know nobody."

The proposition rather appealed to Myra at once. It would mean something to move 160 miles from home, but she always did like her brother Levi. Living close to him wouldn't be a bad thing, and then, too, it might be a help to Jeth in more ways than one. And Myra liked Levi's new wife.

Instinctively Myra thought about the church. Maybe this was God's way of helping Jeth make the change. Without mentioning her thoughts to anyone she prayed earnestly that night that if it was God's will they move to Granger, Jeth would be ready to do so without any persuasion on her part.

"Myra," began Jeth one evening when he came home from work. "Guess I'll drive over an' tell em' we'll go. Shall I?" Jeth dropped his dinner bucket on the table and pulled off his jacket. "If that's what you feel we should do, Pop," answered Myra. "They seem to want to help us all they can."

"I'd rather see where I'm goin' first, but I guess it's a fit place."

"You know it must be a fairly nice place, Jeth, or Levi wouldn't have been satisfied there."

"You mean then that you're willin' we should pack up an' go?"

"Willing, Jeth?" cried Myra trying desperately to hide her emotion. "I asked the Lord if it was His will we should go, to make you willing."

"Huh?" Jeth pulled a chair back from the kitchen table and sat down hard. "You surely didn't—" he looked Myra full in the face, "didn't pray fer me—to lose my job—did you?"

"Lose your job, Jeth? Why, I should say not. Did you?"

Jeth nodded. He reached up with one hand and smoothed the wrinkles out of his forehead.

"Why?" asked Myra.

"Don't know exactly, Me and Russie an' Sim all three got laid off. Pundle jes' said work was gettin' scarce."

"It must mean then, Pop—it must mean we are supposed to go."

* * * * *

"I'm sorry, Miss Butterfield," Millard hesitated at the schoolhouse door, "but I'll not be in your eighth grade in the fall."

"Why not, Millard?"

"We're moving to Granger."

"When?"

"As soon as possible. Maybe in a week or two."

"And why are you moving there?"

"To take care of a farm my grandfather bought."

"I'm sorry to have to give up another eighth grader. And you. Not only you but Liticia and the boys, too."

He thought he heard her voice quiver. He did not dare look up. Millard hurried out the door. He wouldn't want her ever to guess how he dreaded leaving her. There was something so refined and cultured

48

about Miss Butterfield. Her manner was gentle and yet she was firm. There was something about her that he liked. Was it her size, the way she combed her auburn hair, her step, her voice, her high cheek bones, her smile? Millard could not say, but he knew he would never forget her. If he ever loved any girl she would have to be like Miss Hazel Butterfield. All to himself he had thought that more than once, and now as he hurried from her presence and that winsome smile, that disappointed tone in her kind voice, he thought it again.

But Millard wasn't fourteen yet. Just the same, a boy thirteen, a boy as serious-minded as Millard Grinstead, was old enough to start forming personal opinions and ideals. Of course he would never let anyone know how he admired Miss Butterfield, nor what it was about her that was embodied in his ideal. Somewhere out in his future, his future that seemed far removed from his present, maybe he would meet a girl like Hazel Butterfield, smart, but sweet and understanding. The thought of it intimidated him. He'd not let himself even look toward a girl. Not for years and years.

* * * * *

No one could blame the Grinsteads if they moved to Granger, although some quick to pass comments did say, "Jeth won't get ahead even if his father-in-law does put him on a good farm." Other of the more optimistic turn of mind said, "He may make good now that his boys are getting old enough to help him."

For all the drawbacks and losses in their married days Myra Grinstead was not downcast or bitter. Never had she taken the hopeless attitude. With her silent wishing that they would be better fixed financially, she possessed the grace to take things as they were, make the best of their circumstances, and appreciate Jeth's trying at least. All men couldn't be A-No. 1 managers. Maybe if they moved to an altogether new community things would take a turn. Jeth's shoulders had been dropping a little more each year. His once black hair was fast turning gray. He would be white before he was sixty.

Myra prayed. She wasn't sure, but she thought perhaps Jeth did, too. At least, the sale brought more than either of them had anticipated in spite of the fact that most of their things had been used before they had been given to them.

* * * * *

Uncle Levi and his wife Christina did their best to help Jeth and the family get settled. They did it willingly.

49

"We're going to make you like it there," laughed good-natured Christina, "or else we'll die trying."

"I don't see how you folks could do more than you have done," answered Myra. Her entire face spoke the appreciation she felt but her words failed to express.

"And Sunday we're going to take you to our church and you're coming to our house for dinner."

"But you can't be having us over there all the time, Christina. Look what all you've done for us already. Enough is enough."

"We can't do too much for you now on the start, Myra. Levi is so anxious to help you. You have six children and he has none, and he is very fond of them all. When you once get on your feet you'll entertain us," Christina laughed.

"We certainly will." Then after a moment's pause Myra added, "I do hope we can keep things looking nice around here like I'm sure Uncle Levi had them."

"It will probably look a lot nicer with so many to help. Those two big girls of yours—my, see how Orpha has the windows shining. I wish we had a big girl like her. And Liticia is doing a wonderful job at the dish-pan. Not a lazy bone in her, is there? Liticia, maybe your mother will let me hire you once in a while if I need a little help."

Licicia smiled, "Maybe so, Aunt Christina. I imagine I'd like working for you."

"If we'd stayed here I might have had to have a girl most of the time. Levi promised before we got married that we'd move to a smaller place. And there's no use in a man killing himself when it's not necessary. Now look out there, Myra. Homer Jo and Millard are taking turns with the rake. The yard looks better already. I think there's a good measure of the Winegar energy in that Millard boy. See how he's showing Homer Jo how to do it? God bless him. He's a fine stout-looking boy, isn't he?"

Myra didn't answer. She hurried across the room to pick up Glen, who had fallen flat on his face. But she smiled when she planted a warm kiss on his cheek.

* * * * *

From the start Jeth liked the church and the pastor. Myra was pleased.

"Rev. Ambers," Levi drew the minister aside after the service. "I'd be glad if you'd give my brother-in-law and his wife a little special attention before too long. They hold their membership in the church near Doddridge, but they are interested in coming into this denomination. They've been considering it for years already. For the sake of their children, the older ones especially, I hope they make up their mind soon."

"Thank you for telling me, Levi. I understand they bought your place."

"My father bought it. No, Jeth's not fixed very well financially, but he has a nice bunch of children, if their mother is my sister! I'd do most anything for them."

"Well, thanks for telling me, Levi. I'll do what I can."

* * * * *

"Mother," said Millard that evening, "do you know what I wish?"

"No, I don't, Millard. What do you wish?"

"Well, I wish I had those books that got burned."

"So do I, Millard. The next time I write to Grandmother I'm going to remind her that if she wants to please you on your birthday—"

"Myra, I wouldn't do that," put in Jeth, "Millard likes to read too well to suit me."

"Not—not when he likes to read worthwhile books, and that's the only kind Grandmother ever gave any of the children." Myra looked hurt.

"But he's gettin' in such a habit fer readin', it'll make him lazy, if he don't break off from it. That was one thing I was glad got burned."

"Why, Pop; why, Pop Grinstead!" gasped Myra. "I didn't know you felt quite like that about it. You can't mean that the way it sounded. Surely not. I'm glad Millard likes to read."

"Well, I'm not. He'll get other notions inter' his head an' he'll never be satisfied to be a farmer."

"I don't just get your point, Pop," Myra said, picking Glen up in her arms. She took a chair and started rocking him. "Put your head down, honey. Well, anyway," she added looking up, "now that Millard's gone on up—I'll say this yet, Pop—it might be a good idea if you'd read more. It would help you in more ways than one."

"What's one?"

"It would help you out a lot in your English, if nothing more."

"Why English? What do you mean?"

"Well, you could learn to express yourself a little better. I mean you could use better grammar." Myra's voice was very soft. She held little Glen closer to her.

"Well," scowled Jeth, "what's wrong with my grammar? I speak as good English as I kin' an' no one ever had no trouble as I know of makin' me out. I ain't got no use fer these smart people who have ter be so nice about their talk nohow. Millard's smart enough an' I hope your mother don't go to the work an' send the children a lot more books. Millard should go to bed when it's bedtime, an' not sit up an' read."

Myra pressed her lips against Glen's soft head and rocked back and forth. Why discuss this any further? She never did like arguments. This was one of the points on which she and Jeth differed.

Myra liked to read. She must have been born with the desire, for her mother before her was a great reader. Myra often read the children's school books with a healthy desire to learn what she had not learned when she had gone to school, or to brush up on facts forgotten. She took special pains to correct herself in the wrong pronunciation or misuse of a word. In fact, she asked her children to correct her when they noticed her make a grammatical error. Myra saw no use in not knowing all she could just because they were common and poor. Neither could she see why it would be a sign of pride to be able to use correct English. Once before Jeth had stressed that point. She was a little embarrassed sometimes, but Myra loved Jeth anyway. She could overlook his poor grammar.

* * * * *

Millard tossed.

One tear oozed from the corner of his eye and fell on his pillow. He tried to swallow the lump in his throat, but it would not go down. He heard the clock downstairs strike eleven, then twelve. He felt sad and lonesome and dejected. He could hear Richard and Derwood wading knee-deep in sleep in the other bed, and Homer Jo beside him was also enjoying that sweet unconsciousness. That very morning he had listened with interest to the teacher of the young boys' class while he explained the lesson on "Transformed Bodies." Never before had Millard thought so much about death and dying. The teacher had also discussed realistically the mystery of some who would be changed without dying. Then the sermon on "Christ My

Life" which followed was equally as interesting. Simon Ambers was no inferior preacher. Though humble in spirit, he was well versed in the Scriptures and his delivery was forceful and clear.

Now and then in church that morning Millard had pinched the end of his fingers trying to hide his emotion. No one could see his fingers, for his hands were hidden under his tightly folded arms.

That afternoon he had listened to the conversation between Uncle Levi and his father. There was something about Uncle Levi that he liked. Not just one thing—but many. Well, in fact he liked everything, even his bald head. It wouldn't be too bad being bald, if he could be as nice a bald man as Uncle Levi. Millard noticed that his uncle was not only jolly and thrifty and kind, but he was also spiritual, more so than any other ordinary layman he had ever known. Of course, Millard didn't know many. He wondered how men got to be like Uncle Levi. Perhaps they read a good many books about great characters.

If only his books hadn't burned.

Why hadn't he thought of grabbing one or two of them? Especially the best one, "Special Friends of the Lord." That told about great men, and what made them great. How he wished he could read a while. That's what he had wished all the way home.

His soul, though young, reached out for something. He knew not what. He had not forgotten the talk with his mother back in the early winter before the house burned. He could not say exactly that he had heard the voice of God calling him as yet, and yet—he felt as though He might. He had told his mother he would want to join the Rugsbush Church if he joined any, but now they had moved away. But the church at Granger was almost like the Rugsbush Church—same denomination—same creed—same practices. Pop acted interested.

Then why didn't Pop take steps to join right away? Seven months ago Mother had said Pop was dissatisfied with himself and his own church, and Mother had said something, too, about Pop and conviction. Millard wondered what that was, to struggle with conviction. It must be something that makes a person uncomfortable, maybe like trying to get your breath when you couldn't. Millard didn't know. He felt mostly happy. Maybe a little sad, wondering,wishing, longing to know things he wanted to know. How he wished he could talk to Pop. If Pop were more like Uncle Levi, he believed he could.

And then! For the moment he had almost forgotten about it that Pop didn't like him to read. He just said he wished he had those books that got burned. Pop had seemed so good-humored all day. They had had such a nice time at Uncle Levi's place, and the people at church had made them feel welcome.

Ever since the fire Millard thought Pop was more gentle and less critical. Things had been going along quite smoothly.

And now! Oh, how he wished he hadn't mentioned anything about reading where Pop had to hear it. He didn't like arguments any better than Mother did. Millard wondered what Pop would say if Homer Jo begged for a book.

Millard tossed.

Sometime before the clock struck two he fell into a troubled sleep.

Chapter 9

BEFORE Myra got around to writing her mother a letter, the box came.

From Grandmother! Homer Jo lugged it in from the mailbox.

"It's real heavy. Must be sausage."

But before they had the top paper packings all out Myra could see it wasn't.

"Books! Books! More books!"

Homer Jo whistled. Baby Glen grabbed. Myra's heart pounded as she tried to hide her joy and pride. Liticia's eyes danced.

"Won't Millard be pleased? Why, there are more than six. There are nine. Let me go and tell him. They're for his birthday."

"No, Liticia." Mother fought secretly a woebegone feeling that struck her. Pop was outside, too, and would hear. "Let's surprise him and lay them under his pillow."

"All nine?"

"All nine?" echoed Homer Jo.

That would never do. On second thought Myra knew full well it never would.

"Let's put just one up there. This one, 'Special Friends of the Lord,' and the others we'll put here on the mantel."

"Sure thing, because look here Mother, my name's in this one. And look here's one with Richard's name. Why, there are names in all of them."

"You're right Homer Jo. Even Glen's name is on this one, 'The Story of a Raindrop'. But Millard's name is in three books."

"Why?" Homer Jo's eyes opened like saucers.

"That's because Grandmother knew Millard's books got burned. It's not that she likes Millard any more than she does you, Homer Jo, or you, Liticia, or you, little Glen. Grandmother Winegar's not like that. Never. But Millard's birthday books were burned, you know. These I suppose are to replace them."

"I'll put Millard's three under his pillow. "Let me, Mother," Liticia begged. "Just to surprise him tonight."

Mother hesitated, then nodded consent. She'd talk to Millard and warn him not to sit up late. He must not. He was a growing boy and needed his rest, and there was much to be done on the farm before school started.

Pop was busy from morning till dark, but surprisingly happy. More than once a day Millard's will spurred him to work to the best of his ability when he thought how much nicer it was to be working at home and eating at Mother's table than to be working for Mr. Anthony Beabout. He would try his utmost to do everything the way Pop wanted it done. He would give Pop no occasion to call him lazy. He would never say again he wished for a book in Pop's hearing.

But there was no use in trying to hide books or anything else from Pop. Myra didn't believe in undercover living. It made folks tense and ill at ease. It would stimulate wrong attitudes in the children and lead to a division in the home.

Richard was reading his book when Pop came in for dinner. So was Homer Jo. The news would choke Homer Jo if he couldn't tell it. He whispered it in each ear but Millard's. Finding his was to be a surprise. "So don't you tell."

"Grandmother sent the children a box of books," Myra decided to break the news herself. It was her very own dear mother who had spent her very own money for them and the books were all good ones.

Jeth had his face buried in the towel when she said it. If he heard, he never let on. He wiped and wiped his face, then both ears.

"See boy. See boy," chirped Glen, approaching his father with his book open at a colorful picture. Pop peeked over the edge of the towel and cleared his throat.

Ignoring Glen's chirping, he said, "Let's eat."

Naturally Millard wondered if he didn't get a book. Why shouldn't he? But he wouldn't ask. Not there. Not if he burst.

Mother's glance across the table assured him she knew something nice, so when he drew back the covers that night he was not completely surprised.

"Three!" Millard wanted to jump and shout and whistle, but he did none of it. Lying stomach down he started reading.

At 9:30 Pop rapped on the stovepipe.

"Yes?"

"Your light out?"

"It's going to be."

"How soon?"

"Right away."

"You see that it is."

*　*　*　*　*

The last Sunday in August, Jethro and Myra Grinstead were received into the church at Granger, and given the right hand of fellowship. The members stood in a mass expression of welcome.

Jeth had promised to forsake his beloved pipe, hard as it would be. He'd try, though it would be far worse than having his teeth pulled. You couldn't stick those back in again once they were out, but a pipe you could. Almost a week before they were received into church he had thrown it out behind the strawstack, but he had watched where it had landed. He hoped none of the horses would tramp on it and smash it. The next morning at daybreak he found it, wiped it off carefully, tasted it, then hid it on the ledge above the barn door, the back barn door.

*　*　*　*　*

"We will try to have patience with you, Mr. Grinstead," Rev. Ambers had said that Sunday morning in the counseling room. "We would like to keep our congregation free from this habit, but if you should be overtaken sometime, remember there is an Advocate who is ready to plead for you, and help you into victory. Your wife is ready to help you, and I am sure your children are, too."

Myra nodded.

"And we're all ready to help you. So God bless you both as we go into the chapel. You may sit close to the front."

*　*　*　*　*

Myra had told Jeth that if he could prove to her he could be a better Christian in another denomination, then she would follow. That was fourteen years ago. It was more than just the pipe that held him back. Maybe she was expecting too much of him to take the lead. Hadn't she promised to stand by him in everything that was worthwhile?

Hadn't she given her whole self to him for better or for worse? Why not take the step together? True, Jeth was the head of the house, but the head needs good substantial support. For the sake of the children she must not wait any longer.

"Will you do it if I do?" she had asked one evening.

"Do it when?"

"Right away."

"Tonight?"

"We couldn't tonight. Sunday, Jeth."

"Yes, this coming Sunday. Rev. Ambers said he is ready whenever you are."

Jeth looked bewildered. His jaws twitched. He rubbed his hands.

"You can give it up, Jeth," Myra's voice was gentle, soothing. "You think you can't, Jeth. But you can, by God's help." She looked at him pleadingly. "You've never really tried." Myra bit her lip. Maybe it did sound rather hard. But that's honestly how she felt about it.

"How do you know?"

"Have you?" she asked.

Jeth drew a deep breath. His shoulders sagged. He made a doleful sound like a raven far away.

"I've tried lots of things you don't know of."

"Have you, Jeth?" Myra put an arm across his shoulder. She stroked his silvery hair. Maybe he had. Maybe he'd tried and she never knew it. Maybe lots of times.

"Jeth," she said softly, "Jeth, dear, I know. Give me the pipe and I'll dedicate it to the Lord and—"

"An' what would He want with it? If it's not good fer me, much less for Him."

"Maybe that's not the word I wanted. I mean give me the pipe, Jeth, and I'll tuck it away for you, and tell God that's the last time you'll use it."

"There are others in town."

"Of course, Jeth. Towns are full of pipes, and what goes in them, too. But if you would just give it to me, then I'd help you overcome. Oh, Jeth, don't you see what I'm trying to tell you? I want to share this trial or burden or whatever with you. I do, Jeth."

"But it's no trial, Myra. An' it's no burden, an' I said I was a quittin', an' I am." He tapped the toe of his shoe on the floor.

"You have already? Oh, Jeth, is it really true? You've actually begun to quit? Where is your pipe?"

"Are the children all in bed?"

"Yes."

"I throwed it away."

"Really, Jeth? Oh you dear Jeth."

"Well, don't act so surprised, Myra. I told you long ago when I once make up my mind I'd do it. Let's talk about somethin' else now. I met Paul Auckers on the road yesterday an' he's wantin' a boy ter—"

Myra's arm dropped. She drew up a chair.

"—help him this winter, and Millard's just the boy he's lookin' fer." Jeth completely ignored Myra's startled look. He hurried on. "Millard can go to school from there. I know he's set on that, an' I told Auckers so. It's the thing fer him to do."

"And—and—you can spare Millard here? Why, Jeth, he's your main helper. We want to make it go on this farm."

"We'll manage. Orpha's able to do 'most everythin' Millard can, an' Homer Jo, he's no child. What we got all these boys fer, if they can't get out an' start rustlin' fer themselves? Auckers is all right. If we'd stayed at Doddridge, he'd be over at Beabouts now."

"He would?"

"Yes, he would."

Myra's voice echoed back to her like in a great tunnel.

"He would?"

"Yes, he would,for I had him hired. Then things got changed."

"Yes, everything,didn't it? And Sunday we will be taken into the church together, Jeth? It's best I'm sure, that we do it together. I see it now, for I do want to help you bring up these children right. We must not be divided on anything. Jeth, we must stand together."

Jeth's face softened. He looked handsome. He looked kind. He looked pleased. He reached over and took Myra by the hand, "You mean that?"

"Yes, I do. But you see about the church, you were never quite ready before—were you?"

Silence.

"Guess not."

"And although I'd lots rather keep Millard at home with us, if you insist he should go over and work at Auckers, Jeth, I don't want

59

to act mean or stubborn about it."

God love Myra, pretty Myra Winegar Grinstead, now mother of seven. Had she ever acted mean or stubborn? Jeth thought about the pipe above the barn door. He'd throw it in the pond tomorrow. He'd throw it there and let it rot in the mud. "It's bedtime, Mother," and he patted her on the shoulder.

* * * * *

When Jeth informed Millard he was to be ready to go over to Paul Auckers at four o'clock, he was not taken by surprise. Mother had broken the news to him gently and had discussed it over the kitchen sink.

"It was Pop's suggestion, Millard."

"I know."

"You know that?"

"Yes."

"It's not so far but what you can come home now and then. And you will."

"Of course."

"I want you to."

"I'll have to."

"They should let you come home every Saturday night and be here on Sundays."

"Do you think they will?"

"I'll do all I can to see that you may."

"That will help a lot."

"We must see to it that you get to church. You will want to see Orpha baptized."

Millard looked away. He tried to act absent-mindedly, for the moment.

"I put your three books in the bottom of your box. And a Testament. I do hope you won't have to work too hard." Millard saw tiny tears coming to his mother's eyes.

"School!" Millard dreaded starting at another place. They had to change so often. He bit his lip. He wasn't going to give way to his feelings and make it still harder for Mother. "Wish Miss—Miss Butterfield would be the teacher. Then I'm sure I could make it somehow."

"Never cross bridges before you get to them. You may have one as nice."

"Couldn't be. It's nearly four o'clock. Are all my clothes packed?"

"I think I've forgotten nothing. How I dread to see you leave! I hope you say a prayer every night before you go to bed." Millard felt the warm pressure of his mother's soft hand on his upper arm. He smelled some fragrant, delicate shampoo on her wavy hair. Mother was a good mother, a good woman, a queen, an angel of a mother. How he loved her! He'd brace up for her sake. He'd do anything for her sake. "We'll miss you at breakfast in the morning."

Millard wanted to tell her he'd miss being there, too. He wanted to tell her he thought she was nice and grand and beautiful. He wanted to tell her that hers was the best cooking a boy ever could eat anywhere, but the lump in his throat had grown as big as an orange. He wanted to tell her he was glad she and Pop had joined the church together and that Orpha was going to be baptized.

He couldn't.

He couldn't say a word.

He picked up the box and hurried to the car, cap in hand. "Good-by, Ticia." He did not look back.

* * * * *

Paul Auckers was a stocky full-faced man of about fifty winters. Everything about him spoke strength—from his thick russet brown hair to his finger tips. His voice was strong and positive, his step firm, his eyes like blue steel. He used plenty of profanity, even when he was jovial. It just rolled out naturally.

Mrs. Auckers was quite refined and rather attractive after you learned to know her. Her dark eyes had a snap in them that meant she wasn't afraid to tackle anything. She was slender and blithe and smiled without trying.

"Your name is Millard. Mine is Neta. You may even call me that if you want to. I was Neta so long. Mrs. Auckers—well, I can't get used to it. I'll show you your room. You may come up with me. Manasseh has the room at this end of the hall."

"Mannaseh?"

"Yes. Manasseh is our regular hired man. His full name is Virgil D. Vanderbilt Mannasseh Gerlach." She laughed. "We call him Nas. Nas snores, Millard, but I doubt if you'll be bothered over in this room."

She swung open the door at the farther end of the hall. He

entered. She followed. The room smelled of dried rose petals or strange spice.

"This will be your room, Millard. I never saw you before, but I believe we're going to have good times together. I never had a brother and I never had a son, though I often wished for both. Put your clothes in the dresser drawers the way you want them. Here is the closet. Supper is always at 5:30. Do you have an appetite?"

"I don't know."

"Don't know? Well, we'll soon find out then." Laughing, she tripped down the stairs.

Chapter 10

PAUL, he's such a kid. Don't you work him too hard."

Paul Auckers rolled up his blue denim shirt sleeve and felt his arm proudly. "See that muscle, Neta? How did it get that way? By startin' in young. He's fourteen, isn't he?"

"Maybe so, but he's so scared or bashful, I just know he'd do anything you tell him to.

"That's what I want him to do. I'm expectin' that."

"But I know he'd try to lift a barn if you'd ask him to. Paul, remember he's growing and developing yet. Don't make him work too hard."

Paul pinched Neta's cheek and chuckled. His blue eyes laughed. "Bet you'll be wantin' him in here wipin' dishes. That wouldn't be too much for a fourteen-year-old, would it?"

"I might need him in here sometimes. That's in the bargain, isn't it? You wanted a boy so he could help inside or out. Try to get him to talk at the table, Paul. He's so timid it's painful."

"Nas'll get him over that," answered Paul Auckers.

* * * * *

Quickly Myra brushed away the tears. He wasn't going far away. Plenty of boys had started working out at his age. He was well and strong and sensible. If he ever wanted to go away to college, this would help them both get used to being separated. Myra couldn't expect to keep him close to her always. Hadn't she promised to stand by Jeth in everything? She watched him put his box in the back seat and climb in beside Pop.

"Are you going along, Homer Jo?"

Pop nodded.

"I'm comin' along back."

"Just so I know where you are. Good-by, Millard." She waved

and smiled. Pop mustn't know how hard it was for her to see him leave.

If only Pop would have left Homer Jo at home—maybe Pop would have opened up to Millard then. It would have been such an excellent chance, such an opportune time. But Homer Jo always got to go along places. Derwood and Richard wanted to ride along, too, and see where Millard was going to live and work for his board and room, but Pop shook his head and that meant no. But Homer Jo had a way of making that no change to yes often.

"Now he'll never be here to help me with my lessons," lamented Liticia sorrowfully, "and school begins on Monday. I just know I'm not going to like it."

"You've said that before, Liticia, but you always do after you once get started."

"But Mother, I'm sure I won't. If Millard could only go to the same school. Why couldn't Pop have found him a place in this district, if he thought he had to work out some place?"

"That I can't answer, Liticia."

* * * * *

The large spotted dog leaped and sniffed.

He landed his leather paws on Millard's hips, peppering dirt on top of the milk.

"Domino, you——rascal," bellowed Mr.Auckers, "get down there. Millard, from the start, make him mind. He will, too, if I tell him he's got to. Domino, get back there where you belong. Take one pail in to Neta and give one to the pigs over there. Then it's supper time. The washroom's right off the kitchen. Neta will show you."

September first. The cool evening air smelled of ripening apples from the near-by orchard. All along the east side of the house bright colored Swedish dahlias swayed slightly in the pleasant breeze. It played across Millard's hair and whispered through his thick eyelashes. From the open door he could hear Mrs. Auckers whistling a merry rapid little tune that made him feel lighter. Could women whistle like that? He couldn't recall ever hearing his mother whistle. And Pop said he didn't like to hear girls whistle either soft or loud.

"Right in here, Millard. Put the milk on that table. Nas drinks a quart every meal. You don't believe me? Well, you wait and see." Her smile was contagious. From the kitchen came the delicious odor of frying new potatoes and boiling corn, and something else Millard couldn't distinguish. He started feeling a little hungry.

Nas had bushy eyebrows. That was the first impression everyone got. They stood out like great shrubbery-covered window sills over his gray eyes. His nose was large for the rest of his face, and he had one prominent gold tooth in front that shone like the doors at the bank. One finger on his left hand wasn't there. Millard was surprised when from his great body came a soft mellow voice like a warm feather bed. It folded in all around Millard. A man with such a voice shouldn't need to snore.

"Think you can fit in with a crew like this?" Nas asked. Millard stepped back a little so his eyebrows wouldn't brush him.

"I don't know."

"I know you don't. But you'll learn. You'll learn a lot in the next fifty years. Gwin' a join the army?"

Millard stared.

"I don't know. I'm not through school yet. Don't know what I'll do."

"You can talk, can't you? Thought maybe you was tongue-tied," Nas slapped Millard on the shoulder. "Silent tongues never tell lies, not even white ones. We learned that in the army."

Nas filled the basin. "You were here first, kid. Go ahead."

"You go first," Millard said.

"Come on over. I'm crustier. It'll take me longer. Neta there won't give me any grub unless I'm shined up fit fer a banquet." Manasseh laughed through his front teeth. "It's not that bad, kid—a—what's your name?"

"Millard."

"Millard? Millard. Mildewed, Milkweed, ha, ha—"

"Shame on you, Nas," called Neta. "Millard's a nice name. Don't let him ruffle you, Millard. Nas is a big tease and I never refused him a meal yet."

Millard washed. Then Manasseh. Water and lather splashed in every direction.

"You get Nas to tell you sometime how he got such a pretty name," called Neta.

"Can't tell a thing till I'm tanked up, Neta. I'm dry an' dead right now."

"He looks it, doesn't he!" Paul Auckers stepped up to the basin. "Nas's never quit his army talk. Go on into the kitchen, Millard. I see

65

Neta has things dished up. She's not the kind that likes to wait on men, though she waited on me for—"

"Don't tell it Paul," laughed Neta.

"You mean I waited on you that time. Excuse me, little sister."

Mr. Auckers called his wife that only on rare occasions. It always made her blush and smile inwardly. "Sit right here, Millard. Virgil D. Vanderbilt knows his corner."

Millard bowed his head. They were used to having silent prayers at home. Only when capable company came did Pop ask someone to return thanks out loud.

There was a strained awkward pause, a sudden shuffling of feet, then Mr. Auckers said as informally as he could, "Pass the bread, Nas. Help yourself."

The meal was alright. The bed was alright. The pillow was neither too thick nor too thin. The ventilation was perfect.

Millard could here Nas snooze, snooze, snore, then snort. But that wasn't why he couldn't sleep. He closed the door. He snapped on the light and read ten more pages in the blue book. It was a book of short stories called "Gleaming Portals" by Alice A. MacAdams. It was by far the best of the three Grandmother had sent him. He read the story of a poor little waif who hunted for edible scraps in people's garbage cans. After many hardships and knockings and cursing, a rich lady's insensate attitude was changed to pity, and in the end he was adopted and she loved him as her own. He closed the book.

Millard turned off the light and crawled in once more. His mother told him to pray every night before he went to bed. Yes, he had done that. The best he knew how. He wasn't sure he knew exactly. Mother had taught him "Now I lay me down" years ago, but that seemed too short, too narrow, too inadequate now. That mentioned nothing about Mothers or homes or schools or a boy's loneliness in a strange location. He wished he had a book of prayers for a boy of his age. That might help some. Guess God could understand what he tried to say. He was once a boy. Wonder what His voice was like if He'd call. Orpha must have heard it. She had gone into the instruction class and was going to be baptized soon. Maybe he'd hear it someday in school. Or did it always come to people in church? If it came while he was in school, he'd just have to be excused. He'd have to be alone a little.

Tomorrow morning he'd say his table thanks silently before he got to the table. He wouldn't embarrass Mr. Auckers again. God would surely understand and hear his prayer on foot. Or he could say it at night for the next day all three meals in advance.

School. He wished the first day were over. The first was always the hardest—the first of 'most anything—like the first night in a new place. He buried his face in the pillow. It smelled clean and the case was smooth with a slight starching. It smelled something similar to the shampoo on his mother's hair. He grabbed the pillow in both arms, rolled over on his back, and hugging it close to his breast, fell asleep.

Paul Aucker's three raps wakened him.

"Time to get up, Millard. It's 5:30, Aucker's time. Did you hear?"

"Yes, sir. I'll be right out."

There were the cows to bring in (Nas did the milking), the calves, the chickens and the pigs to feed, and water and wood to be brought to the kitchen before breakfast. After breakfast, to Millard's surprise, Mrs. Auckers handed him a tea towel and said, "I just know you're good at wiping dishes, Millard. How do I know?" She read the unexpected on his face, "You just look like it. Set them on the table right here. I'll put them away. Paul said you could. I bargained with him for this. You see (all the time she talked, Neta's hands were working fast) I'm quite a club fan. Paul knew that before we got married, so he can't stop me now. I belong to the Eastern Star and the Ladies' Auxiliary, and the Daring Daughters, and the Granger Art club, and that takes a lot of my time. Your mother doesn't belong to any of them, does she?"

"No."

"I never met her at least. I don't know any Grinsteads in any of our clubs."

"We came from Doddridge. We've been living here just since June."

"Paul's lucky to get you. It's not that he and Nas couldn't get all the work done, but Paul likes to be free for his sports when he takes those notions, and another thing, we both wanted someone young around. Nas is so ancient. You know, someone like you will help to keep us young. We weren't young when we got married, and neither of us can bear the thought of growing old. Nas is forever talking about the army and war, his pranks, and always how he escaped this and that. I think he saw just enough of it to make him egotistical, and he knows he'd be too old to go into it again. I don't want to hear about war all the time. My first a—I lost my first one that way."

"First what?"

"My first husband. No, not a son. I never had a son. Denver and I were married only one month."

"Denver?"

"That was his name. Isn't it beautiful? I never knew another person by that name. I hope I never do. I can't bear to be hearing about war all the time. My, you can wipe them almost as fast as I wash. Take that blue towel for the skillet. Anxious for school to start?"

"No."

"You'd rather stay here and wipe dishes, wouldn't you?"

Millard was dumfounded. He'd never before heard a woman say so much in so short a time. He'd never been around any women. Though vastly different from his mother, Mrs. Auckers possessed something that removed his shyness, little by little.

"Well, I'll try to help you like it, Millard. What grade are you in?"

"Eighth."

"I might have known you weren't in the sixth or seventh. I taught school one year, so maybe I can help you out a little sometimes, but my, you don't look like the kind who would need any help. You look quite capable, but my—oh, you're not this quiet always, are you?"

"Talked your one leg off already, I'll bet, an' startin' in on the second." Paul Auckers stuck his head in the kitchen door. "When she's done with you, Millard, come out to the garage."

"Remember, Paul, I want the car right after dinner."

"I know it, Neta. I want Millard to go over to Baxters for me."

Fresh fear struck Millard. It wasn't cowardice, or fright, but timidity that gave him a strange inferiority complex. He didn't want to tell Mr. Auckers he had never driven a car. He couldn't tell him Pop had never allowed him to drive his. All the other boys his age drove tractors and cars—of course, not out on the highway. Mr. Auckers surely would not expect him to do that without a license.

"Up the back way?" asked Paul's wife. "Yes, Neta, the bridge is fixed at last. I thought Baxter never would get at it."

Intuition and perception were not lacking in Millard Grinstead.

He wanted to learn, he could learn, and he did learn how to drive Paul Aucker's car. All he needed was a little explaining from a patient boss, and Paul Auckers was that. Wouldn't Pop be surprised if he knew!

* * * * *

Grandmother Winegar tore it open eagerly.

"Well, who is this from? Millard!"

"Sept. 6. Dear Grandmother, I do want to thank you for the books you sent me. It seemed like my birthday all over again. I like all of them very much. I am staying at Paul Auckers and go to the Hornback School. The others go to East Dixon."

Grandmother looked up from the paper, "Well, why is Millard staying at Paul Auckers?" she gasped. "And who is he?"

"Well," Grandfather's hands went to his hips. "Read on."

"My teacher's name is Mr. Burns. School started today. It didn't go so good. In love, Millard."

"Of all things," ejaculated Grandfather. "I thought we put Jeth on the farm so the boys could help him."

Chapter 11

I'M going to write to Levi," Grandfather said, walking back and forth across the kitchen. "He must tell me exactly how things are goin' back there. It seems to me Millard would be needed at home. Why don't you write to Myra, too, and ask her how this is?"

"I will. I can't understand why he said it didn't go so good in school. Sounds like he's not satisfied. Poor boy. He always liked school."

"Well, Jeth had it in his head before they left here to put Millard out. Don't you remember what Myra told you?"

"I guess it does help out some, but it seems to me Jeth could have waited till Millard got through the grades. We must find out. Let's eat. Dinner is ready."

"He didn't say in the letter he's workin', did he?" Grandfather cleared his throat nervously. "It says he's stayin' there. But you know that means he's workin', too."

"Of course it does. Who would give a boy board and room free? I must write to Myra." Grandmother Winegar drew a long breath as she pulled her chair up to the table.

It wasn't that Myra's parents objected to having their grandchildren working away from home, but they knew how all these years Jeth had failed to get ahead. They had been willing now to put him on a choice farm with the hope that Millard in particular could help his father succeed. There was no doubt in their minds that he both could and would. Over and over they had swallowed their pride when their son-in-law had to move his family to a smaller place. For years they had talked of helping them out, but as long as Jeth gambled it seemed to them not the wise thing to do.

But did he? Like Myra they never had seen him do it, but they heard. Too often they had heard the same report. For some reason other men making the same wages Jeth did owned their homes and a car besides. What did he do with his money? He did not spend it on clothes or furniture.

Father Winegar could have taken Jeth to town and paid cash for a new car and said, "It's yours, my boy. I know you've had one misfortune after another." But he never felt inclined to do that.

But the night the house burned Myra's father felt like doing anything, everything, when he saw her standing there in the cold crying with Baby Glen clutched in her arms, and Millard so attentive and affectionate to her. And when barefooted Liticia stood crying at his doorstep, he felt like drawing his last cent out of the Doddridge Bank to help them. Grandfather Winegar loved Myra's children and so did Grandma. They loved Jeth, too. Why not buy Levi's farm and give them a trial on it? The ground was in excellent condition. The milk cows were, too. Jeth would have everything in his favor. He must make good. Grandfather saw something in Milllard's face the night of the fire, an expression of stamina and manliness that was outstanding. Surely, now with a son like that Jeth could get on top.

But before Grandmother Winegar had the letter finished, one came from Myra. Grandfather hurried in from the mailbox.

"It's a fat one," he announced breathlessly, holding it in his outstretched hand. "You've got your specks on. You read it".

"Dear Mother and Father," read Grandmother. "The children are all in school, so while Glen takes his nap I'll try to write. A week ago Sunday, Jeth and I were acepted into the _____ church here at Granger. I know you will understand that it wasn't that I wanted to break away from the church I was brought up in, but to help Jeth, and for the sake of the children, it seemed the only thing to do. Maybe I should have been willing to do this years ago, but I wanted Jeth to go ahead first and see if he would live up to it. He really does seem much more satisfied. You may be surprised , too, when I tell you he threw his pipe away, and to my knowledge he hasn't smoked now for two weeks. That will be a help to the boys. I am so glad. I wanted to start family worship, but Jeth doesn't like to read out loud. Orpha is to be baptized in a couple of weeks. She is a conscientious girl and such a help on the farm. Jeth thought Millard should work out for his room and board, and he found a place for him two miles from here. It was hard to see him leave. He's young. The children are all disappointed he has to go to another school. He got to come home yesterday. I'm glad he likes his place. Mr. and Mrs. Auckers are very nice to him, but he was a little homesick anyway. We miss him here so much, especially Liticia. They always were closer to each other than any of the other children. I'm sorry Millard doesn't seem to like his teacher over at the Hornback school. Maybe he will after he gets better acquainted.

I'm glad to tell you the children and Jeth like Brother Ambers very much. He really is a wonderful preacher and makes things so much plainer than Reverend Jacob ever did. I can't believe we'll ever be sorry we moved out here. Levi and Christina have been so good to us, and everybody is friendly. But we surely miss you. Glen talks a lot. I wish you could hear him.

The ladies in the church here have a sewing circle, and they are going to knot two comforters for me next week. Isn't that nice of them? The children are delighted over the books you sent them. I was especially glad for the ones you sent Millard. He still likes to read. He took the books with him. He complained yesterday of a pain in his side. I do hope it's nothing serious. He said one day at school he couldn't eat his dinner. Liticia went over and helped Christina with her fall cleaning the week before school started. We think Levi has a very nice wife. She gave me a little hint once that they might help Millard go on through school if he is interested. I don't know what Jeth would say to that. I wonder what you would think. Of course there's plenty of time yet, but he's in the eighth grade now. Sometimes it seems only yesterday he was in his basket back there by that pretty bay window in our new house. I wish—well Glen is awake now, so good-by and love. Myra."

"She didn't say a thing about how they were gettin' along." There was a tone of disappointment in Grandfather Winegar's voice. "She didn't say how the cows were doin' or whether they were able to meet expenses."

"But she didn't say they weren't either."

"Did she ever?"

* * * * *

"You're going along to town with me Saturday, Millard," smiled Neta, "and I'm going to help you make a few selections."

Millard stopped wiping the coffeepot and stared at her. Then he felt the color come into his face, for he saw Neta's dark eyes were riveted on his twice-patched shirt sleeve.

72

"You need a new shirt," she said softly, "and your socks are practically past darning. Or—" her eyes snapped playfully, teasingly, "are you saving up your wages to get some pretty girl a Christmas present?"

"Oh, Neta," exclaimed Millard. He blushed red. He crossed the kitchen and put the coffeepot on the stove. He glanced at the clock.

"You're saving it for something," she added quickly, "and—I didn't know."

"I'm not," he said.

"Not what?"

"Not saving."

"Not saving your wages, Millard? None of it?"

"I give it to Pop."

"All of it?"

"Of course."

"Then—then—he'll get you the clothes you need. I thought perhaps he'd let you keep part of it."

How could Millard tell Neta Auckers he was one of the shabbiest dressed boys in the Hornback school and that it made him feel sensitive and shy? The sleeves of all his patched shirts were faded and short. Several times he had to stand next to pretty Louise Gresmor at the blackboard in school and work the problems Mr. Burns gave them. Twice he had the answers first, but twice he didn't, and when Louise stood back and watched him finish his problems he knew she was looking at his shirt more than at the board. It made his hand a little unsteady and his mind felt suddenly foggy. There was something about the girl that made him want to look his best. Louise was pretty and neat as a pin. She could not help but notice how worn and threadbare his clothes were.

"I know I need some clothes," Millard's brown eyes looked past Neta. He swallowed hard. His face felt crimson now.

"How would it be then if you get a few things Saturday and you just explain to your father that you needed them, and you give him what's left."

"I don't think he'd like that," Millard answered quickly. "I'd rather not try it. After all, I'm only fourteen."

"But after all—" For some reason Neta Auckers left the sentence unfinished. It was not in her place to put such ideas into Millard Grinstead's head. If the boy felt it was his duty to help his parents

73

with the two dollars and fifty cents a week Paul gave him, she had no right to interfere. Neta bit her lip. "I'll finish, Millard. You'd better go now or you'll be tardy."

Neta stood at the door and watched the boy cross the yard. She noticed that his step was slower than usual.

"O Millard," she called, "Millard, come back. You forgot your lunch."

"I'll be tardy if I come back. Let it go." He walked on backwards. "I'll do without today." Then he ran.

"The dirty shame," frowned Neta.

* * * * * * * *

"Say, Paul." Mr. Auckers and Nas were both in the barn.

"Yes?"

"That boy gets under my hide."

"What boy you talkin' about, Nas?"

"Why, that Millard you've got here."

"Under your hide? What do you mean?"

"He gives me the 'hebies."

"What's that? Talk English, Nas, and maybe I'll understand you."

"Well, he's one I ain't figured out yet, an' I don't like it. I always like to see through folks. He's one of the mighty few that's made me feel dumfounded, an' he's jes' a kid. That's why it gets me so. It makes me half mad sometimes, and yet I wouldn't let him know that fer the world."

"Well, what's so strange or puzzlin' about him?"

"He don't act like a boy fourteen orter. He acts years older. It's no fun tryin' to kid with him. He's so sober all the while, an' twice lately I caught him cryin'."

"Cryin'?"

"Cryin' like a child, Paul."

"Where?"

"Up in his room. Don't you never let him know I told you. He acted terribly embarrassed. Didn't want me ter see him, I know."

"What were you doin' over in his room?"

"Jes' naturally went over. Thought he'd like to hear some of my war stories. All the other kids I've ever met, do."

"An' he didn't?"

"Couldn't tell. He won't get 'thusiastic about nothin'. I ask him if he's homesick, an' he won't say he is."

"Well, will he say he isn't?"

"He turns me off by some clever answer every time. He's got one of them little half Bibles he reads out of every night, too."

"Half Bible?"

"Sure. You know what I mean. The New Testament like all us guys got in the army, if we wanted one. We carried 'em up here in our shirt pockets over our hearts. One fellow called his the new spearment."

"What?"

"Spearment. He said he'd spearment with it, see if it would save his life. I asked Millard the other night if he's trying ter spearment with that half Bible, too, an' I thought he'd look a hole through me. He made me feel, well—I'm not sayin' how, but I can't stand it to let anyone make me feel that way, let alone a kid in his teens."

"Well, I tell you, Nas, maybe you'd better not bother about goin' into his room again."

"He's not goin' ter beat me down, Paul. I'm goin' a figure that kid out if it takes me all year."

"Neta thinks he's a wonderful boy."

"I know that she does. You think I can't tell that?"

*　*　*　*　*

"Can't you figure out a little extra something you could have Millard do over Thanksgiving vacation, Paul, so that I could have an excuse to get that boy a new shirt? He might resent taking it, if I just give it to him for nothing; but you see, if you made him feel he was earning something above his two fifty, he might take it all right. Paul, I've got to get him some clothes. I can't stand it any longer."

"That wasn't in the bargain."

"I know it, Paul, but we haven't any of our own to do for."

"Do you think he's hard to understand?"

"Why?"

"Nas says he is."

Neta laughed. Her laughter filled the room. "Nas? He's the one who is hard to understand. Sometimes I think he's impossible. Millard is utterly different from Nas or any other boy I have ever known; I think he's very interesting."

"Nas said he found him crying a couple of times."

"Crying? crying, you say? Paul, I can't believe that."

Chapter 12

THANKS, Mr. Auckers."

"That's all right, Millard. Be seeing you tonight."

Every Sunday morning Paul Auckers had been taking Millard Grinstead to the driveway of the church. He drove a quarter of a mile out of his way to do this, then went on to town to purchase his Sunday papers.

"You needn't do it, Mr. Auckers. I can walk." Millard had said this over and over.

"I'm goin' after my papers anyhow, Millard, so you might as well ride along. I don't suppose you'd be so anxious to go to church if it wasn't for gettin' to go home with your folks for that Sunday dinner, would you?"

"I could manage to go on home and get there just in time for dinner, I guess — if I wanted to." Millard looked Paul Auckers full in the face searchingly. Those brown eyes seemed to rebuke the older man.

"It's all right, Millard, perfectly all right. I'm not makin' fun, but I just can't imagine a boy your age being interested in going to church every Sunday morning unless it's for something like that. So long now."

* * * * *

Someone tapped Millard on the shoulder.

"Oh, good morning, Uncle Levi. How are you?"

"I'm fine, and how are you, Millard?"

"All right."

"Are you sure?"

"Why wouldn't I be?"

"It's mighty of Mr. Auckers to bring you to church every Sunday morning like he does."

76

"I think so too."

"But I've never noticed you here on Sunday evenings." They were walking up the steps together.

"I go back at four."

"Too bad you have to miss the evening services. They are often the best. Couldn't your father go down after you?"

Millard shrugged his shoulders.

"You're all going home with us for dinner today, Millard. I want to talk with you then." Uncle Levi's voice was strangely kind and mellow.

*   *   *   *   *

How good it seemed to be close to the ones he loved best.

After they got to Uncle Levi's house Mother pressed Millard's hand and said how glad she was to see him. Glen clung to him and pulled his ears and nose and made him chuckle.

"Sit over here on the davenport beside me, Millard," called Liticia. She wanted to throw her arms around his neck and hug him, but she didn't. She just beamed on him admiringly.

"I miss you," she whispered bending toward him.

"I miss you, too, Ticia."

"School any better?" She sat a little closer.

He shook his head.

"Don't you like your teacher any better?"

He shook his head.

"Do any of the pupils like him?"

"I don't think so. Not many at least."

"What's wrong with him?"

"He won't explain anything. And he's always cross. I wish I were through school."

"Our teacher is really nice. I thought at first I might not like her, but I do. I wish you could come to our school. Oh, Millard, I wish it so much. You'd like Miss Yale, I know."

"Be still, Ticia. It's hard enough without you—" Millard cleared his throat to hide his emotion. He crossed his legs. He fumbled with the bottom of his trousers.

"Come on outside, Millard," called Homer Jo. "We want to show you something."

"What is it?" Millard seemed reluctant to leave Liticia. He'd rather stay and talk.

"Come on out and see. Come on, Millard."

"Guess I'd better go see. I'll be back soon, Ticia."

But when Millard returned, Pop and Uncle Levi were occupying the davenport, and Liticia was helping Orpha and Aunt Christina in the kitchen.

"There's room right over on the davenport, Millard. Come on over and join the men folks. I was just telling your father how nice I think it is Mr. Auckers brings you to church every Sunday morning."

"Do you have to pay him for doin' that?" Pop asked.

"Oh, no, Pop. I never asked him to. He goes to town every Sunday morning for his papers, and I just ride along."

"I wondered."

"I was wishing Millard could attend our evening meetings, too, Jeth. Couldn't there be some arrangement made to get him there?"

An awkward pause followed.

"I wouldn't know of any unless Auckers would bring him in," Jeth remarked at last, squeezing the words through his teeth.

"He wouldn't do that, would he, Millard?" asked Uncle Levi.

"Oh, no. Almost always he and his wife go away somewhere on Sunday nights and stay till midnight sometimes."

"You're there by yourself?"

"Nas is there sometimes. Not always."

"Who's Nas?"

"Their hired man. Virgil D. Vanderbilt Manasseh Gerlach is his full name."

"What a name, what a name," laughed Uncle Levi. "He must be quite a character."

"He is. He always talks about his experiences in the World War. That's about all that's on his mind."

"Maybe he's been affected mentally. Do you think, Jeth?" and Levi turned abruptly and faced his brother-in-law. "Do you think that—that's a fit place for Millard to be staying?"

"He said Mr. and Mrs. Auckers were good to him," blinked Jeth.

"But they're not Christians, Jeth, and if they stay out like that Sunday nights and Millard has to be there alone with a man like that Nas, don't you think the environment might not be the best?"

"Well, I don't know," Jeth yawned. "Millard can go on to bed. He don't need to stay up an' talk."

"We ought to find him a way to church, I think," Levi said with feeling.

But why should Uncle Levi be telling Jeth what his boys should do or not do?

"Well, I can't spend the gas to go get him an' then take him back," said Jeth almost resentfully. "I was thinkin' fer the past while now we'll have to cut out some of our night goin', too. Twice goin' to church every Sunday is too much fer—"

"What?" exclaimed Myra, appearing in the dining room doorway. "What did I hear you say, Jeth?"

"Nothin', nothin' to worry about. Do you want me to call the boys in?"

"Dinner is ready."

"Let's go for a little ride, Christina," Uncle Levi announced when it was time for Jeths to leave. "Let's take Millard over to his place. Shall we?"

"A nice idea," she answered.

"Then we'll take Millard over, Jeth."

A somewhat beaten expression crossed Jeth's face that for a moment looked almost perverse or dogged.

"Good-by, Millard," said Liticia rather sadly. She smiled faintly. "Bye, Ticia."

"Good-by," called Orpha and the boys.

"Good-by, Millard," his mother said warmly, "we'll see you next Sunday, if nothing happens."

If Pop said good-by, Millard did not hear it.

Jeth Grinstead may have thought Levi was taking Millard back to Paul Auckers so he could ask Millard a lot of questions about him. If so, he thought wrong, because Uncle Levi did not ask Millard one question about his father. For the first half mile he talked about the lovely evening, the freshness of the air, the naked trees, and the beautiful sunset. "This is the day the Lord hath made; let us rejoice and be glad in it together. And by the way, Millard, do you have a Bible of your own?"

"Mother gave me her Testament when I left."

"That was thoughtful of her."

"I read some in it every night."

"That's wonderful, Millard."

"Nas sorta makes fun of me for doing it—I—I'm pretty sure he thinks I'm queer, but—"

"But you won't let that discourage you, will you, Millard? I mean you won't give up reading it because of him, will you?"

All three were in the front seat. Christina could hear Millard breathe long deep breaths. His body stiffened suddenly, then relaxed. Uncle Levi looked over past his wife, and Millard caught the sympathetic softness of his expression.

"Guess not," he said, but his voice sounded damp with pent-up tears.

"How's school?" Uncle Levi changed the subject. They were halfway there now.

"I don't like it."

"Don't like it? Why not?"

"I don't know. I just don't."

"I'm sorry to hear it. But stick by it anyway, Millard. There are brighter days ahead for you."

"What do you mean?"

"Well, I suppose every boy feels that way about school sometimes, but go on with it regardless, and someday you'll be glad. Wouldn't you like to go through college?"

"I haven't thought much about it."

Millard wanted to tell Uncle Levi his mother had told him once that the first thing to decide was to be a Christian. But he couldn't. Maybe it was because Aunt Christina was beside him.

"Nas says every man ought to be a soldier at least part of his life."

Levi Winegar gripped the steering wheel. He had been a boy once. In a flash he lived a year of his life over.

"I'd like to meet that man you call Nas," he said at length.

"He might be down at the barn now. Shall I go see before I change my clothes?"

"I'll walk along with you."

The large spotted dog came bounding. "Stay back, Domino." He followed the two to the barn. Nas was not there. "Where is he, Domino?" "He may be up in his room. I think sometimes he sleeps on Sunday afternoons, and he might have forgotten to set his alarm."

On the kitchen table Millard saw the note written on a small sheet of blue paper.

"We won't be back till late, Millard, and Nas asked for the evening off. We'll make it right with you for doing the chores by yourself. Your lunch is under the cloth—Neta."

"If I didn't have chores of my own, Millard, I'd stay and help you."

"Oh, I can do them by myself."

"And you really don't mind being here alone?"

"Not much. The worst thing is when I get to thinkin'."

"Thinkin' what?"

"Oh, about when our house burned. I try not to, but sometimes at night I wonder if Mother and all of them would get out if-if it happened over there and I'm not there to help."

"Millard, you shouldn't allow yourself to think about that. It's not likely to happen again. And another thing, my boy, it's comforting to—you know—pray about such things. Have you ever tried that?"

"Why—yes," came his subdued answer.

"We must go now."

"Thanks for bringing me over."

"Christina, there's something about that boy that's different." Levi turned right at the first crossroad. They'd go home the other way.

"I've always said that from the first time I met him."

"I think it can hardly be that he has to be away from home so young."

"Do you think Jeth can really spare him? Isn't he needed there at home?"

"I asked Jeth today, and he said they're getting along fine. He says Orpha can do anything Millard could, and she likes to work outside."

"But, Levi, the boy isn't satisfied there. You can see that. Myra told me the Auckers try to get him to play cards and that fellow they call Nas offers him cigarettes and—"

"What? You mean that boy has to stay in a home of that kind to be able to give his father two and a half a week, and maybe never—why Christina, he might never try to be a Christian, and there must be a reason why he doesn't like school."

"Myra seemed quite disturbed over it today. Did you answer your father's letter yet?"

"Yes, but I didn't realize all this when I answered."

"Myra said Mr. and Mrs. Auckers treat Millard perfectly wonderful, but Levi, don't you see what an influence they'll have on him, what lasting impressions. It's not good for him to be hearing war stories all the time. Another thing, if Jeth is getting along fine why did he say they'd have to quit going to church on Sunday evenings to save on gas?"

*   *   *   *   *

It was after ten-thirty.

"Levi, Levi, wake up. Wasn't that the phone?" Christina shook him gently. "It's ringing. Levi. Who could it be calling this time of the night?"

Out of his first sound sleep Levi Winegar stumbled toward the telephone.

"Hello."

"Yes, what's wrong, Millard?"

"What's wrong, Millard? You're sick?"

"I'll be right over, Millard."

"Come on, Christina, you're going with me. Millard is sick and his folks have no phone. We must go."

Chapter 13

THEY found Millard lying crumpled on the studio couch in the dining room. His face was drawn with pain and both hands clutched his right side.

"He feels feverish, Levi," Christina said. "When did you get sick, Millard?" She knelt beside him and felt his pulse.

"Soon—after—I ate. It came up—some of it. A terrible—pain—in my side."

"What shall we do, Levi?" Christina took off her coat.

"I wouldn't know what to do but call a doctor out."

"It sounds to me like appendicitis."

"Call Dr. Munsell. He'd come."

Christina called.

"He doesn't want to come out, Millard. He says we should bring you in to the hospital."

Millard groaned.

"It might be the best, Millard." Uncle Levi bent low and touched his shoulder gently. "Do you think you can walk to the car?"

"I'll try—but—Pop—might not—like it."

"But if you're sick, Millard, you can't help it, and something's got to be done at once. Come, we'll help you. We'll stop and tell your folks. They might want to go along."

Slowly Millard got to his feet. He might have fallen had he not been supported.

"I—feel—so sick."

"He's dizzy," Christina said.

She grabbed two pillows. They propped him in the back seat. "I'll sit in here with him, Levi."

Now and then suppressed moans came from the boy. The whole world was going round and round like mad.

Levi ran to the door. After several rappings Jeth opened.

"It's me, Jeth. Millard called us a while ago. He's awful sick. I—"

"What?" Jeth acted as though he were only half awake. He rubbed his one eye. "What?"

"Millard is out in the car, Jeth. He has a pain in his side and can hardly walk. Christina called Dr. Munsell, and he said we should him in to the hospital. You and Myra better go along in. You might have to sign, you know."

"Sign fer what?" Jeth's voice was husky.

"For an operation, Jeth. It could be appendicitis, you know.

"Huh? Let me call Myra."

"I was afraid this might happen," Myra said. "Don't you know I told you several weeks ago he complained of a pain in his side?" While she spoke she started dressing.

"I've often had a pain in my side an' it wasn't 'pendicitis. He probably just twisted his self or lifted somethin' heavy."

"Get dressed, Jeth. Hurry. Aren't they waiting on us?"

"Maybe I'd better tell 'em to go an' we'll come."

"Do it then. Jeth, you never get excited." Myra's hands shook. Buttons wouldn't find buttonholes.

"We'll come in our car," called Jeth from the bedroom door.

"All right, we'll go on."

Dr. Munsell was at the hospital when they arrived.

"An operation is imperative," he said after his examination. "Take him up right away." Two nurse aids went after the cart.

"Will one of you sign?" It was the supervisor.

"The boy's parents are on their way," Christina said. "They will be here any minute. He's our nephew."

"We can't wait long," she said. "The doctor said he's afraid it might burst any minute." The aids entered with the cart.

"I'll be responsible for this," Levi said without hesitancy. He looked down the hall. "They're coming now."

Myra came half running. She looked white and frightened. Jeth walked fast, too.

"Be brave, Millard," whispered his mother. She patted his hot cheek as the aids hesitated just a moment before they pushed him out of the room. "And I'll be praying for you, too."

Millard recognized his mother with a groan that meant thanks.

She knew what it meant. Jeth looked shocked and dismayed. His breath came in bunches.

"He's had a hypo," said the nurse. "You may sit here and wait until he comes down or there's a waiting room down the hall to your left. But first I must get the necessary information about the patient. Which one wants to give it?"

Jeth looked at Myra.

"I will," Myra said, stepping toward the nurse.

In exactly forty-one minutes Millard was in his bed.

"Your boy will get along all right," the nurse said assuringly, "unless of course, something turns up we don't anticipate. He'll be sleeping until morning. The doctor will be in to see him before he leaves."

"May we stay?" asked Myra.

"Of course you may. We don't like too many in the room, of course, but the parents are allowed to stay if they wish."

"We'll stay," Jeth said. "Levi, you and Christina might as well go on home an' get your rest."

"Maybe we'd better go back and stay with the children and help Orpha with the chores and get the youngsters off to school in the morning."

Myra looked relieved. Jeth looked troubled, much troubled.

"That's nice of you to think of that, Christina. Orpha will be glad for your help. I told her we'd let them know as soon as we could. She came downstairs before we left, so Glen wouldn't be alone."

"Do Liticia and the other children know about this?"

"I purposely tried not to waken Liticia. You know I thought it would be best if she didn't know before morning."

"Yes, of course. Well, maybe we'd better go then. We'll come back as early as we can in the morning. Of course we'll have to stop by the house and call Auckers. We never thought to leave a note or anything, and no one was there when we left."

"There wasn't?" gasped Myra. "Where were they? Didn't they call you?"

"Why, no. Millard called us himself. No one was there. When we took him back Millard found a note on the table saying they were all out for the night. They might not be home now yet."

"The hired man was gone, too?"

"Yes. And Millard had all the work to do himself."

"Oh, Jeth," Myra's eyes filled with sudden tears. She caught his hand and looked into his face pleadingly. "He mustn't go back there. It's, it's too—"

"Well," Jeth shifted from one foot to the other, and looked at the boy in the white-spreaded bed. How long he looked. His feet were not far from the foot. The nurse was raising his knees. How white, how clean, how peaceful, how perfectly lifeless he looked. What if he'd never wake up!

But Jeth could see his chest rise and fall with steady easy breathing. He didn't look sick now. He didn't look like he'd had an operation. He didn't look like he ever knew a pain.

Myra squeezed Jeth's big hand. It felt warm and strong. A tear fell on her dress. Jeth saw it fall.

"He mustn't, Jeth," she whispered.

"Well—all right," whispered Jeth. "He might as well quit school, too, now since this turned up."

"You got him in here just in time." The doctor stood beside the bed. He buttoned his double-breasted coat.

"It hasn't burst then?" Myra inquired brokenly. It was hard for her to speak.

"Luckily no. I've never had one any nearer to it. I'll see him in the morning. Good night now. Call me if you need me." This last he said to the nurse as he left the room.

For three days Millard was too sick to talk more than he just had to. His mother, reluctant to leave him, was permitted to stay in his room as much as she wanted to. Only while she was near him did she seem to be completely satisfied. She did not try to make him talk. She looked with rapt concentration on her son's face as though she had not seen him for years. The peace on her own was only submerged by apprehension when he was in agony. Though mother of seven, Myra Grinstead did not look haggard or old or toilworn. Her silky black hair fell in soft natural waves above her white forehead, and on her cheeks still lingered that bloom of youth.

On the dresser was a large basket of yellow chrysanthemums Paul and Neta Auckers brought in.

Jeth stayed until almost noon on Monday. Christina brought Jeth and Myra coffee and sandwiches. After that Jeth took Myra to the hospital early every morning and went after her at night. She took one sandwich with her for her lunch. Nothing more.

On the fourth morning Millard greeted his parents with a smile.

"You're better," his father observed.

"Yes, I'm better," Millard replied.

Jeth looked glad. He acted glad.

Somehow it eased the brooding disorder in Millard's mind.

"I'm sorry this'll cost quite a bit, Pop," he ventured soberly, wriggling his toes under the sheet.

"Well—guess it couldn't be helped," Pop answered. "An'," he continued slowly as though searching for words or the courage to say what was on his mind, "we ain't had the sickness some families our size have had. We'll get it paid somehow, I guess."

There were comparatively few times in his life when Jeth Grinstead endeared himself to his son as he did that morning. Millard almost marveled at his father's pleasant attitude. Then he did care? And Millard had not heard him complain once about the extra amount of gas it was taking to bring mother to and from the hospital every day. Warm circles ran round and round Millard's heart. He started feeling hungry. But—maybe Pop meant he'd have to work and help pay the bill. Didn't he say, "We'll get it paid somehow?" Well, he'd be willing to do that.

"I don't know how soon the doctor will let me go back to work," Millard said.

"You're not going back to Auckers," his mother said trying to hide the inward glow of joy she felt in telling him, but in her eyes Millard caught that note of gladness. He looked at his father inquiringly. "Is that so, Pop?"

Groping for a long minute to find his way out of his turmoil of thought, Jeth coughed, then said with an odd expression on his face, "Your mother don't want you to—an' I wouldn't want to see her come with 'pendicitis yet or somethin' worse. She might if you'd go back, I'm afraid."

Jeth's crude way of expressing his approval of Mother's better judgment was accepted with gladness. Pop loved Mother. Instinctively Millard's sensitive nature responded with deep appreciation. He was glad now he got sick. There was pleasure in pain when it proved to him once more Pop wanted to make Mother happy. Pop looked strangely handsome.

"I think Bro. Ambers talked to Pop about this," his mother confided after Pop left, "and we had a letter from Grandma, too, and she said they didn't like the idea of you staying in a home that wasn't Christian, and Uncle Levi said he was praying there'd be a way out for you. But I don't think any of us thought this would be your way out, Millard. And I have something else to tell you." She drew her chair closer to his bed.

"What?"

"As soon as you're able to leave the hospital you're going over to Uncle Levi's till you get strong again."

"Why there?"

"Well, they asked us if you couldn't come there. You see they have two bedrooms downstairs and we haven't. Christina thinks I have too much to do. They talked it over with both of us, and Pop said it would be all right."

"He did?" Millard smiled unconsciously.

"Will that be all right?"

"Well, next to home-it's the best place I'd know of, I guess."

"You see, Millard," his mother said softly—the nurse came in to give him his morning care.

* * * * *

Grandmother Winegar tore it open. Grandfather took his favorite chair beside the kitchen table. "Dear Father and Mother, Myra said she dropped you a card telling about Millard's operation. He's getting along all right. Some of us can't help but feel God had a hand in this to get him away from Auckers. I met Mr. and Mrs. Auckers at the hospital today and they are very nice worldly people. Mrs. Auckers is rather stunning. But it would seem to me their home would not be the kind of home for Millard. He's coming to our place as soon as he is able to leave the hospital. He may stay a month or more. He talks like he doesn't want to go back to school any more this year. If he could start in at East Dixon I think he would like it all right. I was over to their place Monday to help Orpha and the boys, and I wasn't very happy over the way some things looked around there, but I don't want to be too critical. Maybe Jeth does the best he can, but I think, just as you do, that Millard could be a big help right there at home. Don't write and ask me what all I noticed. It must be what we've always said—just poor management. The best milk cow is sick, but that might happen to anyone. I love every one of those children, but I'll try not to show partiality to Millard.

Can't you come and spend Christmas with us? In love, Levi."

Chapter 14

SHOULD we?" Grandfather's one elbow was on the edge of the table and his chin rested suddenly on the palm of his hand. A tumult of thoughts packed his brain. His head moved slowly back and forth with the weight of it.

"Well, could we?" inquired Grandmother, bending forward in her chair. The letter lay in her lap.

"We could, I guess—and—and maybe we should, if we're able and it's not too cold. We'd have to go on the train. We'd have to get someone to stay here or look after things while we're gone. If Jeth can't make it on that place—" Grandfather Winegar got up from his chair and walked to the kitchen door and looked out toward the east, "I have my doubts if he'll ever make it anywhere. Let's plan now to go back for Christmas. I want to see for myself how things are goin' there. Jeth's missin' the best opportunity in his life,if he don't use Millard right there at home. I can't get that through my head why he sends that boy off somewhere else when—here comes Joe Pundle. Wonder what he wants."

"Howdy. Come in."

Joe Pundle removed his cap.

"Howdy, Mr. Winegar. Can you tell me where I could find Jeth Grinstead?"

"I could, Mr. Pundle. How soon did you want to get hold of him?"

"Right away if I can."

"Well, Jeth's left the state."

"Jeth did? When?"

"Oh, the family moved to Granger in the spring. Didn't you know that?"

"No, I didn't know that. I was away myself for several months.

Jes' got back three weeks ago. Well, well. What's he doin' over there?"

"He's on a farm."

"Jeth buy a farm?"

"No, we did. It was Levi's place, an' we bought it an' put Jeth's there."

"But Jeth never liked farming too good, did he?"

"Well—well—" Grandfather Winegar ran his two first fingers around the inside of his blue shirt collar, cleared his throat, and then answered admittingly, "guess he would rather do carpenter work maybe, but you're the man who laid him off, aren't you, Mr. Pundle?"

"I didn't do it 'cause I wanted to-a-Mr. Winegar-but-a-we had that little trouble down in the Daisy Del, you know, an' I got my dutch up an'-"

"I knew nothing of that, Mr. Pundle. This is news to me. Jeth said he an' two other men were laid off at the same time."

Mr. Pundle's mouth was full of tobacco juice. He opened the door and aimed at the ground beyond the porch.

"Sure enough, Mr. Winegar, sure enough." Joe wiped the corners of his mouth. "We'll let bygones be bygones an' if Jeth's way over there, I'll be trottin' on. I'm over here now workin' on that Morris place what burned."

"Rebuilding?" inquired Grandfather with surprise.

"It's goin' ter be a roadside inn, I understand, when we get it finished."

"Who's puttin' it up?"

"I am. I got the job an' I got a bunch of men over there now. I wanted Jeth to help if I could find him. I could use two more men right away. Russie an' Sim aren't workin' fer me no more, so I thought Jeth would—a—a—"

"I meant who owns that place now? Are the Morrises puttin' up a roadside inn where that house stood?"

"Yes, Mrs. Morris an' her brother gave me the contract. Well, I'll be goin' on. When you write, tell Jeth I've got a job fer him any time he takes a notion to come back."

Ignoring the statement Grandfather Winegar called as he stood at the open door, "Do you know, Mr. Pundle, did they ever find out how that fire got started?"

"Who's they?" called Joe Pundle over his shoulder.

"Well, anybody, I guess."

Joe Pundle was in a hurry. "I heard what some think, an' I 'spect you've heard that, too, but I wouldn't say I know, would you?" Then Mr. Pundle laughed and jumped into his truck.

"You're not going to write and tell Jeth what that man said, are you?" asked Grandmother anxiously. She folded the letter and stuck it in the envelope.

"Shall I?"

"No, no. But I would like to know what happened at the Daisy Del."

"No, you wouldn't."

"Wouldn't you?"

"Well—"

"Well, wouldn't you now?" she repeated.

"We're just as well off if we don't know. He's out there now an' Myra says they were taken into the church an' he seems happier, so let's never mention it to her or anybody. I almost wish Joe Pundle hadn't stopped here. Let's fix up to go there for Christmas. I'm gonna find out how much it would cost."

* * * * *

Millard sat in the overstuffed chair close to the window. Now and then he looked up from the book he was reading to watch the winter's first snowflakes which were falling fast. A two-inch blanket covered the earth as far as he could see. Sticky wet snow clung to tree trunks and fences. From the kitchen he could hear Aunt Christina singing. He listened. It was a Christmas carol he had learned in the Doddridge school. Miss Hazel Butterfield had taught it to her pupils and they sang it twice a day for more than a week. Millard laid his one hand over the open page and looked out the window. "Peace on earth and mercy mild; God and sinners reconciled." Clear and beautiful the woman's voice sounded as she sang in joyous manner the story of Christ's birth and mission on earth.

Reconciled. Millard thought. He remembered hearing Bro. Ambers using that word in one of his recent sermons. Line after line Aunt Christina sang. Inaudibly Millard sang with her. The words came back to him. He could see Miss Butterfield's pretty sincere face slightly uplifted, her auburn hair in soft natural waves above the temples, her lips moving as she led that meaningful hymn. The words took on new meaning now as he heard them from the kitchen. He sat spellbound and rapt. "Born that man no more may die; born to raise the sons of earth, born to give them second birth."

Second birth? Second birth! Millard's heart missed half a beat, then raced for a minute. Something seized him and held him completely absorbed. In the quietness of the room a strong belief possessed him that he, Don Millard Grinstead, was a sinner, a lost hopeless sinner who needed something called the second birth. He needed to be reconciled to God. A strange mingling of associated ideas came to his attention one by one, but in the foreground stood his mother asking, "You know what I mean, don't you?" That was the same night she had asked him whether or not he had ever smoked, and she had added so expectantly, so clear-faced and affectionately, that he was old enough now and was going to someday hear God's voice calling him.

For over a year he had been wondering how it would be, how he would feel, what he would do, if that voice came to him while he was in school. Never had he felt like shunning or dodging or ignoring that voice. He did not even shrink from the thought of it. He was open, living from day to day wondering, wondering, waiting.

The experiences at Auckers naturally did not hasten. Something forestalled it, for the message never came through. Nas made fun of his "half spearment". He teased him because he didn't smoke. He told war stories in all their pomp and glory until any normal boy would get a desire to see the rest of the world and have an ambition to serve his country and follow a career that brought him national recognition.

Nas told Millard how he got his long name. Very dramatically and with frequent cursings he related with conceit that each of his names was given him in memory of some distinguished person his father had admired. Virgil was a Latin poet, the Vanderbilts were wealthy folks, and Manasseh was a colored prize fighter and lion tamer in the circus. Besides that (and here Nas laughed boisterously) someone had told him there was a Manasseh in the Bible. The D. stood for Dunihem, his mother's maiden name. Nas proudly told Millard how he started drinking, how he learned to gamble and wrestle, how he once wore a mustache, how he could have had one of a score of women for the asking. He explained all about bayonet practices, bombardments and hiding in trenches. More than once

Millard had wished he could run home—home to his mother and Ticia—and sit on the floor behind the stove and read while the boys played around. He was so homesick several times he felt like crying, but Millard was too big to cry over a thing like that. Why be homesick when Neta Auckers was so nice to him, when he had the best things to eat and a good bed to sleep in? It was something besides that that made him homesick. It was that consciousness that Pop wanted him away from home. He could not understand that. That's the thing that made the tears come, but Nas would never find out why he caught him crying. Millard didn't want anyone to know. But didn't people wonder? Didn't people have eyes and minds? Maybe Paul and Neta Auckers knew. Maybe Nas knew too and that was why they all tried extra hard to entertain him. The thought of it touched the boy's finest senses. He did not want to be pitied. If something could only happen to prove to people that his father did want him back home. Millard was terribly embarrassed when Nas walked into his room and found him in tears. If Pop would have had to send him away from home to work because they were so poor, he wouldn't have minded it half as much. He wanted to go back home because he wanted to be wanted.

Now here he was at Uncle Levi's house and able to sit in an easy chair by the window and read to his heart's content. He would stay until he was strong enough to climb stairs. The explanation had been given that there was no place to put him downstairs at home. That was true. He was satisfied to be at Uncle Levi's home. The place was ideal. Yet Millard longed to go home. He wanted to be wanted there. Mother wanted him back, he knew. Liticia wanted him. But Pop. Why didn't he want him there? Millard wondered until his brain began to whirl. To his knowledge the only thing that Pop objected to was his fondness for reading. Maybe—maybe Pop really was so hard up he had to find him a place to stay. Didn't he act glad that morning at the hospital when he was better? He did. And Pop never complained about bringing Mother in every day—at least not that he heard about it. If he kept on improving as rapidly as he had the past few days, he'd be able to go home and climb the stairs in less than a month.

"I'll turn the light on." Millard jumped. So lost was he in his thoughts he had not heard Christina enter the living room. "You weren't trying to read in the dark were you, Millard?"

"I haven't been reading the past few minutes. I've been— watching the snow." Millard felt warm all over.

"Makes us think of Christmas, doesn't it? Are you warm enough, Millard?"

"Oh, yes."

"You're not getting too tired?"

"No, I guess not."

"We'll have supper as soon as Levi comes in. Too bad your folks don't have a phone. They just must get one. You could call them up and surprise them. I doubt if they'll come in any more this evening now since it's snowing like this."

"I doubt it, too. I don't suppose Pop would like to drive in this kind of weather, and I'd rather he wouldn't try it."

"I must call Dr. Munsell and let him know how you are. I'll do it right now before I forget it. What shall I tell him, Millard?"

"Tell him I'm all right. Ask him how soon," Millard's fingers laced the pages of his book, "how soon I will be able to go home."

"Home? Why, Millard, you're not figuring on going home until after Christmas, are you?"

"Well I—I didn't know how long I was to stay here."

"You're not getting homesick are you, Millard?"

"Not exactly." Millard laughed a dry little laugh. "No-it's not that, Aunt Christina. I think I make too much extra work for you."

"No, you don't. Now Millard, don't you say that again. We're glad to have you here and—don't we act like it?"

"Yes," Millard's face flushed slightly, "you've been very nice to me."

*　*　*　*　*

Jeth Grinstead reached up. It was there above the barn door exactly as he had placed it the night before—the can beside it. He filled it, lit it, and took a long drag. He leaned hard against the doorpost to relax a bit. He must go to town with the eggs and get some bran for the chickens. Driving might be tough, so he needed a smoke to settle his nerves. Myra said she wanted some ointment for Glen's chest. He'd get that at the drugstore. That would give him a good chance to get another can of tobacco. If the roads were too bad, he could call out to Uncle Levi's from the drugstore and ask how Millard was, but Jeth didn't like to talk on the telephone. He'd about as soon walk that far out from town. He'd see how the roads were.

94

He should stop at the hospital and give them some money. He really couldn't spare the money. The sick cow was no better. Jeth detested cows. His hands weren't made to milk. Neither did they fit a pitchfork handle. He hated cleaning out the barn. That should be done, too. If only Homer Jo were Orpha's age! Myra said she thought that was too hard for Orpha. Myra objected. Millard could clean the barn and take care of the cows; Jeth could do carpenter work again—or get a job in town. Millard wasn't a lazy boy when he was out of the reach of books. Millard really could do a lot around the place. They could have a few more cows, more milk, more income, but Millard was too—too— Jeth took a long delicious drag—too knowing, too discerning, too smart, too-

Jeth jumped.

In the doorway stood Homer Jo! Jeth took the pipe from his mouth and held it awkwardly. For a moment he was dazed. He stood speechless. So did Homer Jo.

"Didn't you go to school?" asked Pop.

"No, I have a toothache." Homer Jo held his jaw.

"Then what are you doin' out here with your toothache?"

"Mother said I should come an' see what's takin' you so long or if you drove off when she wasn't lookin'. She wants you to bring home some cornmeal and not to forget the ointment for Glen."

"Well, I was comin' in before I left. You get on back in that house with your toothache or you'll have a real one." Jeth looked completely exasperated and perturbed. He didn't know what to do with the pipe. It felt strangely clumsy and heavy. He didn't want to put it in his pocket, and he certainly did not want to put it back where he got it. Not while Homer Jo was there.

"I—I—thought you threw that away, Pop," ventured Homer Jo with an unnatural grin that mocked his father. At least that's the way it affected Jeth. He felt like slapping Homer Jo—yes, Homer Jo, his favorite son, his pet, the one above all others (except Millard) he never, never would have catch him smoking on the sly. Of all mornings—this when he needed good steady nerves!

"You may go—now," Jeth said in thick, breathy words, "an' see that you say nothin' ter your mother or anyone else on—on this earth." Jeth was gasping for breath. He looked sick and pale.

"Why? Why, Pop?"

"Because—jes' because," shouted Jeth. "Go now, you scamp, you."

Chapter 15

"IT is always easier after one is found out," Jeth had said to himself. Jeth was almost certain that before the day was half spent Homer Jo would tell. Jeth cringed inwardly. He cringed from fear. Fear of what? He chided himself. What should he fear? His own children? Surely not his wife. Not the pastor. Had he not said that if he were overtaken, the church would bear with him and show patience? He had. Then what did he fear unless it was his own moral sense that determined right from wrong? He shook himself. Jeth tapped the pipe on the palm of his left hand and tucked it back on the ledge above the barn door. He had thought once of throwing it in the pond and letting it rot there, but that would be a great way to treat a friendly, comforting, innocent little thing like a pipe! They had loved each other a long time. If he put it away, he'd at least give it a decent resting place.

Lowering his head because of the cold wind, Jeth hurried to the house. Carefully he swept the snow from his overshoes.

"I thought maybe you left already, Jeth," Myra was sweeping the kitchen when he entered.

"I wouldn't go without askin' again if you thought of somethin' else you wanted from town. Homer Jo said you want corn meal. Is that all now? I must be goin'."

"That's all. You really should find out if Auckers took Millard's clothes in yet. If they haven't and Levi hasn't gone after them, you should. You're going to stop to see Millard, aren't you?"

"Well—I suppose I'd better. I hope the road down that way isn't too bad. Anything you want me to tell Millard in particular?" Jeth seemed unusually pleasant. He buttoned his sheep-lined mackinaw and took Glen up in his arms and fondled him a little.

"Oh, I guess not unless you tell him how we all are. You won't forget that ointment for him, will you, Pop?"

"No. How's that toothache, Homer Jo?" Jeth scarcely glanced at him when he spoke.

Homer Jo was perched on the wood box beside the stove. "Well, it still hurts," he whined.

"Maybe he'd better go along in with you and see a dentist," Myra said.

"No, sir, I don't want to go to a dentist. I'll be all right. Pop, wouldn't it help if you'd blow some of your smokin' in my tooth?"

Consternation, horror, and dismay crossed Jeth Grinstead's face with one tick of the clock. Then he looked trounced. He coughed and walked quickly out of the house without saying another word.

But hadn't Jeth concluded before he left the barn that it was going to be easier now that he was found out? Then why be smitten? He wouldn't be. He wasn't. He would shield and handle himself. He would be his own safeguard. Homer Jo was not makin' sport of him. He didn't dare. What did he know about a craving that almost drove a sane man insane? Homer Jo was just an innocent boy who did not realize he injured his father's pride. But, no, he wasn't injured. This was merely an accident. He'd forget it. He hoped Homer Jo would, too. But the futility of that hope stared him in the face. Homer Jo was ten. He was old enough to form notions and opinions and maybe make pretty close estimations. And what if Homer Jo were old enough to have personal convictions?

Jeth gripped the steering wheel and tried to whistle. No worthy tune came within his reach, so he gave it up. All the way to town, Jeth labored with his own soul. He would go home and do away once and forever with the pipe and what went with it, and explain to Homer Jo he found it in the barn and only tasted it for fun for the last time. He must do this if he wanted his boys never to start smoking. He really and definitely did not want any of his boys to get into the habit. It was a bad habit. It was. It lessened a man's resistance against other temptations. He realized it. He knew full well how Myra felt about it. Jeth bit the inside of his cheek to keep back a tear. He could not bear even to think how disappointed his wife would be if she found this out. Through all the years, and especially the last several, she had taken a remarkable attitude. For her sake he must get the victory. Myra was dear to him. He did love Myra. He did want to make her satisfied. She wanted Millard back home. There really was no reason why Millard couldn't be at home to help with the work and finish his term at the Dixon School. He'd be much happier. They'd all be happier. What if the family was large? Some larger ones lived in smaller houses. No one else thought they were too crowded. Only Jeth. That was it. The closeness of things. That pressed in, tight sensation that made a person feel as if were being squeezed all the time.Millard was too knowing a boy to have so close around you all the time. He would soon be a man. His voice was beginning to change already. He would soon be deciding for or against Christ—and the church. He seemed so advanced in some respects for his age. Those books he liked to read made him all the more knowing. Secretly Jeth admired this in his son, and all to himself he almost admitted that if he could get rid of his pipe, he could stand it to have Millard at home.

What a small, insignificant thing to be quibblin' over! A seventy-nine cent pipe! How trifling! But it wasn't the pipe. It was the smoking of it. But what was wrong about that? Plenty of good men smoked all they pleased. Sunday-school teachers smoked. Preachers smoked. If it were a sin, then why was there a difference of opinion and why didn't the Bible say so in plain words, like thou shalt not kill? Whether or not a person liked it was a personal taste, like liking or not liking onions or pepper. It's the way you've been raised up.

Ah! Jeth caught his breath and held it. The one-man debate had been three miles long. Never had it been more tense. The affirmative would win by weight of the argument unless it stopped immediately. Jeth would quit arguing with himself. He'd settle this once and for all and be the master of his own soul. He would prove to Myra and his boys he could quit before any of them followed in his footsteps. That raising up, that livin'-an-example-before-their-eyes religion was the ideal kind. Way down in the lowest corners of his immortal being Jeth Grinstead found that conviction there, and when he brought it to light it shone with dazzling brightness before his eyes. He could not bear to look at it. He batted his eyes and drove on. The snow was well packed and not so slippery as he had feared.

Jeth got the ointment for Glen at the drugstore.

"Nothing else this morning, sir?" asked the broad-smiling gentleman clerk.

"Not today." Jeth looked at the merchandise on the shelves at the right front of the store. There was every brand on display in different sized cans.

"Something in the line of tobaccos?"

Jeth cleared his throat and pulled out his money. The can above the barn door would allow not more than two good smokes. He ought to get a can in case he simply could not resist. He should fortify himself against a nervous breakdown. He could get a small size and hide it away for an emergency. The kind he liked was in a red can.

"What kind, sir?" the clerk followed Jeth's gaze to the front of the store.

Jeth clinched his fist. He scuffled with himself for an awkward minute.

"Oh, I've got plenty of tobaccer. This will be all. I'm in a hurry this mornin'."

*　*　*　*　*

Paul and Neta Auckers sat in the Winegar living room chatting pleasantly. Neta had a gushing, extravagant manner of displaying her personality. She was attractive.

"You look grand, Millard." Neta's cheery smile was contagious. It showed up her dimples and a pretty gold tooth.

"Doesn't he?" smiled Christina.

"How soon do you think you can come back?" asked Mr. Auckers. His tan felt hat fell from his knee to the floor. He picked it up quickly.

"I'll take your hat, Mr. Auckers." Christina hung it on the hall tree. Millard shifted his glance seriously.

"You'd better not count on him coming back, Mr. Auckers," Christina said politely. "We want to keep him here with us until he's really real strong, and, anyway, he's not sure yet about going back to school. He may—well, I guess it's not for me to say what he's going to do. Millard, pardon me. You can speak for yourself. Maybe you haven't decided yet."

"Well, I guess it'll be up to Pop. He did say I better not go back."

"He did?" observed Paul Auckers with surprise. "Then we'll have to do without a boy or hunt up another one. Do you have a brother whom we could adopt a while?"

"I'm afraid not. Homer Jo is only ten, I believe. Not more."

"Oh, I'd love to have a boy that age, Millard," cooed Neta. "Wouldn't you, Paul? They're so pliable and teachable and cute and inquisitive at that age. Let's talk to Mr. Grinstead about it. We wouldn't work him hard, and we'd get him all the clothes he needed and take him places with us. Oh, Paul, we could have the most fun and show him the time of his life."

Neta Auckers noticed the look of startled disapproval on both Millard's and Mrs. Winegar's faces, then added cleverly and confidentially, "We wouldn't lead him into anything that wasn't all right, you know. We know you are church-going people, and we like that kind of boys around. They can be trusted. Nas Gerlach is a rough fellow in his way, but he's perfectly harmless; isn't he, Paul?"

"My, yes; you've just got to learn how to take Nas."

"Say, Millard," exclaimed Neta, "was your side bothering you much before that night?"

"Yes, several times."

"That's just what I figured. I'll bet it hurt you lots of times and you never said anything. Nas said he found you—"

Paul coughed meaningfully. His steel blue eyes spoke reprimanding words to his wife.

But Neta was burning to know why Nas said he saw tears. She wanted to know if he told the truth. She had said she refused to believe it.

"Here comes your father, Millard." Christina met Jeth at the door.

"Hi, there, neighbor." Paul Auckers rose to shake hands with Jeth. "We brought Millard's clothes over. And he says it's up to you whether or not he will be comin' back to our place. You don't need him over there, do you, Mr. Grinstead?"

"Well," Jeth shifted from one foot to the other and scratched his hands, "his mother seems to think his place is ter home. I want her satisfied. You'd better not figure on him comin' back. He don't like school no how, so he might as well quit."

"Oh, no, Mr. Grinstead," exclaimed Neta Auckers genially, "Millard's not going to quit school until he's through. Surely not. He's too bright a boy to do a thing like that. How about your next boy coming to live with us? Homer Jo. Can't you loan him to us for a while?"

Jeth's pipe loomed up before him in magnified proportions, and his boys were watching him around the edge of the barn door. The ledge above was too small to hide it . Should he get rid of his boys or the pipe? It seemed to him he could not be perfectly happy with both on the premises.

"My wife wouldn't hear to that either, Mr. Auckers," Jeth said finally. He heard Millard and Christina each draw a breath of relief. "She's pretty much on keepin' her family around her."

"That's a good idea, Jeth," Christina put in discreetly. "Of course, I never had any of my own, but if I did have I'm sure I'd feel like Myra does."

"Of course," ventured Jeth, trying to sound casual, "when the time comes we'll have to be willin' to see our children scatter out. Some o' the best men had to wrestle fer themselves when they were as young as Millard there."

* * * * *

Not all of a person's thoughts and struggles are easily translated into written words. For days Millard strove with his own conscience. He was certain God was calling to accept His love as a personal gift. At night the consciousness of his sins was almost unbearable. He had no idea it would make him feel like that. He suffered mental agony that brought forth stifled moans. He wished he knew whether or not Pop really wanted him back home. Yet in his anguish he thanked God that his mother loved him so much, and that he was counted worthy of being called. He must settle the question. He could not go on unsaved any longer. There was something about Uncle Levi that made the presence of God feel strangely near.

Then one night he found these words in John: "No man can come to me, except the Father which hath sent me draw him: and I will raise him up at the last day." Millard lay across the bed, the open Testament before him. He read on.

"I will stand for Christ and openly confess Him the next chance I have," he said to himself, and with that determination he fell asleep.

* * * * *

Two weeks passed.

Myra had a needle and thread in her hand. She took Jeth's cap from the hooks.

"I noticed your cap was torn. I'll mend it."

Myra took several stitches.

"It takes a long time for the smell to leave, doesn't it, Jeth?" Myra took two more stitches.

Horrors!

"What smell?" blinked Jeth. He spoke very slowly.

"Your cap smells as strong of smoke as it did before." Her voice was extremely tender.

Horrors!

"Before when?" Jeth took out his pocketknife and started cutting his fingernails. His hands trembled.

"Before we went into the church." Myra kept on mending. She did not look up.

Chapter 16

POOR Jeth. She heard him draw a deep breath.

The children were all in bed. Otherwise Myra wouldn't have mentioned anything.

"I thought by this time it would be aired out."

Jeth cut another nail. He never got excited. He would control himself now.

"Why don't you get a new cap?" she asked sweetly.

Jeth was at a loss to know what to say. Blindly he sought for words.

"If Brother Ambers should stop by some day, he'd think you still smoke. Your coat smells, too."

Myra finished mending the cap—dear Jeth's cap! She hung it up. Her own hand trembled. She could wait no longer, and, turning, threw her arms around his neck. Is that the way it made her feel? Jeth was shocked, troubled, beaten. His arms enfolded her.

"Don't, Myra, please," he pleaded. "It's not your fault. I've tried an' tried. No one knows how I've tried. It's jes no use tryin' to hide it any longer."

"But, Jeth!" Myra drew herself away from him. She wiped her eyes. "I've known it all along," she whispered.

"Myra."

"What?"

"Then why before God didn't you say so?"

"I don't know why I needed to, Jeth. You knew it and so did God."

"Who told you?"

"No one. Could I live with you and not know?"

Jeth groaned.

The clock on the shelf struck ten. A mouse ran across the room.

Only Myra noticed it.

"Well, I venture to say," began Jeth, lapping one word over the other, his deep voice reduced to a still deeper tone, "That there are quite a few men in Brother Amber's church who smoke an' nothin's said about it. If I'm not fit to take the communion, he can tell me so."

Silence.

"How do you feel about it?" Myra's tears kept coming.

"I'm sorry—I haven't been able to quit. That's how I honestly feel."

"You're disappointed in yourself?"

"You're disappointed in me." His voice sounded hurt.

"That's not what I said, Jeth."

"That's what you meant." Jeth sank into a chair. He buried his face in his two strong hands.

"Maybe we'd better move back to Doddridge—an' go back to the other church. It was all right there."

"You don't mean that, Jeth," Myra stood up very straight. "You know you admire Bro. Ambers because he doesn't use tobacco. You know you've said you don't want any of your own boys to use it. You know we all want you to get the victory over this. We'd do anything—anything, Jeth, from Orpha on down to Glen—to help you in any way we know of."

"Stop, Myra! I can't stand it. You make me feel terrible. Don't talk like that to me."

Was Jeth going to get excited? He never had before.

"Dear Jeth, I am not out of fix with you. I've tried to understand all along. I think I do. I am not accusing you. Oh, Jeth," Myra talked very slowly and with feeling, "if I knew you'd take me wrong I never would have mentioned anything, but the boys would think as much of you if you'd smoke your pipe right out in the open, I believe. Yes, I'm sure they would. This way they think you're ashamed of being seen. You can see how they feel about it, can't you, Pop?"

Pop! Oh, why had he ever allowed his children to start calling him that? Jeth felt sick all over. He remembered vividly the day when Russie Richmond called him that and Homer Jo took it up—-Homer Jo, his bright-eyed favorite. It sounded cute that day, and it made him laugh, yet he well remembered, too, the rest of the incident that didn't seem so cute or amusing to him. If all of his children could have been daughters, then none would have been with him at

Flitche's barn building, and girls would hardly be tempted to smoke a pipe because their father did.

Argue, figure, imagine, lament as he would, Jeth could not change the past. He had five sons.

But to answer Myra's question truthfully was a hard thing for him to do.

"I might as well give up," he said at last.

"Oh, Jeth, I knew you would. I'll believe in you. I know you see it as I do. Come, let us have prayer together and go to bed. You're tired." Myra took hold of his arm.

Jeth did not get up. He was stunned. Surely Myra misunderstood him. His mouth opened but without words. His soul cried within him. Would to God he could have meant what she seemingly had understood him to mean. He must tell her. How could he disappoint her again? He felt helpless and unexpectedly confused. If he could only trust himself, he'd let her go on thinking as she did. Myra had a spirit found in few women. How could she believe in him now after knowing how he had failed so often? He must show her. If he had a nervous breakdown, she would take care of him. Then Millard would have to manage the farm. He would not only get nervous(Jeth knew from experience), but he'd also be easily provoked and irritated. He'd get headaches and aches all over.

"Give it to me now, Jeth," whispered Myra.

"Give you what?"

Jeth knew.

"The pipe and all your tobacco. I want to help you definitely this time."

"You—you mean go get them now?" Jeth's arms sagged.

"Yes, dear, I mean right now. You said you might as well give it up, so stick to it and do the thing you know you ought to. If you really meant it—and you—you surely did, didn't you, Jeth—so—-"

"But, Myra. I—I—"

"Don't say 'but', Jeth. Lead me to wherever they are, and I'll pick them up for you. Don't ever touch them again. Make a clean sweep like Brother Ambers says, and break completely away from it tonight. You can. I'm sure you can—by God's help."

Jeth heaved.

"Put on your coat and scarf then," he said.

Was Jeth talking in a dream?

She did. She put them on without delay.

Jeth led the way to the barn. Slowly he opened the door. The ganglia in his nose and tongue quivered as he neared the spot. His mouth watered. No one could possibly know what this would mean to him both mentally and bodily. But the moment had come. He must give it up literally. It is easier after one is found out. Myra might as well know, too, where he had it hid.

He turned on the light.

Jeth reached up. His fingers found the place in the righthand corner on the ledge.

An astonished exclamation escaped his parted lips. His body got rigid.

"It's —it's not there," he said icily. Jeth felt cold all over.

"Is that where you've been keeping it??"

"Yes." Jeth's heart came up into his throat. "Right there. It's gone."

"Who do you think took it?"

"God only knows," he panted. His vital powers seemed to be suspended on a thin thread. He felt sick. He was certain it could have been no one but his second son.

"The little rascal," he said under his breath; "the dirty little rascal. He'll get a whippin' fer this."

But Jeth Grinstead had never yet whipped Homer Jo. There was something about that boy that he adored. He had never been able to cross him. Now this was the way his pet showed his appreciation. The impudence! The brass! The naughty thief!

"Maybe you forget where you put it last, Jeth."

"No, I didn't."

"When was the last you used it?"

Myra would ask that. He seemed not to hear. He acted ruffled.

"Maybe a rat carried it off," she suggested.

"A two-legged rat," muttered Jeth before he thought twice.

"Jeth!" Myra's cry was a stifled shriek. Fear gripped her with terrible claws.

*   *   *   *   *

Millard sat attentive, a serene expression on his face. He had completed the battle weeks before. Inwardly he felt trembly but outwardly he seemed quite composed. There was no doubt in his mind about standing. He could hardly wait until the invitation was given.

He had not seen any of his family in the audience, but perhaps they came later and were sitting behind him. But they were not in church the Sunday evening before. Pop had said they might have to stop going to church twice on Sundays to save gasoline.

A holy hush like a solemn benediction, fell over the audience. It was Don Millard Grinstead's memorable night. He stood. Bro. Ambers nodded. The peace of God flooded his soul, and he knew that moment his sins were forgiven. In simple childlike faith, without any wavering, he appropriated the promises the minister had quoted in his sermon. He had never before known such happiness and quietude of heart.

After the services were dismissed Brother Ambers shook Millard's hand and told him how glad he was he had taken the stand.

"You mean by this you wish to be baptized and received into the church?"

"I think so. There are some things I'm not sure I understand perfectly."

"I'll be seeing you before long. Perhaps right after Christmas. Where shall I talk with you? In your home some evening after school perhaps?"

"That would be all right. I've been staying with Uncle Levi Winegars since my operation."

"I didn't know that."

"I'll not go home until I'm able to climb stairs."

"There are not many steps here."

"No, not many."

"You're getting along all right?"

"Very well. I feel able to go home now. I don't see why it wouldn't be all right, but they want me to stay a while yet."

"Your folks?"

"Uncle Levi's."

"Before I come I'll call to find out where you are."

"We have no phone at home yet. I'm sorry." "I'll call Levi's home then. Good night now. God bless you, Millard."

* * * * *

Uncle Levi approached Millard at the door of his bedroom. He placed a strong hand on his nephew's shoulder. "This makes me very happy, Millard."

The salvation created in the boy's breast gave immediate response to his uncle's spirit with a fellow feeling. The warmness of love the one had for the other now put them on a new common ground, though the one was four times older than the other.

"Does it?" Millard smiled.

"Very. It is the first step which will lead you to your career."

Millard looked at his uncle in surprise. Career? He had heard that word repeatedly at Auckers but never with this association. Nas told him the army offered the best, the highest, the noblest, and most beneficial career any man could ever hope for. Just what did Uncle Levi mean? Millard had never thought about a career until Nas Gerlach mentioned it so often. In fact, the word was seldom in his vocabulary. In the ten weeks Millard had been at Auckers, Nas had talked to him by the hour about choosing a career with a glorious future, about serving one's country which would guarantee any man a ticket into heaven (if there was one) and at the same time give him a chance to see the world and learn how to handle carbines, pistols, guns, bull-dozers, grenades, and powerful machinery of all kinds. It meant you could have fun and learn big things and get big ideas, have big experiences, and at the same time earn money. Millard stood thinking. Nas said he was working at Auckers for the novelty of the experience, not because he had to.

"I have fond hopes for you, my boy."

Millard stood thinking.

"Your mother will be very glad."

"I think she will."

"Too bad they didn't get in tonight."

It rather struck Millard that Uncle Levi did not mention his father. Wouldn't he be glad, too? Surely Uncle Levi meant both of them. Millard nodded.

"I will say good night. If I can be of any help to you in any way, don't be afraid to come to me."

"Sometime I might want to ask you some questions."

"Very well."

* * * * *

"Dear Ticia," It was the first letter Liticia Ann had ever received from her brother. Her eyes widened with surprise and excitement. "Why weren't you all at church Sunday night? I missed you. Guess

108

what I did. I stood. You know what I mean, don't you? Like Orpha did. I've been thinking about it quite a bit—especially since I got sick. Some before that, too. I feel much better now. I'm getting stronger, too, and I'm getting anxious to come home. Ticia, tell mother what I did.

Uncle Levi had a letter from Grandmother today. She said they are planning to come to Granger for Christmas. She said there's going to be a tavern where our house was that burned.

I would call home if I could. I hope they hurry up and get the phone put in. If Pop comes in here before Sunday, please slip me a slice of Mother's bread. Please. So long.

D. M."

Liticia's cheeks glowed. She handed the letter to her mother.

Chapter 17

"**D**ERWOOD," said Myra, "let me hear you say your piece once more before we go. Wait a minute. Are your hands clean, Richard? Homer Jo, your one shoe is untied. Orpha, you put Glen's wraps on while Derwood and I go to the bedroom. I don't want him to forget his piece tonight."

Myra took Derwood to the bedroom.

"'Gently moved until its light,
Made a manger cradle bright.'"

"Right there is where you stumble, Derwood. 'Made a manger cradle bright.' Say it over several times with me."

Derwood said the lines three times.

"Now listen, I'll try to sit where you can see me, and if you think you can't remember when you get to that place, watch my lips. Once more now."

"Come on, everybody," called Richard. "Pop's ready. Miss Yale said we must not be late."

Eight Grinsteads piled into the car and were off to attend the Christmas program at the East Dixon School. Myra was a little surprised Jeth consented to go, but Homer Jo had made such a unique and clever invitation in school (by the teacher's help) and had pinned it onto his father's pillowcase, that he could not refuse. The parents received three other invitations, one from Liticia Ann, one from Richard, and one from Derwood, all delivered in a different manner, but none was quite so unusual as Homer Jo's.

*　*　*　*　*

Jeth still did not know where his pipe had gone. Several times he had been on the verge of questioning Homer Jo, but something withheld him. He shrank from the idea of mentioning anything about it. He anticipated seizing him unexpectedly sometime, but so far the anticipation had never been realized. Jeth tried to watch Homer Jo without appearing too conspicuous. He was positive he sensed a guiltiness in the boy's demeanor. Homer Jo seemed to avoid his father, especially in the barn. Jeth felt tantalized.

Myra asked Jeth several times if he had located his pipe.

"Which one of the boys do you think took it?" she asked that night after they returned to the house.

In an effort to defend himself, he answered, "I didn't say any of the boys took it." Jeth read the worried look in her eyes. He waved her off.

"I know, Myra, but how could any of our boys see up there, an' I'm sure none of 'em knew where I kept it. So don't you fret about that until you know there's something to fret about. I was always careful."

"I heard what Homer Jo said that morning he stayed home from school with the toothache."

"Yes, but he was jes' talkin' to hear himself talk." Jeth bit his cheek.

Then one evening Myra said, "Jeth, I looked through everything."

"Everything. What do you mean?"

"While the boys were in school I thought if Homer Jo did take it, I might find it."

So her mind was still on that!

"But you didn't, did you?" he asked wisely.

"But you said you thought a two-legged—"

"No."

"I hope you never do." And Jeth meant that. He'd rather find it himself.

"What makes you think he might have taken it?" He observed her closely.

"Richard said he talked in his sleep about smoking your pipe."

"Who did?"

"Homer Jo did."

"That doesn't mean he did, Myra. People say all kinds of crazy stuff in their sleep."

* * * * *

After that Pop decided to take the family to the program. It wouldn't be worth much, but it would make them all happy, and since the personal invitation came from Homer Jo, Jeth would do that much to try to please him. He didn't like it that the boy avoided him. He must get next to him.

Or was Homer Jo going to be like Millard, reserved, and hard to understand?

A quarter of a mile from the schoolhouse a tire went flat. Jeth told the boys and Liticia to walk, if they were afraid of being late. Orpha said she'd walk with them and carry Glen. Then Myra said she'd better walk, too, because she didn't want to run any risk of not being there when it came time for Derwood to give his piece.

"I hate to leave you here alone, Jeth," she said. "I do hope you won't get too cold."

"Go ahead. I'll get there as soon as I can."

"Couldn't you take the tire off and run that far on the rim? I hate for you to have to miss part of the program."

"I'll be there in a little while. Go on."

All day Jeth had been upset and fidgety. The constant craving for a smoke had made him nerve-snappy. He felt like saying a bad word or two. He got his tools out and set to work at the unpleasant task. This was worse than milking.

A car stopped.

A man offered his assistance.

"It's tough luck to be having tire trouble on a cold night like this."

"You're right. I'm out of patchin' too. That's the worst of it."

"Let me see what I've got."

The man returned with a can.

"Here's some you can have. Take out what you need. And here, have a smoke. He offered Jeth a cigarette. He pulled out his lighter.

Jeth could not say he did not care for any, although the pipe was his preference. He had been unstrung for days. He could not resist. It looked good: it smelled good: it tasted good.

The man was kind enough to stay with Jeth until he was ready to go again.

"Well, much obliged to you. What do I owe you?" Jeth reached into his pocket. He had some loose change. "Oh, that's all right."

"I should have asked your name."

"Bill Aucker."

"Aucker?" asked Jeth, "Any relation to Paul Aucker?"

"We're brothers. What's your name?"

"Grinstead."

"Any connection to that Grinstead boy Paul's had there for a while?"

"He's my oldest son."

"Yes?"

The man hesitated. He clapped his cold hands.

"Aren't you one of Brother Ambers' members?"

"Yes." Jeth felt suddenly warm.

"I helped him fill silo several days this fall. He's a good man. Heard him talk about you and your boy Millard. If I would have known who you were,I—Well, I'll be on my way. Good luck to you."

Preliminaries had been completed and Miss Yale was ready to announce the first number when Jeth entered. Myra had reserved a seat beside her along the wall. She motioned, smiling.

"Did you get it fixed?" she whispered.

"Yes, a man came along an' helped me out."

Myra looked up in astonishment. Her brown eyes met his brown ones. Wasn't that smoke she smelled?

He did not blink. Something made him encounter her look with a fearlessness he did not know he had. He would explain to her when they got home—this time without shame.

Jeth clapped when the others clapped. He laughed when the others laughed. He tried to act unrestrained, free, clear of guilt.

Derwood got through his recitation without any prompting. Myra was pleased. Derwood did better than any of the first graders. And their other children rightfully deserved the words of commendation the board members made at the close of the program, and special mention was made of Liticia's well-rendered reading.

A number of people shook hands with Jeth, and Myra heard him say he enjoyed the program and was glad he got there in time to hear it all.

*   *   *   *   *

Two days before Christmas a blizzard swept across the eastern states, greatly hampering travel. Levi was not surprised when a telegram came saying his parents would not be coming to Granger.

"I was afraid of it." said Christina. "I'd better call and tell Myra. I'm so glad they have a phone at last. She'll be disappointed,but it would be risky for them to try to come way out here in such weather.

Millard, don't you want to call home again?"

"I can if your busy, but I did call home twice today. Mother said the roads were getting drifted out there. I talked to her around four. If it's snowing and blowing like this, the roads will be closed by morning."

"When I asked them to come," Levi said, "I was surprised they considered it seriously, because Mother never did like cold weather. Maybe they can come for Easter. Let's get together as we had planned and have a good time anyway."

"What if we can't get together?" asked Millard. He walked to the nearest window and looked out. He could scarcely see the road.

Before dawn the calm came. The highway department sent out snowplows, and by Christmas morning all the main roads were passable. Myra called and said the boys and Jeth were working on the driveway and it would be open by the time they got there.

Millard was almost trembling with excitement. He was going home! Home to eat and sleep and be near Mother and Liticia and the rest of the family. It seemed years since he was last inside the house.

He first caught sight of the roof beyond the pine trees at Donnelson's corner. His heart beat faster and harder, and he drew one deep breath after the other as the house came into view. Someone was at the front window; no, two, Liticia and little Glen. They waved. Then the dog came running, bounding over the snow and barking gladness.

Derwood came prancing down the steps to meet them, and, framed in the open doorway, stood Mother in her prettiest apron (a delicate yellow with tiny flowers). Clustered around her were five other familiar faces.

"Merry Christmas to you all," she called.

With a firm step Millard walked up to the house. He appeared well and strong. His cheeks glowed and there was a striking manliness about him. He must have grown taller, too, since he went to the hospital. She had not seen him since he had made his decision. Eager-faced, but serious he caught her outstretched hand, and kissed her.

From the open door came the delicious predominating smell of freshly baked rolls and roast chicken.

"Hello, Glen. How's Glen? Hello, Orpha, Homer Jo, Liticia, Richard, Derwood. Hello, Pop, how are you?"

Pop shook hands, but he did not kiss Millard. He stroked his gray hair. He needed a haircut.

"Homer Jo," Pop said, "you run out there an' help Uncle Levi carry in that box."

"Well, what's in it?"

"I s'pose it's Millard's clothes."

"Why didn't Millard bring it in himself?" Jeth was shocked. What had come over Homer Jo? He had never talked back to his father like that before. He gave him a disappointed look. Millard was shocked, too. Didn't Homer Jo want him to come home?

"I'm sorry," Millard said, "I forgot that box. I'm sorry, Uncle Levi."

"That's all right, Millard. It's too heavy for you to be lifting anyway."

Aunt Christina brought one of her chocolate angel-food cakes, celery, olives, cheese, and a large dish of homemade candies.

What a Christmas dinner they had! Everything from the hot pan rolls to the cake and ice cream was perfect. The ice cream was a surprise. Uncle Levi brought that.

To each of the boys he gave a small toy truck. They were thrilled. The only other gifts they received came from Miss Yale. Jeth never bothered about Christmas or birthday presents. If the family had a good square meal, that was enough. Christina gave Orpha and Liticia each a piece of print, enough for a dress. Orpha's was green and Liticia's was pink. They were pleased beyond words.

"I must show you what they got me."

From the top of his box of clothes Millard brought out a Bible.

"Now I can return the Testament you sent along with me, Mother."

The boys played on the floor with their trucks, the women and the girls washed the dishes. The house rang with gay laughter. Millard sat in one room, then in the other listening, happy, and satisfied. At four o'clock Levi put on his overalls and said he would be glad to help Jeth with anything that should be done.

Jeth objected.

"It is not in your place to come out here and help me. That's what Millard came home fer."

"Of course!" Millard got up. "I'll help you, Pop."

"I'm taking his place today. Millard, you stay in this evening yet.

115

Remember you've got to go at things easy at first. Don't forget what the doctor told you."

"But Homer Jo can help me," insisted Pop. "Homer Jo, get on your duds an' come. Uncle Levi has his chores to do when he gets home."

"Mine won't take too long. Orpha, you don't need to get out in the cold tonight. We can feed the chickens and gather the eggs for her on Christmas day, can't we?"

Quite reluctantly Homer Jo put on his plaid Mackinaw and cap. He would if he had to. Slowly he twisted the buttons through the buttonholes. Orpha handed him the egg basket and he started toward the door.

"And bring in some wood, Homer Jo," reminded his mother.

"Hold on here," exclaimed Uncle Levi wonderingly but half laughing. "What's this thing here, hanging out of your coattail? He reached over and caught hold of something black and hard that had worked out about three inches from the inside of Homer Jo's coat lining.

Homer Jo grabbed his coattail and gave it a quick jerk, and a guilty, condemning expression crossed his face. Rip went the coat lining, and right there in front of ten pairs of eyes stood Uncle Levi Winegar, his mouth wide open with surprise, while he held in his hand Pop's black Yorkshire pipe.

Jeth turned marble!

Chapter 18

"WHOSE is this?" asked Levi innocently. Homer Jo looked at Pop, then at the floor, because Pop's eyes were boring through him.

"It used to be mine," coughed Jeth, "but how it ever got tangled up in that there coat is beyond me." Can marble people talk? His voice sounded cold and haunting. He tried to laugh.

"How did it get there, Homer Jo?" asked Mother. She pressed the wrinkles out of her forehead. Something made her feel queer—top-heavy. She reached for the sink for support.

"Did you put it in there?" she asked.

"Yes." Homer Jo unbuttoned his coat. He bit his lip.

"What for?" she asked.

"Well—I just wanted to — to see how it tastes. Pop did say once it was good for toothache."

Jeth relaxed a little. Marble turned to wood.

"When did I say that?"

"You said, one time, smokin' was the best pain killer you ever tried."

"Oh,———————-! When did I say that?" He came to life.

"You told Joe Pundle that once, an' I heard you tell him you'd rather lose your job an' your best friend an'...."

"That's enough out of you." Jeth crossed the room and took the boy by the arm rather roughly. "You get that pipe and take it right back where you—I mean hand it to me an' don't you never touch it again."

"Never, Pop?" gasped Homer Jo. He drew back and looked up into his father's face questioningly, almost demandingly.

"If you hid a new one out there, then why can't I have your old one to play with? I want to try different kinds so I know which I like

117

best before I get big."

Homer Jo said it all in one breath or his father would have cut him off again.

Jeth never felt so much like slapping one of his children.

"But I didn't," was all Jeth said.

The rest of what he wanted to say paralyzed his throat. Homer Jo got the pipe Uncle Levi was still holding and handed it to his father. All three went outside.

It is easier after one is found out—that is, after the first dreadful moment of exposure. One always dreads that moment, but the afterwards is easier.

Myra decided she must call a family gathering before the children go to bed. It seemed to her mother heart the wisest, the only thing to do now. She loved her children with a peculiar watch-care love. She must do what she could to help her boys grow into stalwart men for God and her girls into beautiful women. That was the only rewarding compensation she asked for. When the children were babies she tried to keep them clean and comfortable. She fed them as well as possible when they were growing, hungry youngsters. She taught her girls how to care for their hair and comb it becomingly, how to cook and clean and sew. The boys must learn from their father how to do a man's work. But when it came to the task of helping to mold character, Myra Winegar Grinstead realized she must shoulder her part of the responsibility with a broad shoulder.

Myra loved Jeth and, although she was sadly disappointed(because he had failed to demonstrate to the children what the power of God could do for him, if he had been willing to surrender all and ask God for His help), she was determined to try to teach them to respect him as their father and overlook this failure.

Myra was hurt, of course, and it hurt Jeth, too, to know he was to blame. Not many days previous he fought tears all to himself on the way to town at the thought of disappointing her, his true, his beloved bright-eyed Myra. Now he tried to deaden his emotions. He still hated to see her disappointed, but it was just "one of those things". It couldn't be helped now.

One time when he was a boy his father set the lantern on a shelf in the washhouse above a tub of fresh sausage. His mother had warned his father that that was a risky place to set the lantern, but he said he'd watch it. But at an unexpected moment the lantern fell. The consequence was that the whole family would have to put up with eating coal-oil flavored sausage or none. Mother said they couldn't afford to throw it all away, and they wouldn't want to sell it, and his father insisted you could hardly taste the coal-oil, if it were eaten with bread and other things. His father admitted he was to blame for the misfortune and not Mother, and he was sorry the whole family would have to put up with it, but it was just "one of those things." It couldn't be helped. He could only warn his boys not to set lanterns above tubs of sausage thereafter.

That was the attitude Jeth took now. The family would have to put up with him as he was or throw him out. He knew of course that would never happen, if they all lived to be one hundred.

After Levi and Christina left, Myra went to the bedroom and closed the door. She was glad her parents had not gotten to come.

"Dear Lord," she prayed, "your Word tells us to cast our burdens upon you and you will sustain us. Oh, do it for me now, and give me wisdom, for Jesus' sake."

Before Jeth came in from the barn, Myra had resolved in her heart she would not cry in front of the children. With a simple entrancing mother charm, so characteristic of her, she started talking in a quiet, unexcited tone. She pitied Jeth, but her pity must not let her ignore her duty toward the children. It would have been much easier to accept the whole matter as a big joke and let the children develop their own convictions as time went on. That's what most mothers would do. They might hear some teaching against the use of tobacco in Sunday school whenever a temperance lesson was taught. She could let the church do the instructing for her. But that was not Myra. She must say something tonight, then drop it. It would never do to be making comments about Pop's pipe every day.

"I'm sure you children do not know how many times your father and I have talked over this matter," she said. "We certainly never expected anything to turn up like this tonight after we all had such a pleasant day together. I'm sure you know your father never would have started smoking if he had known he'd someday have a family like this. But you see, when he was young he had no teaching against it. I knew Pop smoked when we started going together. I didn't think much about it until after we had Don Millard."

Millard felt goose pimples come over his body. Pop had a toothpick in his mouth. He took it out and broke it into several pieces.

"From then on we both felt like we wouldn't want any of our boys to smoke. In fact, I'm sure he's told you that himself."

"He never told me," ventured Derwood.

"Well, he told one of you, and I'm sure he meant it. Didn't you, Pop?"

"Yes, I did."

"And I want you all to know," continued Mother, "that your father has—-tried—to quit, but as I told Millard one time, 'habit is like a cable. We weave a thread of it every day, but at last it cannot be broken.'"

Jeth cleared his throat. He pushed back his chair. But Jeth never got excited. It wasn't his nature. His expression did not change.

"Please, children, do not criticize or condemn your father because he has not been able to break away from this habit. There is only one who can break the cable," she said softly, "and that one is God. With Him I know all things are possible."

"Doesn't God know where the cable is?" asked Richard.

This was too much. Sudden tears welled up in Myra's eyes. She brushed them away quickly. Jeth never had been willing to pray with her about this. He did not care for sentimental experiences, although in his heart he was afraid that might have helped more than anything else.

"God knows all things, Richard, but—" Mother hesitated. Should she say it? "He never breaks a cable as long as someone is hanging on to it. Pop," she said, "don't you want to say something to the children so they will understand better?"

"Well, since we're on the subject, I will say this," Pop began with surprising calmness, "I have said it before and I'll say it again, I'd rather none of my own boys would take to smokin'. It's a habit that is hard to break away from. I started to smoke because I thought it was smart, an' made a man out o' me. After I wanted to quit, I couldn't. I can't work good or feel right without it now. You all might as well know why I do it. It's not because I wanta be smart any more. I jes' get a cravin' fer it— I can't help it. I've tried not to do it in front of you since I promised Brother Ambers I'd try to quit. Then Homer Jo came on me by surprise in the barn one mornin'. I'm willin' to overlook all that, even though it was naughty for him to hunt the pipe an' hide it in his coat like he did, but he an' me settled that part of it down at the barn. He said he wouldn't do such a thing again. I'm willin' to admit I never should have started smokin', but no one ever told me not to."

Then Pop told the sausage story. When he finished, Millard looked at his mother as though he had something to say.

"Were you going to say something, Millard?" she asked.

"Well, that was an interesting story," he said, "but I'm glad Pop's family didn't need to eat coal-oil-flavored sausage the rest of their lives."

Pop smiled. "So am I, Millard." Then his face suddenly sobered. What did Millard mean? Just what did Millard mean? Pop had a specific point in relating the story, but did Millard have a specific point in the remark he made?

"We must all go to bed right now," Pop said, and he got up and walked out of the room.

Don Millard was too interpreting a boy. After the children all went upstairs, Jeth walked back and forth across the kitchen from the cellar door to the window. He looked out.

"You're coming to bed, too, aren't you, Jeth?" Myra asked anxiously.

"Pretty soon."

Jeth felt his black pipe in his hip pocket. Homer Jo told him he would find the little tobacco that was left in the sprinkling can hanging on a nail in the woodhouse. He went out. He found it. He smoked. It calmed his nerves.

After that evening Jeth gave up trying. He explained to Myra as calmly as possible what he had said and what he had meant the night she misunderstood him. From then on he smoked when and where he felt like it. But never in the house. His respect for his wife would not permit that.

*   *   *   *   *

Brother Ambers met Jeth on the walk between the house and the woodhouse. "It's a fine winter day, isn't it, Brother Grinstead?" Brother Ambers smiled pleasantly. He shook Jeth's hand warmly.

"Yes, it is."

Jeth wondered if Levi might have told Brother Ambers. If so, there was nothing he could do about that. It was just "one of those things". The elders could carry him along if they wanted to, and manifest patience if they wanted to, or they could take his name off the church record.

"Is Millard here?"

"He was in the house a while ago."

"I came to have that talk with him."

What could Brother Ambers be wanting with Millard. If he wanted to know anything why didn't he ask him?

"What talk?"

"I told him the night he confessed I'd be seeing him after Christmas. I called a while ago and your wife said it would be all right."

"Confess? What did Millard confess?" said Jeth to himself.

"On Sunday I expect to start instructing all those who wish to be baptized in the next class. The catechism class will be about a six-week course. Will you be willing to cooperate and have Millard at the church by six forty-five?"

"I knew nothin' of this. Millard never told me." Jeth's voice was a little pithy.

Millard was in the woodhouse hunting for a round stick with which he would try to mend his mother's frying pan handle. What was Pop telling Brother Ambers? Hadn't Mother told Pop? True, he hadn't because he supposed she had. He supposed nothing else.

Jeth seemed exasperated. Millard would go out at once and tell Pop he didn't mean to keep anything from him.

Then Pop said, "Well, he would start somethin' like this now when he knows I can't use the gas to go to church twice on a Sunday. I'm pretty hard run since his operation an' all."

Millard could not move. Really? Truly? Wasn't Pop glad he stood? It didn't sound like it. He was sure he heard distinctly every word between the two. Pop's words struck him like a blow.

Discouragement seized him then and there. He wished he could run and run and never stop till he got to the end of the world. He felt wretched and forsaken.

"I didn't know that, Brother Grinstead," Brother Ambers replied. "We have a brotherhood fund, and the trustees, I'm sure, would be willing to help you."

Jeth shook his head. "We haven't been in the church long enough to be receivin' no such help. That's fer widows an' the like."

"Oh, no, brother; you're mistaken there. It's for anyone in the brotherhood who has proved himself worthy and is in need."

"Well, I wouldn't hear to takin' none of it. We'll get along all

122

right in time. The boy's operation was just one of those things that couldn't be helped, so we'll make the best of circumstances; but we can't get to church every Sunday evening, I know that."

Millard was hearing every word. Through the crack in the half-open woodhouse door he could see the two men on the walk. His heart pounded violently and he could not move.

"Maybe I could instruct Millard separately then. Perhaps I could interview him a little every Sunday morning. I'll go into the house and talk to him."

Jeth Grinstead removed his cap and brushed his gray hair.

"You can go in," he said, "but I doubt if it's worth your time, since he didn't think enough of his confession to tell his own father about it."

Millard watched Brother Ambers walk up the porch steps and knock at the door.

Oh,if he could only melt—or disappear as water in the ground never to be gathered together again.

Chapter 19

MYRA opened the door.

"Come in, Brother Ambers. Take a chair. Liticia, call Millard. He may be in the woodhouse. I'm having him do a few little odd jobs for me during vacation, Brother Ambers. Millard's real handy that way."

"How do you feel about the stand your boy took?" Brother Ambers remained standing.

"I feel glad about it, of course."

"You think he's sincere?"

"Sincere? Yes, Millard's sincere."

"Your husband told me out here he knew nothing of it."

"Nothing of it? You mean he said he didn't know Millard was sincere?"

"He said he didn't know he stood."

"He did? Well, I wonder if Jeth is losing his hearing, for I'm certain he was in the room when we were talking about it, Orpha and Liticia and I, the day Liticia got his letter. You see, Millard stayed at Levi's house more than a month, and we didn't get in to church that Sunday evening, so he wrote and told us about it. I must ask him—I mean Jeth. Have a seat."

"I told your husband I was certain the church trustees would be willing to help on the gas situation."

Myra stared.

"It would mean so much if Millard could be there every Sunday evening in the instruction class with the others. I will give him a catechism to study at home, of course, and it may be, too, that he understands well enough to go on without the class instruction, but it would be best to have them all there every time we meet."

Myra stared. She could feel the color creeping out on her face and neck.

"I—" she weighed her words carefully, "I wish Jeth could see it that way that we could spend the gas to go to church on Sunday evenings, and save on something else, if necessary. I wonder if Liticia can't find Millard. I thought he was in the woodhouse."

"Well, I can go out there."

It was impossible for Millard to collect himself immediately for presentation to Brother Ambers. The blow to his sensitive, retiring nature had bruised him too badly. His sincerity, his zeal, his heart of unspoken love, lay at his feet crushed and bleeding and he could not gather them up.

Why had Uncle Levi omitted his father's name? Millard had tried to suppress the fear that Pop wouldn't be glad he had stood. Pop would be glad, Millard felt certain. It would help him carry out Pop's one hope that he wouldn't start smoking. It would help him be an example to his younger brothers. It would give him something to be true to. That was one of the things he had asked Uncle Levi about— why he thought it was wrong to smoke when so many, many church members did.

Millard was open to instruction and advice, and he really wanted to know. Uncle Levi had explained to his satisfaction that smoking was a bad habit because it was a waste of money, offensive to some, detrimental to the mind and body, it lowered a person's resistance to other temptations, it often accompanied the drink habit, and it marred a person's testimony for Christ. Millard remembered them. Maybe Pop's smoking explained why Pop wasn't as enthusiastic and happy as Uncle Levi? Millard wanted to know what Uncle Levi meant about his career. He had told him he meant his life work, his calling.

His calling? Millard felt sure now he'd never have a calling, not the kind Uncle Levi had in mind. He had said he would help him go on through school, if he wanted to go. The future had beckoned, drawn, and inspired him until now. The present. Oh! It seemed so useless, so hopelessly broken.

"Brother Ambers is here now, Millard." Liticia's voice was strangely affectionate. Millard tried to swallow.

"Why, what's wrong, Millard? You knew he was coming. Did you find what you wanted?"

Millard swallowed.

"What's wrong, Millard? Aren't you coming in? Mother sent me out to call you."

Millard made a low, deep sound, as though in pain.

"Why, Don Millard," cried Liticia dashing close to him. Reaching up she placed a slender trembling hand on each shoulder and looked up into his face beseechingly. Was he hurt? She saw no blood, no wound. "What on earth has ever come over you? Tell me. Tell me, Millard." There were tears in her pleading eyes.

Liticia was so pretty, so young, so untainted, and promising! Health and a happy future seemed to be throbbing in her body. If he told her, she might never try to become a Christian. He loved her too much to say anything that might influence her in that direction. Everything might go lovely for her. To his knowledge Pop had never discouraged Orpha in any way. That's why he had refused to believe Pop wouldn't be glad he stood. He wouldn't want to lessen her love for Pop. Pop must have it in for him for some reason. He felt discouraged. How could he face Brother Ambers again when his own father had no confidence in him? Disappointment and defeat quarreled with his convictions like two wild beasts, leaving him deluded and confused.

He shook his head. He took her hands off his shoulders and held her out at arm's length.

"I can't," he said.

* * * * *

"So you're out doing some carpenter work?" With hat in hand, Brother Ambers made his appearance in the doorway. "You know the Lord was a carpenter's son, and I suppose He, too, mended things for his mother."

Liticia ran to the house, leaving the two alone.

The minute Brother Ambers reached the open door, he could see the extraordinary intensity of feeling and dismay on the boy's face. He was a very observing man. Brother Ambers possessed, from varied experiences, a practical knowledge of the technique of dealing with human hearts. They were more delicate and marvelously made than musical instruments. They were capable of enduring almost unlimited sorrow, pain, hate, or love, and also joy. They could be helped into changing from pain and fear to peace and happiness. What string could he touch now to bring out the sweet, rich melody he knew lay in the heart of this brilliant-faced youth? True, he had not known the Grinsteads long.

126

He noticed Millard's lip quiver.

Perhaps he and his father had had some difficulty just before he arrived.

"You remember I told you the night you stood I'd be out to see you during Christmas vacation."

"Yes, sir."

"It is still your intention to be instructed for baptism, is it not?"

"I've decided to put it off—until sometime later." Millard's own voice sent a heartbreaking shock through his body. He shivered.

"You have? Would you mind telling me why, Millard?"

"I—cannot tell you now."

"Is there something I can help you with—today or any day? I am here to help you in any way I can."

Why not unburden to Brother Ambers and tell him all his dreams and struggles from his earliest recollection until now: how he liked to read and his father's objection, how he longed to be good and honest and pure and unselfish, how he wanted to learn about life and God, and to know how to find and win and be worthy of the true never-ending love of some good girl? Why not tell Brother Ambers he couldn't understand Pop and that that was the reason he was sad and discouraged? Brother Ambers looked as if he might be able to understand and give a boy advice. But—no—he wouldn't understand. He couldn't. Uncle Levi would come nearer understanding. He would unburden to him sometime.

Millard heard heavy footsteps on the walk. It sounded like Pop.

Millard shook his head. "No," he said; "there is nothing."

Brother Ambers was disappointed. He had failed to touch the right string. Was Mr. Grinstead right in his prediction that he would be wasting his time with the boy? After all, he hadn't known the family long. He'd make a study of the case.

"The night you stood I thought you certainly seemed sincere."

"I absolutely was, Brother Ambers, and when I understand something—and—when God calls me again—I'll start all over," Millard's voice seemed dripping with tears, but his brown eyes were dry and sad as he looked straight into Brother Amber's face.

"My boy, I'm sorry—I'm sure there could be a solution to your problem, if I knew what it was, but good-by and God bless you, Millard. And whatever you do, don't grieve the Spirit of God. You want Him to call you again, don't you?"

"Yes—sometime."

* * * * *

Grandmother Winegar was humming her favorite hymn when Grandfather came in with the mail. He took his accustomed place by the table and handed it to Grandmother to read.

"I expect it's all about their Christmas without us."

"Dear Father and Mother,

Your telegram, of course, was not a complete surprise, and in view of the weather and your age, maybe it was wise of you to stay at home. If possible, plan to come for Easter. Christmas here was cold, and there was lots of snow. However, we were able to be at Jeths for dinner, and we all had a nice time. Millard was so glad to get home again, but we surely did enjoy having him here with us for a while. I wish we could have kept him here. He made a public confession the first Sunday evening he went back to church. That was two weeks today. A happier boy you never saw. I'm very fond of him.

Jeths didn't get into church this morning. I called, and Myra said Jeth couldn't get the car started. We might run over after a while, and I'll see what I can do. Jeth's not much of a mechanic. Now that Millard's back home, maybe together they can manage their work a little better. Of course, I hope Millard can go to school the second semester and finish the eighth grade. Jeth seems to think it's useless, but we very much want him to finish.

Of course, it's not for us to say; and when we go there maybe I say a little too much sometimes. After all, a man is the head of his own house and the father of his own children, and suggestions are not always too highly appreciated, especially from close relatives. I must learn to use discretion with my love. Orpha is a hard, willing worker and quite pretty. The young men seem to take notice of her and her black wavy hair. Liticia will soon be very attractive, too. Myra keeps the house spick and span, as you can imagine, but the barn—enough said!

Yesterday I had a severe headache. I never had anything like it. It put me to bed for a while.

How have you been these days? Take good care of yourselves and keep on thinking about coming out for Easter. God be with you till we meet again.

Lovingly, Levi."

128

"Now isn't that like Levi? Always writing things to keep us wondering;" and Grandfather Winegar leaned back in his chair to wonder.

*   *   *   *   *

An astonishing, unbelievable thing happened three weeks after Christmas! Uncle Levi took his sudden departure to be forever with the Lord. It happened so quickly—right after supper—almost before he reached the davenport. Christina was dazed. All day he had been unusually happy and talkative. It could not be true! And so soon after their happy marriage. He had been brim full of hope for tomorrow— and now death! Was it necessary? Was it kind? Was he actually dead? His stillness would kill her, too. She screamed, but he paid no heed. He had complained of a pain in his head when he got up, staggered over to the davenport, and lay down. That was all. A sweet, undisturbed peace tranquilized his dear face. She stroked his forehead. His spirit was gone. He must be where headaches are unknown. As in a dream, Christina called Doctor Munsell—then Myra—then Brother Ambers. The news spread. Everyone was shocked. But no one could remedy her loss or bear her sorrow. They could sympathize as best they knew, but the pain was hers to undergo. Christina felt so alone.

Next to Christina possibly no one was touched like Millard. He was completely baffled. Why God would take away a good man like Uncle Levi shook the foundation of all his convictions. Why was he taken before he (Millard) had a chance to unburden to him? He admired no other man more highly. No one else's advice did he value so highly. Next to his mother, no one had taken such a personal interest in him and his future—his career as had Uncle Levi. For days, Millard could neither think nor reason. In secret places, all alone, he cried in fresh agony under this new soul torture. His loss was not like Aunt Christina's, but it was real, personal, gigantic. He could speak of it to no one.

In the sad-faced procession that followed the casket to the cemetery, one fourteen-year-old lad's face stood out from all the others with a look so grief-stricken, it was as though some irrevocable, undeserved penalty had been pronounced upon him. Was this to scourge him? No one knew. No one guessed. No one could understand.

Miss Yale helped Millard make up the work he had missed.

When the day came to go back to school, Pop let Millard make his own decision. Since the boy had his heart set on getting a diploma, it would be better to finish now than to take the eighth grade all over again.

* * * * *

The clock struck three. Glen was taking his afternoon nap. Tired and worried Myra sank on a chair. She dropped her head in the circle of her two arms on the kitchen table and was thus when Jeth entered.

"Are you sick, Myra?" Jeth's voice sounded anxious. Levi's sudden death was still fresh in his mind. He came close and put a hand on her shoulder. "Are you crying?"

"No," Myra lifted her head.

"What's wrong? Don't you feel good?"

"Not very. I worry about Millard."

"Why?"

"He doesn't seem to be well. And he acts sad most of the time. You haven't noticed?"

"He acts like he always has."

"Oh, no, Jeth; I'm afraid he's discouraged. Ever since that day Brother Ambers called to see him, he has seemed different. Liticia says so, too. Something happened that day. Do you know what it was?"

"No. I do not."

"Brother Ambers asked me yesterday if I knew why he decided to drop out of the instruction class, and I said I didn't exactly."

"Exactly?"

"I try to guess till it makes me feel sick. He's keeping something from me, and I can hardly stand it. Christina said she was positive Millard knew what he was doing and really wanted to join the church."

"Well, who all have you been talkin' to about this? Maybe that's what makes him act—or makes you think he acts different. I wouldn't like to be talked about either."

"Oh, no, Jeth. That's not it. Why don't you talk to Millard?"

"Me?"

"Yes."

"He acts like that always around me. He never did have anything to say."

"I'm afraid he's working too hard, too."

"Workin' too hard when he's in school?"

"I mean mornings and evenings. I wish you'd take him to the doctor for a checkup. Millard's not feeling right."

"You mustn't worry like this over Millard, Myra; he's gettin' old enough to look after himself."

Chapter 20

DIGGING post holes was a tiresome job, but there were many tiresome jobs that needed to be done on a farm, and Millard would not shrink from any of them. As long as he lived at home he would help Pop do anything there was to be done. The sadder he felt, the harder he worked. He would do all he could to keep things looking like Uncle Levi had had them, and like Grandfather would like to have them now. Before he and Grandmother had gone home after the funeral he had given Millard some suggestions. Grandfather was too badly broken up about Levi to say a whole lot.

That was why Millard was more determined than ever to keep his struggles to himself. He would not tell Liticia what he had heard Pop say to Brother Ambers lest she feel hard toward Pop and maybe spurn God's voice when He called her. Pop was neither affectionate nor unkind to Liticia. He was rather disregarding. Whether or not he was glad Orpha had joined the church, Millard didn't know; for his father had never expressed his approval or disapproval of that any more than he did of what the girls wore. He might not express himself if Liticia stood, but if he should and it would affect her as it had him, Millard would certainly pity her.

Another thing, Millard knew his mother would feel bad, if she knew what he had heard. She was very tenderhearted and sympathetic, and she would think Pop was unkind. It might hurt her as badly as it had Millard. He wanted his mother and father to feel good toward each other. He'd suffer anything before he'd mar such a feeling. He'd let Pop make her think they couldn't afford to buy so much gasoline. He'd let Pop make her think he didn't know anything about Millard's confession. Pop had spoken the truth when he told Brother Ambers Millard hadn't said a word to him about it. Maybe, after all, Millard was at fault. He should have taken Pop into his confidence, at least make an effort to do so. But Pop never made the slightest kind of an effort to talk to him about anything but work.

* * * * *

Millard rested on the handle of the posthole digger. He felt pain all across his abdomen. Mother had been questioning him too frequently. He must hide his feelings more. If he told her how he felt, she would insist he do less work and lighter work, and evidently Pop thought he was able. He must prove to Pop he wanted to help him get ahead—and especially since the operation cost so much. And since Pop let him decide about finishing school, he'd try all the harder to help him mornings and evenings and on Saturdays. There were only two postholes to be dug. Grandfather had purchased a new gate to replace the broken one at the north end of the garden. The new one was wider than the old one,so the posts had to be set over. That was better than making the gate smaller.

It was a spring-like Saturday, even though it was the first of February. It made one think of making garden and fixing fences. The minute Mother had mentioned the garden gate that morning, Millard decided to fix it unless Pop had something else more important for him to do. Hanging the gate was right in line with a carpenter's work, and Jeth wouldn't have minded doing it, if Millard would dig the postholes.

From the kitchen window Myra could see Millard resting on the handle. He rested so long that she decided to go out and see what the difficulty was.

"This is too hard for you, Millard."

"It is a little harder than I thought it would be."

"The ground is too hard and you will hurt yourself."

"I guess not."

"Did the doctor tell you you could dig postholes this soon?"

"He never said anything about digging postholes, but it's not much harder than some other things I've been doing."

"It worries me."

"What does?"

"The way you work. You're doing too much."

"I want to help Pop."

"I know you do, Millard, but you've got to take care of yourself. You're young and you've got your future to think about. You might hurt yourself for life."

"Oh, Mother, no; please don't worry like that about me."

"You have pain right now, don't you?"

"Well—" Millard tried to laugh.

"Put the digger down and come in and rest a while. This doesn't have to be finished today. I told Pop the other day he ought to take you to the doctor for a checkup."

"Oh, no, Mother."

"Are you sure you feel all right?"

"I'm a little tired right now."

"But have you been feeling all right since Christmas?"

They walked toward the house together.

"I hardly know what to say. Maybe I feel about like anyone else does after an operation. I don't know. Mother, please don't worry about me. I'll be all right. I'm afraid if I don't work Pop will find me a job somewhere else, and I don't want to have to go back to Hornback to finish school. Don't tell Pop I don't feel all right."

"I already told him I don't think you act just right."

"Mother!"

"I did, Millard. I want you to be happy and well. Brother Ambers asked me why you aren't going on with the class." She could not put off insisting any longer. "I wish you'd tell me, Millard. Everyday I've been expecting you to tell me and still you don't." She looked up at him.

"Something must have happened that day he came out to see you, but I don't know what it was. You've seemed different from then on."

"And you told Pop that, Mother?"

"Yes."

"What did he say?"

"He said he thought you acted like always and he didn't know of anything that happened. Did I do something, Millard?"

"No, Mother, no. I never said anyone did anything."

"No, but Liticia said she knows something happened. Before Brother Ambers came hadn't you fully decided to be baptized?"

"Mother, I do not mean I do not trust you, and it's not—that I want to be stubborn—but—will you promise me something?" They were almost to the house now.

"If it's something within my power."

"Well, it is. Will you promise?"

"Yes."

"Then promise me that you'll never ask me again—"

She gasped.

"Why, Don Millard Grinstead!" He took his mother by the arm.

"You'll never ask me again—why I changed my mind. But you'll pray—that something will happen that I can be baptized—before I die."

"Why, Millard! What do you mean? That sounds like you think—" she shuddered. "Millard!"

"Mother," he whispered with feeling, catching her plump hand in his, and squeezing it. It expressed to her his tender love, and she realized as never before the worth of a boy's soul. There was an incomparable something about his manner.

* * * * *

It was not Brother Ambers method to beg anyone to join his church. Undoubtedly, in a year or two Millard would understand better and make a new start. In the meantime he would try to understand the Grinstead family.

On Sunday he shook hands with all of them as they passed him in the vestibule. Millard did not shy away from him, but when Brother Ambers took his hand and looked into his face, he noticed a mysterious sadness on it. The boy seemed to have grown a year older in a few days.

* * * * *

Jeth had never yet refused to take any of his children to a doctor when they were ill. He was a little anxious over Myra. She had always been so well and energetic.

"If I take Millard in to the doctor you go along, too. Maybe you need a tonic or somethin'."

So Myra went along.

"You've been doing too much, son."

Myra was almost certain that's what the doctor would say.

"I'll have to have your Dad watch you a little closer for a while." The doctor winked at Jeth. "Boys this age think they can work as hard as their Dads. You don't want another operation, do you, Millard?"

"No, sir."

"Then take my advice and be careful for a month or more yet. If you lift something and it hurts you then it's too much for you. I suppose your Dad tells you this every day, so listen to him. Do you hear?"

He gave Myra some medicine for her nerves. Every day, especially after Christmas, Myra longed for an ideal relationship in their home. She wondered where she had failed. She read stories of beautiful family life and wondered why theirs couldn't be ideal, too. No matter how poor they had been, or how often they had been forced to move, or how humble their places of abode, she thought home should be the happiest, most contented place on earth for everyone in the family from the oldest to the youngest. She did not believe in partiality. It never made for pleasantness.

In spite of all her prayers, Homer Jo was getting naughtier every day. He talked back to Pop, and that hurt Pop pretty much. Pop had to smoke more than ever. He seldom wanted to go to church on Sunday evenings, and on Sunday mornings he seemed to go out of a sense of duty or to please the rest of the family. After the shock of Levi's death wore off, he regarded it as just one of those things that happens the world over every day. From the day the doctor said Millard had to be more careful about working too hard, Jeth said Millard should find a job some place else as soon as school was out. Pop never said so, but his attitude made Millard feel he was anxious to get rid of him. Millard thought about this in school, and sometimes he could hardly concentrate on his lessons. Again and again, while trying to study, his young heart faltered between returning hope, fresh gloom, and new doubts. He was certain his mother was keeping her promise to pray for him, but his father's attitude and dwindling interest in the church perplexed him more and more.

* * * * *

Spring came. Myra was studying her Sunday-school lesson. In the quarterly she read that the secret of every ideal home lay in the fact that the entire home life was built about a strong spiritual center, the work, the play, the company, even the daily conversation. Myra thought. Without Jeth's cooperation the spiritual center of their home would crumble. What could she do? The father and the two oldest boys were not happy. With eyes half-blinded from concern, she entered the bedroom and dropped upon her knees beside the bed. If only Millard could stand up and take a man's place in the home and help her in this spiritual building—but soon he would be leaving again. Jeth was fixed on that. His mind was set and Millard knew it.

* * * * *

Liticia watched Millard combing his brown hair. It was soft and thick and dark, much darker than her own. His shoulders were straight and broad. He looked strong. Millard was handsome. But not as clear-eyed and eager as he used to be. Why must Pop be sending him away again when there was work, always work to do at home? But then she was going away, too—over to Dogerdys for the summer. Mother could spare her, and Pop said it would help on the grocery bill, if there were two less mouths to feed. She might have to work harder than if she worked for Elisha Grape for Mrs. Dogerdy was lame in one leg and had a bad case of asthma. She might have had a chance to work for Aunt Christina, if Uncle Levi hadn't died.

Everything seemed so different now. No more going to Uncle Levi's for Sunday dinners. Church didn't even seem quite the same with neither of them there, for Aunt Christina had gone to live with her sister. Maybe she'd never come back to Granger to live again. Mother said she was a thousand miles away now. Liticia loved Aunt Christina almost as much as Millard loved Uncle Levi.

"We can call each other on the phone sometimes, can't we, Millard?" She was watching him comb his hair.

"Maybe so."

"I'm so glad I'm leaving since you are."

Why? He looked at her in surprise.

"It doesn't seem right here without you."

"It doesn't?" He put the comb in his pocket.

"No."

"You'll have to get used to it, Ticia, for I may never come back again."

"Never come back again!" she gasped.

"I mean, to stay. Of course, I'll come back every chance I get on Sundays."

"Do you suppose Mr. Schultz will bring you in to church like Mr. Auckers did?"

"Probably not. I don't know."

"What will you do if he doesn't?"

"I'll do the best I can. What are you going to do?"

"Pop promised to come by and pick me up every Sunday morning, and he'll take me back on Sunday evenings, if it isn't nice enough for me to walk. I'll get to come home every Sunday."

"You lucky girl."

"Won't you?"

"I don't know. I don't know the place or the people. I don't know what I'll have to do or how much I'll make or if I can come home Sundays, or anything. It would be out of Pop's way to drive past Schultz's place and pick me up, and anyway it would take too much gas."

"But if we both hand over our wages, that would buy plenty of gas."

"But Pop wants to buy two new tires and a cow."

Chapter 21

WHEN Millard went to work for Mr. Schultz he had an honest desire to live right. Uncle Levi's life and the church both challenged him to be true to his convictions. In his heart he meant to read his Bible occasionally and keep on praying grounds with the Lord. He'd keep himself pure and true and fit for the time when he could go ahead and be baptized—when he'd be old enough to convince Pop he was sincere. When he'd be of age, he'd keep his wages and buy decent clothes. He'd have his own car and buy his own gas. He'd go to church then every Sunday night. He'd go by and pick up Ticia wherever she was working, so Pop wouldn't need to bother about stopping for her. He had a burning desire to be nice to someone, and now that desire centered around his pretty sister, Liticia Ann. Rather unconsciously he longed for a friend, somebody to whom to be true, someone to serve and look up to, someone who would love and inspire him. Passionately he desired to make his life count in altruistic service. He felt quite strong again.

William Schultz owned a dairy farm, and Millard was asked to help deliver milk on Sundays. Mr. Schultz would make no concession. It was his religious duty to take care of both his cows and customers on the Sabbath day as well as any other, and, anyway, ninety percent of the people who did go to church did it out of custom, and the other ten percent went to prove to the first group they were as religious as they. He could be as good as either group,and worship God in his heart without going to church. His employees could do the same.

That was the kind of reasoning Millard heard from the start. He was quite unprepared for it. Pop got him the job. Didn't he know he'd have to work on Sundays? Didn't Pop care?

A month of surprises, one after the other, wondering about his own experiences during his illness and convalescing days at Uncle Levi's, working with ungodly men who cursed and smoked continually, certainly did not strengthen Millard's early convictions, sincere as they had been. He was offered cigarettes and derided for not taking any, even though he was a minor. No boy likes to be called a sissy or angel wings. The reason Uncle Levi had given against smoking that appealed most to Millard, was that it spoiled a person's testimony. But what if you didn't have a testimony to spoil? He thought about the cable: "at last it cannot be broken". Millard pondered. And wasn't it exactly so in Pop's case? When Pop had boys of his own and wanted to quit, he could not break the habit. Now he didn't try anymore. Let the boys call him a sissy, he would not start weaving the cable. Maybe someday he would have a little son.

Millard got Saturday afternoons off. He walked home. It was no less than four long miles each way, but he disregarded the distance, because his mother's smile and that one supper at home were recompense enough. Once in a while he hopped a ride, but most of the cars on the road were heading the opposite direction toward town. The first of every month Millard handed Pop his total earnings, fifteen dollars, or, if Pop wasn't at home when he arrived, he gave the money to his mother, and Pop got it from her. Pop was away more often than he was at home. He always went to town on Saturday afternoons to get the week's supply of groceries and whatever else was needed and often did not get home in time for supper. Consequently Millard seldom got to see his father.

And he very seldom saw Liticia, because she went home only on Sundays. Talking to each other on the telephone wasn't very satisfactory, because Mr. Shultz made it clear to all his men that the telephone was to be used for business only, for he would be receiving calls from new customers since his recent ad in the newspaper. Liticia called right during the dinner hour so she would be sure to catch Millard while he was in the house. She always asked sweetly, "Would you call Millard Grinstead to the phone, please?" Mrs. Schultz's eyebrows lifted questioningly, and the men teased Millard about his girlfriend who posed as his sister. The seventh time she called, he decided to walk over to Dogerdy's the next Saturday afternoon and explain to her why he had so little to say.

"Millard, I won't call anymore if you'd rather I wouldn't."

"But you understand how it is, don't you?"

"Yes, of course I do. But you see I didn't know. And I never get to see you anymore. I think it's cruel."

"But—but what shall I do? Pop got the place for me. I had no choice. Mother called up and talked to Mrs. Schultz one day about letting me off on Sundays so I could go to church, and she just laughed at Mother. I didn't know it though until Mother told me Saturday."

"It's cruel," cried Liticia. She followed him to the gate. She couldn't linger long, for she had to take a cake out of the oven soon. "I hate him," she cried.

"Who?"

"Pop!"

"No, you don't. Why, Liticia. You mustn't talk like that. If you hate someone, that's as bad as to kill, and you wouldn't kill Pop. You know you wouldn't."

"No," she said repentingly, "of course I didn't mean kill, but it's mean and cruel, anyway, that you have to work on Sundays. Pop ought to find you another place. Mother said Sunday she could hardly stand it to think that one of her own children would have to grow up like a heathen right here in this country."

"But I have my Bible, Liticia. I'll never be a heathen now, and anyway, how could I be with a mother like we've got?"

"That's what Pop said to her. You've got your Bible and you can read that, and you'd learn more than if you'd go to church, anyway."

"Well, that's where Pop's all wrong. And it's no fun trying to read your Bible when the other fellows have the radio on full blast and the room's full of smoke, or they throw shoes across the room and knock it out of your hands."

"Oh, is that the way it goes there?"

"There are five of us in one big room. Ted Watermen and Willie Strege have one bed. Art Bickel and Roy Ludwig have the other one, and I sleep on a cot. You'd be surprised if you knew some things. The only time I'm ever alone is when they all go to town—and that is rare. They usually take turns with Willie's car. Two of them go on Tuesday and Friday nights, and the other two go on Monday and Thursday nights. Some fellow from town comes out and gets Ted every Saturday afternoon and brings him back sometime before morning. If they do ever all leave, then Alfred comes up and hangs around."

"Who's Alfred?"

"That's Shultz's boy."

"How old is he?"

"He's eleven. But Liticia, don't tell Mother all this."

"Why not?"

"She has enough to worry about. It's not her fault. Liticia,you won't, will you?"

"I won't promise."

"Please."

"Why?"

"I told you why. She would worry and it wouldn't change things anyway."

"It ought to."

"Yes, but it wouldn't. Promise me or I won't come over here to see you again. Every time there are five Saturdays in a month I'll come to see you unless it's raining hard or something like that."

"That won't be very often then."

"It's the best I can do, Ticia. I like to get home, too. Mother expects me."

"I know. Millard, you need some new clothes."

"As usual."

"I—I" she choked, "I do—I hate him but—not the killing kind."

"Ticia Ann, you naughty—" Millard caught his breath. He felt like clasping her in his arms. "You know I made a big doctor bill for Pop to pay."

"The last time I was home," Liticia whispered, for she saw Mrs. Dogerdy hobbling toward the door, "Orpha told me that Eugene Sagester asked her for a date and if Pop objects, she's—"

"Liticia," called Mrs. Dogerdy in a shrill piercing voice, "your cake. Your cake! Come quick."

Liticia jumped and ran swiftly into the house.

The next time Millard went home his mother gave him a new shirt, two pairs of socks, and a pair of overalls his father had purchased.

"I'll try to persuade him to get you a pair of shoes, too."

"I need a pair. But I ought to go along and try them on. Tell him to wait until I get here to go to town next Saturday."

But the summer was almost over before Jeth took Millard along to town. He said he wanted to wait until McKeyne's had a clearance sale. By that time Millard was tramping the ground.

Millard often wondered how he'd feel in a brand-new suit of clothes, a nice suit that really fit. All the other fellows had dress-up clothes. He had outgrown his Sunday outfit, which had been ill-fitting and far from dressy-looking when it was new. His father must have purchased it also at a clearance sale. Jeth wasn't too particular about his own clothes, and he had no eye for choosing quality of materials. Myra could have selected much better clothes for very little more, but she so rarely went to town that she hardly knew where the stores were located. Pop always bought the boy's clothes, that is, what they didn't order from the catalogue, and then Jeth always checked over the order carefully to see that his wife had selected the cheapest of the items listed.

Since Millard's Sunday trousers didn't reach his ankles and his coat sleeves were tight and short, why should he even want to go to church, if he would have Sundays off? He'd feel self-conscious and ashamed. The girls would stare, and the boys would, too—maybe snicker or whisper. He'd never ask Pop for Sunday clothes. If Pop didn't mention it first, he'd do without until he could buy his own. If they really were so poor that Pop couldn't afford to buy decent clothes, it would help worlds if he'd say so and add that he was sorry. But his silence was discouraging. That I-don't-care attitude was worse than discouraging. It was degrading. Millard felt humiliated, despised.

Four months passed, and Millard could not go to church once. Brother Ambers noticed with disappointment the dwindling interest Jeth Grinstead took in church activities. His mind seemed to wander even during the Sunday-school class discussion, but his wife's countenance was always earnest, yet grave, and whenever she smiled, it was not as spontaneous and buoyant as before. Sometimes she seemed to be in prayer. Although Jeth did not try to avoid shaking hands with Brother Ambers, he did not seem eager to. He was always in a hurry to get to the car and start home.

Brother Ambers decided to make an effort to call on Millard. His varied experiences in dealing with people's personal problems gave him no solution to this one. Each time he was on the verge of questioning Mrs. Grinstead, something withheld him. He seemed to read in her face the closed-door look, and he decided not to insist on her opening up to him.

Twice he drove past Schultz's dairy truck on Benton Street. The third time he saw Millard coming out of the Crescent Lunchroom. He parked and got out of his car quickly.

"Millard."

Millard stopped abruptly. "Why, hello, Brother Ambers." He tipped his hat.

"So you're delivering milk?"

"Yes, sir.

"Every day?"

"Every day."

"Sundays, too?"

"Yes, sir."

"We've been missing you at church."

Millard smiled faintly. Did someone miss him? He wanted to be wanted. But that was a preacher's talk. He probably said that to everyone he met.

"You don't deliver milk on Sunday evenings, do you?"

"No, sir, but I have no way to come to church."

"If I would provide the way, you'd come, wouldn't you?"

"I'm afraid not, Brother Ambers. I appreciate your interest in me, but I couldn't come now. I just couldn't possibly."

"Millard, you keep me guessing. Could you give me an idea why you say you could not possibly come even if I provided the way?"

"I could tell you why, Brother Ambers, but—it is a very personal reason, and it would make me feel very bad to have to tell you. I'll come back to church as soon as I can."

"Is it the same reason that kept you from coming into the church?"

"No, sir. I would still come to church, if I could. I suppose my folks come every Sunday, don't they?"

"They are usually there in the morning, but not often in the evening. Your sister was there last Sunday night."

"Orpha?"

"Yes."

"How did she get there?"

"She was with a young man. I think it was Eugene Sagester, if I'm not mistaken."

"Is he any good?"

144

"Do you want your sisters to go with a good kind?"

"I certainly do, Brother Ambers. I want them both to go with the best—or none at all."

"I could not say that Eugene is the best. Millard," he said kindly, "what you expect of your sisters, you want to do, too."

Chapter 22

THE room was full of gay optimism. Even the flowers on the wallpaper seemed to be smiling. Ted, Willie, Roy, and Art were all talking and laughing at the same time about their fun at the carnival.

"Never been to a carnival?" shouted Willie Strege, the loudest of the four. "Kid, what you livin' for? You'd never in your life catch me givin' all my pay over to my old dad the way you do."

Millard felt crimson.

"You're all older than I am, too," he ventured.

"Yes, but I got to keep all I earned when I was your age. I'd balk. Fifteen, an' never been to a show, never been to a carnival, or a dance, or a circus, never tasted a cigarette. Whew!" Willie whistled. The other three joined him.

"Ever been to a fair?" asked Ted, grinning tormentingly.

Millard felt like walking out of the room, but he was in his pajamas. If he got up, the splits would be more noticeable. He was on parade enough.

"No." Millard shook his answer at them. The fingers of his thoughts struggled to hold him together. This was not the first time he had been made the object of both scorn and pity. The four used him every day as a target for their jeers and taunts. Singly none of them scoffed him to his face, but in a group each added to the fire of sarcasm. The one led the other on. Millard felt hot under their revilings. He wanted to back away from the heat.

"Well, I can't see that it's any worse to go to a carnival than to gamble," put in Roy with a jab.

Millard got up on one elbow. What fresh torment could they discover? He lay down and turned his face to the wall and acted deaf, but Roy's words stung him in the back with uncertain meaning.

* * * * *

The autumn grain had been cut and the hot winds blew across the stubble fields. Millard wiped his forehead as he walked along the dusty road toward home. In his pocket lay his month's wages tightly folded.

"Mother should never hand it over," he said to himself. "She needs things for herself. Someday I am going to give her most of what I earn."

He felt well and strong, but, oh, if he could only be happy, too. Why couldn't he be? The other boys joked and laughed and whistled. They sang giddy, sensational, popular songs about girls and love and glittering fun. One day they sang a new song about "Charlie was known by the company he thought nobody knowed he was keepin'." The boys sang it around the barn, in the milkhouse, and in their room when they were getting ready to go away.

The things that shocked Millard six months ago surprised him no longer. He took for granted that there were only a very few boys in the world who didn't talk and act like the Schultz gang, and he was one of these very few. It gave him that minority consciousness boys do not like. A terrible loneliness enveloped him. He had no promise to be true to, no pledge, no vow, no affiliation with the church—nothing but his own conscience and his mother. Now that Uncle Levi was gone, she was his main inspiration. The Bible Uncle Levi had given him for Christmas was tucked carefully in the bottom of his box under the cot. It was useless to try to read it in the room. It only invited sacrilege.

Derwood saw him coming. He had been watching for over an hour. He ran to meet him.

"Do you know what?"

"No, tell me."

"Guess." Derwood caught Millard by the hand.

"Is it something good?"

"I guess so. I don't know."

"Don't know? Is it something you like?"

"I guess so. It's a baby girl."

"Sure enough? Where is it?"

"At home. It came in the night."

Millard's steps hastened. A little sister? Thank God it was a girl. Mother's sweet, open face looked up into his, and a gentle smile

147

played around her lips. How thankful he was he hadn't burdened her with all his heartaches and discouragements. She had cares enough of her own.

"How tiny, oh, my! Have you named her, Mother?"

"Orpha wants to call her Carrie."

"Wouldn't that be all right, Millard?" Orpha asked.

"It depends on what Mother wants. If she likes it, it's all right with me. Here's your money, Mother. Where shall I put it?"

"Lay it over there on the dresser. Pop's around here someplace. You say my money?"

"I wish it was yours. Orpha, I saw Brother Ambers in town one day a while back, and he told me someone else besides Pop took you to church the other Sunday night."

"Oh, yeah, and what else did he say?"

"I asked him if he was any good."

"Well, Millard Grinstead, wasn't that pretty nervy?"

"I don't think so, Orpha. I wanted to know. I told him I wanted my sisters to go with the best or none at all."

"My, my, Millard. You must think we were all born upstairs, but we're about as common as anyone in seven states. I'll wait and see what sort of girl you pick."

"I don't think I'll ever pick any."

"You mean by that you don't think you could ever find one good enough?"

"No, I didn't mean that."

"What did you mean then?"

"I mean I wouldn't want any but the best, but I doubt if I'll ever deserve that kind."

"Why, Millard," exclaimed his mother, "why do you talk like that? Do you mean—"

What had he said now to frighten her? He certainly hadn't meant to.

"Oh, Mother, don't be alarmed." Millard tried to chuckle away her fears. "I haven't begun to think about girls yet, and no danger! I won't either until I get some decent clothes, so that might be a long time yet, maybe years. I'm never going to get married."

"You're not?"

"No, I'm just going to work and hand my money over to you. I'll keep enough to support myself, and I'll give you all the rest."

"You must think you're going to make big wages," exclaimed Orpha, arching her black eyebrows and rolling her big brown eyes.

"I expect to make a lot more than I am making now," he affirmed. "And I hope to tell you I'm going to be making some money before long too," asserted Orpha. Millard had never heard Orpha speak with such boldness. She looked unusually attractive and her brown eyes snapped. "By the time Mother's able to do the work alone I'll be eighteen and so—"

"You mean you're going to work out?"

"That's exactly what I mean, but I'm going to find my own job. Pop's not going to find it for me."

"The boys can't help Pop do everything that needs to be done and go to school too."

"Pop doesn't like it on the farm anyhow, not one this size. He'd rather have a small place close to town like we had back at Doddridge and do carpenter work again; and, anyway, I can't stay at home and work like a man the rest of my life, when other girls are earning as much in a week as you're getting in a month. Not anymore. I need decent clothes, too. I'm surprised Eugene asked me for a date."

Millard stood speechless. Could this be Orpha, his modest, quiet-mouthed sister?

"Clothes don't make the girl," Mother said softly.

"No," agreed Orpha, "but they do after all. At least they help a lot. When you go out you like to look like somebody—even if you aren't. Millard just got through saying he wouldn't start thinking about the girls until he got some decent clothes."

"Millard," broke in Mother, "pull up that chair and sit here beside me. Tell me honestly whether you are getting along all right?"

"Yes, I am."

"You are feeling well and all right?"

"Very well."

"You get good things to eat?"

"Very good."

"Do you have a good bed?"

"That's nothing extra. It's a cot with a mattress on it. It's all right."

"Does Mr. Schultz treat you nice?"

"Yes."

"Do you get along with the other men who work there?"

"I get along with them—yes. Why?"

"They're a pretty rough set, I suppose."

"I suppose they're like all other fellows."

Orpha left the room. She had cookies to bake and a dozen other things to do.

"They all smoke, I guess?"

"Oh, of course. Who doesn't, Mother?"

"You don't?"

"No."

"I'm glad."

"I might, if it wasn't for that. I know you don't want me to. Then I think about that cable, too; at last it cannot be broken—but then," Millard looked down. He fumbled with his shoestring. "If you never get married—and have boys of your own—it would not be quite so—"

She reached over and caught him by the arm.

"Millard, whether you marry or not, it will make me very happy if you never start. Anyway that is something you know nothing about. Of course, you will get married someday. In a way I guess it sounds ridiculous to be talking like this when you're not sixteen yet."

"I soon will be."

"Yes, and I'm going to do my best to help you get some new clothes, Millard. And I'm going to insist again that Pop find another place for you, where you won't have to work on Sundays. It just can't be right. We're going to live to regret this, I'm afraid. When Pop comes in I'm going to ask him to cut your hair before he goes to town."

"He usually goes earlier than this, doesn't he?"

"Yes, usually. But I'm sure he didn't leave yet."

"He always cuts it so short."

"I suppose that's so he won't have to do it so often."

"But, Mother, Pop's cut my hair only twice in the past six months. Mr. Schultz has been cutting it for me."

"Millard! Well, I have to wonder what Mr. Schultz thinks. You poor boy, I suppose he thinks you're neglected, doesn't he? Pop's coming now, isn't he, Millard?"

Pop was smiling when he came in, and his unusual pleasantness almost startled Millard.

"Sure, I'll cut your hair, Millard. Come on out on the porch.

What do you think of the baby?"

"I think she's pretty nice. What do you think of her?"

"Well, I think she's a dandy."

"Jeth," Myra said, "I wish you'd do something."

"What's that?"

"I wish you'd take Millard along to town and get him something he could wear on Sundays."

"On Sundays?"

"A boy his age likes to dress in something besides work clothes all the time. His best trousers are way too short. Jeth, Millard will soon be sixteen. It's been six months since he has been to church. You ought to find a job for him where he doesn't need to work on Sundays. Can't you do that, Jeth?"

"Do you know of another place, Millard?" Jeth asked. Pop did not look stern. His voice was so mellow it almost sounded rich.

"No, I don't. I haven't tried to find another place. I thought I was to stay with Schultz until you told me to leave."

"Well, your mother ain't satisfied with you there, and she didn't like fer you to work at Auckers either, so I'm almost afraid to try to find another place. You'll never find a place that's perfect, that's fer sure. Schultz never told me you'd have to work on Sundays when he hired you. If you can find a place where you can make as much an' like it better, go ahead an' change. I want your mother satisfied."

What? Did Pop really mean that? Warm circles ran around Millard's heart. Once before Pop had said something that made him dear to his boy. That was in the hospital.

"Let's go get that haircut then an' go to town. Did Schultz pay you?"

"Yes. It's on the dresser."

"I suppose it'll take most of this to get you a suit, but—I want her satisfied."

Myra was almost dumbfounded. Jeth had been unusually attentive the whole past week. When he came home from town the previous Saturday he brought along a large sack of oranges and fresh perch because Myra said she was hungry for some. More surprising than that was the contents of a package he laid on the bed. It was an inexpensive but pretty rayon bedspread, rose at that, Myra's favorite color. That, he said, was what had detained him, he had started home, then thought of the bedspread.

"Are they paying more for eggs this week?" asked Myra, admiring the bedspread.

"No, but I've been savin' up fer such, an' Liticia's been wantin' you to have one. Workin' out puts all sorts of ideas in her head."

"Aren't you afraid working out puts all sorts of ideas in Millard's head, too, Pop? Aren't you afraid, Jeth, someday you'll regret you hired him to a man like Mr. Schultz who makes him work on Sundays and so soon after he got discouraged?"

"I don't know why he got discouraged when I let him come back home an' finish school where he wanted to. Didn't I do that jes' to please you an' him both?"

"Just the same, Jeth, Millard's pretty young to work out among men who make no profession and where he has to miss going to church month after month."

"That ain't as bad, to my way of thinkin', as to have him work fer a man who claims to be a Christian an' ain't. I might have put him in such a place."

Myra's intelligent brown eyes widened. They spoke one page after another. Jeth said no more.

And now was he actually going to take Millard to town to get him a Sunday suit? From the bedroom Myra could hear Jeth pleasantly asking Millard about the milk route.

Chapter 23

ALTHOUGH the suit was shoddy, Millard was grateful for it. He did not expect Pop to get him the best in town. They got home in time for early supper. Orpha hemmed up the trousers while Richard washed the dishes (Derwood wiped them, bless his little heart), and Millard mowed the yard. He mowed as fast as he could, for rain clouds were gathering into gray blankets, and the leaves on the poplar trees were turning wrong side out.

"I'd better take you back," Pop said. His lazy brown eyes seemed to be nibbling at a tasty idea. "You and your suit'll both get wet if I don't."

"I'm afraid so, too."

And they would have, for the rain dropped like dimes before Millard was finished with the yard.

"I won't be back right away, Myra," Jeth called as he was going through the kitchen door. "I forgot the milk strainers, and I've got to get some tonight yet."

*   *   *   *   *

On a Saturday night in November Alfred Shultz came running up the stairs saying his mother wanted Millard to come down.

"I'm sorry, Millard, I suppose you were ready for bed, weren't you?"

"Yes. But that's all right."

"William isn't here this evening, and the boys have all gone out, too. I just had a call from the Blue Plazzo asking for twelve quarts of milk and some cream tonight yet. Hard telling when the boys will get in, and I know when William gets home he'll be dead tired. If you were older, I'd have you take the Nash and go in with it yourself, but the insurance we carry won't allow anyone under twenty-five at the wheel, and William's particular, so I guess I'll drive and have you go along to take the milk in for me. It's so hard to find a parking place along there on Saturday night, I'd have to carry the milk for blocks."

"That would be too much, Mrs. Schultz. Sure I'll go with you."

"I could take Alfred, but he's just ready for his bath."

"No, no, I'll go along."

The closest she could get to the Blue Plazzo was in the alley.

"I guess I can stop here till you run in with it. If I do have to move, I'll just drive around the block once and be right back."

"All right."

Millard started with the milk. He hesitated. In the parking space behind the restaurant he noticed a car exactly like his father's, same make, same color, same kind of a break in the right front fender. It sent a sickening wave over him. Why would Pop's car be parked there this time of night? From remarks he'd heard Art and Ted make, things went on in the Plazzo that weren't too good. Art talked once about the side room and gambling. Oh! It just couldn't be that Pop would be in there. If he didn't have to hurry, he'd wait—he'd hang around in the alley and see who got in that car. The license would tell, but, to be truthful, he had forgotten it if he had known once.

Millard put the baskets on the ground to open the back door. A warm odor of frying hamburger and sliced onion curled around him. Ordinarily it would have made him hungry. From the front of the restaurant came hilarious laughter and loud jazz.

"Right there in the icebox, kid," sniffed the thick-lipped night cook. He wiped his mouth on the bottom of his dirty apron.

Millard put the milk and cream in the icebox and hurried out. Mrs. Schultz was not there. Until she drove around the block, he'd watch. Maybe Pop would show up. He stood thinking. Should he go around to the front and look in? He walked over to the car and tried the door. It was locked. A bulldog jumped up on its hind legs and barked a merciless warning. Millard dropped his hand and stepped back. He knew it was not Pop's car, and all the way home he was glad he had been mistaken.

But the next time Millard went home Pop was driving a different car. He said he had traded the week before for a better one, so perhaps after all that was Pop's old car he saw parked behind the Blue Plazzo.

* * * * *

Mr. Shultz acted somewhat displeased when Millard told him he

154

had promised to work at the neighbors starting the first of the year.

"Haven't we treated you right here?"

"Yes, sir."

"Will Fred Boetcher give you more than I do?"

"Not much."

"More time off?"

"Not more, Mr. Shultz, but I won't need to work on Sundays."

"I see. That's it. You've still got church in your head. I guess you can't get away from that early training, can you? Well, all right, Millard. I hope you and Fred get along, but I know this, he'll work you harder than I do any of my men, if they do work on Sundays. He'll work you that much harder on Saturday, I'll bet."

It was late. He had walked two miles against the wind. He slipped in and took a back seat close to the center aisle. He hardly knew where he belonged. Everything looked strange—even the walls and the frosted windows. His heart pounded unhappily. Good. No one seemed to notice or recognize him. The man beside him shared his songbook without nodding. Millard searched the congregation. Where were the folks?

Prayer—then the swinging door opened and in filed Homer Jo, Richard, and Derwood. They walked briskly up the side aisle and sat with a group of other boys near the front. On the opposite side of the church Liticia walked up the side aisle, then Mother, carrying the white shawled baby in her arms, Glen trailing bashfully behind her.

Millard stopped breathing. How dear she looked, how motherly and good. Was he dreaming? Was this Sunday? Was he actually sitting on a church pew, dressed in a Sunday suit? He ran his hand along the front of his coat to see if it was buttoned right. It was. The swinging door opened again and three men entered, and the third one was unmistakably his father. Millard knew without turning his head. Pop found a seat three benches in front of him. How gray he was. Pop getting old already?

The atmosphere seemed almost awesome. As the next hymn was being sung a strange dread came over Millard. The chorister had a singular, almost holy look on his young face. His voice was rich with expression. He must know God. All the older women looked so righteous that it gave Millard an unrighteous feeling. Maybe he could slip out without being noticed. He felt so out of his sphere,and yet not forbidden. Mother would be glad when she discovered he was there. He searched her out. Through the heads and shoulders he caught a glimpse of her profile and her black wavy hair. Everything inside of him felt warm. He wanted to be good because she was. He tried to relax.

Primary classes passed to the basement one at a time with their respective teachers. From near the front center aisle a young woman rose to lead her class of little boys. Something about her caught Millard's eye. Was it her auburn hair or her high cheekbones? He did not recall ever having seen her before. She made him think of Miss Hazel Butterfield, who was intelligent and refined, yet sweet and understanding. The girl had on a soft navy dress and in her left arm she carried her Bible and a brown purse. She looked happy—as though she loved her assignment. As she passed, her eyes met his for one fleeting moment. He was almost frightened—not at the girl—but at himself. Some unknown force within his soul rose and swelled around an ideal he had been trying to forget he ever had. For an instant he was thrilled. Then he laughed at himself rebukingly. The glance was only an accident. He straightened his shoulders. But during the remainder of the morning service, and especially during Brother Ambers' sermon, Millard caught himself wondering if he'd ever meet those eyes again. He wondered who she was and where she lived.

Perhaps he should not have come to church where he would have to see so many good people, for now a new and fiercer fight would be waged daily between his imaginations and doubts and purposes. Outside of his mother and Liticia, what living symbol of purity had he to help him attain his hidden desires? Already another power was seeking his defeat. Hadn't he told his mother and Orpha he doubted if he would ever deserve the best? The girl, whoever she was, whatever her name, looked like the best; whether he ever saw her again or not, she made him conscious of the fact that she stood above him. Her countenance had that unstained look on it. And who was he? He hurried out.

"Oh, Millard, you got here!" Liticia clasped his hands. "Are you going along home with us?"

Her eyes danced with happiness.

"Will it be all right?" "All right? Why not? It's ages since you've been home on Sunday. Let's go to the car. It's cold standing here. I was invited out for dinner, but when I saw you here I told Melodie

Ann I would go along home with her some other time."

"Who?"

"Oh, Melodie Ann Brooks. But I can go home with her some other Sunday. Mother and I have been wondering all week whether or not you really would get to come. We've got all kinds of things to tell you, and I know you'll think little Carrie is getting cuter all the time."

"I didn't notice Orpha."

"She's working in town."

"Where?"

"Oh for—I forget the name—but the people who own the Broadway Bake Shop. She started Thursday morning."

"Did Pop—"

"Yes Pop took her in. She said she was going to work out as soon as she was eighteen, but she didn't locate a job as easily as she thought she would. She finally found this place for three seventy-five a week, room and board, every Thursday afternoon and every other Sunday off. This is her Sunday to work. Move over. Here they come."

"Maybe there won't be room for me."

"Of course there'll be room. Richard can sit in front between Pop and Mother. You can hold Derwood. Glen always wants to stand, anyway."

While Pop took his Sunday afternoon nap, Mother rocked on her favorite rocker, the boys played on the floor, and Liticia talked to Millard for an hour. She beamed on him admiringly. How tall and handsome he looked! How straight the part in his pretty brown hair! She drew him to the corner of the dining room.

"I'm so glad Pop got you the suit," she said softly.

"You don't hate him for that do you, Ticia?" He looked at her with such a searching expression that she hung her head. Her cheeks got red.

"No, I guess I shouldn't have said it—but you don't understand," she was almost whispering now.

"Understand what?"

"Well, I was just trying to say I felt sorry for you. Millard, I want to ask you something."

"What?"

He waited.

"Well—when you stand—in church," she picked at the corner of her handkerchief, "do you have to confess everything?"

"What do you mean—everything?"

"Every little thing?"

"Like what?" Millard felt almost numb. Why was Liticia asking him this?

"Like that," she whispered.

"Like saying you hated Pop?"

She nodded.

"You never told him that, did you?"

"Oh, no."

"Or anyone else?"

"No. No one but you."

"Then don't tell anyone else. You've confessed it enough, I should think. Are you—are you," Millard cleared his throat, "thinking of standing?"

"I might. If I could just be sure I could live it—I would. If we could be baptized together—" she looked at him shyly now. "You've always seemed nearer to me than Orpha. When I get through school I wish we would do things together. I wish I could find a job where you work—and—"

"But you must not wait on me, Liticia. If you want to be a Christian, don't wait on anything or anybody."

"Then why did you?"

Millard did not answer.

"Don't you remember what Miss Butterfield used to tell us, Millard?"

"What was that?"

"That story about the old man who always gave other people such good advice?"

He remembered it well. The old man had a remedy for everyone's ills, but used none of them himself. Millard squirmed. "By the way, Liticia, who was that girl in church this morning who looks like Miss Butterfield?"

"Miss Butterfield? Who do you mean?"

"She went downstairs with a class of little boys. She has auburn hair."

"Oh, that was Melodie Ann Brooks, and you're right—she does look like Miss Hazel Butterfield."

Chapter 24

MILLARD did not like the idea of Brother Ambers providing him a way to or from church. His sensitive, retiring nature could not accept that. Since Pop expected him to work out for his room and board, he'd be as independent as possible. He wanted to be a man. He'd walk, and if the weather were too severe, he'd stay in his room and read. He was utterly opposed to being the object of mercy. Pop never wanted to go to church on Sunday night, so in order to get back to Boetchers by suppertime he had to leave home no later than three. After the chores were done it was too late to start out to walk to church. The winter was long and unusually severe. Millard often missed going to church.

The voice of God which once was clear and distinct seemed to reach his ear now as through a maze or curtain. It did not interrupt him with such breath-taking haltings as formerly. One day not long ago he had been deeply touched over the experience of losing his favorite uncle. Although he still felt that loss, time was healing the wound. Whenever he went to church he saw young men who were destined to make good because everything was in their favor. They could go to college if they wanted to. Their fathers would help them through and give them farms besides when they got ready to settle down. They were appreciated, loved, and wanted.

Every time he saw the girl with the auburn hair, Millard wanted to make good. He noticed once she was sitting beside Liticia and when she smiled a dimple showed in her one cheek. Her manners were ladylike and gentle. What did Liticia say her name was? Melodie Ann Brooks? Did a girl ever have a prettier name? He wondered. He wondered what her voice sounded like. He wanted to know, but he never put himself out to try to find out. Foolish thought! How ashamed he would feel if anyone could guess. She probably came from a refined well-to-do family. Her father was undoubtedly a man of sterling character. Millard looked down. The enemy of his soul sent him the feeling of renunciation and with it despair, superstition, and bitterness. If Pop would only be different, be sincere through and through——

* * * * *

Didn't he see her?

He almost bumped into her. "Hi, Pop." She was just passing the Blue Plazzo as he came out. He stopped abruptly.

"Why, hello Orpha. Aren't you workin'?"

"Not today."

"I thought you had Thursday afternoons off. Ain't—ain't this Saturday?"

She laughed.

"Of course it's Saturday. How are all the folks at home?"

"All right. How come you have today off?"

She seemed embarrassed. She fumbled for words.

"Well—I'm out of a job right now."

"I see. Coming home tomorrow?"

"Oh, I'll see once. I can't promise."

The attractions of the city kept Orpha more and more away from home and the church. Slowly but certainly the surging tide of amusements caught and held her in a current. Something else far more thrilling than Sunday school and church captured her attention, and that something was Jack Fondwell. He was tall and dark and pleasing to her eye. There was no reason why she shouldn't marry him after he declared his love, and convinced her that two could live more economically than one. Of course Myra was disappointed that Orpha didn't find a husband in the family church, but she told her mother she wanted to transfer her membership to Jack's church in town, because it was so much handier. Everybody worshiped the same God anyway. If Pop was disappointed, he did not express his disappointment out loud. When Myra broke down and cried over the letter Orpha wrote and mailed the day after her marriage, Jeth said without emotion, "Well, she's made her own bed, now let her lie in it. I'm not goin' to tell any of my children who to marry or not marry. I wouldn't cry over that."

Spring came and in the class of converts that knelt for water baptism was Liticia Ann Grinstead, aged fifteen. Jeth's unconcernedness about his own spiritual status did not keep him from doing his duty in providing a way for the rest of the family to get to church once each Sunday in the morning. Besides wanting to save on the gas bill he was bothered with night blindness.

Fred Boetcher took Millard along to town to help him unload a motor that needed repairs. Then Fred decided to get a haircut. While Millard was waiting he walked up the street. Across a window in bold red letters he read. COME IN. THERE'S A PLACE FOR YOU IN THE C.C.C. CAMP. INVESTIGATE TODAY. A man on the opposite side of the window noticed the bright-eyed lad and motioned, smiling. Millard stepped inside.

"Are you looking for an opportunity with our training program?" he asked, smiling agreeably.

"I have a job with Mr. Fred Boetcher."

"How old are you, son?"

"I'm seventeen."

"Through high school?"

"No, sir. I never went to high school."

"This is exactly the place for you then, because you can learn a trade while you earn. What is your name, son?"

"Millard Grinstead."

"Well, Millard, the C.C.C. Camp will provide a way to start you off toward some successful career. You will get your uniforms, excellent meals, recreation of all kinds, with some basic military training every young American wants. Your supervisors are men of outstanding skill and character, and you get thirty dollars a month."

"Thirty?" Millard looked at the man in amazement.

"Thirty dollars, yes, sir. You have parents you are helping?"

"Yes, I do."

"The checks could be made payable to your mother or your father. Twenty-five to them and five to you."

Millard thought.

Five dollars a month to keep? Twenty-five for Pop? or Mother? Wouldn't that be better than fifteen? And uniforms furnished? Then Pop wouldn't have to buy his overalls and shirts.

"Hundreds of boys just like you, Millard, are taking advantage of this opportunity. You will get to work on large-scale projects, such as bridge building, road construction, or forestry. Your instructors will be both military and civilian personnel. They are men who are proud of fellows like you, good looking and physically fit, who have been deprived of high school privileges. Here are pictures of the camp out here off of Highway 91. You've surely seen it."

"No, I haven't been out that way."

"Well, here you see the boys in the mess hall, and here they are in their bunks reading and listening to the radio. Here is the instructor's office and reception room. The boys are entertained every week, so there's not a dry time for anyone. Religious services are conducted weekly—What are your ambitions, Millard?"

The man rested on one arm and looked Millard full in the face.

"Maybe that's a hard thing for you to decide by yourself. If you are undecided, then why not sign up today and join the gang the first of April?" The man shoved an application blank before Millard and handed him a pencil.

Should he? Millard hesitated. Would Mother care? He was sure Pop wouldn't. He had said he could find his own job if he made as much as Mr. Schultz paid him.

"You see, son, it all boils down to this. The opportunity is yours. The government is doing this to help you and your family. Here is a list of the boys from this county who signed up today. You probably know most of them."

To be truthful Millard knew practically none of them. His eyes scanned the paper.

"Doesn't it sound good to you, Millard?"

He could not say it didn't.

"I guess it does."

"You can have five dollars a month to buy your knickknacks. If I'm not mistaken, they furnish you with some cigarettes."

"I don't smoke."

"You don't? Then you probably do your work well and fast. Some boys are always losing time lighting their cigarettes. You know what I mean." The man laughed. He fumbled with a pack in his shirt pocket, but he did not take one out.

"You'll never be sorry, but of course if you don't want to, someone else will take your place and you'll be the loser."

Millard took the pencil and with a trembling hand printed his full name, Grinstead, Don Millard.

What could Fred Boetcher say but that he would have done the same thing? It would be a good experience for the shy, sensitive boy, and besides, although the boy deserved all he would get at the camp, it was more than he could pay. He had a notion to offer him a raise if he would stay another year, but according to news reporters the problems of the past would undoubtedly be repeated. The past eighteen years had been a fateful one for too many nations. This C.C.C. Camp was a forerunner to the draft, so why not let the boy go? Fred Boetcher would be loyal to his patriotic convictions. Millard seemed so innocent. This would prepare him for the future. Secretly Mr. Boetcher was thankful his tiny twin boys lay sleeping peacefully in the Mt. Carmel cemetery. Death had seemed cruel at the time, but time heals such wounds.

* * * * *

Life in the camp was something new for Millard. He was never alone. At first the closeness of the other boys made him feel tight all over. How could he relax? Their careless talk surprised him, and their unashamed exposures shocked him. None of them read a Bible or said a prayer before they crawled in for the night, so why should he? He would say his lying down. He really hadn't much to pray, except for God to take good care of Mother and Liticia and the rest of the folks at home. Once he almost asked God to bless Melodie Ann Brooks. Some of the boys had pictures of their sweethearts on the walls at the heads of their beds, and most of them had pictures of some pretty girl in their billfolds. Millard didn't have a billfold. He might get one after he got his first check. All the boys talked about going to town to spend their money then. Some of the boys had pin-up girls on the walls. Some had pictures of women they called their mothers. They looked gay and young, and some had flowing hair. Millard had no picture of his mother. He wished he had one, but hers would seem quite out of place there. Her face was so gentle and plain.

Millard enjoyed the food after the 'tightness' wore off. At first nothing tasted just right. He enjoyed the morning exercises, the drills, the brisk walks, and the baths. The work was not too hard. Vigor of a young man's strength tingled in his entire person. He could do anything the other boys could do—almost. Sometimes something around his incision hurt, but he never let on.

A lot of the boys went home on Sundays. Those who didn't have folks or friends hitchhiked. Millard often got a ride as far as Donnelson's corner. He could have gone home on Saturday after-

163

noon when his turn came, but he didn't want to eat too many meals at home. Pop was always mentioning the high cost of living.

Once when Millard went home Melodie Ann was there. Liticia had brought her along home after church. Millard's hands and feet felt clumsy and too big.

"You've never met my brother, Millard, have you, Melodie?" asked Liticia, leading Millard toward her.

"Not that I can remember." Smiling, she extended her slender hand.

"I'm glad to meet you, Millard." Her deep blue eyes met his.

Her voice! It was beautiful.

"I'm glad to meet you, too." What had he said? He had said it and he couldn't take it back now. But how could he be glad? She could never mean anything to him—and yet—how could he forget her now? She had that something he had often dreamed of finding since he knew Miss Hazel Butterfield. The little red brick schoolhouse back at Doddridge in Harper's Valley, the curtained windows, the blackboards, the teacher's desk—even the hooks in the cloakroom where he hung his wraps—stayed in his memory with a sacred meaning because of that teacher. One time when he had the earache in school, Miss Butterfield drew him aside in the cloakroom and whispered low, "I'll pray for you tonight, Millard, that your ear will be all right in the morning, so you won't need to miss."

In the morning his earache was gone.

Could this girl do a thing like that? Could she pray and get answers, too?

"I don't think I ever told you, Millard," added Liticia, "Melodie is Brother Ambers' niece."

Something like a bolt went through Millard's body. Then she was somebody good, unapproachable, higher than the best.

"Niece?" he asked. She saw his eyes widen. He drew back.

"By adoption," she said in a low confiding tone. "Brother Ambers is not my real uncle. I was taken out of a home for orphaned children when I was three years old. My mother is dead and my father did not care for me, so I was put out for adoption."

Millard's heart jumped to his throat. She, a girl as sweet and beautiful as—as that—not wanted!

Chapter 25

THE fact that Melodie Ann Brooks was an adopted, once unwanted child did not lower her any in Millard's opinion. On the
other hand, it sent him a small fraction of courage. It had somewhat
of a lifting effect on him. He still felt unworthy to be so near to her,
and imagined that because of her own experience she wore that
gentle, understanding look so few girls had, and that he noticed as
readily as her auburn hair. Was there a chance that they could ever
be on common ground—ever say more to each other than what had
already been said? She followed Liticia to the kitchen to help with
the dinner preparations, but her voice lingered in the room.

"Now, Mother," Liticia said, "we can finish the dinner. You go
on in and visit with Millard."

"You do that, Mrs. Grinstead," added Melodie. "I will help
Liticia."

And so they sat and talked. Millard held little Carrie on his lap
and smiled at her sweet baby ways. It hardly seemed possible so
small a creature was his own sister. Mother looked young and rosy.
The soft spring breeze through the open south window played across
her wavy hair.

"How do you like camp now, Millard?"

"It's all right since I'm better acquainted."

"Are you still working on the Turtle Lake road?"

"We will be most of the summer, I think. I drive one of the trucks
now."

"You like that, I suppose."

"Of course."

"There wouldn't be any chance of—oh, what am I saying? Of
course, I know they wouldn't let you do that."

"Do what, Mother?"

"Oh, use one of the trucks so you could get to church. I don't suppose they'd think of allowing such a thing."

"No, Mother. They couldn't start a thing like that. The fellows drive the trucks only with orders from the supervisor." He read her thoughts and added quickly, "They have a chapel service for us every Sunday morning at nine. This morning a ladies' choir from some church sang three numbers and a man played the piano."

"What else?"

"Us fellows all tried to sing along with him. I mean some of us did. 'Onward Christian Soldiers'—that's about the only song they ever have us sing together—that and one other."

"Why?"

"I don't know. I guess they're the songs the fellows know best, but—" he caught himself. Why tell Mother how some of the fellows jeered and mimicked after the ministers were gone? He didn't. He would never do a thing like that. He wondered secretly why no one ever led the good old hymns he partly knew, "Nearer My God to Thee" or "In the Cross of Christ I Glory." Those were the two songs he'd heard his mother hum sometimes about her work. The ministers who talked to the boys told more funny stories than Scripture in an attempt to be entertaining. He'd better not tell Mother that either.

"I do wish you could manage to get to church." Mother bent forward and touched his arm.

Millard swallowed hard.

"If Pop would—" Millard heard him coming and did not finish.

If Pop would what? What was he about to say? Yes, if—Pop would—would make a number of things different now and would have before in all the days since Millard was a little child. But Myra wondered the rest of the day what Millard was going to say and didn't. Didn't Millard know he was soon going to be a man—yes, her boy, her oldest son would soon be a man who must disregard all the "if Pop's" and do what he knew was right. As intelligent a boy as he had always been, couldn't he see, couldn't he learn, couldn't he profit? He must make his own decisions. He had his own soul to answer for. He was no longer unaccountable. Long after she went to bed, Myra still wondered and thought. Homer Jo was thirteen now. Soon he, too, would be a man. Already he was self-willed and disobedient.

"Jeth," she said the next Sunday morning, "if we would start a little earlier couldn't we go around by the camp and pick Millard up so he could come to church with us?"

They were at the breakfast table. Jeth dropped his knife.

"He didn't ask me to."

"I know."

"You know? Why? Did he ask you then?"

"No."

"Then how do you know he wants me to?"

"I just thought maybe."

"But did he say so?"

"No. But I told him I wished he could get to church and he started to say, 'If Pop would—' Then you came in and he never finished. I thought maybe he meant if you'd come after him, he would. Since you get ten dollars more a month now, couldn't you use some of that for the little extra gas it would take, Jeth? Just once a week?"

"I was right here. He could have asked me if he had wanted to get in ter church very bad. How does he get home? I don't get him."

"I know. He says he gets a ride up to the corner with a Mr. Wilson who comes this way every Sunday."

"Then why can't he hop a ride ter church? There's corners over in that direction to hop off at."

"Maybe so. I mean yes, that's so, Pop, and maybe that isn't what he meant either."

"Hard tellin' what that boy meant."

"It's our duty to encourage our children to go to church. It's our duty to help them get there—to go out of our way to get them there," Myra added.

"After they're as big as he is?"

"He's still our boy, Jeth, and you accept his checks."

Jeth meditated. Myra's pleading brown eyes searched for his. He must make her satisfied.

"I couldn't hardly get around to it this mornin', Myra. You should have said somethin' sooner. It's all of six miles out there and back to church. I might have ter fix a tire yet. It's a nice mornin'. He could walk."

"But if he stays for their chapel at nine, then starts to walk, he wouldn't get there in time either."

"He could make it for the preachin' or start out right after breakfast. I think he could find a way if he was awantin' a way very bad."

Something was choking Myra.

"That's—that's what I'm afraid of—now, Jeth," she faltered, "I'm afraid he's losing interest in the church."

It was hard for her to control herself.

"Now don't worry, Myra," Jeth said; "you always take things too seriously."

"Too seriously?" she gasped.

"Most boys like ter sow some wild oats while they're young. He'll settle down someday and hunt up the church."

Oh! Jeth shouldn't talk like this in front of the children. Homer Jo's eyes were fast widening. So were Richard's.

"Is Orpha doing that?" she asked sadly.

"I don't know. She's young yet, too. She'll come ter her senses when it's time. I'm not agoin' ter worry over Orpha. Jack Fondwell can do that now."

"Jeth!" whispered Myra. "A daughter's a daughter until she's dead."

"Well we'll go by fer him next Sunday," Jeth said, frowning slightly. "We'll all have ter get around earlier. We must help your mother ter be satisfied." This he added glancing around the table.

* * * * *

"Dear Mother and Father," read Grandmother. "The strawberries are about over. I've canned fifty-one quarts. The garden looks good yet, but we need rain. I didn't get to church yesterday. Glen was sick. He must have eaten something that upset him. The rest of us are well.

We had a card from Orpha Saturday. They have gone to Whitville, where Jack found a better job. Orpha writes so little, I wonder if she is happy. Of course she never did like to write.

No, it wasn't my wish that Millard work at the camp. I had nothing to do with it. Jeth told him he could find his own job and he made his own decision. Jeth didn't care. I'm not well enough posted about the setup to know whether it's all right or not. There are so many things I do not understand. The thing I don't like is that he seldom gets to church. He says he likes the work all right. Sometimes I have to wonder about some things, but I try to take all my worries to the Lord. Maybe if you'd write to him sometime it might be a help. You know Millard always did like to read. He says they have a library at the camp and can have plenty to read evenings if he wants to. Of course, I have no idea what kind of books they are. It seems my boy is—I hardly know how to express it—but he's sorta getting out of my reach. I know too little about him any more, and what he's doing, but of course I must remember he's almost a man. It seems impossible. Sometimes when I hold Carrie in my arms she reminds me so much of Millard when he was a baby. I wish you'd pray for us all. I know you do, but remember Millard especially. I'm sure he has struggles that nobody knows anything about. I can see it on his face. For one thing, he's fighting conviction. I know this letter is too much about Millard, but this is on my mind, and I had to unload a little. He's either a good bad boy or a bad good boy. I hope I live to see all my children saved. When I see some children going astray and both parents are seemingly fully consecrated I shudder for ours. Liticia has a nice friend. She is Brother Ambers' niece. That's a help to her.

Sometimes Jeth says he wishes we lived on a smaller place and he could do carpenter work again. I wish he could be satisfied here. It is best for the boys.

Liticia is finished with the grades now. She's working for Mrs. Dogerdy again. I thought I could hardly spare her, but Derwood helps me pretty good and Glen does a lot of little things, too. I know I shouldn't say it, but sometimes I almost wish I could keep them little and around me.

Does Christina write to you often? Her letters to me are always so sad. It seems she is reconciled, but she can't get used to it. You knew her sister and husband brought her back when she disposed of her things. The place is rented, but I feel sad every time we drive past. Millard thought so much of Uncle Levi. Carrie is calling for her bottle, so good-by and God bless you. With love, Myra."

* * * * *

"Come on, D.M., try one." He held out his half-empty pack.

Millard ignored him. He wiped the sweat from his forehead and dumped the gravel.

"It would be good for what ails you."

"Nothing ails me."

"Then try it for the fun of it."

Millard shook his head.

"You don't know what you're missin'. Who you tryin' to be so good fer? Your mother?"

Millard felt red, purple. He wanted to hit Crow Maxton on the

169

mouth.

"I know," laughed Crow. "Say, you guys," he hollered at the top of his voice, "do you know what D.M. stands fer, huh? I found out. Darling Mama. That's it." Turning to Millard he grinned sheepishly and said in an undertone, "Come on, kid. Show the guys that you're as tough as the rest of us."

Millard wet his lips.

"I can work as hard as the rest of you without smoking," he said, "and I'm money ahead."

"Gonna be a miser, a tight wad?"

Millard's anger subsided a little. He'd rather be called a tight wad than the other.

"If I was a tight wad," he said, "I'd save my money and sponge off of you. Thanks, but keep your cigarettes."

Similar experiences were frequent. Not one other boy in the camp went through what Don Millard Grinstead did, because he was different. He was the only boy who did not smoke, the only boy who had never been to a carnival, the only one who did not swear, the only one who did not know the taste of liquor, or how to play cards. A few others could not dance. Some, but not many, could say they had never been drunk. What should he do? Leave the camp? He did not want to do that.

Millard was taken by surprise. He was standing on the steps when the car stopped in the driveway.

"Doesn't this take too much gas, Pop?"

"Your mother said I should."

He looked at her. "Mother did?"

"Didn't you tell her you wished I would?"

"No. Why, Mother, when did I say that?"

"Didn't you say you'd come to church if Pop would —" She read his look of utter astonishment. He got in the back seat. "Wait a minute. I'll have to run in and check out."

His mind was in a whirl. Is that what Mother thought he meant to say?

"You mustn't bother to do this again," he said after they were on their way. "This is too much."

The day after his father had come to get him to take him along to church (to satisfy Myra), Millard was fired with questions.

"Was that your Dad an' Mother?" inquired a nosey-face boy they

170

called Stuffy.

"Yes."

"Was that plain-lookin' little woman your mother?" asked Bob.

"Yes," answered Millard.

"Whew. No wonder you're so good," put in Tom. "Mine ain't that holy lookin'."

"I didn't know you were a member of that church," Bob said.

"I'm not," answered Millard, "I'm not a member of any church."

After that it was easier. Was D.M. a bad boy trying to be good or a good boy trying to be bad? The boys stood whispering, asking each other.

Chapter 26

L ITICIA and Melodie Ann saw each other every Sunday. After the Sunday-school hour they sometimes sat together for the remainder of the service. Each had discovered in the other traits of character that attracted. They were happy even in silence. The one was a blonde. The other had a maiden's crowning glory of auburn hair.

"You haven't gone home with me for a long time, Liticia. Can't you go along today?"

"I'd love to, but I'd have no way home after church."

"Home?"

"I mean back to Dogerdy's. My father just never wants to come in the evening."

"Why?"

"It's the gas. He says it takes too much, and he wants to go to bed early."

"I think the best sermons are in the evening. Bro. Ambers has started a series of sermons now on discipleship. He makes it so plain. I never did understand a lot of things he explains. You would be interested I'm sure."

"I know, too, I would. Melodie, there a thousand things I would like to have explained to me. I am full of questions. I try to figure out the answers to some things till I think I'll—"

"Things like what?"

"Oh, Melodie Ann, you'd be shocked if I told you what all. I must go. Pop is beckoning to me. He doesn't like to wait. Mother is expecting me to go along home with them. You know it's the only time I get to be at home. Couldn't you go along with us and have your brother come after you again? I hate it that it's this way, but I can't help it."

"Wait a minute; I'll go ask him. I'll see what Mother says."

Melodie Ann was soon back.

"Liticia, are you sure your folks won't object if I go along? Ask them first."

"Did Marlin say he'd come and get you?"

"Yes."

"Mother, it's all right if Melodie Ann goes along home with us today, isn't it?"

"Certainly."

"Pop?"

"Why, certainly," he echoed.

And so Millard met her face to face again, the girl with the winsome smile and gentle understanding face, the girl of his secret dreams, whom he could not forget. He was sitting on the porch steps when they came home.

"Don Millard, why weren't you at church?" asked Liticia. Her words struck him like a hard blow. What answer could he give? The girl's blue eyes were like stars shining on him in the night. Their radiant lights were exposing him and all his unrighteousness. He could not run and hide. And there was Melodie Ann. There was some power to her character that held his attention. She would surely influence his entire life—his destiny. Instead of answering Liticia he stood up to tip his hat, but he had come bare-headed. He nodded. He was not expecting to see her today. Was his hair combed properly? He had not answered Liticia. He did not want to lie. He did not want to admit the truth. He would not say he deliberately stayed away from church to avoid possible conviction. Neither would he say he would have been there if Pop would have said just one word to let him know, or just one word to indicate he wouldn't take the same kind of attitude if he should stand again. The words he had heard from the woodhouse were written in his memory with indelible ink. They would not fade away. Several times he thought he could forget; then something new would happen to make them plainer. Didn't Pop have any confidence in him? Didn't he care at all whether or not he went to church? Didn't he put any worth on his soul? He knew Mother wanted him to be a Christian. But she did not know what he heard Pop tell Bro. Ambers. If Millard would not have heard, Pop still would have said it. And he surely said what he meant. The meaning of it all — that was what mattered so. Every slight before or since enlarged the meaning. He was unwanted. Even now as Pop got out of the car, the boy felt as though he were not welcome at home.

"You told Pop not to come after you again," Liticia continued coming up the steps. "You said you would find your own way. Couldn't you find a way this morning?"

"I might surprise you sometime, Liticia," he said. "Hello, Melodie Ann."

"Hello, Millard."

Millard felt ashamed. Wasn't Melodie Ann an unwelcomed child and an orphan? Yes, but someone found and took her when she was little, nursed and loved her, helped her into the kingdom. She was not unwanted now. Maybe she didn't even remember her father. Pop was a professing Christian. It made a difference in the world. He had expressed his feeling to brother Ambers. "I doubt if it's worth your time." Oh! Those words were branded deep into his heart. Could he ever be worth anybody's time? Would God take time to fool with him?

* * * * *

Mother had prepared a pan of ice-box rolls the night before. She stuck them in. They could bake while the girls finished the rest of the dinner. Soon the house had the delicious yeasty smell of homemade bread. They would melt in your mouth with buttery goodness. It was good to be alive now and know the delightful sense of hunger with satisfying food within sight. The day was perfect. Not too hot or windy or rainy. All nature seemed happy and contented. Nothing hurt. Why not be happy? Why not forget every sadness and injustice with the night — lie down and sleep and wake up new and leave all bad forever asleep? When Millard looked at Mother and Liticia and Melodie Ann Brooks that did not seem impossible — but in a moment like a flash the struggle was on again, like an unexpected attack from the enemy. He had seen and heard too much. He would not try again until Pop made the first move.

After dinner the girls took a walk out through the garden down to the grove. A log offered a good place to rest.

"You said you wondered about some things," began Melodie.

"I do, Melodie Ann. I wonder why I was ever born and what I'll ever amount to, and what life is all about. I wonder why God allows this and that and whether or not He knows our futures, I mean all the

174

little things that will happen. I wonder about God and death and heaven and how God can be God. I wonder about my family and why everything is the way it is, and whether or not I'll ever be a mother. I wonder about Orpha and how Mother stays so sweet. I always felt close to Millard for some reason — closer than to any of my other brothers—closer than to Orpha. I wonder about him all the time."

"Why?"

"Because he was going to be baptized, then changed his mind like that." She snapped her fingers.

"Why?"

"That's what I don't know. He won't tell. Something happened to make him sad. He changed so quickly. But for that matter he's had things to discourage him before. I thought he was sincere. You'd think he was, too, if you'd read the letter he wrote me while he was staying at Uncle Levi's."

"Have you tried to find out?" She seemed interested in Liticia's problem.

"Of course. His indifference now worries me. And yet he wanted me to go ahead. He's glad I went into the church."

"Don't you have any idea what has discouraged him?"

"Oh, Melodie, I hate to tell you this, but I am afraid it's about — you won't tell anyone, will you?"

"Not if you tell me not to."

"I — I'd better not tell. He might not want me to. He never likes me to say an unkind thing about anyone. He's just that way."

"That's an excellent quality, isn't it, Liticia?"

"Yes. But he suffers things all to himself. It would help if he'd confide in someone."

"Doesn't he confide in your mother?"

"He used to more than he does now. Yet he dearly loves Mother. I know he does. It worries Mother, too."

"Doesn't he confide in your father?"

"My father?" Liticia's hand clasped her throat. "No — not in him. I wish he could."

Her eyes filled with sudden tears. "Oh, Melodie Ann, will you help me? You seem so close to me."

"Help you what?"

"Help me pray for our family?"

"Of course, I will. And I believe —"

"Believe what?"

"That things will come out all right someday."

"Oh, do you?"

* * * * *

Since Millard knew there was little or no chance for him to attend high school, he decided to stay in the camp. He enjoyed the work, and the supervisors all seemed to like him. Even at unskilled labor there were plenty of opportunities to display his abilities and trustworthiness. One time after another he was recommended for some responsibility because he did what was assigned to him without complaining, and he did his work quickly and well. After the first year he was seldom ridiculed because he did not smoke. After the second year some even admired him for the firmness of character they called grit. Occasionally Millard found his way to church, and every time he saw his ideal girl he went to bed to toss in wakefulness. There was a sincere, indefinable beauty about her young face that made him feel he wanted to worship God and pray. Whether he hammered or sawed, drove a truck or helped set the poles, trimmed trees or ran the power lawn mower, the light on her face kept the glory of a noble woman's love alive in his heart. He could never be satisfied with any lesser kind.

But! Millard was working hard and making no progress spiritually. Some other worthy man would come and win for himself that glory of her love. He was conscious, very conscious, of a void in his soul, and he knew he was out of harmony somewhere in that divine plan for his life. Over and over he wished now he had ignored Pop's conversation with Brother Ambers and done the thing he had started out to do. Why had he allowed that to discourage him? Unless he could be bigger and stronger than the thing that got him down, where would he land? The thought sometimes horrified him. This looking back all the time to the day of disappointment was robbing him of faith in himself.

Millard tossed and thought.

He would stop going to church altogether and see if he couldn't forget everything, forget that he ever had convictions, forget Pop ever hurt his feeling, forget Melodie Ann Brooks and everything about her. He tried to close his mind. Maybe the best way to forget would be to go to a movie on Saturday night.

Millard sat rapt, tense, startled, thrilled. It was a fascinating, zooming picture about a young man who wanted a chance to do something big in some fascinating science. He had no high school education and came from a poor family, but because of his high I.Q. and a good character, he was offered a chance in the United States Air Force. Aviation became his career. In a short time he was an outstanding aviator — admired, applauded, honored, advanced. Millard enjoyed the picture. He would never forget it. He would go again.

Was there some truth to all the things Virgil D. Vanderbilt Manasseh Gerlach told him? He recalled his dramatic orations about war. Nas didn't ever seem to have a worry or a care. He joked and laughed and lived carefree. No ideal girl made him conscious of his unrighteousness.

Millard found himself in a state of mental confusion. What he would do he did not, and what he would not do tonight, tomorrow he did. He could not understand himself.

* * * * *

The probability of a world war had been written about and talked about and expected so long, and so many critical situations had been overcome by skillful diplomacy, quelling people's fears, that when at last the declaration was broadcast, few were prepared for it. To many it came almost as a thief in the night. Some were panic-stricken when the order for immediate mobilization was issued to the United States Army.

Myra rocked little Don Millard in her arms and sang over his cuddly soft head. She was not panic-stricken. She felt like singing because her son was too young even to know what guns and war were. By the time he was grown the world would surely be sick and tired of war, and permanent peace would be established. Nations and powers and peoples would have learned their lesson. The armistice was signed.

But Myra Grinstead was as sadly disappointed as millions of other mothers who had small sons in that day. Despite what was accomplished, all that was lost, all the was suffered at home and abroad, the most intelligent diplomats and powers could not prevent the tumult of events that led up to the second world war. Every man seemed caught in the horrible fine-spun web.

With anxious eyes Myra watched the papers. Don Millard was no longer a baby on her lap. He was no longer a school boy. He was a young man now and old enough to register and not a Christian! Her mother heart was tense with dread.

Chapter 27

THE state fair was widely advertised by handbills, and posters and radio. All the boys were going. Millard had never been to a fair. He did not care particularly to go with the gang of fellows. He did not enjoy their boisterous, flippant talk, their constant smoking, and their foul stories. Millard went to the fair alone.

He was standing alone, resting a bit, watching the swarms of people move back and forth like young wheat with the wind.

"Enjoying the fair?" Millard turned quickly, for he had not heard anyone approaching from behind. The officer removed his cap and wiped his forehead. His grey hair was cut "butch" style. He had a healthy, well-fed face, and his eyes were blue steel. They were piercing and fearless, but soft with a touch of humor and human understanding. The officer's voice was deep.

"Yes, sir."

"I suppose you know without me telling you that I'm the recruiting officer stationed here to assist young men who are interested in enlisting, or have you already?"

"No, sir, I haven't."

"I'd guess you're old enough."

"Yes, sir."

"Married?"

"No, sir."

"I know you've been thinking of it then."

Millard shifted. "A little," he answered.

"Come over here to the station and I'll give you some of our literature."

They did not need to walk far. The officer stepped behind his counter.

"What's your name, son?"

"Millard Grinstead."

"You live around here?" "Yes, sir."

"You see, Millard," he began, using his familiar personal warm up, "it is the policy of the United States Army and Air Force to encourage every young able-bodied American to enlist and help to make ours the best and biggest and strongest army of the world. We're all going to have to work together to get this accomplished. Never before in history has the United States Army offered her young men such wonderful opportunities to earn and learn while in uniform. Have you any college training?"

"No, sir. I've never gone to high school."

"Have you wanted to, or don't you care about school?"

"Oh, yes, I've cared."

"That's all right, Millard, you can get instruction in almost any academic course while serving. Later, if you wish you can get credit at many of our colleges and universities. You can choose something you are especially interested in or vocational studies. You look smart and ambitious, Millard. You look as if your mental test would rate high."

Millard blushed. He did not especially appreciate the flattering words.

"We've learned a lot about young men during the last world war," hurried on the officer. "The men who enlist always make the best soldiers. We've learned a lot about new devices, new ways to keep the boys well and happy and entertained during off-duty hours, new methods of fighting the enemy, new everything. Have you any plans for your future?"

"No, sir."

"Then do the wisest thing you've ever done in your life, Millard; enlist today. You'll get fifty dollars a month and a chance to see the world, but better than that, you'll always have the satisfaction that you've done your part to help save our country. Do you have home folks?"

"I'm the oldest boy. There are nine in the family."

"What a noble thing for you to do, Millard, to help protect your family from worse than — well, you know what's going to happen unless we do our utmost and do it now. Of course if you go into the army it does not mean necessarily that you'll have to go into combat. But we've got to prepare. You understand all that without my telling you. We've got to have thousands of soldiers for coastal guards. We must have an ever-increasing number in our nation's military establishments. No other organization can do more or offer more for her soldiers. You find out what you really are when you join the Army or Air Force. They teach you to be original, self-reliant, yet able to cooperate with a group and take orders. You learn to be keen, quick, and efficient. It'll bring the best out of you—stuff you never knew you had. Don't let the other fellows beat you to it. Enlist today, Millard—Grinstead, did you say?"

"Yes, sir."

Millard stood thinking. He'd been hearing plenty of discussions and pledges of allegiance to the flag. A "new and free world for our children" was seen on every hand. To most of the boys war was talked about as sort of a valiant sport. Some of them said they would not miss it for anything. What would Mother say?

"Is there any question you'd like to ask me? I'm here to answer it if I can."

Millard cleared his throat. He smoothed his hair.

"My Mother would be the biggest problem."

"Why so?"

"Oh, I have a feeling."

"She'd be proud of you. That's only mother nature to hate to see her boys leave home. Mothers cry when their boys go off to college, too, and I've seen some cry when their boys get married. My mother cried once when I went north on a hunting trip. Ha! She was afraid I might get hurt, but say, she was plenty proud of her boy when I came home with an elk and had my picture in the paper."

But the officer did not understand and Millard could not explain. How could he tell him that his mother had a conscience against fighting, that her Bible said, "Thou shalt not kill," and he was a part of her? But he might never have to fight or kill. The war might be over before he got that far. Some of the boys even hoped they'd get a chance to fight.

"Could I have my money sent in my mother's name?"

"Absolutely. She could get forty a month. Do you have a life insurance policy?"

"No, sir."

"You'd take one then. That would make her feel satisfied."

Millard shuddered. He'd heard that expression before. He

181

doubted very much if that would play any part in her being satisfied.

"Think how thrilled your mother would be to get a picture of you in uniform, say from Texas or wherever you'd be stationed, and a necklace or a pillow top with 'Mother' on it, or some rare perfume or a vase. I know how mothers exclaim about those things. It gives them something to look forward to. You always have a chance to work up in the Army. If you're the honest, clean boy I think you are, you've got the chance of your life, Millard. Enlist now and help us. We're bound to conquer. Someone has to whip the devils, and it'll take brave, strong young men just like you. It's exactly what your mother really and honestly down in her heart expects of you. I know women pretty well. I hear mothers every day say, 'If I had ten sons I'd give them all to help make and keep our nation free for democracy.' You don't want to be called yellow or a slacker or wait until you're drafted. The manly thing is to enlist. That's the true spirit of democracy. This is the war to end all wars."

Millard thought of little Glen, just old enough to begin reading about cats running after rats, and dogs running after balls. He should never need to read about war in the daily newspapers or know the harshness of anything. His little hand should never manipulate a gun or a bayonet. He hoped all his brothers would live in a world of peace. More than that, he wished — they would all find and keep that soul peace he did not have.

Millard's thoughts were in a turmoil. He could not understand himself. He had read books and magazines until he did not know what he believed. Slowly he printed his name. Grinstead, Don Millard, age 20.

He might as well tell her the first chance he had. Sunday morning Millard went to church. He would convince Mother he still had an interest in the things dear to her heart, that he respected her faith and Liticia's. He'd go along home with them and break the news to her gently. Surely she must be thinking this would be the likely thing he'd do. He was in the no-getting-out-of-it age and he could not claim any rights for exemption. His obligation was to go, so why not go before he was told to?

The steaming dinner never smelled more delicious. Little Carrie was dear. Mother said she looked like him, but Millard could not see it. Everything she did and said was cute. She clung to Millard's neck and planted a loving kiss on his cheek.

He waited until he was ready to leave and Pop had gone to the barn.

"Do you know what I did the other day, Mother?" He looked down at her. How soft and creamy her plump cheeks were today.

She followed him to the door.

"What did you do?" She tilted her head a little with a premonitory air, and drew a long deep breath.

"Did you — enlist, Millard?"

"How did you guess it?"

She grabbed his one arm and laid her head against his shoulder.

"Didn't you want me to, Mother?"

Oh, was she going to take it like this? He had hoped so she wouldn't. "It was the only thing to do, Mother."

He could feel her breathing heavily. Was Mother crying? That he could hardly stand.

"I'll send you forty dollars a month, Mother. You can do anything you want to with it. You can buy more strawberry plants or chickens or anything you want to."

"It's not the money I want, Millard."

She lifted her head and leaned hard against the door casing. There were tears in her brown eyes, and her cheeks were flushed.

"What — then?"

"You've known me so long — and don't know — what it is I want more than anything else in all the world?" The agony of her soul was written on her dear face.

"Oh, Mother." Why must she take it so hard?

She looked into his face beseechingly.

"I'm doing this for your sake," he said softly.

"No," she cried, "I don't want you to. I don't want any of my children to fight for my sake. I want them to love and be ready to suffer not for my sake but for Christ's and the Gospel's. Millard, you do not know what all you'll have to take part in and — and you may never come back."

"Mother!"

"You don't know anything about war. You were a baby during the other one. There's no victory without deaths."

"But I may never get out of the states, Mother. At the rate they can kill now, the end may come before we know it."

"Maybe so, but I doubt it. You remember, Millard, what you

asked me out there on the walk the day you were digging the post-holes?"

Yes, he remembered. He remembered too well all that happened that day and the days previous. He remembered how startled she had looked at him when he said it. He meant it then. And he still meant it.

"Yes."

"I've kept my promise."

"Thank you."

"You still want to be saved before —"

"Yes, of course."

"You have no conviction you ought to get right with God before you go?"

"I can't now. Mother, don't worry about me. I'm not going to leave yet."

"Then can't you change your mind, Millard? Oh, please think this over seriously, won't you? I never dreamed when you were little I was raising a boy to become a soldier to take up arms."

"Someone must fight, Mother. Do not grieve. I am no better than anyone else's son."

"You're not? My child, you are to me. This sounds absurd, I know. But I think I've prayed more for you than a lot of mothers have for their sons. You have grandparents who are interested in you, and this would disappoint Uncle Levi if he knew. I would gladly see you go into Civilian Public Service Camp. I want all my boys to serve the government and the nation in anything that's Scriptural."

"Well, Mother, I know you're right, even though I can't see everything the way you do. The way I look at it, it's my duty to go into the Army. I have no conviction against it. I don't like to disappoint you, but I'd have no reason to give for not going. Every boy who asks to go into the C.P.S. Camp has to have a genuine reason to give for not going and live up to it."

After Millard left Myra went to the bedroom and closed the door softly.

"We've failed," she cried, "dear God. I don't want to excuse my part of the blame, but send him through real conviction so that he will be saved before — he — Oh, don't let him die."

Her eyes were red when Jeth came in.

"What's wrong, Myra?"

"Millard enlisted."

"He did? How soon will he leave?"

"I forgot to ask him."

"You mustn't feel bad, Myra."

"I can't help it."

"It's just one of those things, an' we can't help it."

"Jeth," she said, looking into his face earnestly, "don't you think together — we might have been able to?"

Chapter 28

SIMMERING in the heat, Millard walked toward home. He had a pain in his eye sockets, and sometimes he seemed almost blind. He wanted to cry like a child. But he didn't know about what to cry. He could not understand himself. He picked up a blade of grass and chewed on it. He straightened his shoulders. He must quit this foolishness and face facts as they were, like a man of his age. Leaving home wasn't so bad. Joining the army was going to be a glorious adventure. He'd be ashamed to have anyone know he was so ridiculous. What absurd thoughts. He would get home before the folks returned from church and take one last mental picture of the farm. Did the other fellows feel this way? He doubted it.

At the wooden bridge over Lone Creek he stopped to look at the sparkling water as it tumbled and laughed over the stones. Nature was not nervous or tense. He crossed the bridge and went down over the grassy bank to take a drink. It was pure and refreshing. He felt a wild craving for something satisfying. His soul reached out to something intangible — unattainable, unexplainable.

Ahead he saw a car beside the road under an oak tree. Too bad to have tire trouble on a hot Sunday morning. Maybe he could help the man. He could wash when he got home.

He caught his breath in astonishment.

Oh, powerful remembrance. Must he see her face before he left? Beside the man stood Melodie Ann Brooks. This was not the way her family usually took to go to church. She did not recognize him until he removed his cap. Her mouth opened with surprise.

"Why, Millard, I did not know you. Daddy, this is Liticia Grinstead's brother. This is my father, Millard."

Of course she didn't know him. Millard wasn't certain he knew himself today. What fate had caused this incident that the tender sweet influence of herself would follow him the more now? He had been trying to forget. Her eyes met his, tormenting his restless soul. All his unrighteousness seemed bared to her whenever he stood in her presence.

"You'll be late for church, won't you?" he asked, trying to compose himself. Sweat broke out from every pore.

"I guess we will now," Mr. Brooks said. "It never rains but that it pours, but we've all got to take rain sometimes." He chuckled.

What did Mr. Brooks mean?

The girl hastened to explain.

"Aunt Hattie had a stroke this morning, and we took Mother over there." She motioned east.

Who was her Aunt Hattie? It mattered not. Nothing relative to her was to matter.

"I thought you didn't live down this way," Millard remarked feebly.

Why let her know he ever thought about where she lived? He must go on.

"I'd be glad to help you, Mr. Brooks, if I can," suggested Millard, not certain whether he meant it or not. He must go on.

"I think I've about got it now. Thanks."

"I'll be on my way, then," Millard said slowly, "and good-by, Melodie Ann. Tonight I'm leaving for an army base in South Carolina."

"Oh, I hadn't known!"

Was there a note of disappointment in her voice? It sounded like a child being disappointed because of an unanswered prayer. Tormenting thoughts pressed in upon him. Millard felt senseless for a minute. He had told Mother he had no convictions and now — so near the time to leave must he be pricked again? Why did she make him feel so uncertain of himself? Why was she so righteous, so Christlike? Didn't she know he was going to help fight for her safety, and her future security? Didn't she know he was among the first in the eyes of America? The note of disappointment was the same as Mother had in her voice. Towering imaginations towered higher and higher.

"This evening, Millard?" she echoed quietly. She stared at him with widened blue eyes. "The twentieth of August? Well, good-by then — and God be with you." She held out her hand.

He walked the remainder of the distance home as in a trance, wiping the perspiration from his forehead, unbuttoning and buttoning his suit — not knowing what he was doing — and hardly thinking. Not until he reached the garden gate did he take himself in hand. He walked through the garden and looked at all the vegetables. Mother wanted more strawberry plants. She must get some. Mother should get whatever she wanted. He stopped before the bed of beautiful gladioli. He rubbed their velvety petals between his fingers. He walked through the barn and out to the chicken house. He picked up an egg and looked at it. He used to like eggs soft-boiled when he was little, dipping Mother's home-made bread in that salty goodness. Millard hurried past the woodhouse, on into the kitchen. One of Carrie's little sandals lay on the floor. He picked it up and looked at it. Tiny beside his big ones! One of Mother's aprons hung on a nail beside the pantry door. He touched it. There were Pop's rubber boots in a box under the sink. His feet were as big as Pop's now. Would the boots last until he got back?

He went upstairs and looked at the beds. Homer Jo and Richard slept together in this one; Derwood and Glen in this one. Liticia slept in the other room when she was home. That was not often any more. Beside her dresser was a little printed clipping fastened with a pin to the wall. Millard stepped close to read it. "A friend is one who likes your success, but your failures endear you to him the more."

He read it the second time. He stood at the window and looked down the road. The car was gone. Would she be that kind of friend? Vain thought. They were not friends at all. They were scarcely acquainted.

He went down and walked through the house again. Next Sunday he would be in South Carolina. He looked at the bed where Mother knelt to say her prayers—prayers for him. The faded rug on which she knelt was a worn braided rug.

He felt hot.

Was he feverish?

He got a drink.

He'd sit on the porch steps and wait for his family to come home. The panting dog sat beside him. Millard looked at his recently purchased watch. It was inexpensive but would serve the purpose. He cleaned his finger nails.

A cloud of dust—yes, they were coming.

Mother looked long at his face and mentioned nothing about this being his last Sunday home. His younger brothers gazed at Millard, half shyly but admiringly. Liticia was unusually quiet. Several times she seemed on the verge of telling him something, then walked away.

Mother scarcely ate any dinner. Millard hoped she wouldn't do that after he left. Pop watched her and tried to talk and act pleasant. In this way Pop would be good to Mother. Millard could be confident of that, for he had never known Pop to mistreat her. There were thousands upon thousands of husbands far worse than Pop. Some of the fellows had parents who didn't live together, and they had to go one place to say good-by to one, and to another place to say good-by to the other. Pop had a few shortcomings, but he was not mean to Mother.

"You'll write every week Millard," said his mother.

"I'll try to."

"I fixed up a box for you. A few things to nibble at on the train."

"We'll take you in," Pop said looking at Mother when he said it. Once more Pop endeared himself to Millard. He didn't say it as though he were glad to get rid of him, but to please Mother.

The hour came. Parting was the worst part of leaving. It was worse than the separation would be. All there was to say had been said.

"Millard," Liticia drew him aside.

"I want to tell you before you leave that Marlin will be leaving soon too." She blushed a peach pink.

"Marlin? Marlin who?"

"Marlin Brooks. You know, don't you? Melodie Ann's brother?"

"I don't know him very well. Where's he going, do you know?"

"He's going to a C.P.S. camp."

"Oh!"

"I thought you might like to know we'll be writing to each other."

"What? You mean—you mean you're friends like that?"

"Well—sure. Isn't that all right?"

"I—suppose—it's very wonderful." He looked away.

"It would be nice if you and he were going off together."

"Don't say such a foolish thing, Ticia, or did you mean you wished he was going with me to Fort Jackson?"

"That's not what I meant," she whispered softly.

Oh, where was the glory, or splendor, or honor of being one of those first in the eyes of America, if in Liticia's eyes her friend Marlin Brooks had made a better choice! Who was he trying to please! Couldn't they all see he was going for their sakes! Were they all blind to his love!

*   *   *   *   *

Men, Women, and children of all ages and classes were milling around the railroad station. Fellows and girls were walking arm in arm laughing and talking. Several girls were tripping around collecting soldier's autographs. Grief-stricken mothers were crying softly trying desperately to smile in spite of their tears. Some of the boys were prancing back and forth, shouting like impatient children; some were munching candy; some just stood with their loved ones, waiting. Women were fanning. Men were smoking. Everyone felt sticky. The train was an hour late.

"Let's sit in the car and wait," suggested Millard.

Mother and Liticia agreed, for they did not anticipate standing in the crowd for an hour, and little Carrie was getting sleepy. Pop and the boys got out and strolled around. Everyone seemed restless, impatient, anxious to be done with the suspense. Was this the first picture in the drama of war?

The three in the car talked about insignificant things—about the kind of dog a lady was carrying in her arms, the stillness of the air, and Millard's watch. All the time their hearts were burning within them with things of far more significance.

At last. Shouts rose high. Men grabbed their bags. There were kisses, good-byes, more tears, a few pitiful shrieks, and the throng jammed in one direction.

Millard smelled the fragrant shampoo on his mother's hair when he kissed her good-by.

"Don't cry, Mother." It was all he could say. Sudden tears were blinding his own eyes. He didn't realize it really would be so hard at the last. He'd been bracing himself all day, all week.

He felt awful.

He couldn't stand to see her cry.

He'd have an infinite remembrance of it. She did not scream in high notes like some women, but sobbed softly, shaking her head sorrowfully.

"Don't forget, Millard," she whispered, "every night—I'll keep—that promise."

He pressed her plump hand in answer.

"Ticia, good-by. Write to me sometimes. Tell me—the things you think I'd like to know. Be good now."

She could not speak. Every word, every letter lodged in her throat.

He must go or he'd be the last one on. "Good-by, Pop, and all of you. Take good care of yourselves. I'm sorry Carrie fell asleep."

"It's just as well—Millard," cried Mother. "She doesn't understand."

"When you write to Orpha tell her I'm sorry I couldn't tell her good-by. Boys, be good to Mother and help Pop."

He hurried away.

"Come on, D.M.," yelled someone at the opposite end of the coach. "Back here's a seat." It was nosey- faced Crow. He'd had a little to drink. In his hand he held several cheap romance magazines. After the train started he handed one to Millard.

"Here, boy, if you won't smoke, try one of these."

They hadn't gone far until one of the boys pulled out a mouth harp and started playing the "Missouri Waltz." Soon some of the others joined him in chanting. One large soldier, who looked older than the rest, hummed a beautiful deep-throated bass accompaniment.

Chapter 29

"MOTHER, have you heard from Millard yet?"

"Yes, we got a letter yesterday. It's up there on the shelf beside the clock."

Liticia curled up on the end of the davenport to read.

"Dear folks at home,

Well, how are you all? Fine, I hope. I think about you every day.

Our trip was pleasant all the way. Fort Jackson is a big place. It covers 54,000 acres, also 200,000 acres of woods where we take part of our training. We are kept busy, so no one has a chance to get homesick. We are in training every day. We get up at 5:45, eat breakfast at 6:00, make our beds and start out at 7:30. We have indoor and outdoor classes and lectures, and after supper we can go to various recreation centers.

There are swimming pools, lakes where we can go fishing, and hobby shops where we can make things. Then there are ball diamonds, libraries, snack shops, theaters, and bowling alleys. We can go to town twice a week, just so we get to bed before 11:00 p.m. I seldom stay up that late. This is quite an experience for one like me who has never been away before. We are furnished with all kinds of reading materials and plenty of music. I want to learn to do some fancy diving and join the life-saving class.

After the first six weeks of basic training with combat instructions those who pass certain tests will be sent some other place to training schools for leadership. We are being watched all the time by combat-tested officers.

I surely can't complain about the meals, and I'm certain I'm not losing weight. We get to meet some generals sometimes, and they really do praise us. I took out a $1,000 life insurance policy. If I do have to go overseas I'll take out more.

Did you all go to church on Sunday? We have a chapel here. The chaplain told us Sunday we were all born to struggle on this earth and there is no perfect place but heaven, so we must all laugh as we learn to fight. Once a week they give us a band concert.

Don't forget to write to me. Tell me what you all are doing. Mother, I enjoyed the good things you put in the box. The fellow beside me said he never tasted such a good home-made cookie. I'll write again before too long. Tell Liticia to write to me. Did Marlin leave yet? Love from Millard."

* * * * *

Often in the evenings after supper Millard walked out along the river path. He had a love of nature in his heart, and in his finger tips a caress for flower petals. Somehow his spirit within revolted against the harshness of his training. Their realistic combat maneuvers, carbine drills, and closing-in practices on hidden machine guns all seemed too beast-like for real action. He hoped he'd never have to fight. He was not weak in body or sissy, but Millard had a gentle soul; he was a lover of peace and beauty and books.

The corner drugstore was a favorite place for the boys. One could buy anything there from postage stamps and popcorn to champagnes and mixed drinks. Half a dozen feminine beauties with laughter in their eyes and smartness in their walk waited on tables. The soldiers liked to touch them as they passed and hear them say a cute word or two. These girls were everybody's darlings and nobody's sweethearts.

One evening Millard went into the drugstore to buy some stamps and a tablet. He saw a soft-backed notebook, and he bought it for a diary. The juke box was playing some light music, the place was blue with smoke, and someone had evidently told a prize joke, for everyone was laughing hilariously. He took the notebook and started down the street and walked out toward the park. He found an empty bench and sat down. A dozen or more youngsters were playing in the wading pool. He watched them for sometime, pencil in hand. The voices and laughter of the children splashing and tumbling in the water was better music than that in the corner drugstore. He must write, for dusk was creeping around fast, and one by one the dripping youngsters were being called out of the pool.

A diary had never appealed to Millard before, but a fellow had to give vent to his feelings some way. He'd hide it in his duffel bag.

He might throw it away, too. Some of the other fellows started diaries and let each other read them. He wasn't going to pass his around. He began to write:

"A month since I left home, thirty days and thirty nights of clock work. We're a big human machine. Must take a lot of brains to work it all out. Seems senseless in a way, these make-believe massacres. Personally I think it's hard to imagine the enemy and get fired up. How could a fellow kill without being mad—without cursing? I wonder."

Millard closed the notebook and sat in deep thought. A soldier came strolling along with one arm around a little blond. He had seen the same soldier the night before with a dark-haired girl. Was Millard the only boy who didn't have a girl friend? Some of the fellows wrote to two or three and were constantly watching for another. Slowly Millard went back to his headquarters. He pulled open his duffel bag. Opening the notebook once more he jotted down two lines.

"There's a pretty girl I can't forget;
When I get back home, I'll win her yet."

* * * * *

"Dear Millard,

It's nice of you to write and tell us about yourself and what it's like where you are. I'm working now for the Elmer Felter family. They have three small children, and I get more money here. I was home Sunday and everyone is well. Of course, I know Mother writes everything to you. Marlin is in Belton, Montana, now. I haven't heard from him yet. It's absolutely nothing but friendship between us, and I don't know yet how often we'll write to each other. I suppose his experiences will be quite different from yours.

The lightening struck Schultz's milkhouse Monday night and caused considerable damage. Glen seems to like school all right, but Homer Jo can hardly wait till he's through. He is talking already about being a soldier like you. Melodie Ann's Aunt Hattie was buried Sunday afternoon. Pop still wants to leave the farm and do carpenter work again. I can't think of any more news this time. May God bless and keep you. Lovingly, Liticia."

* * * * *

"Dear Liticia,

Well, I'm way down south where the cotton grows, camping in the woods, eating and sleeping outside. It seems like ages already

194

since I left home. I wonder how Marlin is getting along in Montana. Most of the fellows here make some pretty bad remarks about the C.O.'s, but one boy, Luther Bradley, told me he wishes now he'd taken that position himself, but his minister didn't give him any encouragement. Three Gideons were here Sunday and handed out Testaments to all who wanted them. I took one. I left my Bible at home. I didn't want to ruin it and I have enough to lug around anyway. These are a nice size to fit into our shirt pockets. Ticia, how's Mother taking everything? Is she reconciled to me being where I am now? Best wishes. Your brother, Millard."

* * * * *

"Dear folks at Home,

Just a few lines to let you know I'm well and I hope all of you are too. I had a letter from Liticia last week. I tried to write several times before but was just too tired. It's ten weeks now since I left home. Maneuvers ended last night, and we will be loading up and moving to Fort Knox tomorrow. Part of the company will go by train and the rest by truck. I will operate the net control station which is in the captain's car. My pay was raised ten dollars a month.

Well, how are you all anyway? How is little Carrie? Don't let her forget me. It is real warm down here and dry. We always have good meals. Thanks for your letters, Mother. It's nice to hear from you every week. Tell everybody hello for me. A lot of the boys are talking about furloughs already. You tell Homer Jo to get it out of his head to join the army. We're apt to be on the move a lot from now on. We were in Texas for a while. Pop, if you ever see Fred Boetcher or William Schultz or Paul Auckers tell them hello for me. How's everything going for you on the farm? Mother, I told you you should spend what you want to out of the money I send home. If you want to know it, I'd rather be working on a farm than down here on maneuvers. I really am tired when evening comes. Some of the boys went in to Columbia tonight, but I was too tired to think of it. With love to all. From Millard."

* * * * *

"Diary:

I never was so tired. More rifle practice, swamp wading, and bridge building. God help this war to be over before Homer Jo is old enough to go. I doubt if I'm making a very good soldier. It's awful to be lonesome in a crowd this size. There's a sweet charming girl

195

named Melodie Ann. Someday I might woo her. I will if I can."

*   *   *   *   *

A puzzling expression crossed Millard's face as he looked at the letter. He sat on the edge of his cot and tore it open.

"Dear Millard,

A few weeks ago I had a letter from your mother telling me you were in the army stationed way down south somewhere. I was surprised and pretty much upset about it for a while; then I decided to commit you to the Lord. If Uncle Levi would have been permitted to live, he might have been a big help to you in making decisions. I've never been able to figure out why you were not baptized and taken into the church."

Millard's hands trembled. He cleared his throat.

"Since Uncle Levi is gone, let me know if I can be of any help to you spiritually or otherwise. It would make me very happy to know I could be a little help to one he thought so much of. Enclosed is a bill to buy some stamps or socks or even candy, if you are hungry for some. Write to me sometime, if you find a chance. God be near you all the way through. Sincerely, Aunt Christina."

Millard felt hot, then cold. Fond memories to the past made him feel like seeking some secluded spot where he could lie down and relax. The five dollar bill was inside a little printed tract. On the outside was a picture of Christ's bleeding, nail-pierced hand hanging above the dark world. Millard's heart thumped as he read:

"Christ loved and prayed for His enemies. Do you?" Millard bit his teeth together hard.

"He rejoiced though He had nowhere to lay His head. Do you?

He went among the poor and lowly to lead them to God. Do you?

Christ rejoiced, though all forsook Him and fled. Do you?

He denied Himself comfort and ease that others might find peace to their troubled souls. Do you?"

"Yes," said Millard to himself, "that's exactly what I'm doing now. I'm denying myself comforts, and — no — no, I'm wrong. I'm not here to help others find peace to their souls. I'm here to learn how to kill them before they have a chance to find peace. I'm here to help send our enemies to hell quick that we might live in peace and comfort." He read on.

"When Christ met a person or company of persons He talked to them of eternal things. Do you?"

"Oh, this is for preachers," thought Millard.

"He said an account must be given of every idle word that men shall speak and never engage in foolish talking or jesting. Do you?"

"Christ was brought as a lamb to the slaughter and He opened not His mouth but patiently endured mocking and shame. Do you?

Christ was separate from sinners. Are you?"

"No, of course not. I'm a sinner myself." Millard shifted.

"Christ had such love for those who crucified Him that He prayed, 'Father forgive them; for they know not what they do.' Have you such love?"

Millard read on.

"For whosoever will save his life shall lose it; but whosoever will lose his life for My sake, the same shall save it. For what is a man advantaged, if he gain the whole world, and lose himself, or be cast away? For whosoever shall be ashamed of me and of my words, of him shall the Son of man be ashamed, when He shall come in His own glory, and in His Father's, and of the holy angels. Read Luke 9:23-26."

Millard sat on the cot with his head in his one hand, the tract in the other.

"What are you reading, D.M.?" Someone grabbed the paper out of his hand. "Great ———, Where'd you get hold of this?"

"My aunt sent it to me. Don't tear it, Hal. She's a good woman. She means it all right. Give it back."

"Well, doesn't she know Christianity's out of business during war?"

* * * * *

"Do you hear from Millard?" Melodie Ann tried to ask without showing much interest.

"The folks or I hear from him every week. You hear from Marlin, don't you?"

"Yes, don't you?"

"I've had three letters. When is Marlin's birthday, Melodie Ann?"

"The tenth of March. Why?"

"Oh, I just wondered. I don't want to forget to send Millard a birthday greeting. I was thinking of his and I just wondered about Marlin's."

"When's Millard's?"

"The fourteenth of December."

"Oh. Does he really like it in the army?"

"Melodie Ann, I don't know for sure. How could he?"

"I don't know. I just wondered."

* * * * *

Diary:

"Nothing would suit me better than to hear this was over. I dreamed last night I was talking with Uncle Levi and that then we went to church together. The dream was too short. I hate this play killing, but what can I do now?"

* * * * *

"Dear folks at home,

Fort Knox is full and running over. There were twenty-one trainloads of soldiers, thirty-five cars in each train, and fifteen hundred vehicles in our division and another division is also here. I will be going to school again soon, I believe in New Jersey, for more radio technician work. I got another raise. The trip through Tennessee was beautiful. Possibly I will get a furlough about Christmas or New Year. They tell us they're going to give us as good a Thanksgiving dinner as we could ever hope to get at home. I'm always glad for your letters, but I'm sorry to hear Pop hurt his hand. I surely hope it won't be long in healing. If I could, I'd gladly do his work for him. I was much surprised to get a letter from Aunt Christina. How is Carrie doing? Do you think she remembers me?

With love and best wishes to you all, Millard."

* * * * *

"Dear folks at home — Mother and Pop and all the rest,

Hello to everyone. We are only seventy miles from New York City now. For a while I couldn't tell you where I was, I was pretty sick for several days and couldn't work. One evening on the street in Trenton I passed two C.O. boys. I'm pretty sure of it, because I overheard them talking. I wanted to stop and have a conversation with them, but I didn't quite have the nerve. You asked me what we had for Thanksgiving dinner. Well, turkey and dressing, gravy, sweet potatoes, olives, a salad, coffee, ice cream, and pie. Then they passed out chewing gum, candy bars, and cigarettes. I traded my cigarettes for candy. Thanks, Mother, for the box of cookies you sent me. They were very good. Some were broken, but the crumbs were good anyway. The boys in my billet all had to have some. I must go to bed.

Love, Millard."

Then a telegram came one evening from Fort Dix, New Jersey. "Meet the 7:30 A.M. train Wed. Millard."

Everyone in the Grinstead family except Pop was excited. Pop never got excited (except once). Richard and Derwood helped their mother straighten up the house, and Pop promised to bring some ice along home from town so they could have homemade ice cream. The boys promised to crank it. Myra phoned Liticia and told her the good news.

"Don't you think Mrs. Felter could let you off a day or at least part of a day? Ask her. I don't know how long he'll be at home. — Oh, she said you could? Well, good. We'll stop by, then, on our way home from the train depot."

✱ ✱ ✱ ✱ ✱

As the train neared Granger, Millard felt trembly, excited. Oh, if he were only going home to stay, to take off his suit and put on civilian clothes again. But he would not dare breathe such a thought to anyone. He had a strange yearning that made his blood restless. He must brace up and hide such feeling. He should be proud he was a soldier in the United States Army. He would be, for the United States Army had accomplished great things in the past century. He leaned forward and looked out the window. In the early morning light he saw them standing beside the depot, and on Mother's face he caught a glimpse of eager anticipation.

Chapter 30

THEY hadn't changed much in three months time, only to be the dearer. Mother looked more motherly, little Carrie smarter. Pop looked well and a wee bit more gray. The boys smiled with silent expressions of excitement and admiration.

"Hello, everybody, hello! Hello!"

"You look well, Millard," Mother announced, pleased and smiling.

"I am. I've never felt better in my life."

"I'll carry your bag," offered Homer Jo. "The car is right over here." He led the way.

Liticia was watching at Felter's door, ready to dash out. She saw them coming.

"Thanks for letting me off, Mrs. Felter," she called as she opened the door. "I'll be back tonight before too late. Let the ironing go. I'll do it tomorrow."

"All right."

"Millard."

"Hi, Ticia."

She crowded in beside him. The car was full.

Pop let the boys off at the corner. If they hurried they wouldn't be late for school, and if they were, the teacher would excuse them. Soldier brothers did not get to come home every day. Teachers throughout the country counted with a tinge of pride the boys they'd had a part in helping become good American citizens and good soldiers or sailors. Miss Yale liked the Grinstead children.

"Wasn't that nice of Mrs. Felter to let me come home today, Millard?"

"It certainly was."

"I saw Fred Boetcher yesterday," Pop said over his shoulder.

"You did? How's he?"

"He's all right. He asked me how long you were gonna be home an' I said I didn't know."

"How long can you stay, Millard?" inquired Liticia.

"I've got to be back by a week from Monday."

"Fred wants ter see you, Millard," Pop said.

"He does?"

"He's got a job fer you."

"A job? Doesn't he know I've got to go back?"

"I mean fer while you're here. See?"

Yes, Millard saw. He had dreamed of coming home and helping Pop with his work. He had fully intended to show Pop he had no hard feelings toward him. Regardless of any hurt feelings in past years, Millard was going to consider them all as never having been hurt, and the offender as never having offended. This now could mean but one thing; that he was more welcome to work away from home that at home. He was going to tell Mother to make him a bed on the floor and he was going to offer to pay room and board before the day was night. Pop couldn't wait until they got home? He had to tell him with his back toward him?

Millard swallowed twice, three times. Insulting thoughts tormented him.

"I'll call him up when we get home," he heard himself say.

"Well," Mother said objectingly, "we want you with us while you're here."

There seemed to be a difference of opinion. Pop coughed with resentment.

"Well, I thought maybe you'd be wantin' some extra cash fer a pair of shoes or somethin'," he ventured.

"That's right, Pop," answered Millard absently, at the same time wondering why he had come home at all. "I do want to get a new pair of dress shoes before I go back."

Millard could see Mother was hurt worse than he was.

"Come back here, Carrie, and sit on my lap." He held out his arms to her. He must hide his feelings. Mother mustn't know how disappointed he was. Why hadn't he thought about the probability of his being in the way? It surely must be more than the cost of the food he'd consume in eight days. Perhaps Pop thought he knew something he wasn't to know. Well, if he did he never passed it on.

"You had to get up early, didn't you, Carrie? You know your brother, don't you?" He pinched her cool cheek.

She smiled yes.

"I'm going to buy or borrow somebody's camera and take your picture." He held her close to him. "Will you smile for me when I take it?"

She smiled. She laid her head against his shoulder bashfully.

"Ticia's picture, too?" she peeked up into his face.

"Yes, I want to take Ticia's picture, too, and Mother's and Pop's and everybody's."

"Everybody's?"

"I mean in our family. So I can remember how you all look."

"Why?"

"I might not get back again for a long time." He swallowed hard.

"How long?"

"I don't know, Carrie. Nobody knows."

"Nobody?"

"Here we are already. Who lives here?" Millard pointed to the house.

"I do an'—an'—us, an'—we're gonna have ice cream." Millard squeezed dear chubby little Carrie and chuckled close to her ear. He must hide his disappointment. All the way home he had imagined eating Mother's cooking for eight blessed days. He was hungry for her rolls, her corn bread, her potato soup. Mrs. Boetcher was a good cook, but not so good as Mother.

"Did you bring the ice home, Jeth?"

"That's right, Myra. I fergot it. I'll go back an' get it."

"Mother, you aren't making ice cream just because I came home, are you?"

"Well, why not? Didn't you just tell Carrie you might not get back for a long time? Don't you like ice cream any more?"

"Oh, of course, but you mustn't go to all that extra trouble and expense." He fumbled in his pocket.

"Here, Pop, let me pay for the ice."

But Pop shook his head. "Keep it. I guess we can afford to do it onct," and a faint smile played around his lips.

The house inside looked just as he remembered it. Nothing new, nothing placed differently. The freshly scrubbed pattern in the kitchen linoleum came up to meet him in a friendly manner. He put his duffel bag in the corner of the dining room. He hung up his coat and cap. The house had that singular familiar home smell. He would fill his lungs with the sweetness of it while he could.

Mother had the pancake batter mixed. The table was set for three.

"Pop and the boys are early. You see the boys wanted to go along in to meet you," Mother hurried to explain. "That's why there's a stack of dirty dishes. Liticia, did you eat?"

"Yes, I had breakfast. Mother, you and Millard and Carrie sit down. I'll make the pancakes and fry the eggs. Why didn't Pop wait and eat with you, too?"

"He said he gets a headache to wait, he said. Maybe you're hungry for something else, Millard. Would you rather have something else besides pancakes?" She took his arm.

"Mother, anything suits me. I'd be satisfied with a cup of tea if that's all you had. The pancakes we get don't taste like yours. Oh, you want up on my lap again? Carrie, I believe your hair grew while I was away." He stroked her little head. "By the way, I've got something for you in my bag."

"What?"

"Shall we get it while Sister makes the pancakes?"

He carried her to the dining room. Her eyes widened as he opened his bag and drew out a package.

"You open it."

"Oh," she exclaimed with childish glee.

"Do you like it?"

"Y-e-s."

"Go show Mother. Tell her it came from New Jersey."

"A doll. Isn't that nice, Carrie? You will like to play with it. Did you tell Millard thanks?"

"Thanks."

"You're welcome. Mother, I brought you and Liticia each a handkerchief."

"Millard, you shouldn't have done this."

"And here's a box of candy, too. It isn't much, but I wanted to bring you something."

"Isn't much? Why, Millard? Why did you do this?"

"I wanted to. Most of the boys have someone — a — this is to tell you how I appreciate your letters."

"Will you have a cup of coffee, Millard?"

203

"Please."

Mother bowed her head. Millard bowed his. He had enjoyed many a meal, many a beautiful sight, but he would enjoy but one Mother. There was something so tender, so mysterious about her silent prayer. Somehow it took all the fearful misgivings out of his restless mind.

"How's Marlin getting along?" He could wait no longer to ask her.

"All right. Melodie Ann heard from him since I did. He's due a furlough, too, any time." Liticia drew up a chair. "Here's the syrup, Millard. Marlin said he signed up to work in a hospital unit."

"What's that?"

"Well, instead of doing soil conservation work in a C.P.S. camp, he will be an attendant in a mental hospital, because he'd rather work with human beings. It's different from soil conservation or forestry or road building, you know, dealing with people."

"You say a mental hospital?"

"Yes."

"How much would he get?"

"Fifteen dollars, I believe. He gets only five now."

"A month?"

"Why, certainly. Not a day. I wonder if there might be a chance of you seeing him while you're home. I wish you could. Melodie Ann said Sunday he might bring another young man along home with him when he comes."

Millard looked up sharply.

"What for?" He had a strange, tense feeling. He had a deep craving to know something. It nipped his appetite. He took a sip of coffee. His throat felt tight.

"Just for friendship's sake, I guess," she answered.

Millard wouldn't mind talking with Marlin Brooks who was corresponding with his sister. He would like to have conversation at length with him about his conscientious scruples against fighting, but—he was not particularly interested in meeting the young man who might be coming along for friendship's sake.

He might have known. What else could he expect? It was ridiculous that he should harbor such envious thoughts. Vanity of vanities. Why had he ever seen her face?

"Mother, your breakfast is very good."

"Tell us about yourself, Millard."

"What shall I tell?"

"Everything. Is it like you thought it would be?"

"Well, no, it isn't exactly. But Mother, I didn't come home to talk about that. I came home to get away from it for awhile. Tell me all about yourself."

He didn't want to tell her the harshness of maneuvers in simulated combat and machine gun practice. He didn't want to tell her about wading swamps up to his knees, and about pistol drills. He didn't want to tell her about the movies he'd attended, nor the loose vile stories he'd heard and how hard it was to keep his mind on better things. How could he explain to her his mental and soul struggles and his awful loneliness on off-duty hours?

"Have you been getting yourself anything with the money I sent home?"

"Millard, that's your money. You'll be needing it when you get home. You might want to buy some clothes or maybe a car. I'm putting it away for you. I have Pop to look after me."

"And you're getting along all right?"

"We have enough. We get along, Millard; unless it's a case of necessity I'm not going to spend that money you send home. Someday you'll be wanting a little home of your own."

He laughed a crippled, forced laugh.

"Pop still talks about getting off the farm, but Grandfather wants him to stay here. Did you ever hear from them?"

"I had two letters from Grandmother and one from Aunt Christina."

"You did?"

"I had one from Bro. Ambers, too."

"Oh. A nice letter?" "Well, yes, it was. He said he thought he didn't do his duty by me and if I came home he wanted to have a talk with me—but—"

"But what, Millard? I'll ask Pop if we can't have them here for dinner Sunday."

Millard got up and walked across the kitchen. "Don't, Mother. I'll wipe the dishes for you, Liticia. Tell me what you know about Orpha."

"She certainly doesn't write much, does she Mother?"

"No. She tells us so little about herself. As far as we know they still live at Whitville. She has never been home since they moved. Millard, you'll never neglect writing to us like that, will you?"

"I'll write whenever I can."

"You'll promise me that?"

"Yes, Mother, I promise."

Liticia, Mother, and Millard talked all afternoon. Mother prepared the ice cream and Richard and Derwood froze it when they got home from school. Millard wanted to do it, but Mother said the boys wanted to,and she wanted to keep him near her while she had the chance. After supper Fred Boetcher was coming over after him. Millard had called Fred and the arrangements were made. Glad as she would have been to do so, Mother would not need to get out the comforters to make a floor bed. Not even once. He'd come home Sunday for dinner, but he'd slip a dollar under his plate to pay for it.

"Mr. Boetcher," Liticia asked, "could I ride along as far as Felter's?"

"Why certainly, certainly. Come right along. Are you working there?"

"Yes, sir."

"Well, Mr. Grinstead, I'm glad you suggested this. I'll get a little extra work done now that I was goin' to let go until spring. I just supposed when your boy came home you wouldn't let him out o' your sight. Looks mighty like he'd be goin' across before long."

Millard felt a poignant pain circle his heart. So it was Pop's suggestion! He drew Mother aside in the kitchen. She looked as if she were going to cry.

"Don't invite Bro. Ambers here on Sunday," he whispered.

Chapter 31

MYRA Grinstead spoke in low tones. "Brother Ambers, Millard came home Wednesday." "Is that so? I'm glad you told me. I'd like to see him. He wasn't here today, was he?"

"I didn't see him. He's working for Fred Boetcher."

"You mean he came home to stay?" "No, he's going back Friday." People were wanting to shake the pastor's hand. She must not talk long.

"I'd like to see him before he goes back."

"He said you wrote to him."

"Then he got my letter. I wondered. I feel an obligation toward your boy." Bro. Ambers' voice was serious. "I've failed to get next to him," he said softly. "I regret it ." His voice was almost a whisper.

She must move on. People standing near by might hear.

Brother Ambers, who usually understood and appreciated human problems and had helped hundreds of others, was unsuccessful with the Grinstead family. It bothered him.

But he had so many parishioners that he could not afford to let it trouble him greatly. It was difficult to help someone who wouldn't accept help. Hadn't he offered to help Jethro Grinstead? He wondered sometimes what going the second mile included. But he must make an effort to see this boy, Millard, and have a talk with him. Brother Ambers' sister had mentioned to him several times that Liticia Grinstead had requested Melodie Ann and Marlin both to pray for her brother. Once in a prayer meeting someone handed in Millard Grinstead's name as an unspoken request. If Brother Ambers remembered correctly, it had been his niece, Melodie Ann.

* * * * *

Every bit of snow had disappeared and the day was almost like spring. Millard wanted to go to church, but no, he would not. He wanted to see Melodie Ann, yet he wanted to forget her. No doubt Marlin and his friend would be there. He must dismiss that girl from his mind now and forever. He left Boetcher's house in time to get home about twelve thirty. He'd walk with shoulders erect like a well-trained soldier should, and think of nothing in particular. In his hand he carried a borrowed camera. He could not go back to camp without a few pictures. When the other boys pulled out snapshots of their families and showed them, it made his own loneliness more poignant. Seeing other's loved ones only increased his longing. He wanted something in his own pocket that was familiar, dear, near, near as his own blood. He'd take a picture of Mother to give him courage some day. He walked briskly past the spot in the road where he had hesitated one hot Sunday morning in August, talking to Melodie Ann and her father. It seemed years ago instead of months. He wouldn't think of it. He wouldn't. She'd be smiling at someone better, someone more righteous than he, someone more worthy. Millard looked straight ahead. He would not care. He dare not care. Who was he?

* * * * *

Mother's dinner as usual was delicious, but somehow Millard couldn't eat much. Neither could his mother. Her glances meant something.

They told him whole chapters of sweet, warm, caring words he tried to interpret. Pop and the boys and little Carrie ate heartily and talked freely. The baby of the family usually gave suggestions for conversation, and the boys all liked to hear her talk—tried to make her talk.

Leaving the family this time was going to be harder than leaving them had been the first time. This would be his last meal at home for a long time—hard telling how long. Fred Boetcher had prophesied that nothing but serious illness would prevent him from going over-seas now, and Millard had a feeling Fred was right.

He tried to absorb into his memory cute little things Carrie said, and the picture of Liticia's pretty clean-cut face, pink with the bloom of womanhood. She was a beauty. She was his sister. He was proud of her. The boys all looked healthy and bright. Pop was a strong handsome man. What an ideal happy family they ought to be!

Why weren't they? Millard wondered. He lingered on each face around the table. They had never had any serious disputes of which he knew. To his knowledge Pop had never really mistreated Mother. Pop loved her in his way. Homer Jo had been Pop's pet for years, but now not one of the children spoke to their father like Homer Jo did. Millard was surprised.

Millard pondered, and thought, and thought. The long standing problem Pop had over his tobacco—well, yes, of course, there was something around that whole situation that didn't conform to a standard of family perfection, and Pop did have other temptations, but why, why, couldn't they be an ideal happy family?

Millard tried to enjoy his pie. Mother knew he liked butterscotch pie, and she had made it especially for him. It was delicious—but the question was pressing on his mind—why couldn't they be one grand happy family with a mother like Mother was?

Oh, bitter, bare thought! Millard winced. He must be the reason for the unhappiness. He wished he knew why. He wished he knew what it was about him that made Pop ill at ease in his presence. Why did Pop always want him at any other place than home? Pop did not ask him any questions about army life like he thought perhaps he would. Of course, Homer Jo did—but didn't Pop have any interest in him? Hadn't his absence endeared him to his father?

Oh, to be welcome! What a wonderful, wonderful feeling that must give a boy to come home and be welcomed by both his father and mother, to be received with gladness by both, and have a personal interest shown him by both.

Would Pop treat Orpha like this, if she came home? Instinctively Millard's heart went out toward her. He pitied her if she felt like he did. Did she? Was there a reason why she wrote so seldom and had never come home? He had been away; perhaps he did not know everything. He must write to her. She had never been close to him like Liticia was, but if he hadn't promised to work four more days for Fred Boetcher, he'd look up the bus schedules and go to see her. Maybe she was disappointed or lonely, too. Perhaps together they could figure out what it was that kept their family from being happy. Millard looked again at each one seated around the table. Dear little Carrie should never know anything but joy and contentment. She was so sweet and young and innocent. Pop seemed to love her; at least he held her on his lap sometimes. He smiled at her often. The next time Millard came home he would spend at least one whole day with Orpha. She was his sister, too. He must get next to her. Maybe after he left, the rest of the family would be perfectly happy. Mother and Liticia made all the expressions of regret about his leaving. Pop didn' express himself one way or another. It was best he was going back; yes, best.

"Marlin won't get to come home for a month yet," Liticia said to Millard after dinner.

"Did you hear from him?" He looked down into her lovely face.

"I had a letter yesterday. The boy he wanted to bring home with him isn't going to come after all."

"He isn't?"

"No, he and his girl friend are going to attend her sister's wedding. I think I have it right. Anyway, there's to be a wedding, and he's going to that instead of coming here on his furlough."

Millard stared. Had he heard correctly? The boy had a girl friend. And he hadn't been in church after all? And he wasn't interested in Melodie Ann Brooks? Bewildering thoughts tormented him. He had been so determined to forget once and for all.

"I—understood you to say," he stammered, "he was coming along for friendship's sake."

"Oh, did I? Well, maybe I did. Why, what's wrong about that?"

"Nothing. Nothing. I guess—I misunderstood what you meant."

"Well, I surely didn't mean to leave the wrong impression, Millard. Did you think I meant he was coming along because he was interested in—in some girl around here?" She caught him by the arm.

"Well, I didn't know. I—I thought perhaps it was Marlin's sister."

"Melodie Ann isn't interested in anyone. Marlin gets almost provoked at her sometimes. She turns down every boy who asks her. She says she's never going to get married."

"Why?"

Liticia laughed. "Well, I don't know, Millard. Melodie Ann has high ideals. She is sometimes hard to understand, I think. She says that when the right one asks her she'll know him, but she's afraid he never will."

"I see." He cleared his throat nervously. "Afraid, you say?"

He walked to the corner table abruptly. He picked up the camera. "Now I want all of you to come outside with me. I want to take your picture. Carrie, get your doll. You said you would smile for me, didn't you? Come, all of you."

"Me, too?" asked Pop.

"Why, of course. Mother, you look all right. Leave your apron on. I like that one."

★ ★ ★ ★ ★

"Why, Millard, you're not eating." Mrs. Boetcher passed the meat platter. "Take more."

"No, thanks. I've eaten all I care for."

"But you've eaten scarcely anything. You are excited about leaving, aren't you, Millard?" she said sympathetically, more as a statement than a question.

Millard could not answer. He had tried to work hard the past week and dismiss everything but his work from his mind. It seemed he could not hold the thoughts back. They trickled in. Now the hour to leave was drawing near. Tearing away was going to hurt. He wished he had a pill he could swallow to deaden his finer senses a little.

"Fred, you answer the telephone."

He did.

"Someone wants you, Millard."

He took the receiver.

"Me? Hello. It is? When did you get home? You did? I'm afraid I can't Marlin. Thanks. I'll be leaving in about an hour. Yes. Well, I don't know; I wouldn't be surprised at that. How have you been getting along? You are? That's what Liticia told me. Yes. Yes. Well. I'd be glad to have a talk with you, too. No. Well, it was mighty nice of you to call me, Marlin, and good luck to you. What? When I get back we'll get better acquainted? Thanks. Thanks. Good-by. What? Yes, the folks are coming to take me in. Good-by."

Millard's heart pounded till his chest hurt. He gathered his things together and stood waiting at the door. "We'll get better acquainted—when you get back."

"Don't look so sober, Millard," Fred stepped close to him. "You must brace up and smile." He slapped him on the shoulder. "This is the noblest, grandest thing a young man can do, to leave home to fight for us who remain here. God'll see you through."

"He will?" asked Millard huskily. "How do you know?"

"He takes 'em all through who lay down their lives, I mean jobs an' homes or whatever, for a cause that's right—an' this can't be wrong. So long now, Millard, an' thanks for helpin' us out. I'll be

211

askin' your parents about you now and then. Cheer up, now; God's on our side, we all know that."

* * * * *

Millard held Carrie on his lap. It helped to hide his feelings. Mother wiped tears all the way to the depot. The boys watched Millard with wondering eyes. How important one must feel to be a soldier. Liticia sat tense, now and then biting her lips.

"You can't guess who called me up a while ago, Ticia," he said softly.

"It was Marlin."

"How do you know?"

"He called me first."

"You didn't tell him to?"

"Oh, no, he asked for you and I told him where he could find you. What did he have to say?"

"He said he was sorry he couldn't get to talk to me before I go back."

"What did he have to say to you?"

"He called to let me know he got home late last night. He'll see me on Sunday. Oh, I wish you could have stayed over Sunday yet."

"I wish lots of things."

* * * * *

"Oh, Millard!" Mother threw her arms around his neck, and sobbed on his shoulder. "You're going—too far away, I'm afraid."

"Don't, Mother, please." They lingered beside the car.

"But it hurts me that you couldn't have been at home with us while you were here."

"I wanted to be."

"I know. It doesn't seem right. Be good, Millard. I'll always be praying for you."

"Yes—I know."

"And, oh, I hope—"

"What, Mother?" Pop and the boys walked on toward the train.

"I hope you'll not need to—kill any mother's son. They all love their boys—mothers do, regardless who they are."

"Oh, Mother." Was this why she was crying?

"I hope—I won't," he answered thickly. "Don't think of that. Don't read the newspapers. I'll write. Don't worry, Mother." How could he tear her loose? He was glad he had a mother who loved him

212

this much, but he must go.

He must go!

Oh, infinite remembrance! His heart was bleeding with hers. As the train turned the bend, he looked out the window and saw Liticia leading Mother back to the car, and both were wiping their eyes. Millard leaned back in his seat and closed his eyes. Was there glory and comfort and joy in this sort of grief? There must be, for they had been drilled into believing it. The boys had all received printed matter with prayers on which assured them there was a silent peace in spite of doubts, protection in every danger, eternal reward for every sacrifice, forgiveness for every sin committed. The God of peace and happiness, the Father of all mankind, understood these abnormal circumstances and had abounding mercy. Didn't Mother know about this comfort and peace of mind? He would send her a copy of a prayer the next time he got one.

* * * * *

"Diary:

"A strange feeling possesses me as the time draws near to leave shore. How I wish I could have seen Orpha. My heart is full of love for her and all the family. We will be far, far apart now. The pictures mean much to me. I'd give a fortune for one of Melodie Ann. I might have seen her if I'd have gone to church. Am I a fool? Good-by, America. Oh, am I a fool? God in heaven, can you understand a creature like me? If so, have mercy."

* * * * *

"Dear Folks at Home,

It seems a long time since I've heard from home. It's five weeks. I'm somewhere in Ireland now, but from now on I won't be able to let you know where I am or what I'm doing. Send all my mail to New York. It will reach me in due time.

We had a nice voyage and good Christmas dinner. The people here are very friendly and this is a most beautiful country. You have an idea what I'm doing, don't you? There's no use for me to tell you anything, because it would be cut out. Did you get the picture I mailed you from New York? That was quite an experience—that ride in the subway.

Our dollars here are worth $1.20 each. Mother, I wish I had a dish of your good ice cream tonight. It might be a long time before I see you all again. Tell Liticia to write to me soon. Send me a letter air mail. It's so hard to wait so long. Be sure to write my address plainly—Sgt. Millard Grinstead, 83465120, Company A, 2nd Battalion, A.P.O. 48, New York City, N.Y. With love, Millard."

Chapter 32

DEAR Orpha,
  Maybe you will be surprised to get a letter from me from Ireland. I've been here a month now. I've been in the hospital for two weeks. I had to have a minor operation. I hate to tell Mother, but it's nothing serious. Did you get the letter I mailed you from New York? I surely haven't had many letters from home yet. Please write to me, Orpha. I'm really sorry I didn't get to see you when I was at home. If I had to do it over, I would have come to see you regardless. I wish you could have been at home the day I took pictures of the family. Carrie surely is cute. Have you seen her lately? Orpha, why don't you go home sometimes? Mother said you won't write often either. I've never met your husband. I hope you are happy. Send me a picture of yourselves. Time gets heavy for us at a place like this. It may be a long time before I see you again, Orpha. There's a movie actor here in the same hospital. We're alike in some respects now. I did not give up a $375,000.00 a year job to fight for peace and security, but I gave up something worth more than that. Maybe you don't know what I mean, but Orpha, God knows. I'm a little homesick perhaps. Write to me, 83465120, Company A, A.P.O. 48, 2nd Battalion, New York, N.Y. Love, Millard."

* * * * *

The days dragged on like months—sometimes dreadful months. There were all kinds of sicknesses soldiers could get away from home, diseases they never dreamed of having. One young boy with brain fever cried out pitifully at night like a lost child whining for his mother. Some let out oaths of anguish in their distress and disgust. Many wrote love letters in mad spasms of loneliness. Some drew pictures of girl's faces in hearts on the bare walls. Some printed names on the bedsteads. The nurses rebuked them half teasingly and slapped their hands in fun. The bare cream hospital walls were monotonous. Some of the soldiers who weren't too sick played cards, some read, some were despondent and refused to read anything. Each day some were dismissed and others admitted.

What was wrong? Why did strong, healthy young men get sick, men who had never known sickness at home? It wasn't fair. Good care and good food didn't compensate for their loneliness and bewilderment. The nurses did what they could to cheer the boys, especially whenever the cart removed a buddy to the death ward.

* * * * *

Millard held out his hand anxiously. All the boys were yelling for letters. He did get one!

"Dear Millard,

It was my full intention to see you and have a chat with you while you were home on furlough. I did not know you were at home until your mother told me Sunday morning after church. She told me where you were working, and on the day I planned to come to Boetchers I was called out of town on special church work. I regret very much having missed seeing you, Millard. I want you to know you are in my thoughts and prayers, and if I can be of any spiritual help to you, do not hesitate to let me know. It seems to me there must have been a reason why you gave up so suddenly after your confession, but I have never been able to learn why. Whatever it was then, Millard, do not allow anything to discourage you when you decide to live for Christ again. Not only do you have loved ones in your family who are praying for you, but your name is also often mentioned in our weekly church prayer meetings. When you get home I want to have a good long talk with you by all means. Very sincerely, Brother Ambers."

Millard folded the letter slowly and stuck it back in the envelope. Was it true that his name was mentioned out loud in prayer meetings? Did anyone care that much about his soul? Did, did—Melodie Ann—attend those prayer meetings? His pulse quickened, he straightened his legs. Pent-up feelings broke out in sudden coughing. He buried his face in his pillow.

"What's come over you, Grinstead?" yelled a boy from the second bed on the other side of the ward. "Shall I call for help, D.M.?"

"No," answered Millard sitting up on the edge of his bed. He stuck the letter under his pillow.

"Sandy, do you always understand yourself?"

"What are you talking about?"

"About anything. Sometimes don't you get impatient and—and wonder when we'll be out of here—and—home again?"

"Shut up. Who don't? Didn't I hear the doctor say this morning you'd be out next week?"

"Yes, out of here."

"What you fussin' about then? Come on over an' play a game of cards. Come on. You can walk a little now."

"I'd rather read, Sandy."

"You read too much. That's what's wrong. Lay down some of those books of wisdom and philosophy. Here, look at this." Across the bed came a comic magazine.

A nurse entered with a box in her hand.

"Here's a package for Don Millard Grinstead," she announced.

Millard almost sprang out of bed and reached with both hands. It was a box of Mother's home-made cookies. He passed them around to the other fellows.

* * * * *

Diary:

"I don't feel good tonight. Seven weeks of European training. It's been pretty rough. I'm glad I can't write it home. It would make Mother sick. Mother is a dear. Thank God for the pictures. Nothing is pretty here but nature. The sunset is beautiful tonight. The wind through the tree tops sounds like harp music in the distance. The clouds have strange faces. It seems peaceful; then in the day we make this beautiful country the devil's playground. My nerves are on edge tonight. I have an unforgettable dream of that sweet girl, Melodie Ann Brooks."

* * * * *

"Dear Liticia,

Well, sister Ticia, the boys have all gone downstairs to a movie. I mean those who are able. I'm in the hospital again this time with a skin disease. I've lost some weight. Break the news gently to Mother. It is nothing serious. I get as good care as I could get in any hospital in America. That's what they tell me.

I can't write you anything. Mother told me in her last letter that

217

part of one sentence was cut out. I'm being treated fine. I'm still somewhere in Ireland. I think I can say this that I went to Londenderry one day last week; also was in Belfast. If possible, send me a few air mail stamps and envelopes. I can't get any here. Then you could hear from me oftener.

Ticia, that was a wonderful letter you wrote me about Marlin's visit at home. If you've found a good Christian friend, stick to him. Love must be a wonderful thing, Ticia. I've seen plenty of the cheap stuff, and I know that's not the kind I'd want. Marlin must be doing a fine work in the hospital unit.

Say, I had another letter from Orpha. I wish you'd try to go to see her. I think she's really homesick, but she thinks Pop doesn't want her to come home. She let me know she's not so happily married. Yes, I read my Testament. Orpha said she sent me a package six weeks ago, but I have not yet got it.

Ticia, I could write you pages and pages, but there's no use. I know better. Thanks for the poem you sent me. I liked it. I read a lot since I'm in the hospital. When I get to feeling stronger I'm going to learn to weave some fancy belts. I'm glad you pray for me. I surely wouldn't say I don't need it. In love, Millard."

* * * * *

They had been on the troop ships four days. At dawn of the fifth they could see the scalloped coast of Northern Africa. Millard had not slept much all night. He felt restless and worn. The thrill of expectancy made some of the boys rigid and tense, others blank, some distinctly forlorn. In the distance they heard low reverberations like thunder. Some cowered. Was it true that the Germans had guns that could mow men down like grass at a distance of fifteen miles? In the early dawn balls of fire rose in heavens and whitened the sky with a moment's blinding glare.

Just before disembarking the commander called the men together. He said slowly, resolutely to the men, "In a few minutes you men will be on African soil. In a short while you will be seeing action, most of you for the first time. You're among the first American troops to engage the enemy. A word of warning to you: I'll tolerate no cowards in the ranks of my company. You've already been briefed in regards to your objective. Any man that fails to carry out a direct order from myself or an order from one of the noncoms will be court-martialed. We'll do this thing up right. I don't have to

218

wave a flag in front of you. You all realize what this paper hanger is trying to do to the world. I expect the best from each one of you. Good luck to you all."

Determined resolutions seized most of the company. In the muck of the morning they could see ambulances threading their way back and forth through the trees and odd sod-roofed huts. Millard's nerves felt jumpy. He must get a grip on himself. He must fight down this fear in his soul. All the boys on the ship were too splendid to be torn by steel or fire.

A village could now be seen. To the right, pretty red poppies brightened the grass. Suddenly something rocked the universe! A meteor-like explosion followed in a split second. Millard thought it would almost pull the stars and moon down from the heavens.

"What's it all about, D.M.?" whispered a young sapling of a boy crouching close to Millard.

"To defend our liberty, Bob," he answered with terror. "Don't you remember what's been told us?"

The air smelled of acid and something bitter coated their lips—dust of powder. There was tense waiting and stiffening of muscles as the boys walked down the gangplank. The explosion could have been fifty miles across the desert. Men and women, some old, some young, like dried up prunes, were standing along the shore motioning in strange sign language. They wanted to carry bags, guns, cameras, anything for the American soldiers. They had nimble feet like cats that could walk rope bridges. They smiled and seemed not concerned that in the near distance war was raging. The Americans would save them.

A second and a third burst of flame tore upward in the distance; something black blew to pieces and fell like a plastic toy. No one could tell where it drifted.

"March in the vigor of youth. March like real Americans!"

* * * * *

"Liticia, here's the last letter from Millard."

"When did it come, Mother?"

"Yesterday."

"Oh, dear, I do hope he's not still in the hospital."

"Read it out loud."

"Haven't you read it yet?" "Yes, but I want to hear it again," Mother's voice wavered.

"Why, what's wrong, Mother? Is he worse?"

"Oh, no. Read it. He's far away and in dangerous territory. Oh, Liticia," and Mother sank into a chair.

"Dear Ones at Home,

"Merry Christmas to you all. I'm farther than ever from home now. I'm spending Christmas in a pup tent in North Africa. I've had no mail for six weeks. It's an awful long time to hear nothing from home."

$$* \quad * \quad * \quad * \quad *$$

"Well, Mother, why doesn't he get the letters we write?"

"I can't understand it unless our letters are not delivered. Go ahead and read."

"Tell everyone hello for me—everyone I know who might inquire about me. After we left Ireland we saw Scotland and Wales; were in England and Liverpool and visited the city of Oran. Did I tell you I took out another life insurance policy before I left New York? This was a $5,000 policy."

Liticia looked up. "Don't cry, Mother."

"Oh, it sounds so uncertain. Read on."

"My, I feel so far from home. Did you hear about a shipload of soldiers' packages and supplies being sunk? Well, I guess that's where mine went that Orpha said she sent me for I never got it."

"Then do you suppose he never got the Christmas package we sent him?"

"Maybe not. Does he say anything about getting it?"

"No. Read on."

"She wrote me several very nice letters. Did she come home for Christmas? I hope so. I wish you'd —"

Liticia looked up again. "Mother, please don't cry."

"I can't help it today. Go on."

"— you'd all get together and have a picture taken and send it to me. I wonder how big Carrie is now. Mother, did you get the hankie I sent you from England? Please tell Homer Jo to get it out of his head
_____"

"Oh, so part of this has been cut out. What do you suppose it was?"

"Well, from something he wrote once before I suppose he wrote that he was to get it out of his head to join the army."

"That must be it."

"Oh, Homer Jo talks about it constantly. He can hardly wait." Mother looked sad. She rubbed her hands. "Liticia, doesn't it sound to you from different things Millard's said that he almost wished now he wouldn't have enlisted?"

"It does in a way."

"Read on."

"If you care to hear from me sooner, send me air-mail stamps and envelopes. Of course I can send my letters free, but you won't hear from me as soon that way. Pop, I hope Grandfather persuades you to stay on the farm. It's a nice place to be. We have Catholic and Protestant chapel services every Sunday. The chaplain's office is in the Battalion Headquarters building. Anyone who wants personal help can go there for interviews."

"Do you suppose Millard has?" asked Liticia.

"I don't know. Read on."

"I'm sending you a program of the chapel service we had today. Today we all read the prayer on the back."

"Shall I read that too, Mother?"

"Yes, read it."

"Almighty Father of the universe, give me the courage and self-faith to do what I am asked to do. Give me joy and cheer in my own heart that I may keep my brother from being blue or discouraged. Lift my mind and spirits that I may serve Thee as well in war as in peace. Help me feel Thy presence wherever I may be and no matter how far from home. In trials or in times of fear or in the midst of destruction I know Thou art with me. I will never be afraid. I trust my life, my loved ones, my future plans in Thy hands. Thou art kind. We pray for victory and as we work and fight for it, we will not lose our determination to preserve the good and to set free the oppressed. We love freedom and a better way of living, and the beauty of the human spirit. Almighty Father, send us out bravely to the tasks that lie ahead. For Jesus' sake and in Jesus' name. Amen."

"Did Pop read this letter?" asked Liticia.

"I don't think so."

Chapter 33

HITLER knew what he was after and had definite plans for attaining his objective. The middle East was one of the grand prizes of Nazi strategy, and Hitler had promised to reveal a "secret" weapon which would shock the world. But American arms and industry quickly produced a weapon which astonished Hitler into shattering Rommel's vaunted mechanized forces. Three weeks after a recommendation came from Africa, shipments of new weapons were sunk on their way to Egypt; these were promptly replaced by materials urgently ordered by the president. Large numbers of M-7's, with a speed of more than thirty-five miles an hour, and guns that hurled their shells seven miles were rushed to North Africa. These were placed at less than twenty-three yard intervals on a six mile front, and fire on the German line was opened. Fifty thousand British troops with their twenty-five pound guns advanced only a few miles in two weeks until the Allies landed in North Africa.

After the fall of the city of Oran, the Germans rushed troops to Tunisia by air. Allied forces raced eastward. Italy and Germany succeeded by ship and plane to reinforce their Tunsian battalions with 60,000 men. The Allied line ran from the Mediterranean south to the Gulf of Gabes. Allied tanks, artillery, and tank destroyers were more than a match for the German and Italian weapons.

On the third day things looked serious. Millard felt sick as he saw men falling in front of him — comrades, buddies from his own battalion, fine young Americans. The first boy he knew to go was Jackie Peters, who had shared some of his mother's homemade candy only three weeks before. He saw Jackie running about an eighth of a mile ahead of him when an explosion tore like a wild flaming dragon with fiery tongues striking in every direction. When the smoke sank down Millard could see that the boy's right leg was blown off just below his knee, and both of his arms were dangling and bleeding. The lad did not drop down and die immediately. With some strange sort of human courage, he jumped twice on one leg toward Millard, crying pitifully, and then fell with his face to the earth.

The sight chilled Millard.

"My God!" he cried.

Two dreadful hours of massacre followed. Desperately Millard tried to fight down the fear in his soul. His eyes were wild with terror, and he wiped his face with his dirty handkerchief. He saw one boy lying with wide open eyes staring blankly at the sky, and blood running from his neck till it made a pool on the ground. Three days ago they had eaten breakfast together. The atmosphere felt thick, and tingled his cheeks like electricity. All around him men scrambled for safety or fell flat on the ground. Millard crouched behind a bush. A storm of fragments flew over him. Appalling noises followed. Screams of wounded men grew louder and louder. In wild anguish his mind was torn with fright. Men's faces looked like ghosts. There were curses and stifled moans; a burst of flames on yonder hill; bellowing convulsions of earth, and blackness — blacker than night.

* * * * *

Diary:

"So this is war! Oh, hideous sights! I'm tired and sick, and I can't sleep. Is God here in Africa? Mother, did you pray for your boy today? Home sweet home and Mother are what I long for."

With trembling hands Millard put the diary in his duffel bag and then looked at his snapshots. He must write a letter.

"Dear Folks at Home,

It is eight weeks since I've heard from home. Why don't I hear? Can't somebody send me an air-mail letter? Please. I wish I were home. I've seen three days and nights of action. It's useless for me to write any of it. Someone sent me a good-luck chain letter. Some American soldier started it, and it's gone around the world four times now. The one who breaks this chain will have bad luck. I'm to send it and four copies of it within twenty-four hours to persons I wish to have good luck. The letter says a boy won $1,000 and failed to pass it on and lost it. What do you think of such a chain? Well, I don't believe much in it. If I have good luck at all, it will come from above.

How are you all? I'm glad you are safe in the good U.S. We had turkey for New Year's dinner. We don't get eggs over here for our breakfast. The hens lay golden eggs — they are thirteen cents a piece. How is everyone? How is Carrie? Tell everyone hello for me. Please write. In love, Millard."

* * * * *

Sleep was out of the question. Every time Millard closed his eyes he saw fire and falling wounded boys screaming in intolerable pain. He lay with his hands behind his head.

Suddenly a terrific crash almost lifted him off his bed. The whole camp vibrated. Chips of cement fell from the ceiling to the floor. Boys fell flat and crouched together, clawing at anything they could catch hold of. Off in the distance the whole desert was ablaze and the earth was spitting clods high up into the air like black rain. The boys crept outside. This was their night off duty. They were worn and almost senseless. They sat outside till daybreak, talking in low tones. They were too frightened and terrorized to sleep. Far off in the distance the sounds of violent battle kept up till dawn. Then silence.

The Americans were camped on a wide plain between two jagged ranges of mountains whose rough peaks towered toward the blue sky. The plain along the foot of the mountain was spotted here and there with red poppies and yellow daisies. The American soldiers fought like tigers, but sly Rommel's army drove them back one hundred miles, for Rommel had seventeen soldiers to the Allies' one, and they came roaring through the mountain passes like lions; soulless, brutish, indescribable. The situation was grave.

Millard had a feeling of isolation. He yearned for something. A thousand ideas haunted. He wanted safety. He tried to remember the words of the printed prayer. There was something in it about not being afraid in the midst of destruction. They were in deadly peril. His division faced a line twenty miles long. At right angles and west lay hills with peaks, some of them 2,000 feet high which were held by the enemy.

By some strange turn in the whirling vortex of the war, the Germans and the Italians under-estimated the strength of their opposers. The American boys fought desperately to hold mountain passes as long as possible without getting trapped. For three more days artillery bellowed and echoed in the high hills, but the enemy was held back at each successive attack.

Millard was going to do his level best now since he was in it. He fought hard to hold the Axis forces back. His face, encrusted with dirt, was sweating and haggard. He was tired. There was a tormenting restlessness in his thoughts. Mother had said she hoped he wouldn't need to kill a mother's son. She had cried over the idea. Now he was in the midst of this glorious adventure — oh, was it a glorious adventure? Was it? His bronzed dusty face, parched from thirst, was swollen. With wild, desperate efforts he tried to carry out Lieutenant General Montgomery's orders to destroy once and for all the enemy forces. Caught like rats in a trap, the Germans and Italians hit out in every direction, but the General sent out orders with high compliments that kept the American boys' fighting spirits high. "We'll show them boys what our army can do!"

"We've got plenty of tanks, D.M.," shouted the boy nearest him. "We'll smash 'em up an' cripple 'em till they get the bloody dose they deserve. Come on. To —————————; we'll smash right through them."

Behind the antitank guns, scattered in a semicircle from the sea to the mountain passes, was a field of artillery. Behind those heavy guns was plenty of armor in reserve. In front of all the infantry screen, a cunning trap was set where all sorts of unpleasant things could happen.

Night fell. The boys were asked to pray that the enemy would be foolish enough to walk into their trap. Some men were sent along the edges of the roads with their automatic rifles. All night Millard saw men being killed. Boys were knocked down around him like tenpins. Balls of fire rose to whiten the sky; then everything was profoundly dark and he could hear wailing and cursings, and cries of dying men. Would he get calloused to misery and suffering?

He saw gaping wounds and torn flesh until dirty wounded men loomed out of nowhere, and the whole place seemed a yawning chasm of death. He groped along, scared almost senseless with the smell of death. The night seemed like years — long years of explosions and fire and cries. Every noise hurt his soul until he almost wished for death. Near daybreak the report came that they had killed 5,000 men, destroyed fifty-two enemy tanks, and that there were only 100 casualties of their own army. Not one tank had been lost. With daylight came sight. Millard saw unconscious boys gasping for breath, some vomiting, and trying to get up. Ambulances were threading their way over the battlefield gathering up the wounded and hurrying them to the hospital. The enemy received a fierce mauling, but the fight was not over.

* * * * *

In cold sweat Millard took up his pencil to write. His body shook with fear.

Diary:

"God knows I might be in pulp any minute, too. I'm tired, tired to death tonight. I hope I won't need to go out again. I wish it would be over tonight. I have to wonder if I've just made a ghastly failure of my life. The birds of death just missed me several times."

* * * * *

Millard tossed. Sometimes he shook all over. Most of the other boys drank beer and went to sleep. The last words they heard before they dropped off were words of praise for their gallantry. It helped very little, for their tempers were frayed and their nerves were ready to snap.

Millard's legs were cold, almost numb. His eyes were swollen, and he ached all over. He thought of home and Mother and a certain girl with auburn hair and high cheekbones. Did she read the paper? Did she have any idea he was in the thick of action? There was nothing tender, nothing beautiful, nothing feminine in the camp. Only horror and livid terror and misery. Was there glory when his comrades were crushed and mangled in African dirt? Who would pay for this? Wouldn't the Germans who lived through this, if any did, be cursed to the third and fourth generation?

The other boys were taking their turn now. It sounded as if they were pounding the earth to pieces out there. Millard must not let this unnerve him. Though hideously strained by terror and suspense, the other boys were sleeping; why couldn't he? One had laughed before he lay down and bragged about knocking the liver out of the enemy, but his laugh sounded grotesque and weird to Millard. If this kept all summer, he would lose his mind. He wished he could find magic wings and fly home.

* * * * *

A letter! Millard tore it open feverishly.

"Dear Millard,

I am sending you an air-mail registered letter to tell you Grandfather Winegar was buried this afternoon. He was sick only a few days. We got word Sunday evening at five and we drove to Granger in the car, leaving Monday morning at four o'clock. It was a large funeral. Homer Jo stayed at home to do the work. We must go back home tomorrow. Grandmother is quite resigned to her sorrow, but is sad anyway. He was a good father to me.

Grandmother said he often talked about you and was always anxious to hear you were all right. I dare not let myself dwell too much on what could happen to you. I must only pray that God will spare your life for a good purpose and call you to give your heart to Him before it is too late. Liticia went along with us to the funeral. Pop would like to come back here to Doddridge to live and do carpenter work again, but Grandmother talked him into staying on the farm for the present.

Millard, you know Homer Jo really expects to join the army before long. He can hardly wait. He has been smoking for some time now. My talking is to no effect, it seems.

Liticia and Marlin seem to be very fond of each other. I am glad for Liticia. In the last letter I had from Orpha she said she was sick. I wish she would come home, and I pray constantly that all our children will be united with us again some day. God take care of you, Millard. Very lovingly, Mother."

Millard read the letter twice. So Grandfather was gone! He would never see him again. He was undoubtedly in some happy paradise where Uncle Levi had gone. Father and son were together in heavenly bliss.

Stark thoughts engulfed him. Would they suffocate him; a lone tear crept to the edge of his eyelash and hung trembling. He must get some rest today. Some of the boys were going out to bathe and relax in an old bath tub they had found and dragged over the desert sands. They could hear the rumble from the front like distant thunder. So it was not over yet. He must sleep somehow. Disappointed, he turned from one side to the other. At last he fell into troubled unconsciousness, dreaming he was groping along in the dark, falling over wounded, mangled bodies, and then carried away in a pool of smoke.

*   *   *   *   *

"Do you hear from Millard?"

"Let her read the last letter, Liticia."

"Oh, Mrs. Grinstead, I didn't mean you should let me read you letters. I just — wondered, you know."

"Of course you can read it, Melodie Ann. You can understand it better than if we'd try to tell you. My, it's a long time since you've been here."

Liticia found the letter beside the clock.

"Dear Folks at Home,

I'm thinking especially of you today, Mother, because I know it's your birthday. I know it's a month or more since I last wrote, but if you'd know what all I've been through you'd understand why. I'm all right and well. ——————————— ——— I've been right up in the thick of it and helped in seven engagements. You wouldn't believe what's been going on here right in the midst of beautiful nature. I hope and pray God will bless all American arms as He has here in Africa. You can't imagine how good it looked to us to see Germans giving up by the thousands. We've learned a lot about the enemy's ways of fighting, and things looked plenty tough for us for a while. I will have heaps to tell when I get home. I've seen ——— ——————. Please tell Homer Jo ——————————————- to join the navy. I could tell you a lot, but it's no use. This won't be cut out, I know, that we've won every battle since we learned how to hold all mountain passes with our artillery fire. Did you read about it in the papers? Over 40,000 prisoners we took. Say, what a sight to see them shaking their heads and asking us where we got our artillery. I was in ——————————-. I'm operating a radio now. I'm lonesome to hear from home. It seems I hardly get any mail. If you were here you'd realize what it means to hear from home and you'd realize, too, what it means to know someone prays for you. I was very sorry to hear Grandfather died. He is, no doubt, better off than any of us. I don't suppose I'll come home till it's all over. It is grand to have Italians friendly to us. They would rather be our prisoners than fight us. If things keep shaping up the way they have, the Germans can't last long. How are the chickens and crops back home? Say, the U.S. would look mighty good to me now. Does anyone ever ask about me? How are Liticia and Marlin getting along? Tell everyone who knows me hello, and please pray for us over here. Love, Millard."

Melodie Ann drew a long, deep breath and put the letter back in the envelope. Her cheeks were flushed. She stood at the window and looked out toward the sky.

Chapter 34

THE boys were almost dying from thirst. They would have been afraid to drink much of the water sent to them in the water carts if they had not had water purification tablets they all carried with them. Without them water could be a dangerous fluid.

Climbing mountains when one was heavily burdened with weapons was terrible. But thirsting for water was worse. Frantic officers telephoned the medical corps. Something had to be done. Battle was inevitable. The soldiers plodded on. Water! Water! Finally soldiers saw a cart of water arrive. It had lime in it, which helped to quench their thirst.

The climb was a dangerous one, the mountain strange and unexplored. It was dark. Only a few stars shone dimly. Millard stumbled and fell, but pulled himself up quickly. That afternoon orders from the general were, "The real battle will start soon. Likely tomorrow. Do your full duty with faith in God. Let us go forward to victory and drive the enemy into the sea. Remember boys, millions of people are listening for wireless news today, so let's give them good news."

Up and up. Then dangerous jumps into the dark. Scaling ladders were built to hoist supplies. Spotting towers were put up for observers who used powerful field glasses. The boys worked frantically tugging forty foot towers in the dark. Millard would be stationed in one of these towers.

"It's tough, boys, but it'll be worth it," came the commander's encouraging words.

The harsh drone of a plane was heard several miles away. It circled, then roared down to within a few feet of the ground. Guns cracked; red tracer bullets streamed like fire from the mouth of a dragon. The plane zoomed toward the sky and dropped butterfly bombs, fifteen or more fiendish-looking things with aluminum wings. They looked like mad bats as they spiraled to the earth. Millard held his breath. A second later a series of explosions cracked like mammoth fireworks and shrapnel sprayed high, then fell.

The night was awful. It put new uneasiness into Millard. But little did he know yet what war was. That night was terrible, but the next forty eight hours were to be hideous. The heavens and the ground were swept by fire and terrific explosions. Men were blown to bits. Billowed in smoke, dust, and bursting shells, the desert became a raging unspeakable sight, incomprehensible to anyone who never saw bombardment at its height. Men crawled on their stomachs like mad dogs clawing with their hands and teeth in raging terror and agony. Bombers roared overhead, guns thundered from the desert below. Sometimes it looked as if the angry sea coughed up old tree stumps and all sorts of filth. Terrific flashes and fire spurted like great fountains. The whole world seemed on fire. Millard felt terrible, almost savage. The universe was going to be blown to bits any minute. Sand mines exploded almost every second.

Millard was in the armed reconnaissance battalion. He had to be at the front, the most dangerous position of all. It was his duty to report by radio from lookout stations the exact position of the enemy. When orders were given to advance, he had to go first. Which was worse; to operate a machine gun or to tell in what direction to fire?

In black darkness of soul he saw men being hurled into eternity hour after hour, day after day. He could not lie. This was his duty to the government to spot the enemy. He felt as if he were stripped naked of all the moral power and intelligence he ever had, but he reported truthfully. Maneuvers in the south and in Ireland had been nothing compared to this. Fragments flew and whipped around him. The air was rent with explosions. The scene was unearthly. Why was he helping to blow up the world? The whole place was becoming one great, screaming, howling stage of intolerable misery. It was an open grave, and he'd be falling into it any minute, too. The sight and noise were appalling. Closer and fiercer became the battle. He felt an anguish in his soul no human could describe.

"Advance again," came the orders. How close must he go? Must he even see the whites of their eyes! Almost blindly he ran to the next tower and climbed into it. Gasping, he sent back the report of positions. Another attack on civilization might end the job. He was weak, thirsty, and wild with fear. Nothing but God alone could keep him from being hit this time.

* * * * *

Myra tried to hum as she went about her work. Every hour of the day she committed her boy to God. "Don't let him die, dear Lord, but if he must be taken, help him get saved before that hour should come. I know some will be taken, but somehow, God, it seems to me Millard was born with purpose."

She was humming when Jeth came in with the mail.

"No letter from Millard yet?"

"Nothin' but this paper today."

"I wonder why we don't hear. I wonder if he's in the hospital again? Jeth, when you go to town, bring me home a few more air mail stamped envelopes."

"You've used up all I did bring home?"

"Yes, you didn't bring any lately."

* * * * *

Before dawn of the third day a gray drizzle of rain started falling. The Americans were pushing Rommel back steadily and surely to his last standing position. His doom was written. They were hammering him to certain death. They had fought by moonlight, in dust storms, and they could fight in rain, too, if necessary. In the past week Rommel had lost 30,000 men. The American forces had won every battle.

* * * * *

"My God," Millard caught his breath and held it. In the early dawn he could see dead bodies everywhere — literally heaps of them, Germans and Americans. Did they know why they were fighting, these boys who loved life and health and home? Did they? Millard wanted to scream! Close to him was a young light-haired youth, rain smearing his blood-clotted face. He stumbled along. As daybreak brightened the earth, the terrible sight became more visible. Men lay face down — their clothes soaked in the rain. Millard became almost wild with terror! The whole place was an open graveyard. Would this be his end? Would he be killed — perhaps today! Why was he helping kill these men? Oh! He passed a boy who reminded him of Ted Waterman. He looked away then turned and looked again. It couldn't be Ted. Impossible.

What anguish, what insufferable pain! An almost unintelligent fear took hold of Millard. A feeling of remorse, shame, and bitter reproach flooded his soul. Why were human beings set against one another like this? Had these dead men really known why they had been trying to kill? Had they been as blind and ignorant and unknowing about the whole matter as he?

What a death to die! What sorrow, what disappointment! What havoc! Perhaps some of these boys had girls at home, girls they loved and hoped to marry. Maybe some of them were married. Millard's soul cried out in agony. He felt exhausted, stupefied. The whole sight was horrible, repulsive. How could he ever wipe it out of his memory? The other boys cursed, cursed plenty as they stumbled along. They had to say something to strengthen their taut nerves and deaden their senses to the awful sight and stench. It was getting still more terrible.

Was this what made them first in the eyes of America, to help kill the dirty German dogs, then walk on them? Was there no other way to settle disputes than to kill and shed blood? Could anyone answer his question? He could not feel like some of the other fellows seemed to. They cursed thankfully and the sight, though bewildering to them and horrible, only fanned their hate to finish the dirty mess.

Millard stood stock still. His whole body trembled. He panted for breath. On the slope in front of him lay a stout man clenching his fists till his fingers were white at the knuckles. Between his moans and gurgling he was grinding his teeth. He was lying in bloody sand. His brown eyes screamed at Millard. Never, never in his life had Millard seen a man who looked so much like Pop. The man was trying to say something to Millard. He was in insufferable pain.

"Sonny," he cried pitifully, "do it." He moaned.

"Do what?"

"Finish—me up."

"What!" Millard stood motionless—frightened!

"Please, sonny." The German could speak a fair English. The man couldn't have looked more like Pop had he been his twin.

Millard felt sick in every joint and muscle. His abdomen hurt, so did his spine, his head, and his heart. He felt he would froth at the mouth with fear.

"Have—mercy," cried the man, "you—put me down—this low. Please end it—too."

"I did?" cried Millard. "How do you know I did it? I—I didn't."

"Please, sonny. You've got a gun there."

Oh, God! Wasn't it Mother's last wish he wouldn't need to kill a mother's son.

"Mister," choked Millard; "mister—you look—like—my pop. How could I kill my—own—pop?"

Millard knelt in the bloody sand beside him. He laid one hand on the man's forehead. It was cold, wet.

"I didn't mean to kill you - if - if I did it, Pop - mister."

Tears filled Millard's eyes. They ran like rain down both his cheeks.

"You can have-all-that's in my pockets-sonny," he gasped, "if you'll only - end - it - for me. God knows - I'd rather let you - live - live. Son, I'd do it for you - if - I'd knocked—you down, first."

Millard somehow got to his feet again. What should he do? The man's brown eyes begged him pitifully. The agony on his face was more than Millard could bear.

"Shut those - brown eyes, mister - and - and - God forgive me," Millard screamed! He closed his own eyes and shot!

Millard couldn't believe it.

He waited a minute before he opened his eyes. The deed was done. He'd done it. He'd done it! He'd killed some mother's son!!

Crying like a child Millard took out his dirty handkerchief. He laid it gently over the man's face.

He reached into the dead man's coat pocket and pulled out a billfold. It was black leather, a much better billfold than Millard's own. He opened it. On one side was a picture of a calm sweet-faced woman, and on the other the man's picture and name. Emil Agustav Duerr, M. A. So the man was not just a common nobody like he was. He was an educated man, a teacher, and he had called him "sonny."

Millard shook with sobs. He cried out in his disturbing anguish. He put the billfold into his own pocket.

Pent-up feeling from his earliest recollection broke out. This was too much. He felt as if he'd go to pieces. Why did he have to go through this? As he stumbled on still crying, a thousand faces came before him and everyone of them was the face of his father. He wanted to go back and gather up that man and give him a decent burial. He wanted to bathe his handsome face and big strong body tenderly in warm water, put a suit on him, and send him home to his wife in a nice casket. She was probably at home watching for mail, waiting for him to come back and help her plant the garden. Perhaps in agony she'd get the word some day that he gave his life for his country and Hitler.

"Sonny." Oh, why had the man called him that? His own father never had. It made him love that man who was only following orders to kill the Americans. He hadn't wanted to kill any more than Millard wanted to.

Perhaps his home was a happy one. No doubt it was. Maybe they laughed and sang together—Emil Agustav and his wife. Maybe they had a little girl like Carrie. Maybe—a thousand and one things.

"What are you sobbin' about?" a soldier caught up to him. Millard tried to collect himself.

"Let's not talk about it. This whole thing makes me feel awful. Would Christ shoot a man?" Millard smote his breast.

"What?" asked the other.

"Would Jesus Christ kill a man - a - I said a man who - I don't want to talk about - it - I said."

* * * * *

That evening the boys were ordered to lie down and sleep. They would go no farther that night. They had come out to a good spot to set up a bivouac and would wait for further orders. Perhaps the enemy was afraid to start again, knowing his doom was at hand.

Millard had fallen into his first sound sleep for a week. He was completely exhausted. The experience of the past few days made him pallid and worn.

A bomber.

A terrible explosion!

The next thing Millard knew he was picked up and dropped fifty feet away. He tried to sit up. He batted his eyes. Was he torn completely in two? For a moment he thought he was. He tried to move his toes. They were still on his feet, but were his feet on his legs? Were his legs still fastened to his body? What happened? Was the world coming to an end? Had he been killed and was this hell? Had God forsaken him?

He tried to claw the ground.

He fell backwards. Ah! Ha! "No matter what it costs, boys!" Isn't that what the officer had said? Where was he now? Was he blown to bits, too, wondering whether or not he was dead or still alive, in hell or still in Africa?

Blinding flames burst upward. A film of dreadful smoke sank around him. Where was he? In the sea? He was falling, falling. The world was falling. Was he going crazy, or was it a dream? He heard falling metal and something like dirt flying, then sharp cracks like lightning. Was it the devil's whip?

Oh, agony of agonies! Would he ever march again in the vigor of youth like a real American? Would he ever see home and Mother again? Never. He was dying. He knew it.

Yet he kept on breathing. He wished he could - die - die now - but no - he wasn't ready to die. He was going to accept Christ before he died.

He opened his eyes. Boys were huddled everywhere like sheep without a shepherd. He felt petrified.

Oh! So he wasn't dead? No, he remembered he had tried to snatch a little sleep - a little sleep to give him more nerve for the coming engagement. He sat up. He moved his hands and arms. They were still on his body—but stiff and weak. He coughed. He spit on the ground. It wasn't blood, was it? He tried to get up on his knees. They felt strangely weak, too. He never had felt like this before.

"My God! My God," he cried. "Peace - peace in my soul. Oh, help—me find it—before I die. Oh, God in heaven! Who said there is—glory afterwards? Why have I come to help in this bloody mess?" He fell on the ground limp; his lips still moved in prayer.

* * * * *

After the eighth engagement in which Millard had a part, a personal message came from the army commander, "I want to express to you, my soldiers of this army, whatever your rank or employment, my sincere thanks for the way you have responded and fought. We have never possessed such a magnificent fighting force, and you are today being spoken of in every home in the world. I am proud of you. Your brave and brilliant work and devotion to duty have made these outstanding victories possible. My triumphant cry is, fight like this to the end."

Chapter 35

MYRA Grinstead hurried in from the mailbox. In her hand she
carried two letters, one addressed to Mrs. Jethro Grinstead
and the other to Mr. Jethro Grinstead, and across the front of the
letter to Jeth was printed in Millard's own handwriting, "Personal."
She held her breath as she opened hers. What could this mean, these
separate letters? Millard had never written a personal letter to Pop
before.

Pop never wrote to Millard. Pop didn't like to read or write. He
seldom read Millard's letters. He either listened while Myra read
them or waited to be told what they contained. What now? It had
been a month since Millard had last written.

Myra sat beside the window. The clock on the mantel struck ten.

"Dear Mother,

Greetings to you in Jesus' worthy name!" Myra caught her
breath. She held it. Millard had never written such a salutation
before. Her breast rose and fell. Glad, glad tears filled both eyes. She
wiped them with the corner of her apron so that she could see to read.

"I am glad to tell you your prayers for your boy were answered
at last, for I found Christ and have been baptized in the name of the
Father, Son, and Holy Ghost."

Myra's arms broke out with goose flesh.

"I have been praying for a long time for real conviction. (Censored) I have prayed to God for conviction and at last,

(Tears streamed down Myra's plump cheeks now.)

He sent it to me and called me with His sweet voice. Oh, Mother
dear, I know you've kept your promise to pray for me, and perhaps
without those prayers (Censored) I have confessed all my sins and
have received the assurance that they are forgiven, yes, even the
worst one I committed. I ask you to please forgive me for every

wrong thing I've done against you, and I am sure you will. I am sorry now I didn't go ahead and get baptized when I was going to, but it was my own stubborn nature. How I long for home and this war to close. Oh, how good a real bed would feel again and how good some of your homemade bread would taste! Please pray that I will soon get to come home and won't be (Censored). I was baptized today by the army chaplain, and I'm sending you my certificate, so you can see it really is true. I told you I was coming into the army with (Censored). Forgive me, Mother. I marvel that God took such good care of me and kept me from harm until I gave up all to Him. I had to help play a very important part in nine major engagements here in Africa. I was in the group that had to report to draw on artillery fire in (Censored). I dare tell now since it's past. Mother, I won't write more. Just be happy with me that I've found Christ precious to my soul before (Censored). I wrote Pop a personal letter. I hope he, too, will be glad, but whatever his reaction, I am determined by the grace of God to live out and out for Christ the rest of my days; and when I come home you'll see I am a changed boy and the peace of God is upon me. Pray that I will get to come home before many months, and that men will not make war any more. In love, Your son, Millard."

"P.S. Tell the folks who might be interested in me what I've done in Jesus' name."

*   *   *   *   *

"What's wrong, Mommy?"

"Nothing is wrong, Carrie, dear."

"Then why are you crying, Mommy?"

"I'm crying because I'm happy, dear. Millard gave his heart to God way over there across the ocean."

"Why?"

"Because God wanted it."

"Is that why you cry, Mommy?"

"Sit down here beside me, Carrie, and I will try to explain to you what it means."

Myra was talking to Carrie when Jeth came in. He looked up in surprise.

"Have you been—cryin'—Myra?" he asked.

She held it out to him. "Here's a letter for you, Jeth."

"Fer me?" He did not reach for it. "It's not fer me, is it?"

"It's addressed to Mr. Jethro Grinstead and it's marked personal, so that surely means you, doesn't it?"

"Well." Jeth took the letter and looked at it musingly. He scratched his head. He stuck it in his inside coat pocket and walked out. Myra watched him hesitate at the garage, then slowly he walked to the barn. He entered and closed the door.

"What's in his letter?" asked Carrie.

"I wouldn't know, dear," answered Mother, and as she spoke she drew her youngest child close to her and pressed her lips on her soft flaxen hair. "I hope it's something nice like is in mine."

Jeth stood at the barn window and looked at the letter in his hand. He did not tear it open quickly but acted as though he dreaded doing it. Slowly he got out his pocketknife and slit the end. He drew a long, deep breath, then another. It was not a page, not two, but more.

He found a box and sat down. He never did like to read. Millard had a pretty good hand. He could make it out well enough. But Pop never did like to read.

"Dear Pop,

Greetings to you in the name of Christ my blessed Saviour."

Pop took off his cap. He dropped it beside him. He held his breath. What in the world?

"I've just got to write you a letter and get something off my mind. I just finished writing a letter to Mother to tell her I was baptized today by the Protestant army chaplain in our battalion. I found Christ one night after a bomber went over and the blast threw me fifty feet in the air and knocked me unconscious. That is an experience I could not go through again without the knowledge that I am forgiven of all my sins and ready to meet God. I prayed all the rest of that night, and confessed all my sins— "

Jeth shifted on the box. He sniffed.

"until I found peace in my soul. I wish now I would have gone on when I first confessed my love for Christ, regardless of what I heard you say—"

Jeth's hands got unsteady. The pages shook. His stomach felt queer.

"to Brother Ambers that day he came out to see me. I was in the woodshed and heard what you said to him, and that's why I didn't go ahead and receive baptism them. It hurt me, for I thought I was sincere. I told myself I wouldn't try it again until you made that right with me, but when a person sees all I've seen, you don't care what anybody ever said or did against you, not even your own father. All you can think about is to get right with God.

I'm not writing this letter to show you up or excuse myself. I see now I had the wrong attitude. I held it against you in my heart, Pop, all these years. Sometimes I didn't hold it against you, but after all, way down in my heart I did. Sometimes I thought I had a reason to feel hurt and hold off from God; but the night God spoke to me it came before me big as a mountain that I couldn't let that stand between me and God. I had to lay it down and count it as nothing. I could not afford to lose my soul over a little thing like that. I have forgiven you from the bottom of my heart, Pop, and God spoke peace to my soul when I did. I never told a soul what I heard you say to Brother Ambers that day.

"I also(Censored). I killed a man. He was a wounded German soldier, and when I passed him he begged me to finish him and I did."

Jeth coughed nervously.

"I try to wipe it out of my mind, but I don't know if I ever can. What makes it so hard is that he looked very much like you, Pop."

Jeth stood up. He leaned hard against the window casing. He felt weak. His eyes got misty. He gulped for air.

"He looked like your twin- I declare he did, and he called me Sonny."

A tear trickled down Jeth's cheek and hung trembling on his whiskers. He hadn't shaved yet that day. He pulled out his red bandanna and blew his nose. He wiped both eyes.

"I can't describe my feelings. I felt awful. He was a nice-looking gentleman. I could tell that in spite of the mess he was in. I was beside myself. I was frenzied and horrified, yet the poor man was suffering. So I did it. Oh, Pop, I killed a man who looked like you."

Pop's tears were rolling now. He wiped his eyes. He had never been an emotional person. He couldn't stand much more of this.

(Censored).

"Many things were put in my mind that I cannot write now. I am tired. Please help me pray for peace. I've seen the light, and I must follow it with my cross."

Jeth was too weak to stand any longer. He sat on the wooden box to finish the letter.

"Pop, for a long time I have felt that our family was not so happy as we could be. I do not blame you or anyone. If I am the cause of it,

I wish you would tell me what I could do. I want to do my part. The nicest thing I could think of would be news that there's an end to this—. I want to come home and be received into the church. Another thing that would make me very happy would be if we could get better acquainted. Pop, you're my father and I'm your son, but it doesn't seem to me like we know each other very well. God has filled my heart with true love for all men and especially my own father. I hope I can lie down in peaceful sleep tonight. God bless you, Pop. I cannot tell you how happy I am since all my sins are forgiven and I have peace of mind. In love, Your son, Millard."

Jeth Grinstead put the letter on the box beside him and buried his face in his big strong hands. He shook with sobs. Something he did not know he possessed welled up within him. It made him warm all over. It made him suddenly come to life.

The storm of antagonism that had so long blocked his pathway to the natural beauties of life broke loose. The noonday sun shining in through the window casement cast a soft shadow on his gray hair. His one hand relaxed while the other sought his bandanna once more. The homely cobwebs in the corners of the window quivered as the breeze blew in the cracks. They seemed to throb with the emotions in his own breast. It was unlike anything he had ever before experienced.

For several long minutes he sat watching the cobwebs fluttering—thinking. A little bird hopped on the window sill, looked at him with beady black eyes, nodded his head, and flew away.

Jeth picked up the letter and read it through again. He sat. He looked at his watch. Was it dinnertime? He wished he wouldn't need to eat. Food was the farthest thing from his thoughts.

Once more tears streamed down his handsome face, Jethro Grinstead's handsome middle-aged face.

He must gather himself together. He must act like a man his age and intelligence. He stumbled toward the door. He must go in or Carrie would be running out to call him for dinner. Myra would naturally be wondering what was in his letter.

Oh, tearing, naked thoughts. Oh, agonizing, intolerable, closeup thoughts! He, too, must find peace of mind and soul at any price. He knew it now.

A storm of flying fragments of ideas flew past him. His was not a battlefield of war; his battlefield was his own soul. He stood by the barn door thinking. One night Myra had come with him to that very spot. Dear Myra. She so sincerely had wanted to help him be a good father, a better example to the boys.

The pipe was not on the ledge above the door. No, it was closer to Jeth than that. It was in his pocket where he could fondle it whenever he wanted to. They'd been friends a long time—dear friends, pals. And now Millard wanted to come home to get better acquainted with his father. In fancy Jeth saw smoke envelope him like a great milky pool, a whirlpool sucking him in. It enveloped him. He seemed powerless to stem his imagination. The smoke would pull him into a bottomless whirlpool unless—. He opened the barn door and went slowly toward the house.

Myra saw him coming. The magnetic warmth of her sweet personality met him at the door. He did not need to fear Myra. She had been a real companion, a true helpmeet.

He might as well be frank. She could see his eyes did not look quite right. She'd been crying, too.

He came close to her. "Myra," he said putting an arm across her shoulder, "you and Carrie go ahead an' eat. I want to shave. I don't feel like eatin'."

"Why, Jeth! Why not, Jeth?"

"I don't want to eat now, Myra. I've got somethin' I want to attend to."

"Aren't you going to tell me what it is, Pop?"

"I want you to go with me. You and Carrie eat, then change your dress, Myra. I want you to go with me."

Jeth walked across the kitchen. What was it? Myra had noticed that his voice faltered. This was something extraordinary. Myra had never known Jeth to act like this. The pressure of his hand on her shoulder had felt different from his usual caress. His hand was trembling a little. Myra had felt it distinctly. There was a strange, loving accent in his voice. It made her warm all over.

"Come on, Carrie, dear, you and I will eat. If Pop isn't hungry he doesn't need to eat."

"Maybe we could let Carrie stay with—Melodie Ann Brooks fer a while," Pop suggested. "I'd rather not take her with us."

Chapter 36

THE trees were beginning to bud but the wind was chilly and damp. As Jeth and Myra passed Lone Creek the water was laughing in the bright sunlight as though jubilant spring had come. Two geese rose from the bank of the brook at the noise of the car. The world was alive with color, and noises, and moving wings.

"You won't mind staying at Melodie Ann's house a little while, will you, Carrie?" asked Mother gently, at the same time still wondering where Jeth was going.

"I like Melodie Ann."

"What if she's not at home, Jeth?" Myra asked.

A disturbed expression crossed Jeth's face as though he were trying to knot a string and the ends didn't meet.

"Then I don't know," came his answer. "Since Aunt Christina is gone — we, sorta miss her, don't we?"

Jeth's voice was strangely mellow. He had never said such a thing before. Maybe Jeth thought such things, but never expressed them — could it be? Something was melting years of struggle out of his face. Myra sat in awe and amazement all the way — wherever they were going. Jeth was not acting queer or disturbed exactly. His face looked sad — yet distinctly gentle. He stopped in front of Brook's house.

"You take her in, Myra. Jes' ask if she can't stay with Melodie Ann while we do a little business in town."

"Of course, Carrie can stay here. Come in, honey. What a nice surprise. How did you know I was lonesome? I'm here all by myself this afternoon."

"We won't be gone so long, I don't think," smiled Myra.

"Well, that's all right, Mrs. Grinstead. Don't hurry with your shopping. We'll get along all right, I'm sure. Won't we, Carrie?"

She took the child to the bedroom. "We'll put your wraps right here like this. What have you been doing all morning?"

"Oh, playin' with my doll."

"Your doll?"

"It's the one my brother got me, my biggest one. You know that one?"

"You mean — Millard?"

Carrie nodded.

"He's far, far way. You know that?"

"Yes, I know. He's in Africa, isn't he?"

Carrie nodded.

"Let's go out in the living room, Carrie. Here's a little chair just your size. See. It was mine when I was your age. Try it. It just fits you, doesn't it?"

Carrie nodded.

"Do you have a little chair like this at home?"

"I got a stool. It's not like this."

"I'm sorry we don't have a doll here for you to play with. Let me see. What can I give you to look at? Would you like to look at some pictures?"

"I don't care."

"Here, sit up on the davenport and you can look at some while I finish this letter to Marlin. I had it all done but the last line when you came."

"Mommy got a letter from Millard today. Two of them, an' one was for Pop all by himself."

"It was?"

"Mommy cried when she read hers an' —"

"Cried? Is - is he hurt?" Melodie Ann's hand went suddenly to her throat.

"I guess not."

"Then why did - your - Mommy cry, dear?" she said, rebuking herself.

"It was all about his heart."

Carrie climbed up on the end of the davenport. She started looking at the pictures. The album more than filled her little lap.

"His heart?"

"About givin' it to God." Carrie looked up innocently into Melodie Ann's face.

"Did - he, Carrie?" Melodie Ann's voice had a catch in it. Her breath came in a gasp. She sat close beside the little girl on the davenport. "Tell me - all about it. You say — your biggest brother - Millard - gave his heart - to God?" She bent forward.

Carrie nodded.

"Way over there where - where war is at an' her was - you know her got bap - a - a." She punched her first finger into her cheek thinkingly.

"You mean baptized?"

"Yes. Baptized with water - cause Mommy told me it was in the letter all how it was - an' everythin' that made him glad, cause Mommy prayed each day he would."

Melodie Ann's heart thumped. She looked at the wall but saw nothing.

"Oh, Carrie." Unbidden tears welled up in the girl's blue eyes. She fought to keep them back. She hurried to the kitchen. She took a drink.

She came back.

"Are you sure, Carrie?" She had to hear it repeated. She couldn't believe it by hearing it once.

The child looked up questioningly.

"Huh?"

"Really, did your brother get baptized - over there in Africa?"

"Mommy showed me the paper."

"What paper, honey?"

"Where it was written down that he did."

"What do you mean, dear? Who wrote it down?" She sat beside the little girl.

"Why, the preacher. It was written on a paper with lines around the edge like this." Little Carrie went round and round with her finger. "An' Mommy can put it in a picture an' hang it on the wall if she wants to."

"Oh, Carrie, isn't it just wonderful! Your Mommy cried because she was glad then, didn't she?"

"Yes, glad. Why - why," Carrie looked at the bigger girl in surprise, "you needn't cry, too." Melodie Ann looked away quickly. She bit her lip.

"I know. I - I won't." Something was tugging at her heart. Tears wanted to come.

"Mommy said glad tears aren't hot, but sad tears are."

"I know." Melodie Ann's one arm went around the child beside her. "No, glad tears aren't hot. Does Liticia know about your brother?"

Carrie did not answer. Perhaps she did not hear.

"I know who this is." She pointed to a picture.

"Who?"

"Marlin."

"That's right."

"I like Marlin. Don't you?"

Melodie Ann laughed.

Carrie looked through the picture album like a child her age would. She wasn't too interested in most of the pictures.

She found one that took her attention.

"Who is this little girl with a doll?" "That's me when I was , oh, about seven, maybe."

"Don't you still have it?"

"No, I don't, Carrie. One time I dressed it with pretty clothes and gave it to a little girl who was sick in bed for a long time."

"What was the matter with her?"

"She had rheumatic fever."

"What's that?"

"It's a disease that made the little girl's legs hurt, and she had to be in bed a long time."

"An' she couldn't walk?"

"No, she couldn't walk for a long time. Her parents carried her out on the porch sometimes when it was nice and warm."

"Mommy said when summer comes an' it's warm again she hopes my brother will come home."

"She did? Shall we put these pictures away and make some candy or popcorn balls?"

Carrie slipped off the davenport. Her eyes danced. "Let's do that."

* * * * *

Brother Ambers answered the doorbell. He had on his overalls.

"How do you do, friend Jethro and Sister Grinstead." Brother Ambers extended his hand and shook both of theirs cordially. "Won't you come in?"

"Are you too busy to talk a little?" Jeth asked.

"Not at all. Not at all. Take off your coat, Sister Grinstead."

"Thanks, I'll just leave it on."

"I'm sorry my wife isn't here. Please have chairs. I just took her to the dentist a bit ago and while she's there I thought I'd do a little job she's been after me to do. You'll excuse my overalls."

"That's all right," Jeth began. He rubbed his trembling hands. It was hard to begin but he must. He knew why he had come. "I - I had a letter from Millard this forenoon," he hesitated. He seemed to be groping for words. He swallowed hard.

"You did?"

Jeth stroked his face. He pinched his cheek.

"She had one, too." He motioned to Myra. He might as well be frank and outspoken - straight from the shoulder. "I haven't read hers an' she hasn't read mine."

"Strange," thought Brother Ambers. There always had been something rather unusual, stiff, reserved about this man, Jethro. He never had been able to get next to him. What now? Was there family trouble? For Sister Grinstead's sake Brother Ambers wished his wife were present. He might need a good helpmate. Of all the problems that a minister must encounter, family troubles are the most heart-rending. But Jethro's wife did not look vexed or perturbed; she had a deep-settled peaceful expression on her face. They did not look as though they had been quarreling.

Brother Ambers waited.

"I reckon he told her in hers about bein' baptized over there in Africa by the army chaplain."

Brother Ambers glanced over to Jeth's wife and she nodded.

"Least ways that's what's in mine, an' — " Jeth cleared his throat. He brought his left foot up on his right knee. He gripped his ankle. He looked at the floor. How should he say it? It had to come out. It had to if it killed him. He never knew before he was capable of such emotions. Was this the way Millard had felt?

"I'm surely glad to hear this," Bro. Ambers responded warmly. "This is, you know, what we've been praying for."

"He's been through some pretty tough stuff - a - Brother Ambers," Jeth continued still gripping his ankle. "He was throwed fifty feet from the blast of a bomber one night, an' then he also killed a man."

"Oh, Jeth," Myra caught her breath. "Did he, Jeth?" Her eyes filled with sudden tears. "He didn't say that in mine. Oh, I'm so sorry — so sorry."

"That part was," Jeth's lips trembled, "too much fer him - I guess." Jeth pulled out his handkerchief. He blew his nose.

When a man gets Jeth's age, does he get emotional? Myra stared. What had come over her husband? She felt very tender toward him.

"That night he decided it. I come here to tell you, Brother Ambers, that —" (Jeth's foot dropped to the floor. He unbuttoned his coat at the bottom.) "that I done the boy wrong by the way I talked to you."

"What do you mean — the way you talked to me? When?"

"That day you came out to the house to see him an' I said it weren't no use fer to go in an' talk to him, an' all that. Surely you remember."

Of course, Brother Ambers remembered. How could he forget? But Myra looked surprised. What was Jeth talking about?

"He says he was sincere an' wanted to go ahead then an' be baptized - but - he was in the woodhouse an' heard us talkin' an' I didn't know it."

Myra sat motionless. This was what Millard wouldn't tell - not even to Liticia? Jeth saw Myra's look of astonishment.

"He says in his letter he never told no one."

"Well, I often wondered why he gave up," remarked Brother Ambers. "He never seemed to want to tell me."

Jeth cleared his throat. "I come to tell you, Brother Ambers, I had - no reason - to say what I did. If he'd gone ahead - an' been baptized then, he'd never have gone into the army maybe — an' he'd never - had to kill a man - an' go through all this."

Silence.

Jeth was wiping his eyes. He drew one long painful breath after the other.

"I'm glad," he said at length, "that Millard's got peace now — but — Brother Ambers, I — ain't got it."

Silence.

"I've not had it fer years - in fact," he was crying now, "I've never - really - had it - fer sure."

Jeth reached into his hip pocket.

He pulled out something.

It was his black Yorkshire pipe and a can of tobacco.

247

He got up and took several steps toward Brother Ambers. Brother Ambers got up to meet him. Jeth held out the two things which were so hard to part with, those two long-loved friends of his, and placed them in the minister's hands.

Myra's heart jumped. She sat fascinated. For years she had hoped, dreamed, prayed to be stirred by just such a scene as this. In the past few years she had almost lost hope. It had seemed useless.

"That's one thing that's been standin' in my way, I reckon." Jeth sat down again. His voice was unsteady, almost feeble. "I - I want to get rid of it. She knows I've tried it - before - but it's got an awful hold on me. I want - you - to pray fer me, Brother Ambers, that's why I came here."

"I'll be very glad to pray for you, Brother Grinstead. I'll do everything I can to help you. Shall we kneel right now?"

"Not yet. I have another thing to tell you, Brother Ambers. I'm ashamed to say it - but - Millard knows this, too. I don't know if he's ever told you or not."

"Millard has never told me anything about you, Jethro."

"Never?" gasped Jeth.

"Never."

"Well, it's happened mor'n onct, an' I know you wouldn't approve of it. Before Millard comes home I've got to be different about this, too."

Silence. The clock ticked the seconds away.

"There's no use fer me to do this - unless I do it up right, Brother Ambers."

"That's right, Brother Grinstead."

Silence.

Brother Ambers waited.

"I'm ready to help you in all your problems, and I'm sure your wife is, too."

"I know that, Brother Ambers," Jeth blew his nose again. "That's why I brought her along. I have never been the Christian that she's been - but I want - to try to make - a happier home - fer her an' the children."

Jeth stopped.

Myra waited to hear what else he was going to say.

Chapter 37

MYRA wanted to cross the room and put her arm around Jeth's shoulder. She wanted to tell Brother Ambers Jeth had been a good husband to her in spite of a few things. She wanted to shout her fidelity, but she did none of these things; she was too amazed. Was what she had heard true? Did Jeth feel that their home could be happier, and did he really want to do something about it?

It was evident Jethro Grinstead was going through a real struggle.

"Myra don't know it, Brother Ambers," choked the man, "but - I've - done some gamblin' - too."

At last it was out. He relaxed a bit.

Myra did not jump or gasp. She did not even look surprised.

"Or did Millard - tell you?" Jeth asked in a throaty voice.

"No, Jeth," Myra answered softly. "Millard never told me anything about you. If he knew it he never told me."

Jeth seemed somewhat relieved.

"Millard did tell me already, Jeth," she continued, "that he wished you'd talk to him more. He would like to feel close to you like fathers and sons should." She fumbled with her gloves. Jeth leaned forward and covered his face with his handkerchief. Then he looked up suddenly.

"Myra," he said in a tone that was little above a whisper, "would you mind if I'd talk a while with him alone?"

"Not at all, Jeth. Shall I go to the car?"

"No, you needn't do that," Brother Ambers said. "You stay right here. We can go to the basement. I want to look at the fire a little anyway."

Jeth followed Brother Ambers to the basement. He stood with one hand on the work bench. He must not detain the minister much longer. Brother Ambers put in two shovels of coal and faced the man who stood several inches taller than he. Since this confession was voluntary, he was going to let the rest of it be so. He waited, not knowing what to expect next. Truly the Spirit of the Lord was working.

"I'm sorry to say this, Brother Ambers," began Jeth, heaving, "but I've - I've never felt right toward Millard."

"You haven't? Why?"

"Well, - before he was born his mother spent so much time in prayer - it worried me."

"Worried you. Why?"

"Well," Jeth moaned, "from the start I had a feelin' he was born fer a special purpose."

"We've all been born for a special purpose, my dear friend."

"We are?"

"Yes, but just what had you in mind? Tell me more."

"Well, it's hard fer me to explain - what I mean. I'm no hand at puttin' thoughts into words - but - when Myra prayed so fer months - I had a feelin' that that boy was gonna likely be a preacher someday." Jeth drew a long breath.

"And what of that? You didn't want him to be?"

"No, I didn't."

"Why?"

"'Cause I wasn't livin' - like I should - to be the father of a preacher, Brother Ambers - an' I couldn't stand it to think maybe — someday he'd be sayin' things that would —" Jeth smote his breast. "Don't you know what I mean?"

"You mean you thought maybe Millard would preach against things like smoking and gambling and it would condemn you?"

"Yes. Yes. That's it. It's worried me fer over twenty years. There always was something about that boy that made me - what shall I say, uneasy, an' - unhappy. He always liked to read books - an' I didn't want him to. He always was such a sober boy - an', oh, I can't explain it, but I've been fearin' this. I thought sure if he went to the army I'd - he'd - an' now he's gone an' been baptized an' —" Jeth was shaking now.

"You mean," Brother Ambers put a hand on Jeth's shoulder, "you feel God has saved his soul, and He's going to use him in some definite way, and you've felt all these years he was born to fill a special place, and do a special work for God but you fought the idea?"

Jeth nodded. He could not speak.

"Would to God the world had more mothers like your wife, Brother Grinstead. This would be a better place to live, if more wives would pray like you said Myra did for her unborn son. I suppose many times she thought her prayers were not heard."

"I - I want to clean up before he comes home. I want to - to treat him - like I ought to. If he's gonn'a make a - preacher someday I've got to - be fit - to listen to it." It was hard for Jeth to control himself.

"Levi was goin' to send him on to school, I think if he wanted to go an' - now that's all off. Millard's not a child, you know, but he don't seem to care a thing about girls, so when he comes back - I want him to help me on the farm - sorta be like partners - if he's willin' an' get things goin' a little better."

"Millard would like that, wouldn't he?"

"He always did like home - an' he's orful fond of his mother. He says - fer me to try to help the other boys from goin' inter the army - but - Brother Ambers - it's - too late now."

"Too late?"

"Homer Jo thinks of nothin' else. But we've got to be movin' on, Brother Ambers. I'm takin' too much of your time. I know I haven't been a very good member, but I'm glad you didn't kick me out. I want to do better from now on."

"If you've told me all you want to, shall we go upstairs then and have prayer together before you leave?"

"Yes, sir." Jeth hesitated at the bottom step. "Someday if you have time - would you write to Millard - an' tell him - I came in here an' made this - right - with you? I'm no hand at writin' letters."

"I will, Brother Grinstead. I'll do all I can to help you into the happiness you want. I'll be glad to write to him."

* * * * *

Millard's face shone with a heavenly radiance when he got up from his knees. The chaplain took his hand and held it a moment. "God bless you, my boy, and the peace of His love be upon you from this day forth."

Millard did not know the chaplain had spoken a memorized line. "Thank you," he said.

Millard took out his handkerchief and lightly brushed the water of baptism off his shoulders as he walked slowly back to his pup tent. He had never before known this soul happiness. He knew his sins were all forgiven, not by the application of water on his head but by his personal faith in Jesus Christ.

The two day rest from fighting surely was wonderful, but no one knew how much longer it would last. The fellows were just waiting for orders. Did Rommel back into the Mediterranean? Indeed not. He was too cunning to do a thing like that. He had backed toward Egypt so the orders could be coming any time to pursue him there.

Millard stood outside his pup tent, gazing at the long purple rays stretching to the north and to the south of the late setting sun. Slowly they were fading into black. For three dreadful days and nights he hadn't even had time to think about the sunset. Perhaps the sun had set in the west, but he had seen nothing but fire and blood and hellish explosions, obscuring the sun, moon, and stars.

Must he go back to the front again? Would he be called out tomorrow or the next day or the next? Maybe tonight yet? Millard groaned within him when he thought of all that had happened in the past month. He shivered. This newly found peace and joy in his soul was something too precious to lose. It had cost too dearly. He had prayed in bitterest agonies until dawn that night after the bomber explosion threw him and sent him near death. Not until he was willing to overlook everything Pop had ever done and promise to be baptized and follow the Lord truly, had peace come. Now he knew in his inmost soul what more he must do. He would wait until after supper.

It was not going to be an easy matter. If he ever needed divine help, he did now. Dropping on his knees inside his tent he prayed until the sweat trickled down his temples. So soon after his baptism must he be tempted even as Christ was?

"Oh, God," he cried in his sincerity, "I want to be true to my promise to Thee. Undertake for me by Thy mighty power some way, somehow, and give me words of wisdom according to Thy printed Scripture here in my pocket. If it means death, even that would be an easy thing compared to the thousand horrible deaths I died out there the other night when I was yet lost."

After supper Millard walked back to his pup tent again to be alone once more.

"Come on, Grinstead," called several boys as they passed his tent, "let's go get some beer."

"No, thanks."

"Come on. We might not have another chance like this soon again."

"I don't care for any beer."

After the boys were out of sight he started toward the chaplain's headquarters.

He knocked on the door, although he could have entered without knocking.

"Come in," called the chaplain warmly.

"Thank you," answered Millard politely.

"Oh, so it's you, Millard, isn't it?"

"Yes, sir."

"I had a cousin by that name. Millard Goldsmith. He was a great singer. What can I do for you, Millard?"

"I came, sir, to tell you how happy I am since I'm baptized. It's wonderful to have peace. I was in torment before I gave up."

"Take a chair, Millard. I'm glad you're happy."

The chaplain tilted back in his chair and tapped his fingers on his desk.

"But," Millard cleared his throat, "in order to keep this peace I found out there the other night, I've got to obey my conscience."

"I see. And just what do you mean, Millard?"

"I mean, sir, that the Bible says I should not kill, and my conscience won't let me do it any more."

"You mean—" the chaplain let his chair legs drop to the floor with a thud. He looked Millard straight in the face and bent forward when he spoke.

"I mean," Millard said without faltering, "that after all I've seen and gone through recently to find peace, that if I would disobey the Word of God and go back to the front and help kill more men, I believe my soul would be cast into the bottomless pit."

"Wait a minute, wait a minute, my boy. Where do you think you find anything in the Bible to make you believe a thing like that? My Bible tells me that David was a man after God's own heart and he killed. And there were other great men of God who were warriors and God blessed their armies."

"I know, sir, but that was all in the Old Testament. I have not read anything about Christ killing in the New Testament."

"And did you feel like this when you joined the army?"

"No, sir, I didn't. I joined the army with practically no conscience against war, although all along I hoped in my heart the war would close before I had to take part in the actual fighting. My mother said when I left home the last time that she hoped I wouldn't need to kill any mother's son."

"Well, now I suppose a lot of mothers possibly said that same thing, but she surely didn't mean you'd be doomed if you did. Don't you know killing in times of war isn't like going out and shooting a man because you're jealous of the girl he's got?"

"You mean then that the words of Christ don't hold good in times of war?"

"If they did, my boy, where'd we all be tonight? You don't mean to tell me you think all our boys who've already laid down their lives since this is on, who laid down their lives a living sacrifice for their country and for the safety of others, are doomed!" The chaplain almost shouted the words.

"It is not for me to judge others, sir. I am only speaking for myself," answered Millard softly.

"And how many did you actually kill? Do you know?"

"I worked mostly in the towers the past few weeks."

"Then you did not even operate a gun?"

"No, sir, but I spotted the locations of the enemy and sent reports back, so they'd know just where to fire."

"Well."

"And I did kill one German who was already wounded."

"Well."

"He was badly wounded and would have died anyway, and as I passed him the other morning he asked me to finish him up."

"And that condemns you?" The chaplain frowned a frown of disappointment.

"I will never be able to blot it out of my mind."

"But you don't mean it condemns you, surely."

"Not now. I asked God to forgive me, and I know He has, but from now on I cannot help to kill."

"You mean you're going to be a traitor?"

"No, sir; not that."

"A deserter then! You mean you're going to forsake your duty? Haven't you given your pledge of allegiance to the United States government?" he shouted.

"I did, yes."

"And you mean it wouldn't bother your conscience to refuse to take orders?"

"Not if those orders conflict with the Word of God, sir. I am more afraid of disobeying Christ now than I am of disobeying the government."

Chapter 38

THE chaplain ran his fingers through his thin hair. The muscles in his cheeks twitched nervously.

"Are you sure, Millard," he said at length, eyeing the young man in front of him carefully, "are you sure," he repeated, "that you aren't a bit unnerved? Let me call the doctor. Perhaps he could give you something to calm yourself a little."

"It is not a doctor I need," Millard answered clearly. "The other night when I was blown fifty feet and knocked unconscious and I didn't know for a while whether I was in hell or not, I really was unnerved then. My soul was in a judgment too unbearable to think of long. Peace came after I promised God I'd lay down my gun and forgive all men, even those who seek my life, not before. I cried and prayed for hours. It was terrible. Have you never felt like that?"

The chaplain got up and walked back and forth in front of his desk, his hands in his pockets fumbling coins. His countenance was not indignant, not contemptuous, but strangely agitated.

"No," he said abruptly. Then he sat on top of his desk. "I am very sorry to learn that one in our battalion has formed such ideas as you have. It is somewhat disturbing, or I should say disappointing, or still rather unfortunate that one who carries your rank and has proved so efficient, should now even think of deserting his post of duty. Do you want to be sent home with a dishonorable discharge?"

Millard did not answer.

"Don't you think your parents, your home town, your local board, would be heartily disappointed?"

"I would rather have the disapproval of men than God, sir."

Again the chaplain walked back and forth.

"What would you do if you'd be put in a guardhouse?"

"I'd stay there until I was released."

"It would be mighty unpleasant and mighty lonely there, my boy."

"My Lord would be with me, sir. I read in my Testament that Paul was put in prison and so was Peter. They did not consider it a disgrace or a tragedy. I decided before tonight that if this stand costs me my life that would be an easy matter compared to a death in sin and disobedience. Eternity is awful long, Chaplain, to run the risk of spending it in the wrong place."

A strong but slightly unsteady hand came down on Millard's shoulder. "Have you been seeing apparitions, my boy?" he asked.

"What do you mean, sir?"

"Have you been bothered with seeing things that aren't? Strange figures — like ghosts at night?"

"I've seen enough that actually was. I've seen my own soul trying to die a thousand deaths, begging to die, but God told me the soul will never die and I'm still here. My body will die but not my soul. The soul of that man I killed, where is it tonight? It haunts me when I think of it." Millard dug his fingernails into the palms of his hands.

"But you told me God forgave you." The chaplain bent forward and waved his hand dramatically.

"He did but — the man had a right to live as well as I. He was not trying to kill me because he wanted to."

"How do you know?"

"His eyes were kind, sir — and he told me as much."

"A German, you say?"

"Yes, sir."

"He could say as much at his last, perhaps." The chaplain laughed a dry laugh. "He knew he was down. The Germans are deceitful. You should not talk like this. I could make it bad for you, but —" he hesitated. He seemed to search his thoughts for words. At last he spoke.

"Wouldn't we be in a pretty mess if everyone took your attitude?"

Millard sat thinking.

"Supposing all our men would say tonight I can't kill another German? Supposing everyone would refuse to take up arms?" he asked. "I know that day will never come as long as the world stands. There will always be those who will fight. My Bible says there will be wars and rumors of wars until Christ comes."

"Are you better than the other boys?"

"No, sir. I've been a sinner and - and I'm only a sinner saved by grace."

Staggering thoughts made the chaplain restless.

"How God spared my life through nine engagements," Millard added feelingly, "is more than I can figure out. It was only by the prayers of my mother and perhaps a few friends at home, and by God's great mercy, that my life was extended until today so that I could get baptized."

"Let me ask you this, then. If you are no better than the other boys, do you take this position then because you don't want to get out there and die with sinners?"

"I said, sir, it is not death that I fear, but to disobey God. Is there not some way out for me?" Millard's eyes filled with sudden tears. He fought desperately to hold them back. "I believe it is my duty to obey every law of the land that does not conflict with the Bible. I've read a good bit as I had opportunity before we came here to North Africa. It is not that I shrink from hard work or danger, but I believe God wants me to help to heal the wounds of war, but not to help wound. I came here to you tonight for spiritual help and advise, not to argue with you, sir. Today you baptized me in the name of the Father, Son and Holy Ghost, and all three of them have put it on my heart to come to you to tell you this, that it would be sin for me to kill again, and if I do, the Holy Spirit will be grieved, and it would be just like helping to drive nails into the hands of Christ on the cross again if I did."

"How do you figure that out?"

"I did not figure it out, sir; it's in the Scripture that we should do unto others as we would be done by, and also inasmuch as I do to the least person it's the same as doing it to Christ. I would not kill Christ."

"But you're twisting and confusing the Scriptures, Millard," said the chaplain. There was tension in his deep-throated voice and his gray eyes looked tired. "That verse has to do with helping some poor person in need of food or clothing."

"I know - but - oh, sir - who am I to tell you this? You are above me, I know, and I respect you very highly, but it also says inasmuch as ye have done it not, and Christ prayed for those who sought his life. How can I love my enemies and pray for them and yet kill them?"

The chaplain did not answer. He pulled out his watch and looked at it.

"I have heard and read some," he said after an awkward pause, "about the conscientious objectors. They are a peculiar group of people who are causing the government a lot of trouble and making for themselves a lot of unnecessary comment. Their arguments are good for peace times, but they are senseless now. There are exceptions to every rule. We can't just fold our arms or all get down on our knees and pray that the Germans won't come in and take everything we have, and kill our wives and children and burn up our cities. You don't just let the mosquitoes crawl all over you and suck the blood out of you. You kill them, don't you, and snakes, and the like?"

"But those don't have souls, sir."

"It almost seems sometimes that some people are brutish enough not to have souls. The Germans and Japs ought to die like beasts."

"But they do have souls, sir. We talk about sending them to hell and we don't mean their bodies. That goes back to dust like the animals do. It's the souls of men I have no right to send to destruction. God is love, and since I'm saved in His love I must testify to His love." Millard found himself saying things he had not dreamed of saying. Surely it was the Spirit of God within him. "Couldn't I - maybe - get a job driving an ambulance? I have a friend in the states who is a conscientious objector and he volunteered to serve in a mental hospital, not because he was a coward or afraid, but because he has a conscience against fighting men. He would fight fire or disease or flood gladly. He is very happy serving in a hard place and he gets only five or ten dollars a month, I forget which."

"You infer that - that's what you'd rather be doing then?"

"Well, he is giving his time and service, and the government has made this provision for those who feel they cannot fight. You see, sir, he is putting his love for Christ into actual reality. He expressed it every day to his patients. That is what I feel I must do, too. I must express outwardly the love I feel in my heart. I cannot see how I can obey the Bible and love my enemies and at the same time kill them."

"Haven't you heard of a man killing his crippled or deformed child because he loved them so, or even a beautiful wife because he saw she was going astray?" The chaplain's face was getting flushed now. "I say that love can absolutely kill. These young men in our regiment all love their homes, their parents, their country with a true love. I know it." The chaplain's hand went palm down on his desk. He look a little sharp. "What kind of Bible have you been reading?"

Millard pulled it out of his shirt pocket. "This is it, sir. It's a Gideon Testament like all the boys get. Isn't it the same as yours?"

"Of course. Put it back. I guess it depends on who reads it and how. Three blind men touched an elephant . You know the story, no doubt. One felt its tail and said he had hold of a rope, another touched his trunk and said he had hold of a tree. The third touched his side and said it was a wall. They were all as sincere as they could be, but who could condemn them because they didn't interpret their sensations correctly? God himself wouldn't hold them accountable for that. The greatest of men perhaps don't see or interpret the Scriptures alike in every detail. You're getting down to fine points here. You're like the blind man. You've got hold of one verse. Do you know, Millard, what I'm trying to help you to see?" He squeezed the words out through his front teeth.

Millard stood up erect and looked his superior straight in the eyes. He took one step toward him with a confident look on his face. "Allow me to differ with you a little, sir, I - I beg your pardon, for I did not come to argue, but I've searched the New Testament as a whole, putting all the words of Christ together with open eyes and an honest mind. One verse tells me to submit myself to the government and to pay tribute, but to give God what belongs to Him, and that's obedience to Him first. Peter and John disobeyed the government to obey God. The whole New Testament teaches love and good will to all men, even our enemies. I must love those who persecute me. The only way to make an enemy a friend is to win him with kindness. The Bible says we should honor all men and again that God is no respecter of persons. The souls of the Germans are worth as much as your soul or mine. I've read and read and prayed and looked at this whole problem till I know I don't think the elephant is a tree or a rope or a wall, as you put it. It's an elephant, sir. I see the light and cannot deny it. The light is revealed to us in the truth of the whole Word of God, sir."

"Well, my boy," said the chaplain huskily, rubbing one hand over the other. "I've been stationed up here to encourage the boys in this battalion - to build up morale in this time of special distress and danger. I mean to do my duty as a good soldier of Christ." Again the palm of his hand smote his desk. "I was happy to baptize you when you came to me today, but I must confess I've never run up against anything quite like this. I don't know what else to do with you but report you first to the doctor. I think you've been reading too much. You know a person can be intemperate in that, too. Before we came over from Ireland did you spend a lot of time by yourself, or did you get out with the other boys?"

"I've always been somewhat of a reserved nature, sir. I have always liked to read a great deal."

The chaplain sat on the edge of his desk. He sat deep in thought. A group of soldiers went by laughing and shouting in half-drunken vociferations.

"In there's that kid," Millard heard one say. Then he heard another say something about beer and they all burst out in boisterous shouts.

"Well, I tell you, Millard," blinked the chaplain, running his one hand unsteadily through his thin hair again, "supposing you go back to your tent and have a good night's rest. Don't read your Testament tonight. Let your mind just rest a little. Try to forget everything but the prayer. Do you have a copy yet of that printed prayer we passed out in chapel this forenoon?"

"Yes, sir."

"You were there, then?"

"Yes, sir."

"Just read that over once or twice and then try to sleep. That's what you need Millard. You've got yourself all worked up tonight. This won't do. Do you know what I thought when you came in here?"

"No, sir."

"Well, most of the boys who come to me for help have trouble with their sweethearts or wives or some sex problem. You have nothing like that bothering you?"

"No, sir. I - I"

"Wait a minute, Millard." The chaplain stepped close to him and touched his sleeve with the tips of his fingers. Maybe at last he was at the root of the boy's problem. His face lit up with new courage. "Tell me the truth, son," he said. "Are you fretting over some girl and you want to make yourself believe you can compensate by taking this kind of an attitude?"

Millard stepped back in astonishment. He caught his breath and held it.

"No, sir," he answered. "I have no sweetheart."

"You never had any?"

"No, sir."

"You should. This is an abnormal situation. You must get interested in a girl. Girls do wonders for men. You must find you a girl, Millard."

"Here?"

The chaplain laughed.

"Can't you think of a sweet little thing you know back in the states?"

Millard blushed. He shifted from one foot to the other.

"Can't you?"

"I can think of one, sir - but - I've never written her a letter. She doesn't know - I think she's sweet." His voice dropped almost to a whisper. He looked toward the door.

"Go back to your tent and write her a letter then tonight. Get your mind off yourself and you'll soon feel better. Just try it. Listen now. You come back tomorrow evening and tell me how you made out."

"And you won't report me to the doctor after all?"

"I'll wait twenty-four hours first and see how you feel, Millard," he said sympathetically. "I hate to turn you over unless it's absolutely necessary. I really want to help you."

Millard walked toward the door.

"And what shall I do if the call comes before tomorrow night and — I cannot go?"

The chaplain shook his head.

"This world is made up of some awful queer people with some awful queer ideas," he said, "and I'll have to have some information on how to —" He left the sentence hanging over Millard's head.

Chapter 39

MILLARD limped. For days he had been suffering from a pain on the bottom of his right foot, but not like this. He could scarcely walk. Hobbling painfully on his heel he reached his pup tent. He dropped on his bed and removed his shoe. The lump was more than twice as big as it had been that morning. The pain was going to his ankle. He felt it going to his knee. Searching in his duffle bag in the dark he found his flashlight and his diary. Elevating his foot on his blankets he lay on his stomach.

He hadn't written in his diary for weeks. Not because there wasn't plenty to write, but because he hadn't had a chance. With the aid of his flashlight he wrote in spite of noise outside the tent.

Diary:

"Thank God I was baptized today, and I just got back from having a talk with the chaplain. I do not know how things are going to work out for me, but one thing I know I am determined to hold to is this peace that was so hard to find. I must not lose it at any cost. God help me. So the chaplain thinks it would help me to have a girl, a sweetheart. Little does he know the girl I admire would not help in the way he thinks, but rather in the opposite. She is all tenderness and love. Her sweet life has influenced me to make this decision. Only God will ever know how she has helped me tonight. Did she send·up a prayer for me? If not, the picture of her lovely face in my memory has made me want to be a good man. Someday, if she is not taken, I will prove to her I am sincere. The letter I mailed to Pop - what will he say? Oh, God, help him to believe in me. If he refuses to read it, I'll at least have a clear conscience. If he reads it and it makes him mad, I cannot help it. I had to write what I did."

Millard snapped off his flashlight and lay musing. He was glad the other three boys in his tent were out. At last he snapped on the light again and wrote in his diary.

"In vain I've tried to forget her face;
  But it came before me in every place,
In deepest hell on darkest nights,
  With Christ's and Mothers. All three were bright.
I long to be stirred by her dear sight
  Could she see - could she tell - I've seen the light?
That holy light that comes from above
  Where there's nothing like war, nothing but love?
Oh, Melodie Ann, you may never know
  Why God has allowed me to suffer so;
But this I know within my breast
  You've helped me to vict'ry and peace and rest."

He reached in his shirt pocket and unfolded the prayer the chaplain told him to be sure to read.

"Almighty God and Father, the Creator of all things visible and invisible, look down on me here today, and keep me faithful to my duty until my great task is completed. Raise me above the stress and strain of war until I continually feel Thy hand of watchful love on me. Help me to keep my dignity as a good soldier, and never stoop to anything that would bring dishonor or reproach to the country for which I am serving. We together thank Thee for victories won, and pray for greater victories tomorrow. Help me never to know fear or discouragement when others are called to give their lives, knowing Thou who lovest life, and peace, and all things beautiful, wilt reward according to Thy good pleasure, in the name of Christ, Amen."

Millard did not read the prayer a second time. Somehow it did not satisfy. He must word his own prayers. He slipped the prayer into the back of his diary. He put the notebook in the bottom of his duffle bag and knelt in prayer.

He tried to make himself as comfortable as possible. His foot pained a lot. By flashlight he read the entire eighth chapter of Romans, lingering at the eighteenth verse. He read and reread that verse, "for I reckon that the sufferings of this present time are not worthy to be compared with the glory which shall be revealed in us." He snapped off his flashlight and dropped into a peaceful sleep.

In the morning Millard could not get his shoe on. He hobbled stocking-footed to the mess hall. His foot hurt much worse than the night before. He must see a doctor.

"There's nothing to do but operate on this foot," the doctor said frankly, "we can't let it go. How long has this been bothering you?"

"I've felt it for some time, but it never bothered me a whole lot until this past week. Yesterday it hurt so bad I could hardly stand on it, and last night it hurt very much."

"Well, we'll have to put you in a hospital. There's infection in there."

"How long will I be there?"

"I don't know that. It all depends on how extensive the operation will be. Of course, you won't be able to put your shoe on again for maybe ten days or even two weeks. It's a shame and a half you won't be able to help chase that tricky Rommel and his men into hell's last fire, but I guess you'll have to just be lazy for a while." The doctor slapped Millard on the shoulder. "Report at once to the hospital. I'll take care of this as soon as possible."

"And what do you think it is, doctor?"

"It looks and feels like some kind of growth under this callous. I'm not able to say until I go in there. It might not be anything serious."

Millard hobbled back to his pup tent, and, in spite of the pain, he had a new unwritten song of thanksgiving in his heart. Could it be that God moved in this strange and unexpected way with His hand of mercy for one who sincerely wanted to love in action as well as word?

From his hospital bed Millard could hear the constant distant reverberations like thunder, and could see the fire of guns against the darkening sky, even though the field hospital was perhaps twenty miles from the battle. He could smell the oily smoke when the wind swept it across the desert. Even at this distance the noise of war seemed hideous. A few vultures with naked heads and long bills, hungry birds of death, circled in the near distance, screeching in high shrill notes before they swooped to the earth. From the hospital window Millard watched the birds. What were they looking for? Some flesh to devour? Everywhere - anywhere seemed the close call of death.

The operation itself was practically painless. The doctor used a local anesthetic, but now the pain was severe. Yet Millard was very conscious of the fact that there were hundreds of boys worse off than he. His misfortune had been nothing compared to many around him.

In the first bed to his right was a man whose haggard face was drawn in pain and his breathing was labored. In the second bed was a man his face and both hands wound in white gauze, and there were puckers around both eyes. He'd been crying until the bandage on his face was wet. On the other side of Millard's bed was a man who must have been in the hospital for some days. One leg was missing, and the other was in a cast. His blanched face, which was damp with a nervous sweat of anguish, had a look of doom on it. Beyond him sat a lad on the side of his bed, his thin bare legs dangling, and his hands shaking as though he had palsy. He looked as though the horrors of war were unbalancing his young mind. There was a weird, pitiful, captured look in his eyes. Wasn't he some loving mother's dear boy? Probably a month ago, he did not shake at all; and now it seemed he could not stop shaking. When Millard felt better himself, he'd try to talk to the boy. He seemed so young and weak and wan.

Millard's foot hurt. Wouldn't he get a pain pill to tide him through the first night? If he were at home, where he couldn't hear those everlasting explosions, those terrible roaring planes, and those hideous land mines blowing up the earth, maybe the pain would not be so severe. He felt every vibration in his foot. How it must hurt those who were torn and broken and half murdered, brought in to be patched up and mended to live the rest of their days in mutilation. The lad that shook, would he ever be able again to enjoy life? Millard saw him staring out of the window as though his soul was speaking one continuous unuttered oath of anguish, Millard pitied him, not himself.

A storm of dust or smoke rose high in the heavens in the distance, and a bellowing series of faraway explosions echoed and re-echoed. The lad shook till his teeth chattered; then he let out a cry of terror. It was an appalling sound. Sweat broke out all over Millard. If he were able he'd go over and talk to him. A man over in the corner in the vilest language he had ever heard.

"The devil's raving like mad tonight, ain't he?" shouted someone in the opposite corner.

"An' I hope to God, Rommel an' all his black angels will be put into the blackness of blackest hell where he can't ever see his way out," answered yet another. Must Millard hear such talk for two weeks?

While the man was speaking another patient was brought in. The boy was half conscious. His starry eyes were bulging and his temples were both swollen. He was coughing as though he would choke, and he was spitting chunks of brown blood in a pan the nurse had given him. Two nurses put him in the last empty bed in the ward.

As darkness crept over the continent, the field hospital sounded like one howling place of torture as moans and curses and cries came from everywhere. It never subsided. The lad who shook became one pitiful bundle of intolerable agony. Was it going to be as awful as this day after day? Was there ever going to be an end to sorrow and murder, slaughter and suffering? At least, he, Don Millard wasn't out there on the front helping to kill more men. But these around him were all boys the Germans and Italians had tried to smash up, and didn't get it done. Shouldn't he hate them for this? No, for the wounded Germans and Italians far outnumbered these. Even with all their suffering and loss, the Americans were ahead. "Is there a God somewhere?" cried a man in the ward in a loud insistent voice. No one answered. He was probably talking "out of his head" anyway. Past the open door went the death cart. It had passed twice before in the last hour.

Millard would ring if he knew where the bell was. Maybe there were no bells here. Couldn't he have a pain pill just the first night? He could feel the surgeon's knife cutting to the bone. He felt sick on his stomach. He was not afraid to suffer. He was not even afraid to die. But his supersensitive nature made him too sympathetic to the pains of others. Except that he knew the Lord and had peace in his soul, this whole thing, so indescribably weird and horrible, would sap the very strength and will power out of him. No wonder the most exciting magazines and pictures of feminine life seemed dull and uninteresting to the other boys when the whole world was being blown to bits in one mad convulsion after the other. The sight of torn human flesh and blood was chilling, weakening, disturbing. No wonder men who did not know God cried out, tormented by fantastic apparitions. Not long ago these same boys had laughed and sung and bathed their fine strong bodies in the warm sunshine. In Ireland they laughed at the movies and danced with pretty girls who came to camp to be hugged and smiled at.

What good did laughing and dancing and movies do them now in the depths of this wicked, filthy, broken world!

Millard wished he could tell all the boys about Jesus Christ and

His power to save. Christ could give them perfect peace in spite of all this. Millard knew He could because He had done it for him. But didn't they have Testaments of their own? He saw only a few of the boys refuse to take one when the Gideons passed them out. Didn't they read them? Did they read but, like the blinded man at the elephant, only try one verse and give up because they couldn't understand what they read? Millard could recall seeing only a very few of the boys reading their Testaments. Most of them carried them for a good luck charm.

Millard pondered and thought.

A nurse came in. She lit a little oil lamp that gave a small blue flame. The man in the second bed to Millard's right looked ghastly in the dim light. His hands across his breast had dreadful long fingernails. Millard watched. Was there really life under his drawn parched lips? Even while Millard watched, his faint cold voice cried out in wretched helplessness, "You - cur - you - old - swine - I'll - get you yet." Was he dreaming or was he delirious?

Millard motioned to the nurse. "Couldn't I please have a pill tonight to help me get a little sleep?"

"Are you in pain?" she asked.

"Yes, ma'am."

"Where?"

"In my foot."

She lifted the cover to make sure he knew what he was saying.

"I'll see," she said and hurried away.

Presently she returned with two small capsules and a glass of water.

"Thanks, miss."

"You're welcome."

She made her rounds. Others got pills and some got "shots". After what seemed to Millard an hour, he fell into a deep, dark, but peaceful sleep.

✳   ✳   ✳   ✳   ✳

Liticia tore open the letter. She'd waited for a long time, longer than ever before.

"Dear Ticia,

Greetings to you in Jesus' name. Have you heard about my baptism? Surely Mother has told you, if she got my letter. I haven't heard from home now for more than five weeks. Why doesn't someone write to me? How glad we'll be when this war is over. Everyone wonders how much longer it can last. Ticia, war isn't (censored). Do you pray for peace? I'm so anxious to get home.

Well, I'm in the hospital now (censored) I had an operation on my foot a week ago. There was an infected growth on the bottom of my foot, I could not wear my shoe so the doctor cut it out. As soon as I dare walk they are going to make some kind of a sandal for me. I doubt if I'd be able (censored) about finished up I think. It surely sounded good to me to hear that the Italians and Germans both surrendered by the thousands. I had a feeling it would go that way. I was right in the thickest of nine major engagements. (censored) escaped death and accident so far. I did not get a scratch, only bruises from stumbling and falling. I suppose this growth on my foot came from walking and tramping so much, but (censored) I don't know but I can (censored) How is Marlin getting along? Say, why doesn't Orpha write to me? Does she write to you or go home? I think I must hear from some of you before many days. Either you don't write or my mail is being tied up somewhere or lost. Ticia, remember me in your prayers. In love, Millard."

Chapter 40

IN the final battle some 300,000 German and Italian troops were driven from a series of strongly fortified mountain positions by about two thirds their number of British and American troops. Of the 400,000 enemy troops, only a few made their escape to Italy. About 350,000 surrendered with their great stores of weapons and ammunition. The Middle East had been saved, but vast rows of graves marked the route where American boys laid down their young lives on the shores of the blue Mediterranean waters.

Millard knew that it was alone by the hand of God he was not among those thousands planted in African soil. The longer he stayed in the hospital the more conscious he was of the fact that God had kept His guardian angel watching him, especially during those last days on the front. The casualties had been heavy enough. To see the wounded brought in was heartbreaking, sickening. Ambulances were always coming. Cries and moans were a continuous sound. The lad who shook got so excited that sometimes he stuttered. He would probably always shake.

Millard limped on his sandal over to the boy's bed. He sat down beside him and took hold of his one flabby arm. The boy stiffened.

"Don't," he cried in fresh fright.

"I won't hurt you," Millard said gently. "I'm your friend."

"Uh," the lad drew back and stared out of his faded, fishy eyes.

"Don't be afraid of me."

Millard stroked his hand.

"Who k-k-killed me in my s-s-s-sleep?" he stuttered. "D-d-did you?"

"No one killed you. You are alive. See, alive like I am. Touch me. We are not dead."

"Uh."

"We are in the hospital, friend, cheer up. Maybe the worst is over now. Maybe we'll get to go home someday before long. Where do you live?"

"Live? Where? Who c-c-could l-l-live among so many d-d-dead? They t-t-tried to k-k-kill me in my s-s-sleep 'fore I had a ch-ch-chance to run. T-t-twice they k-k-killed me."

"What's your name?" asked Millard.

"Uh," The boy twitched. "It's lost, everything's - lost," he cried pitifully.

"Everything like what?" asked Millard.

"M-m-my pictures an' everything."

"You had some pictures? Who were the pictures of?"

"They k-killed her, too. An' s-s-she was s-s-sweet an' s-sleepin', too." He stared up into Millard's face with his half-dead eyes that had such a taken-away look in them.

What could Millard do for a lad whose mental sense was slowly but surely slipping? Couldn't something be done for him to bring him back before he was completely unbalanced? Millard had noticed he didn't eat enough to keep a bird alive. He never smiled, always shook, and looked frightened out of unseeing eyes. What was it that bore so on the boy's mind? Who was the sweet "her" he thought was killed with him in sleep?

Oh, the tyranny! Oh, the cruelty! Oh, the agonies of hatred and war! What monstrous crimes in which boys like this one were involved. Once he must have enjoyed life and home and a girl who was pretty. He did not look like the sort of a lad who liked bloody things. Who started this detestable, damnable mess? Could it ever be rectified? Couldn't some nation budge from its own selfish opinions and make peace? Surely no human beings really wanted war. Weren't all the soldiers, Germans and Italians and Japs, as well as the Americans, anxious to go to their homes, and home-cooked meals, and love?

"I really wish I could help you," said Millard, rubbing the lad's arm gently. "Would you like to look at a picture of my mother and father and little sister I have back home?"

The boy's mouth dropped open. He did not answer. Millard went to his coat on the nail beside his bed and returned with the picture. In blank anticipation, the lad took the picture and held it close to his eyes with his two shaky hands. He dropped it in utter disappointment and bit his own wrists in tense anguish. Millard did not dream it would affect him this way. He meant it well. He felt almost like a scolded dog now. What could he do for the poor lad? He tried to think.

"The Lord is my shepherd, "Millard said suddenly, soothingly. The boys arms dropped limp at his sides. Millard sat closer so he could speak softly in his ear. "I shall not want," he said. "He maketh me to lie down in green pastures — nice, shady green pastures, soft and smooth like velvet, and He leadeth me beside still waters - peaceful waters that are clear and cool, where there is no night, for the waters are the river of Life, where God is, and there is no night, only peace and joy." The boy sat listening. Millard continued. "He restoreth my soul, too, and leadeth me in paths of righteousness for His name's sake. Yea, though I walk through the valley of the shadow of death."

"Uh." The lad stiffened again. "They k-killed us; they d-d-did. You see who it was? In the valley of death - at night - an' took her away?"

Millard gave up. Sweat from fearful thoughts, terrifying thoughts, broke out on his face and neck. What would become of this lad? And the hundreds of others who would be in mental darkness the rest of their days.

Disappointed, Millard limped away. He walked down the hall only to see with his own eyes more pictures of despair, suffering, and hopelessness. Here were some slightly wounded, hobbling around like himself. Next were some feebler ones, propped up on pillows or on elbows, trying desperately to get interested in a cheap story or Christian Science. There lay the feeblest, belching and choking with gas pains, some dying possibly from internal hemorrhages. Everywhere, everywhere, were torn, disfigured, racked, and dismembered men. Once they had all been robust, physically fit with nerves like blue steel. Now their nerves were worn till they were thin and brittle. They could snap at anything - little things.

* * * * *

Myra read the letter to Jeth.

"Dear Folks at home," (censored)

"Why, Jeth, all this first line is cut out."

"Today I got a letter from Orpha. It was three months old. I was glad to get it anyway. Today I went to an African village, my first trip to town for a long time. I am able to walk quite well again. I do not know how much longer we will be here, but the way things have been shaping up I wonder if we might get a ride down the streets of Berlin yet before we come home. Don't any of you write to me any more? Don't you think I like to hear from home, or what is wrong that I don't get mail? I wonder and wonder."

"Well, that's strange," Myra gasped. "He thinks we're neglecting him. Poor boy. But I've been writing every week."

"Brother Ambers told me Sunday he wrote to him," Jeth said.

"And I know Liticia has written."

She continued the letter. "You can't imagine how homesick I am today. It seems like ten years since I left the states. Nothing would suit me any better than to find myself on a quiet little farm once more milking cows and feeding chickens and living at peace with all my neighbors. This is my last sheet of paper. I could not find any in town here, so please send me some and some envelopes, too. Some of the boys trade cigarettes for paper or stamps. I have nothing I wish to trade.

"It is so wonderful to know (censored) to look upon. (censored) We had a mess of lice to get rid of, too, and that isn't (censored). I wish I could help them all but there're too many. Well, how are you all? How are Orpha and the boys? How is Carrie? I've not heard from any of you since I told you I was baptized, but I won't let that (censored). I have to wonder if you ever got my letters. I wrote one to you, Mother, and one to Pop, too. Did you get them? Your loving son, Millard."

"Well, well," said Jeth, "write him another today again and send him some paper. If there isn't any here I'll go get some. What becomes of the letters you mail him? And I would sure like to know what all that was that got cut out.

* * * * *

Millard couldn't wait until he got to his pup tent to read it. He tore it open and sat on the ground.

"Dear Millard,

Marlin got to come home over Thanksgiving. He had many interesting experiences to tell about his hospital work. He gave a talk in church. Pop and all of them were there to hear it. I told you in my last letter how different Pop seems. I hope your foot soon heals. Millard, I have something to tell you. Please don't be too surprised,

273

but Marlin and I are engaged."

Millard's breath came fast - faster.

"We are happy and are sure we are meant for each other. The folks think it's all right, and I'm so glad. I'm twenty, you know. Millard, we want to have our wedding soon after you get home. Have you any idea at all when that will be? Of course, if it goes too long we might not wait, because I'd like to have a chance at working in the hospital where Marlin is because there are openings for wives of C.P.S. men. I know I'd enjoy doing that.

"Did you get a letter from Marlin lately? He said he was going to write and tell you how glad he is you turned to Christ, and he is so anxious to get better acquainted with you now. You'll love Marlin; I know you will, Millard. He is grand to me and has such high ideals and he really is a Christian. What do you think of Marlin's request? I told him you were a quiet sort of person, but that I felt almost sure you wouldn't refuse. I've already asked Melodie Ann to be my bridesmaid."

Millard's hands got cold; then his face got hot. The pages shook.

"Of course, she's my very best friend for several years. I want her to wear a soft shade of blue. I think she'll look pretty in that color with her auburn hair. She acted like she doubts if you'll want to stand up with her, but I surely hope you won't refuse. We want to have our wedding in the church because our house isn't large enough. We hope we can have the wedding in June. I pray every day you'll be home by then. It just seems too good to be true, Millard, that God found me such a wonderful friend who wants me now for his wife. Then it seems almost too good to be true that you were baptized. I cried for joy all afternoon when Mother called me up and told me. Hurry home and good-by now. Lovingly, Liticia."

Then they did get his letters. Stirred in his soul by deep feelings and great imaginations, Millard walked as in a dream back to his pup tent and put the letter inside his diary in his duffle bag. He must have sufficient self-control to keep his thoughts on the earth, for soon now they would be pulling up stakes. Pulling out the notebook and taking his pencil, he jotted down a few lines hurriedly.

"What can a mother give to her son?

What can a girl make out of him?

Both can do wonders; both deserve praise.

One gives him life; both keep him from sin.

God bless my mother back on the farm
  May her faith in her boy never grow dim.
And Melodie Ann, He'll bless her life, too.
  She's the girl who inspired my sweet faith in Him."

* * * * *

"Dear Folks at Home,

Christmas greetings to you from Italy. I just got through listening to a speech by King George. Last evening we heard President Roosevelt talk. We are all anxious to come home. We had a quiet Christmas here and a good dinner with turkey and dressing and all that goes with it. We also had fruit and candy and nuts. If only I could have eaten at home with all of you. It was wonderful to get a box from home once again. The homemade cookies are so good I hate to see them get all, but I don't want to be stingy with them. Thanks for the socks and the candy and the stationary. I haven't been getting any mail for a long time, so this package I got helps to make up for that. I wonder why you don't write me more letters. Before we left Africa I had a letter from Liticia mentioning something she wrote in a previous letter which I never got. I'm sure you have written. I wonder what happens to your letters. I want to come home so bad. I wonder what lies ahead for me? (censored) I am well. I am listening to beautiful music. It puts new thoughts in my mind, and makes me want to come home and be the best man possible. Such beautiful harmonies and richness of tones. I can't explain how it makes me feel.

Boys everywhere are writing letters home tonight. Most of the boys have girls. They are lying on their stomachs everywhere in their pup tents, some holding flashlights. All the fellows are anxious to get home and see their folks. We are all going to get treats tonight. I suppose it will be candy and cigarettes. We are to hear a sermon on New Year's Eve, they tell me. Well, I'll be glad to hear one again.

How's the weather back home and what did you do today? It is like summertime here and the roses are blooming. It makes me think of the beautiful "Rose of Sharon" song I heard them sing in church back home. Happiness to you all. Please write to me. Please. In love, Millard."

Chapter 41

A month after Christmas Myra read this letter to Jeth.
"Dear Folks at Home, (censored)

It will soon be two long years since I left the states, and I've seen a lot of things and had many experiences, some pleasant and some not so pleasant. I cannot tell you where I am in Italy, but I'm in the hospital again. (censored) The doctor does not know if the infection from my foot scattered or whether I am allergic to something here in Italy or picked up a germ in Africa, but I've got a rash on both legs that is very itchy and painful, and hard to get rid of. I may have to be here quite a while yet, but I will not complain about this. I get good food to eat. The Red Cross service is very good. Mail is held up a lot when you're in the hospital. I have had only one letter since I'm in Italy and that was the one from Marlin. I was surprised but happy to hear about Liticia's coming marriage to him. I surely hope I will be home by June for the wedding. It is hard to know what to tell you now, for all my letters will be carefully examined. I hope nothing I've written before was cut out. I am happy in spite of my (censored) God bless you all at home and please do write to me. In love, Millard."

* * * * *

During the third week Millard was in the hospital he received a letter from Orpha.

"Dear Millard,

Many things have happened since I last wrote to you, but evidently by some of your letters to the folks, you never got two letters that I wrote. Mother sent me the letter you wrote to her about your baptism. It really touched me a lot, Millard, to think what you had to go through before you found the Lord. I realize we can't imagine half of what you've been through, but I'm so glad you have peace. That's an awful condition to be in, Millard, not to have peace, for I know all about that.

I was very, very unhappy after Jack and I moved to Whitville. I was always afraid. Fear is torment. I was too unhappy to let Mother find it out, so I didn't write home much, and I didn't want to come home because of Pop. Well, I'm back here at home now. You'll be surprised, but I thought I'd write it to you first myself. I came yesterday. Jack and I are separated for good. He wasn't true to me anyway, and more than that he lied to me when he asked me to marry him. I had no idea then he had another wife. Well, one day in Whitville she turned up and claimed him as her husband and demanded money and things. I said I'd step out. It was awful. I came home, and made my things right with the folks, and called Brother Ambers to come out, and I confessed everything to him and I found peace in my soul. Millard, it was no easy thing to do."

Tears rolled down Millard's cheeks. They were not hot tears, either.

"You went through some hard experiences since you left home, I'll venture to say, and so have I. Mine weren't on a battle front, but I've been nearly torn in two by pain and sorrow and disappointments of false love. I won't try to write it all, only I want you to know your letter helped me an awful lot. God used you to bring me to my senses, Millard. I had things to make right, too, a number of things. I cannot undo my past, although I've shed almost barrels of tears over it. You can be glad you are not tangled up in a mess like I got myself into. Pop does not seem to care I came home, but I can't help Mother much. I'm not a bit well. Oh, I wish you'd pray for me, Millard. And hurry home so our family can be all together again for Liticia's wedding."

Millard's tears dropped from his chin now.

"She seems so happy. How different my life might have been if I wouldn't have been so bent on my own ways several years ago. But I feel forgiven now and I want to be taken back into the church. Your loving sis, Orpha."

Millard groaned. He looked out the hospital window and saw rows of beautiful trees set on a distant green knoll. The sky above was full of dreams. Millard loved nature. The trees against the azure Italian sky and the fields below were written in colorful, tuneful, symphonic style that stirred his emotions greatly after reading

Orpha's letter. To the right was a small waterfall, an old fashioned wooden bridge, a mill and flowers bending to the breeze. The music only contributed to his emotions. Did any of the other boys ever feel as he did? He doubted it. Like the cool water tumbling over the rocks the music fell, then hung quivering in shining pools of melody for happy moments before it broke forth again in fresh descents. It quenched his thirsty soul.

"Oh, God," breathed Millard, "help her make something beautiful out of her life yet - as beautiful as the song and the scenery. If I had done differently maybe I could have helped her somehow, but help me do it yet, dear Lord, when I get home. Orpha, my own sister, Orpha!"

He took a piece of paper and started writing. He had plenty of time now.

"Dear Orpha," he wrote,

"Bless God for the peace and forgiveness of sins you wrote about. Well, I'm here in the hospital yet. It's already six weeks since I came here. If I'd walk very carefully I could get to the Red Cross room and write on a table, but I'll just write on my bed this time. Here it is almost like being in a palace after having lived in pup tents in Africa, but that all goes with war. I am not sure, but maybe I am perhaps a tiny bit better. My legs look terrible. The doctor is stumped. By the reports the boys on the Pacific are going right along. How I long to come home! It will seem good to see you all.

God bless you, Orpha, for the courage you had to find peace. There is nothing like it in all the world. I know how hard it is, but it's worth it a thousand times over. I will have much to tell when I get home. I am very sorry to hear about your disappointment in Jack, but the thing that makes me glad is to hear you are back home and happy once more.

I would like to know some things, but I'll just let that go. I've done my duty and I am at peace.

Liticia told me Pop was different and was in church the night Marlin gave his talk about his work in the C.P.S. unit. I wish I could have heard it. I cannot tell you where I am in Italy or what the other boys are doing here. Keep praying that I will get home for Liticia's wedding. Orpha, your letter did my soul lots of good. I certainly haven't had much mail since I'm here. God bless you till we meet again. In love, your brother who cares, Millard."

After Millard finished Orpha's letter he wrote in his diary. He filled one page and then another. Then he lay for a long time looking out the window.

In the morning Millard decided to try to take a walk. His knees would get stiff if he didn't walk. He inched his way down the halls. Here were the boys who could sit up in bed. They were bandaged for jaw and head and face wounds. Some had to suck liquids through straws and talk through their teeth. There were dozens of them.

In another section were those wounded in their joints, men with arms and legs in casts, or stretched up on pulleys. Next were patients with abdominal injuries, those who knew hunger and thirst and couldn't take nourishment yet.

Millard inched along. He passed a large ward of amputation patients. Some were smiling, some looked discouraged, some looked absolutely heartsick, especially those whose both arms were gone. Next were the spine cases. Those were the men who had that hurt, pitiful, blasted look on their faces. It made Millard sick. It was as bad here as in Africa! Would they never get done bringing in the wounded? How much longer could this fighting go on? Weren't the Germans about to their end?

Millard was weaker than he thought. He almost staggered. He must go back. He'd go to the end of the hall yet, then go back. His legs hurt awfully. He could scarcely bend his knees without making them crack open and bleed.

The head nurse appeared in the half-open door. She stopped short: "Well, Mr. Grinstead," she said, "what are you doing way down here? Are you able to be out strolling this morning like this?"

"I think so. It doesn't go too good yet, but if I don't walk some I'm going to get stiff in my knees."

"Well, now you better just slide along on your way back. Listen to me, Mr. Grinstead," and she shook her finger at him somewhat playfully, a twinkle in her dark eyes, "You'd better get on back to your bed before the doctor comes around."

"Nurse, nurse."

She looked back through the half-closed door. She stepped over to the bed.

"What now, Christopher?"

"Who - is it?"

"Who - where?"

"The man - you were talkin' to - to. What's the name you said," he rolled his eyes.

"The name? Grinstead?"

"That's it. Yeh. Tell him to - come here."

She stepped back to the door.

"Mr. Grinstead, the man in here says he wants to see you. Don't stay too long. He's sick," she whispered. "Tetanus," she shook her head. "I just gave him another shot."

Millard entered, sliding his feet. Who would be wanting him? He stood close to the bed. He could see at once that the man although large in frame, was wasted and exhausted from almost insufferable pain. Despair and fear had put their mark on his sick face. He moved one big hand slightly. He seemed too weak to do that, or was the shot beginning to do its comforting work?

"Your name?" he asked thickly.

"My name is Grinstead. Don Millard Grinstead. What's yours?"

The man did not answer.

"Where - you - from?"

"My home is in Granger —"

"Oh." Millard could not be sure whether the man was disappointed or relieved.

"Why?" asked Millard.

"I thought - maybe you come - from Dodd - in - in - Harper's Valley. I knowed - some Grinsteads - there - " It seemed difficult for him to talk. He kept rolling his eyes up into his head and his thoughts wanted to float away, yet he tried to grab hold of them.

"I used to live in Harper's Valley ten years ago. What's your name?" asked Millard the second time.

"Was it on - on - a - Morris place?"

"Yes, we lived in a Morris house not far from Doddridge."

The man stared at Millard for one awful moment, his eyes glassy.

"I'd - never - never - never - do it fer - her - again," he mumbled. "She'll - she'll - ah - you're not - the - one - I - I -"

The nurse came in briskly and tapped Millard on the arm gently.

"It's long enough," she said emphatically, and Millard followed her out of the room. "He mustn't be disturbed again. There are so many who get unbalanced after they've suffered as he has. He's all upset this morning. Now you go back to your bed, Mr. Grinstead, before the doctor comes."

"I will, Miss Maria."

So men must continue to be victims of suffering and disappointment and dementia, because we all want justice and freedom and safety from oppression? Millard had a forlorn feeling when he went back to his bed.

When the doctor made his rounds he looked at Millard's legs with a puzzled expression.

"I tell you, my boy," he said, "we're going to have to put you in quarantine. I'm afraid you might have something here that's contagious."

The doctor called the head nurse. "Fix a place in the isolation tent for this boy, Miss Maria. We've got to put him in quarantine and start a new treatment. Try X-ray. His knees are getting stiff, did you notice?"

"Yes, sir," answered the nurse.

"Did you ever have anything like this before?" inquired the doctor.

"No, sir," answered Millard, "never."

Miss Maria, the head nurse, gave the orders to another who brought Millard a wheel chair. She was a beautiful Italian girl with black hair and rosy cheeks. She smiled at Millard and made two dimples when she told him to get on the chair. She raised the front rest so he would not need to bend his knees.

"They're not so pretty, are they?" she pointed to his legs. She was pretty even when she frowned.

"Not very."

"And I'm to take you for a ride, they tell me. Are these your belongings?"

"Yes."

"Call me Consetta, please."

"Consetta?"

"Yes, sir. What did your mother name you?"

"Millard."

"Millard," she repeated, "and what name did your father give you?"

"Grinstead."

"I must try to remember it. There are so many to learn. They come and go. Is this your bag?"

"Yes, Miss Consetta. I can hold it on my lap."

"Yes, of course you can. Are we both ready now? I must take you to the isolation tent. Some boys call it the jail, for most of them hate to go to that place, but I see you are still smiling."

"It would not help to frown, would it?"

"Of course not. Say it again — your name. It is not so common."

"Millard, or you can call me Don if you wish. That is my first name. Is yours Miss Consetta?"

"Plain Consetta will do. Here we go."

"So long," called a patient on one side. "Be good now."

"So long," chimed three or four more who were able to talk.

"So long, boys," answered Millard, waving his hand. "I hope to see you on our way home before too long, and I hope I didn't give this rash to any of you fellows."

The isolation tent was large enough to hold twelve beds. It was stretched over a wooden floor and was well screened. At one end of the tent were two boys about ready to be dismissed. So unless others came in Millard would be practically by himself. One blessing then, he would not be tormented all day by seeing other men suffering, and tormented all night by hearing their moans and cries.

"I'll come out occasionally to see if you are behaving yourself, Don," smiled the nurse. "If you need me hang this white cloth here on the hook outside this window. You can reach it from your bed. I'm to start the X-ray on you at eleven o'clock. Is there anything you want now before I leave?"

"If you'll put a few things on this stand for me now, I'll be fixed up for a while."

"Yes, what do you wish?"

"In my coat pocket is my Testament. I'd like that handy."

"There you are." She put it on the stand.

"In my duffel bag is a notebook. I'd like that, too. And my pencil and —"

"Well here, I'll let you get out what you want." She put the bag on the stand beside his bed.

Millard ran his hand deep into his bag. He thought he had another pencil somewhere. He found it, and something else too. He had never looked inside it yet. He had felt so awful after that one look at the picture that he had stuck it in his bag and hadn't attempted a second look.

Chapter 42

H E just held it in his hand a long time. Finally he opened it. His hands trembled with peculiar emotions. On one side of the billfold was the picture of the calm sweet-faced woman and opposite hers a picture of Emil, the man who had called him sonny, the man he had known for only a few minutes of his life, but who had made such an unforgettable impression on his memory. Emil Augusta Duerr, M.A., the man he shot.

Millard studied the pictures closely. The woman almost seemed to smile at him. His eyes got misty.

"He would have died anyway, lady," he said to the picture. "Emil was badly wounded, lady, and you couldn't have stood it to - to watch him suffer. You'll forgive me, won't you? God has. Lady, I was beside myself that morning. I was mad with fear. But it was wrong." Hot tears trickled from his eyes and dropped on the pillow. "Emil, I wouldn't have done it of my own accord. And you know that. How can you look so like Pop? Emil, you asked me to do it. Why did you say I could have this? Or was it your watch you meant I should take? I didn't want it. I had no right to take anything from a corpse."

Millard looked inside. Emil had some money in his billfold. Millard counted it. Fifty marks. He pulled out a paper. It was a letter to Emil from Gerda. Was that his wife? Gerda? Was that her name? The letter was written in a beautiful German hand.

"Has the mail come today?"

Millard dropped the letter. He wiped the tears away quickly. Consetta had praised him for smiling on his way to the isolation tent. He mustn't let her see his tears so soon. He felt embarrassed.

"No. But I wish I would get some mail today. I haven't got any for weeks. I can't understand." Millard tried to hide his emotions.

"So many say the same thing, Don. Mail is always delayed at such times, especially when one is in a hospital. My - my - why - you -" she hesitated, "now you aren't blue already, are you, Don? You've been making tears."

Then she had noticed. Millard tried to laugh. "Can you make this out?" He handed her the letter.

She looked at it a moment.

"Where did you get this?"

He told her briefly. He couldn't go into detail and control himself well.

"Can you read German, Consetta?"

"Yes. You can't?"

"No. I wish you'd read it to me if you have time."

"It's not long." She looked at her watch.

"Mein Lieber, lieber Emil," she read. "Es kommt mir vor als eine Ewigkeit seitdem Du abgereist bist. Du kannst Dir gar nicht vorstellen wie schrecklich einsam ich heute Abend bin. Der Sonnennuntergang war einzigartig; ja gradezu wunderschoen.

"Immer und immer wieder stehe ich vor dem Bild und wundere nur ob Du bald zurueckkommst. Du hast noch viel Arbeit ehe es fertig ist. Ich glaube, es wird wohl Dein Meisterstueck. Letzte Nacht trauemte ich wir haettenein Geschaeft und ein Mann aus Amerika sagte meir er wuerde Dir $12,000 fuer Dein Gemaelde geben.

"O, mein herzlichgeliebter Emil! Werden wir wohl je weider so froelich sein wei in meinem Traum! Ich denke immer, wirst Du wohl bei mirsein wenn unser Kleines ankommt? Jeder Brief von Dir versichert mir's. Jeden Abend wenn ich ins Bett gehe bin ich so froeh dass nun wieder ein Tag hin ist. Jetzt sind's nur noch 153 Tagen.

"Heute Abend sende ich Dir, Emil, eine Extrabeilage meiner Liebe. Behuet Dich Gott!

"Deine treue Gemaehlin, Gerda"

"Now you must tell me what it means, Consetta."

"You mean you didn't get it?"

"I can't understand German. I understood a few words, but not enough to know what you were reading. Can't you translate it for me now?"

"Well, all right. I might not be able to translate it exactly, but I think I can just about.

"My dear, dearest Emil.

"It is ages since you left. You cannot know how lonely I am for you tonight. The sunset was of singular beauty; yes, actually too beautiful.

"Again and again I look at the picture and wonder whether you will soon return to finish it. There is still a lot of work before it will be completed."

Millard raised up on one elbow. A stifled exclamation escaped his parted lips, "Then Emil was an artist!"

"I believe it will be your masterpiece. Last night I dreamed we had a shop and a man from America told me he would give you $12,000 for your painting.

"Oh, Emil dear, I wonder if we will ever again be as happy as we were in my dream."

Millard clutched his throat. He squirmed. He wanted to cry out. He wanted to go back to that spot in Africa and try to bring Emil back to life again for her sake.

"Shall I read the rest?" asked the nurse.

"Yes, of course, read it. I'm sorry it affects me this way."

"You are a man of feelings, aren't you, Don?" Consetta said observingly. "Let's see, I left off about the dream."

"I wonder whether you will be with me when our baby comes? Each of your letters assures me you will be."

Millard felt cold all over. He held his breath awkwardly. He broke out with perspiration. His teeth almost chattered.

"Every evening when I go to bed I am so happy that one more day is passed. And now there are only 153 days yet.

"This evening, Emil, I send you an extra portion of my love. May God be with you. Your faithful wife, Gerda."

Millard couldn't help it. He didn't even care now. Silent tears rolled. He reached for a handkerchief.

Consetta's eyes were thoughtful and sad, too. Slowly she folded the letter and handed it back. "Don," she said thoughtfully, "you know we're supposed to hate certain people and they're supposed to hate us, too - but -" her voice was very subdued now, "you know a man like that really doesn't want to leave his home and wreck another man's and kill, any more than our men wanted to kill you American boys." Her big eyes were dramatic. "There are hundreds of thousands of women like this Gerda Duerr who are going to be disappointed. It doesn't seem quite right. And nobody seems to know exactly why we're fighting, but we've got to. We are set against certain peoples ignorantly, innocently, blindly. What's it going to bring us? Say, don't tell on me, Don," she shook her forefinger in his face. She stood close to him. "I've said enough. I get full sometimes. I feel like a hot boiler. Just once in a while. I mustn't. Excuse me, Don, - but - but it's the truth."

"You talk like an educated person, Consetta."

She laughed without mirth. "No, I'm not. I'm plenty stupid. But I've gone to school enough to speak several languages and to appreciate human beings of other nationalities, and can't help but form some personal opinions and convictions. You shall not tell on me, Don," she said quietly, "or I won't read any more letters for you. It's a good thing the boys at the other end have the radio on. They did not hear. It might not have mattered either. But sometimes you have to be careful how you express yourself. You look like a clean, honest sort of man who can think a thing over in fairness."

"Thank you, Consetta. I found the Lord since I left the States. I am a Christian now."

"The Lord? What do you mean? Found the Lord?" She stood up very straight and folded her arms.

"Well, I realized I was a lost, condemned sinner. I confessed all my sins to God one night and He forgave me, yes, even the sin of killing this German artist. That was awful. Then I was baptized by the chaplain and - when I get home I'm going to join the church if they'll accept me."

"You are a Protestant, aren't you? I see your little Bible here on your stand."

"Yes."

Consetta's expression changed. "I must get busy on this X-ray treatment," she said. "I will be as good to you as if you were a Catholic, Don, but I must not discuss religion with you - much as I would like to. I must not. There may be some very good Protestant people, but the priest does not want us to discuss religion with any of them. He is very strict."

Consetta was quiet the rest of the day.

* * * * *

Millard spent much time reading and writing. Many times when he was writing Consetta came in.

"What are you writing, Don?" she asked one day. "You make me inquisitive."

"Oh," answered Millard, drawing a long breath. "Oh, just thoughts I get.

"Well, you must get quite a few," she laughed. "And I trust they are beautiful thoughts."

Weeks passed by when the letter came.

"Dear Litica,

This still finds me somewhere in Italy in a hospital. I send you my best of Christian greetings. There is still plenty of water between us. I was in one hospital ten weeks, then in another one two weeks, and now I'm in still another. My case seems to be a hard one to cure. It is very difficult to get rid of any kind of a skin disease here in Italy. The climate or something has to do with it, they tell me. I have no idea how much longer I'll be here. I get scarcely any mail. The doctors are puzzled about my legs, which are very uncomfortable. There are ten other boys here with the same thing.

"Liticia, you keep on praying that I'll get home for your wedding. This is April already. One day it looks like I'm better, then the next I'm worse. Watch the papers and you can about figure out where the boys are and what they are doing. I can't tell you any of that. I'm very tired tonight for some reason. I listened to a broadcast a while ago, and it seems a shame that in America people are having so many strikes on top of this awful war. I pray this will soon come to an end and for a good cause. It can't end too soon for me. How I long for home and to go back to church again. One day my hopes are up and then they go down. (censored)

"It is twenty-two months since we started across the Atlantic. Many things have happened since that day that I will tell you about when I get home. I am pretty homesick tonight, but I'm happy in my soul. How thankful I am for the pictures I took that day. I suppose Carrie is a big girl now, and I wonder if she'll crawl up on my lap like she used to. How thankful I was for Orpha's letter. I can hardly wait till I can have a good talk with her.

"You ought to see the big grapes they have over here. You would think they are plums. There are a lot of mushrooms, too. They really are delicious. I get good care and good eats, but nothing would taste as good as a slice of Mother's home-made bread.

"I wonder if Mother ever told Brother Ambers about me being baptized over here. (censored)

Say, Ticia, have you started your wedding dress yet? I must get me a new suit. I think I heard the doctor tell the nurse this morning that if my legs don't heal up pretty quick they'll have to send me home. They just won't heal here in Italy. They've tried everything. In love, Millard."

Liticia gave the letter to her mother.

"Oh, Mother, I - oh, of course, I don't want to have Millard laid up, but he would surely get all right if he came home. I must get my dress. Melodie Ann and I want to go to town together."

Liticia's face shone radiantly beautiful in anticipation of her wedding day. Marlin's furlough dates were scheduled, and his letters to his betrothed one were full of love and future plans.

* * * * *

"Dear Folks at home,

"This will not be a very long letter because I am getting ready to leave Italy. Plans are made to start voyage on the Conte di Savoia Thursday. I will drop you a line as soon as I arrive in the States. The doctors all say it's no use for me to stay here any longer. Things will soon be over anyway now, the way things are shaping up. Love to all, Millard."

Myra was thrilled. She cleaned house from top to bottom, washed rugs and curtains, and cleaned wallpaper. Glen and Derwood raked the yard and washed the windows on the outside. Pop painted the kitchen woodwork and varnished the floor in the front room. Orpha helped Litica with her dress, weeping inwardly, secretly, over the soft delicate folds. It seemed sacred, hallowed, and undefiled. Her hands trembled. Orpha wasn't strong enough to do much, but she wanted to make herself useful doing something.

"I wonder what he'll look like, don't you, Liticia? I wonder if he'll look much older."

"He'd naturally look a little older. Oh, I can hardly wait to have him tell us all those things that were cut out of his letters. I wonder if he ever got all we sent him?"

"We will do nothing but sit and hear him talk for a whole day - a whole solid day and hear him tell us all about his experiences."

"That's right, Orpha, you weren't here when he was home before he left. I never will forget how reluctant he seemed to be to leave, and yet he wanted to act bravely."

"Is this the way you want it, Liticia? If I'm not doing it right don't be afraid to tell me."

"That's all right. Wait, let me press that seam open a little. Oh, I do hope Marlin will like my dress and the way I'm making it."

"You don't have any fears, do you?"

"No," laughed Liticia, "not many. Say, I'm going to call Melodie Ann and tell her about the letter, and I want to write and tell Marlin, too."

"If Millard won't come home by June, who is to be Marlin's best man?"

"I don't know if he had a second choice or not."

* * * * *

Myra knew it was from Millard before she read it because of the postmark.

Eagerly she tore it open, standing at the mailbox. She couldn't wait till she got to the house. Glad, glad tears stood quivering in her eyes. The penciled words were blurred, but she could read them through her teary mist of happiness.

"Dear Mother and Pop, Orpha, Liticia, Homer Jo, Richard, Derwood, Glen, Carrie.

Hello, everybody.

Arrived safely in Charleston today. Nice voyage. I'm feeling better already. I am sure it won't be long now until I can come home. I'll write again soon. I'll have to be in the hospital here a little while, but not long. I'm quite sure. It is wonderful to be this close home again. I can hardly wait now.

As ever in love, Millard."

Myra ran to the barn.

"Pop," she cried in glad excitement, "Pop, he's in the States now."

"No!" It was Pop's way of saying it was too good to be true. His lazy brown eyes glistened.

"Here, read it for yourself, Pop."

Chapter 43

TWO days later Liticia got a letter. It wasn't very long, but she welcomed it.

"Dear Liticia,

Thank God my legs are getting better fast since I'm back in the states. It must have been the Italian climate. At this rate I may get home before the first of June. Did you say you wanted your wedding on the twelfth? Go ahead with your plans. If you want to, you can write to me here in the hospital. I'm not the only sick soldier who was sent home. Plenty are worse off than I am. I'll be seeing you before long, Ticia. Just think, it's over three years since I've seen any of you. I can hardly wait. Love, Millard."

Jeth wasn't the kind of man to whistle as he worked, but had he been, he might have joined the merry tune Derwood was whistling. Jeth had never known such inward joy. He was going to show Millard he was different, that God had wrought a miracle in his life, that God was able to break a habit he could not. He was going to try to get acquainted with Millard and treat him like a father should treat a son. He'd let Millard take charge of the family worship when he got home. Myra had long ago wanted a family altar, but Jeth did not like to read. He wasn't used to praying aloud either. Maybe Millard could go ahead with that now. At least he'd give him a chance. Millard liked to read.

Pop would feel shy at first. He wasn't sure he remembered exactly how Millard looked. Of course, he'd know him, but they never had sat and talked at any length. Never! Millard would be three years older now. He'd be a man. Pop had always felt ill at ease in his presence, even when Millard was a boy.

Peace. What a difference now! It was like being set free from bondage. It was. That cable had been strong and heavy, and he had

290

not realized its weight until God had broken it loose from him. How utterly different now! The homely, detestable cows, the stables that always needed cleaning, yes, the entire farm took on a new atmosphere.

Homer Jo wasn't at home any more. He had found a job at a filling station, and roomed and boarded in town. Jeth and Millard would be like partners. They'd plan and talk and work together until Millard would - well - maybe someday want to marry.

But Millard didn't seem to notice girls. It wasn't his nature.

Maybe Millard could talk to Homer Jo about his cigarettes. Maybe Millard could talk to him about not joining the army, too. Homer Jo would not listen to Pop. Pop would depend on Millard for many things now. Everything would be different. Yes, everything.

Peace. How soothing! How restful! Sin and a guilty conscience make men do strange things and pervert their attitudes. Pop determined to prove to Millard how his attitudes had changed. Perhaps in his letter Brother Ambers had failed to make it plain to Millard. Maybe Millard couldn't believe it. That was more than likely. Maybe Millard - well maybe a thousand and one things.

Jeth was anxious for his son to come home. He was as anxious as any of the family, but he dreaded their first meeting. How should he act? What should he say? Should he kiss him like Mother always did? He never had before.

* * * * *

"I want to show you my dress now, Liticia. Come into my bedroom."

"Is it all finished?"

"All finished." Melodie Ann held it up by the hanger.

"It's lovely, Melodie Ann."

"You really like it?"

"Of course, I do."

"Shall I try it on? I want you to see if everything suits you. This is your wedding, and I want everything just the way you want it."

"Oh, I think it will be. If Millard comes home in time and gets his suit, I'll be satisfied."

"You don't think he won't do you?"

"No. He'll come, I'm sure. God has worked out everything for us so far, and he can do the rest. If we knew the day when he would be released from the hospital, we could set the date for sure. We want it on the twelfth, but we could shift it a little. My, you ought to hear Carrie talking about our wedding and Millard's coming home. You'd think it was her own wedding, she gets so excited. It amuses me. She can't understand why we asked you and Millard to be our attendants unless you're getting married too!"

"Oh, that little Carrie," Melodie Ann said blushing. "Now how do you think it fits?" She turned around slowly. A delicate smile hovered around her lips, and there was a rippling luster in her auburn hair. She was a beautiful girl.

"It's perfect, Melodie Ann. And you do look sweet in that shade of blue. Who would have thought three years ago that I would be marrying your brother, and you would be my maid of honor?"

"Well, I hardly thought that three years ago, Liticia. A lot of things can happen in three years. And if you go back with Marlin and work in the hospital, oh, Liticia -"

"What?"

"You'll have so many experiences! Maybe someday your life will almost be like a story."

Liticia laughed. "What's happened already is a pretty nice sort of story, we think. But it's not for publication and never will be. It's our story. I imagine a good many lovers think their own experience is like a story. We do want to make our lives together count for something for others, and that's the best kind of story, don't you think?"

Melodie Ann hung up her dress and stood at the foot of the bed. There were strange longings in her serious blue eyes. "Together - two, like you two - you and Marlin - ought to make things count. I guess - love must be a wonderful thing."

"Of course, it is. I must go now."

"Don't be in a hurry, Liticia. I see your father is busy talking to mine. It looks as though they're on some interesting topic. What could it be?"

"Melodie Ann," Liticia remarked, "you just can't imagine how different Pop seems. Not only seems, but he actually is, and it all started the day he got a letter from Millard."

"Did you read the letter?"

"Me? No. I'd never ask Pop to read it. It was personal. Mother told me that but not what was in it."

"No, of course not. I shouldn't have asked."

"That was all right, Melodie Ann; but no, I wouldn't expect to read it. I'm pretty sure he let Mother read it though, because she just said a lot of it was censored. They wonder and wonder what it was. You remember I told you once how Pop was distant toward Millard. Well, I'm anxious to see how he'll be now. His whole attitude seems to have changed. I think he's really anxious for Millard to come home, too, and he never was before. He's so nice to Mother. He seems worried about Homer Jo, and he's so kind to Orpha. Oh, Melodie Ann," Liticia stepped close to her and took hold of her arm, "Orpha, poor girl, she's not a bit well. I'm dreadfully worried about her. I think Pop is, too, without saying it. Wasn't that nice of Brother Ambers to take her back like he did? Oh, I thought he was so kind about it all. I hope he'll be that nice to Millard."

"Then you really think - Millard will come into the church when he comes home?"

"I surely think so. Oh, everything will seem so different. And, oh, I forgot to tell you Grandmother Winegar wrote and said she would come to our wedding. Think of that. She's anxious to see Millard, too. She always was fond of him. I think she's coming as much to see Millard as for our wedding."

"You mean your grandmother will come out here alone? Isn't your grandfather dead?"

"Yes, but Aunt Idella said she would come with Grandmother. She has never been here. Really, when I think of everything, it's no wonder Carrie gets so excited! I do too. I quit my job Saturday."

"You did?"

"I'm going to stay at home now and get things ready. It's wonderful, Melodie Ann. We must go." And Liticia tripped down over the porch steps toward Pop.

*   *   *   *   *

The doctor came.

"Your legs look a lot better today."

"Have you any idea how soon I can go home?"

"Where do you live?"

"In Granger,...."

"What's your hurry?"

"My sister wants to get married the twelfth of June."

"I see. Can't she go ahead and get married without you?" There was a twinkle in the young doctor's eyes.

"Sure, but they want me for the best man."

"I see. Well, you might be able to make it by that time. You wouldn't want to put your uniform on yet. It would only irritate. But I think maybe you can get home for the wedding. We'll see."

* * * * *

"Dear Folks at Home,

The doctor talked favorably today. This is Friday. He will not come in tomorrow. My legs are improving. I'm happy. It looks as if I'll get home before the twelfth.

This certainly is a nice day. The lilacs are in full bloom now, and outside my window is a mock orange bush like the one Grandmother had by her gate. I wonder if it is still there.

I can almost smell rolls and light bread whenever I think of home. I'll gladly sleep on the floor. I'll be so glad to get home I might not even want to sleep the first night - just sit and talk and look at you all. Many of the boys here in the hospital get company. That makes me more homesick than ever. I've been reading a lot in my Testament. I also read several very good books from the Wheeling Library Service. I have to do something to pass the time. The doctor thought I might walk a little more tomorrow. It's surprising how weak I am from lying around so much. I'm anxious to get out in the fresh air on the farm and work. God bless you all till we meet. With love as always, Millard."

Diary:

"Only God knows how anxious I am to get home again. It is springtime in my soul this morning. Oh, will she know me when I get home? Will she speak to me with her charming voice? Will she believe in me? Or will she be taken? Am I a fool? If she is taken, she will never know I cared. Every day girls come here to see their soldier friends. Some are wives. It makes me wild for love. But I do not want a painted, worldly girl. I want one like Melodie Ann. I need someone to love. Would she ever love someone like me? Maybe I'd better burn this diary before I go home. Why did I ever start it? Well, I know. I had to give expression to my thoughts. It can't be wrong, I guess, to write down my fondness for someone. Marlin Brooks must be a happy man. He's getting a mighty sweet girl - even if she is my own sis! This is Sunday morning; it would make a beautiful wedding day. Will I ever have a wedding day? I hope so.

"Heaven's best gift to a man, I'm sure

Is a wife that's good, and sweet and pure
Her smiles and her voice—"

Millard closed the notebook and stuck it in the bag hanging at the head of his bed. He put his pencil on the stand. The words did not want to come, so he'd finish it some other time. He lay back on his pillow and with pleasant thoughts in his mind soon fell into a tranquil sleep.

*   *   *   *   *

They were all in the car ready to start to church when a gray coupe turned into the driveway. A man got out and walked directly over to Jeth behind the wheel.

"Are you Jethro Grinstead?" he inquired.

"Yes, I am."

The man reached into his inside coat pocket, pulled out a yellow envelope, and handed it to Jeth.

"Oh," cried Liticia joyously, "it's a telegram, Pop; it's from Millard. I just know it is. Maybe he's coming home today." She sat on the edge of the seat with glad anticipation.

"Well, here," Pop handed it back to Liticia, "You read it, then."

Her cheeks glowed. She held her breath in happy expectation as she tore it open.

"Oh," she cried. Her face turned white. White as a sheet.

"What is it?" asked Mother, "Liticia!"

"Oh! Oh!" she screamed. "It says he's - he's - dead!"

"Dead?" asked Pop thickly. He gripped the steering wheel.

"What?" gasped Mother. "Dead! Not Millard!"

"Dead?" cried Orpha.

Liticia almost fainted. She could not read it. She handed the telegram to Pop and sank into a corner of the back seat, weak and dazed. The yellow paper shook. Pop gripped it with both of his strong hands. Slowly he read the sad, bold black words. He read it first to himself. He was too shocked, too overtaken to read it out loud. The family sat paralyzed with sudden grief.

"Jethro Grinstead

"Granger,....

"Your son, Don Millard Grinstead, died in this hospital seven-thirty a.m. today. Remains can be shipped at government expense plus allowances not to exceed fifty dollars for interment after arrival. Send name and address of undertaker by return wire. J.F. Seymore.

1st Lt. M.c. U.S.A.."

Jeth could not read the telegram out loud. He handed it to Myra, and after she read it, he helped her out of the car and led her slowly to the house, but it was impossible to tell which of the two was weeping the hardest.

$$* \quad * \quad * \quad * \quad *$$

It was one of the largest and one of the saddest funerals ever held in Brother Ambers' church. Don Millard's body was sent home in uniform in a flag-draped casket. He had enlisted as a soldier in the United States Army, and he had never been discharged. He was sent home a hero of war.

It could not be true. It could not be true!

But it was true! The corpse in uniform was Don Millard, and no one else. His face - yes, it did look some years older - but, oh, so happy, so contented, so peaceful, so serene, and unclouded! Who could wish him back now?

But they must find out what happened. After the telegram came, they got his letter. It came the next day. But what happened after he said he was improving so nicely and would be coming home soon? The family was broken with disappointment, grief, and anxiety. Oh, mystery of mysteries! Would the hand of God move over the Grinstead home and take away the oldest son, the one Jeth felt was born with a special purpose because his mother had prayed so earnestly before he was born? Would God do a thing like that now when everything was going to be different. Would anyone ever be able to answer their question, Why? Now there was a funeral instead of a wedding!

Jeth was too hurt to talk. Myra all but collapsed. They could do nothing but shake their heads in silent sorrow.

When Melodie Ann heard it, she caught her breath, then ran quickly to her room. She closed the door and cried bitterly. No one would ever know there was something about Millard Grinstead she admired. No one would ever know she saw something grand and worth while and promising in him. No one would ever know how she had prayed for him and had faith that he was going to come back and make good. No one, not even Liticia - no, not even her own mother would ever know how she cared. He never knew. He never guessed. Why tell it now? No one would ever find out about the tears she could not control.

Chapter 44

NO one thought it out of place for Marlin Brooks to sit beside Liticia. Everyone knew he was going to come home for his wedding. He did not expect, however, to come home earlier for a funeral, least of all Millard Grinstead's. Melodie Ann sat beside Orpha. Liticia asked her to, for Orpha's sake. When Melodie Ann cried, folks thought it was because of sympathy for friends, the two Grinstead girls. No one guessed she was saying farewell to a secret love.

Brother Ambers told the congregation that Millard had accepted Christ as his personal Saviour and had been baptized by an army chaplain in a foreign country and that he had written him a letter expressing his gladness. There was no doubt in the preacher's mind that the young man before him was saved. For that reason death was his gain. It was a triumphant passing. There was joy in spite of the bitter disappointment of Millard's family. Millard Grinstead was young, intelligent, ambitious, and promising. Had he lived he undoubtedly would have become a leader in the church. The family had every right to be disappointed. Millard had not come home. This was only his body. There would be no returning.

As Myra sat on the front seat close to her son in the coffin, she lived over in her mind every year of his life. She held him in her arms and felt his wee head in her neck. She kissed his soft cheeks. She smiled at him in his basket in the bay window in their first new house. She helped him learn to walk and picked him up and comforted him when he fell. She taught him how to talk and interpreted his sweet childish babblings. She buttoned his coat and tied his shoes and sent him off to school with his little dinner bucket filled with things he liked most. She helped him pronounce new words in the storybooks Grandmother sent him. She tucked him into bed and sang him to sleep the first time he had to go upstairs at night. She spread him slices of warm fresh bread when he came home from school hungry as a bear. She watched him grow out of one size of clothing into another size. She saw him helping Liticia with her lessons and heard his voice getting deeper.

She saw him dashing into the house the night of the fire and felt him wrapping the comforter around her shoulders tenderly. She told him again how she'd miss him when he left for the first time and saw the sad hurt look in his pensive brown eyes. She saw him sitting in church eager-faced and attentive as he listened to the Scriptures being interpreted. She saw him standing beside her bed the day after Carrie was born.

She saw him on the hospital cart, ill, pale and half conscious. She caught his look of recognition and felt the answering pressure of his hand before he went to the operating room. She saw him coming up the porch steps on Christmas day. She saw his look of sheer joy over coming home and his expression of satisfaction at the table.

She saw him leaning on the posthole digger and heard again all the words they both said. She saw him standing in the kitchen watching her stir the gravy. She heard him calling her "Mother."

She felt his arms around her when he left in uniform, and heard his unuttered groans when he kissed her and tore himself away. She smelled the aftershaving lotion on his face and the sweet freshness of his breath when he told her good-by. She had one last glimpse of him as he disappeared on the train - the train that took him to New York.

She saw and lived again a thousand intimacies with him, her own little Don Millard, her baby, her firstborn, now in the flag-draped casket before her. He had been her baby, her boy, her main support through all the years. He was the one who loved her. He was the one who sent her a pretty handkerchief from England and who remembered her birthday. He was the one who asked her to pray for him that he would be saved before he died - he, her Don Millard, who had written those sweet words telling that her prayers for him were answered.

Oh, what was it he had written that had been censored, she would never know. She would never know what her boy had tried to tell her. She had expected him to come home to tell her. And now he would never come home. Myra Grinstead shook with sobs.

Brother Ambers ended his remarks, closed his Bible and started reading. Myra sat spellbound. She looked up to listen.

"There is no death! The stars go down
To rise upon some fairer shore,
And bright in heaven's jeweled crown
They shine forever more.

There is no death! The dust we tread
Shall change beneath the summer showers
To golden grain or mellowed fruit
Or rainbow-tinted flowers.

The granite rocks disorganize
And feed the hungry moss they bear.
The forest leaves drink daily life
From out the viewless air.

There is no death! The leaves may fall
And flowers may fade and pass away;
They only wait through wintry hours
The coming of the May.

There is no death! An angel form
Walks o'er the earth with silent tread;
He bears our best loved things away
And we then call them dead.

He leaves our hearts all desolate;
He plucks our fairest, sweetest flowers.
Transplanted into bliss, they now
Adorn immortal bowers.

The birdlike voice, whose joyous tones
Made glad those scenes of sin and strife,
Sings now an everlasting song
Around the tree of life."

Myra drew a long, deep breath. It was a breath of willing but incomprehensible submission. Jeth gripped her hand.

Brother Ambers prayed. Then the undertaker carefully folded back the flag, opened the casket, and a long stream of people passed by to take a last view of the Grinstead boy who, the paper stated, had helped to fight for their peace and liberty and security. In the procession were Paul and Neta Auckers, Miss Yale, Mr. and Mrs. Schultz, and Mr. and Mrs. Fred Boetcher who had learned to appreciate him because of his sterling character and willingness to work. Everyone who had known Millard liked him. And many of his friends and acquaintances attended the funeral.

Aunt Christina sent a nice letter expressing her deepest sympathies. She could not bear to come to the funeral. She and Levi had loved Millard as their own. Her own sorrow was still too fresh to come back now for this.

A week after the funeral Jeth and Myra got a letter from the captain of the medical corps.

"Dear Mr. and Mrs. Grinstead,

Please permit me to extend to you and your family my sincere bereavement in the loss of your son, Don Millard Grinstead, who passed away in this hospital from vasamotor collapse.

You may be assured he received every possible care and attention. May you find consolation in the thought that he served his country bravely and faithfully and died in honor and respect. He helped in nine major engagements and is among the first in the eyes of the American people. You may write to the Claims Division, Washington 25, D.C., for settlement of accounts for your son.

"Very sincerely yours, R.H. Hanser, M.A.C. Executive Offices 27th General Hospital, Charleston, North Carolina, U.S.A."

* * * * *

Under the circumstances Marlin and Liticia did the only thing that was thinkable. They slipped quietly to Bro. Ambers home and were married. Mr. and Mrs. Brooks and Melodie Ann went along as witnesses. Aunt Idella and Grandmother, who had stayed for a while after the funeral, helped Myra prepare the wedding dinner without any fuss. No one but the immediate families were there.

Everyone was watching the headlines. At last the news came. The Second World War was ended. There was excitement, broadcasts, parades, marches, music, drinking, whistles blasting, and bells ringing in every city and town and village of the union. It was a night of great hilarity and ostentatious display. Why not shout and drink and cheer when the land of the free, the home of the brave, was once more safe?

After Marlin and Liticia worked a year in the mental hospital they started housekeeping on a little farm on the edge of Granger. Liticia drove home frequently, at least once a week. One morning she lingered on the steps.

"How does Carrie like school, Mother?"

"She likes it fine."

"Do you think Orpha's any better?"

Mother shook her head.

"She went along with Pop to see the doctor. I can't see that she's any better."

"She doesn't look well, but I wouldn't want to tell her. I want to take her along home with me some day again. I know she's sad."

"You can't blame her," Mother said.

"I know. Well - by, I must go now before it rains any harder. I hope you'll like the cookies. I made a double batch. By, Mother."

"There comes the mailman."

"I'll bring it in for you before I leave."

"I can get it, Liticia."

"There's no need for you to come out in the rain. I'll run and get it, Mother."

Liticia returned with a letter from Grandmother and a package.

"What's that?" asked Mother, as Liticia came running up the steps.

"I don't know. It's to Mr. and Mrs. Jethro Grinstead. Did you order something?"

"No." Mother took the package. "I wonder what it could be."

"Open it and see."

Liticia followed her mother to the kitchen. Myra put the package on the table and cut the cord with a paring knife. Inside the heavy wrapping paper was a box.

"Why, that looks just like the box I sent to Millard."

"To Millard. When?"

"Why that was, oh, long ago. The Christmas he was in Italy. Don't you remember? We fixed up a box for him?"

"Well, what is it? This makes me feel queer. You open it, Liticia."

Myra held back in wonder and excitement.

"Why - why -" exclaimed Liticia in astonishment, "why, look, its letters. Here's one to you, and one to Pop, letters addressed and sealed and here's one addressed to Homer Jo. They were never mailed. And what's this? Look. It's a - why, it's Millard's writing. Look." Liticia leafed through the first tablet. Under that one were two more.

"Why, Liticia. Look," cried Mother, "it's pages and pages of something he's written. What can it be?"

"Let me see it. Oh, I can't go home now. I want to read some of this first. This looks like a diary."

"Well, read out loud then. I've got to hear what this is."

Each took a chair by the kitchen table. Myra picked up the letter addressed to her. She tore it open.

"Read this one first." Myra handed Liticia the letter.

"Dear Mother,

Greetings to you in Jesus' dear name. Oh, Mother, why don't you write to me? I know I was a wandering boy and I told you I was coming into the army without any conviction against it. Mother dear, please forgive me. I was not altogether truthful, for I always wondered, and there were strange unhappy (tears streamed down Myra Grinstead's plump cheeks; it was hard for Liticia to read), feelings wrapped around the very thought of death. From the first I prayed secretly for conviction. No one will ever know the soul struggles I've gone through. At last it came, but not in a way anyone would wish for it. I wrote and told you I found Christ one night and accepted Him into my heart. I went to the chaplain and asked to be baptized. He baptized me in the name of the Father, Son, and Holy Ghost. I thought you'd want to know. I thought how glad you'd be to hear it, but day after day I got no letter from you. Ten weeks and no letter."

"Why, I can't understand," cried Myra. "Go ahead."

"You got my letter, for Liticia mentioned it. Mother dear, I have peace. I prayed all night for real salvation and forgiveness from all my sins, even the worst one I committed. I promised God that night I'd follow all the way, not half. It was not an easy matter to go back to the chaplain and tell him my convictions. I asked you to please forgive me for all I've ever done against you. Thank you for all your prayers for me. You will never know the impression you've left on me. I want to come home and be a true Christian. I am homesick. Mother, I hope you can soon set a plate for me at your table."

"Oh!" Myra tried to stifle her cries.

"How anxious I am to know how Pop feels toward me now. I hope I did not write anything in my letter I shouldn't have. Your loving son, Millard."

"Well, I can't understand who sent this and why it's been so long in coming," Myra said, shaking her head.

Myra and Liticia both cried. Liticia put the letter back in the envelope and picked up the first tablet.

"Shall I read some of this?"

"Yes, read it all, Liticia. Every word of it. My boy, my boy," she sobbed.

"Praise God I have been saved. In the name of Jesus." Liticia's voice broke. "I have been saved so truly that I want to do only those things which are taught in the Scriptures. I know I am being watched. I know some think maybe I'm 'cracked', but I am willing to be a fool for Christ now. I know what the will of God is for my life. It has come to me as a shining light and I have true peace that passeth all understanding. The truth of God is a light not seen on land or on sea. It comes from God alone. When the bombers came over me while I was sleeping and when the explosion picked me up and threw me up in the air and dropped me, I was almost torn in two. It was a terrible thing. It was a horrible night, and the judgment of the Lord was upon me, and I knew it was my eleventh hour. It was a 'warrish' battle that day. Finally we got to draw back toward the rear for a rest while the rear guns roared over our heads. I wanted to die. I prayed to die, but I could not die."

"Oh, Liticia," cried Mother, "no, don't stop. Read on."

"I was left only a quivering mass of human flesh, and I was in a hell no man can stand to be in long and yet live. I died a thousand horrible deaths in a thousand hells, crying to God for peace, peace, peace, at any price. I begged for forgiveness of sins, yes, the one of killing that man. I got no peace until I was willing to lay down my feeling toward Pop. The German looked like Pop."

"Oh, oh, Mother," shivered Liticia. "How can I read it?"

"Oh, it was unbearable - a fiendish thing to kill a man who looked like your own father. I thought I would go insane for a while. It haunts me yet, but God spoke that sweet word, 'Yes,' to my soul at last. At last, after I promised I'd obey Him, and not fight any more He gave me peace. I promised. I must keep it. I must bear the true cross of Christ - no matter what the costs. I must keep peace in my soul at any price. If it comes to death, that would be an easy matter compared to the thousand horrible deaths I died and couldn't die. Death without Christ is a terrible thing. I know, for I've seen fear on every hand and men's hearts failing them because of fear.

I have been reading my Testament, and it plainly says I cannot take up arms any more. I will gladly obey every law of the land, but the law of God's love is above that. I would like to help to heal the wounded hearts of this awful massacre - but I cannot help to wound and kill any more. I must pray for the rulers of the nation, but when they tell me to disobey God I cannot do that. The judgment of God is a terrible thing. I've seen many things to prove it. How I long to see multitudes come to this light. I wish men could see what a disgrace war is.

I cannot serve two masters. I must stand for the truth, or I'll fall away. I must give my testimony wherever I go. I must never be ashamed to let others know what tortures my stubbornness got me into. Sin brings sorrow. I tried to make myself think I was going to protect my family and those I love, but God told me I was wrong.

Peace. Peace. It came as a shining light. The peace of God is a blessed thing. It is not only for me but for all mankind. I hope I can tell someone someday. This light must not go out. It is my hope. I prayed in all sincerity that God would undertake for me before I would be called back to the front. He did, but not in a way I expected. I thought I'd be sent home in dishonor or persecuted or cast into prison or even put to death, but God put me in the hospital. It was surely the hand of God. He was merciful to me. I offered to drive an ambulance, but God said, 'No, you can suffer instead - but not alone, for I will go with you through that, and you need not be afraid - no, not even unto death'. Death in Christ is easy. I knew unless I accepted Christ, I would never again hear His call.

God wonderfully spared me through nine major battles with not so much as a scratch. God spoke to me many nights in my sleep in Africa. I suffered untold things in dreams. No one can describe what war is. You have to see it for yourself. It is a hell only which one up in the thick of it, like I was, can know. The wings of death took me to a thousand unbearable torments, but, thank God, peace came as a sweet relief. The voice of Christ came as a beautiful 'yes' to my soul. I can never forget it. How wonderful to go to sleep with peace of mind when I am tired.

When I get home I want to rest and rest and rest. I will ask Brother Ambers if he will take me into the church. If he won't accept my baptism, he can do it over, but surely he will accept it when I tell him of my salvation. It is real. Someday I think I would like to write a tract and tell this experience. Maybe Brother Ambers can help me put it into words. I'd like to save other boys from what I've gone through. There must be some better way. There are boys like myself who did not understand.

I can't forget the man I killed and his wife. He was trying to kill me and didn't know it. Surely he did not want to go to war and leave her. I was in the most forward part of the battle at the very point which split the corners of the valley with the strong mountain fortress. To our right front flank our position split this valley in right angles. To the left of this the valley led out into a broad plain. At that place was the darkest of all experiences, fire and blood and screaming everywhere, and afterwards at dawn Emil lay dying, Emil Augustav, the German artist who loved beautiful things and home and babies and could paint pictures. Someday will we meet at the judgment? I cannot know. I hope he was saved. There must be a better way for men to settle disputes. What is the worth of a man's soul? There is no price. I love all men. I long to see them find the peace I have longed for and have found. I wonder what is going to come to pass. Men who do not love Christ will never help bring the world to peace. If I get well and the war is not over and I am asked to fight again, I will go to the chaplain again and take my stand. If it means death, that will be far better for me than disobedience, which would forever rob me of this peace. The chaplain seemed somewhat disturbed or confused when I spoke to him. I have read my Testament much, but I cannot find anywhere that love should be set aside in times of war.

I think Marlin is doing a great work. If I had gone on when I started, I too might be with him today. I cannot bear to think long on the sights I've seen - young men pushed into eternity without time to get right. How God spared my life I do not know, for always around me and over my head, was death. I must write what's on my heart. Consetta wanted to ask me often about my Bible, but she was afraid to. I wanted to tell her that perfect love casts out all fear. She was very kind to me. Like Peter and Paul I must give my testimony. It is my life now."

"Oh, Mother," sobbed Liticia, "isn't it wonderful! Did you ever suppose Millard would be like this? And - and write things like this, Mother?"

Chapter 45

MYRA Grinstead had never been a woman who cried easily, but now as she listened to her son's voice from paper her finest, most delicate emotions were deeply touched. Something penetrated the very core of her life. She could not withhold her tears. They simply flowed.

For seventeen long months she had tried to find a satisfactory answer to that one question that kept coming back. It rose before her at the most unexpected moments. Sometimes just the twitter of a bird, the odor of her own freshly baked bread, or a glimpse of the garden gate from the kitchen window brought the question up with poignant freshness. The heaviness in her breast never lifted. And now this!

Why was he taken so suddenly on the last lap of his journey back home? Why did the telegram have to say he had gone - when they knew it was going to say he was coming? For months and months she and Jeth had discussed their disappointment until it was threadbare. There was nothing left to say or ask, nothing to do but go on wondering, wondering, wondering, trying to find consolation in the words of the beautiful poem Brother Ambers had read at the close of his message.

Myra was submissive. Over and over she had analyzed her attitude, and she knew she was, yet deep down in her mother heart there was a silent yearning to see her boy a man - alive, saying and doing things. In the stillness of the night she lay dreaming of him coming home and enjoying their new home since Pop had changed. She wished Millard could know Pop now. Sometimes she even felt as though she would gladly forfeit her own life in exchange for his. He was that dear to her. She knew he would have made good. And now - why?

There was a sudden pulse of joy in Myra's heart as she wiped away her tears.

"I always knew, Liticia," she said with intense feelings, "I always knew," she repeated with a faint smile on her tear-stained face, "that there was something good in Millard."

She stood up. She rubbed her plump arms with her hands.

"Read more," she said. "I must hear every word."

"It's really no wonder, is it, Mother, that so much was cut out of his letters, if he wrote things like this?"

"I'm surprised we ever got this at all. I wonder who sent it. What comes next?"

Liticia turned and read the next page.

"Sometimes I wonder if I shouldn't let my life insurance policies lapse when I get home. What I could collect would be used for some worthy cause. There are many things I wish I could talk over with Uncle Levi. Perhaps Brother Ambers can advise me. I am anxious to get acquainted with Marlin, too. How happy he must be knowing he did not help to kill men or destroy homes. Many things have come to my mind in my travels. I have seen part of the world, and it is too beautiful to blow to pieces. Even in Africa after the battle quieted the sunsets were most beautiful. They seemed to try to say that God was peace, and in that place He would give it if men would only read His words of love. Many things have been revealed to me that I feel in my heart and cannot find words to express. I wish I knew how to write."

A picture fell to the floor. Liticia picked it up. It was the one Millard took of the family before he left. It was worn.

"My own prayer."

"What?" asked Myra.

"I'm just reading what it says here in his diary. Look, on this side of the page he has pinned a prayer and on this side there is written 'my own prayer'. See?"

"Oh, that must be one of those printed prayers they give the boys to read. He sent us one once, don't you remember?"

"Oh, yes. Shall I read the prayer Millard wrote?"

"Of course. I must hear it all." Myra half laughed and half cried.

"Dear Father, Thou art truly my own father. I thank Thee Thou hast lifted me out of the pit of sin and death and set my heart at peace even here far from home and in the midst of war and confusion. I am glad that now with tomorrow unknown I can put my trust in Thee, dear Father. Give me courage to stand for the truth as taught in this holy Book. Give me a burning testimony all day and every day even though I am very uncomfortable. Heal me in your will. Your will is sweet to me and I am satisfied. Let me never forget the things I've learned in this experience. Dear Lord, I know I'm going to be tried and tested for the stand I've taken, but help me never to doubt my salvation. May all men come to the truth. Let my life show only love. Dear Father, if I should give my body in war and burn to death as a human torch for my country and know not love, it will count for nothing. Thou art love. In joy I want to go home and serve Thee as long as I live. Please keep my life and soul tonight. In Jesus' name. Amen."

From Myra's breast came a deep breath too great for words. Liticia picked up the next notebook. "This looks like a diary, too, Mother. It must be. Shall I read this?"

"I said I want to hear every word."

Myra sat down again. She sat on the edge of her chair, her hands clasped tightly on the table in front of her. Liticia caught her breath. She held it.

"Why, Mother," she choked, "Mother, why I can't believe this, Millard liked Melodie Ann!"

Myra made no answer. She clasped her hands more tightly.

Liticia read on.

"Why - it's all the way through. Melodie Ann, Melodie Ann. Mother! She knows nothing of this. I'm sure she doesn't. Why - why he actually loved her! Did you know this?"

"No," whispered Myra. "I never knew Millard cared about any girl." A stifled moan escaped her slightly parted lips. Her cheeks were flushed.

"Well, I just simply - can't - read - any more of this - out loud - Mother. Oh! It's breaking my heart! Look!"

Liticia drew up a chair and sat close to her mother. Together - silently they read page after page while uncontrolled tears streamed down their hot cheeks. The diary revealed things they never dreamed: Millard's convictions, his fears, his soul struggles, his new-found peace, his love and devotion to his family, all that and more - his secret love for one in particular, the pretty girl with the auburn hair named Melodie Ann Brooks.

"Why, Mother," cried Liticia putting her arm across her mother's shoulder, "I never knew he could write verses like this. Did you?"

Mother shook her head.

"I'm finding out more - and - more. It's all - so wonderful. It's all so wonderful - to get this - after so long a time."

"Mother, it's only in this one book that he mentions Melodie Ann's name. He says here he was going to burn it, so you know he never intended that anyone else should ever read it."

"Of course - he didn't. That proves he died suddenly. We must not let anyone else see this diary. It wouldn't be fair - or right. Liticia, what shall we do with it? We can't let the boys or anyone see it."

"Maybe we'd better burn it as he intended. Oh - what shall we do with it?"

"You just know it would hurt him if he knew anyone was reading it. Why, Liticia, this was sacred to him."

"Am I going to tell Melodie Ann? Would you, Mother?"

"I don't know. You're sure she doesn't know?"

"I'm sure she doesn't have any idea he cared for her. Think how it would make her feel now, if she found this out."

"It might make her happy - but maybe it wouldn't."

"Are you going to tell Marlin? Are you, Liticia?"

"I tell him everything. Would it be all right to take this along home and show it to him and see what he'd say about telling Melodie?"

"Well, I don't know. Do as you like, but it dare not go any farther. I do want Homer Jo and Orpha and the boys to read what's in this other tablet, though. It might help Homer Jo."

"It should. I wonder what's in this letter to him?"

"I suppose Millard tried to persuade him not to go to the army. I wonder if he didn't intend to mail these letters?"

"He must have. They're addressed and sealed."

"He doesn't mention Melodie Ann's name any place but in this diary, does he, Liticia? So that shows he intended to destroy this. He never expected anyone else to read it. I just can't believe it. I wish Brother Ambers could read some of the other tablet. My boy - my poor boy."

"What do you mean, Mother?"

"Well, we have no idea how lonely he got - all those weeks and months in the hospital - especially when he was quarantined. He did this to help pass the time. I just can't believe it. Oh, what will Pop say? I wonder if the one who sent it read this all first."

"Well, Mother," said Liticia, "I think it was meant to be. It didn't just happen. It couldn't have. I believe God planned that he had to go to the hospital to have time to write all these things. But why were they sent to us now? And why just this? Didn't he have a watch and a billfold or any other things? I can't understand why just this box was sent to us. Do you think we'll ever find out?"

Myra jumped.

"Liticia, there comes someone."

Myra stepped to the window. "It's Pop and Orpha already."

Liticia looked at the clock.

"Have I been here that long? Oh, Marlin will be coming in to dinner and he won't know what has kept me so long. Here, let me put the diary inside my coat before they come in. I'll take it along with me and show it to Marlin."

"Then you're really going to let Marlin read it, Liticia?"

"Well - well - I don't know. Should I? Maybe not. Here, Mother you take it. Quick. Hide it before anyone sees it. But I think I'll tell Marlin. I tell him everything. If he thinks it's all right I might tell Melodie Ann sometime."

Quickly Myra Grinstead slipped the diary behind the clock on the wall shelf. It would be safe there for the time.

"Mother," Liticia's big eyes widened as with some sudden inspiration.

"Yes."

"Do you know - this would make a story?"

"A story?"

"Yes. Millard did not live his life in vain. He did not die in vain. Pop is different now and Orpha came back. And maybe Homer Jo will see things different now, too. Don't you see it, Mother, how Millard's life is just like a story? Why, it has to be. It is, because he found himself in such a tangle and God helped him out of it and through it all others have been blessed. I - I think Melodie Ann should know he loved her, too. Yes, I do. She will be surprised, I know - but - she - she prayed for him. I know that. She cared about his soul, Mother."

Myra's brown, tear-filled eyes took on a soft, warm glow.

"Maybe we could persuade Brother Ambers to write a tract, Mother," said Liticia, "maybe like a little story."

Myra Grinstead's heart throbbed with profound emotions that had warmed her heart from the days before her boy was born until this very moment - rich, deep, fathomless emotions that no one but Millard's own mother could have felt or interpreted. She glanced out the kitchen window and saw Pop and Orpha coming up the walk together in the autumn rain. She stepped close to Liticia and touched her arm. Her lips quivered - not from pain, or grief, or fear, but with hope and a new mysterious joy. "if it would help just one mother's boy like my Millard," she whispered, "I'd be willing - to have it told. It's a story of unspoken love."

THE END

AUTHOR'S NOTE

This story was written by request. The letters were selected from sixty-five letters written by Millard's own hand, which were submitted for reference by the Grinstead family.

Myra wrote to the author of this story, "It will make me very happy if just one boy like our Millard will be drawn to Christ by reading this story. This is my prayer."